Praise for #1 *New York Times* bestselling author

NORA ROBERTS

NORA ROBERTS

DANGEROUS EMBRACE

Published by Silhouette Books
America's Publisher of Contemporary Romance

SILHOUETTE BOOKS

Dangerous Embrace

ISBN-13: 978-1-335-01283-8

Copyright © 2019 by Harlequin Books S.A.

The publisher acknowledges the copyright holder of the individual works as follows:

Treasures Lost, Treasures Found
Copyright © 1986 by Nora Roberts

Risky Business
Copyright © 1986 by Nora Roberts

Recycling programs for this product may not exist in your area.

CONTENTS

TREASURES LOST, TREASURES FOUND

To Dixie Browning, the true lady of the island.

Chapter 1

He had believed in it. Edwin J. Hardesty hadn't been the kind of man who had fantasies or followed dreams, but sometime during his quiet, literary life he had looked for a pot of gold. From the information in the reams of notes, the careful charts and the dog-eared research books, he thought he'd found it.

In the panelled study, a single light shot a beam across a durable oak desk. The light fell over a hand—narrow, slender, without the affectation of rings or polish. Yet even bare, it remained an essentially feminine hand, the kind that could be pictured holding a porcelain cup or waving a feather fan. It was a surprisingly elegant hand for a woman who didn't consider herself elegant, delicate or particularly feminine. Kathleen Hardesty was, as her father had been, and as he'd directed her to be, a dedicated educator.

Minds were her concern—the expanding and the fulfilling of them. This included her own as well as every one of her students'. For as long as she could remember, her father had impressed upon her the importance of education. He'd stressed the priority of it over every other aspect of life. Education was the cohesiveness that held civilization together. She grew up surrounded by the dusty smell of books and the quiet, placid tone of patient instruction.

She'd been expected to excel in school, and she had. She'd been expected to follow her father's path into education. At twenty-eight, Kate was just finishing her first year at Yale as an assistant professor of English literature.

In the dim light of the quiet study, she looked the part. Her light brown hair was tidily secured at the nape of her neck with all the pins neatly tucked in. Her practical tortoiseshell reading glasses seemed dark against her milk-pale complexion. Her high cheekbones gave her face an almost haughty look that was often dispelled by her warm, doe-brown eyes.

Though her jacket was draped over the back of her chair, the white blouse she wore was still crisp. Her cuffs were turned back to reveal delicate wrists and a slim Swiss watch on her left arm. Her earrings were tasteful gold studs given to Kate by her father on her twenty-first birthday, the only truly personal gift she could ever remember receiving from him.

Seven long years later, one short week after her father's funeral, Kate sat at his desk. The room still carried the scent of his cologne and a hint of the pipe tobacco he'd only smoked in that room.

She'd finally found the courage to go through his papers.

She hadn't known he was ill. In his early sixties, Hardesty had looked robust and strong. He hadn't told his daughter about his visits to the doctor, his check-ups, ECG results or the little pills he carried with him everywhere. She'd found his pills in his inside pocket after his fatal heart attack. Kate hadn't known his heart was weak because Hardesty never shared his shortcomings with anyone. She hadn't known about the charts and research papers in his desk; he'd never shared his dreams either.

Now that she was aware of both, Kate wasn't certain she ever really knew the man who'd raised her. The memory of her mother was dim; that was to be expected after more than twenty years. Her father had been alive just a week before.

Leaning back for a moment, she pushed her glasses up and rubbed the bridge of her nose between her thumb and forefinger. She tried, with only the desk lamp between herself and the dark, to think of her father in precise terms.

Physically, he'd been a tall, big man with a full head of steel-gray hair and a patient face. He had favored dark suits and white shirts. The only vanity she could remember had been his weekly manicures. But it wasn't a physical picture Kate struggled with now. As a father...

He was never unkind. In all her memories, Kate couldn't remember her father ever raising his voice to her, ever striking her. He never had to, she thought with a sigh. All he had to do was express disappointment, disapproval, and that was enough.

He had been brilliant, tireless, dedicated. But all of that had been directed toward his vocation. As a father, Kate reflected… He'd never been unkind. That was all that would come to her, and because of it she felt a fresh wave of guilt and grief.

She hadn't disappointed him, that much she could cling to. He had told her so himself, in just those words, when she was accepted by the English Department at Yale. Nor had he expected her ever to disappoint him. Kate knew, though it had never been discussed, that her father wanted her to become head of the English Department within ten years. That had been the extent of his dream for her.

Had he ever realized just how much she'd loved him? She wondered as she shut her eyes, tired now from the hours of reading her father's handwriting. Had he ever known just how desperately she'd wanted to please him? If he'd just once said he was proud…

In the end, she hadn't had those few intense last moments with her father one reads about in books or sees in the movies. When she'd arrived at the hospital, he was already gone. There'd been no time for words. No time for tears.

Now she was on her own in the tidy Cape Cod house she'd shared with him for so long. The housekeeper would still come on Wednesday mornings, and the gardener would come on Saturdays to cut the grass. She alone would have to deal with the paperwork, the sorting, the shifting, the clearing out.

That could be done. Kate leaned back farther in her father's worn leather chair. It could be done because all of those things were practical matters. She dealt easily with the practical. But what about these papers she'd found? What would she do about the carefully drawn charts, the notebooks filled with information, directions, history, theory? In part, because she was raised to be logical, she considered filing them neatly away.

But there was another part, the part that enabled one to lose oneself in fantasies, in dreams, in the "perhapses" of life. This was the part that allowed Kate to lose herself totally in the possibilities of the written word, in the wonders of a book. The papers on her father's desk beckoned her.

He'd believed in it. She bent over the papers again. He'd believed in it or he never would have wasted his time documenting, searching, theorizing. She would never be able to discuss it with him. Yet, in a way, wasn't he telling her about it through his words?

Treasure. Sunken treasure. The stuff of fiction and Hollywood movies. Judging by the stack of papers and notebooks on his desk, Hardesty must have spent months, perhaps years, compiling information on the location of an English merchant ship lost off the coast of North Carolina two centuries before.

It brought Kate an immediate picture of Edward Teach—Blackbeard, the bloodthirsty pirate with the crazed superstitions and reign of terror. The stuff of romances, she thought. Of romance...

Ocracoke Island. The memory was sharp, sweet and painful. Kate had blocked out everything that had happened that summer four years before. Everything and everyone. Now, if she was to make a rational decision about what was to be done, she had to think of those long, lazy months on the remote Outer Banks of North Carolina.

She'd begun work on her doctorate. It had been

a surprise when her father had announced that he planned to spend the summer on Ocracoke and invited her to accompany him. Of course, she'd gone, taking her portable typewriter, boxes of books, reams of paper. She hadn't expected to be seduced by white sand beaches and the call of gulls. She hadn't expected to fall desperately and insensibly in love.

Insensibly, Kate repeated to herself, as if in defense. She'd have to remember that was the most apt adjective. There'd been nothing sensible about her feelings for Ky Silver.

Even the name, she mused, was unique, unconventional, flashy. They'd been as suitable for each other as a peacock and a wren. Yet that hadn't stopped her from losing her head, her heart and her innocence during that balmy, magic summer.

She could still see him at the helm of the boat her father had rented, steering into the wind, laughing, dark hair flowing wildly. She could still remember that heady, weightless feeling when they'd gone scuba diving in the warm coastal waters. Kate had been too caught up in what was happening to herself to think about her father's sudden interest in boating and diving.

She'd been too swept away by her own feelings of astonishment that a man like Ky Silver should be attracted to someone like her to notice her father's preoccupation with currents and tides. There'd been too much excitement for her to realize that her father never bothered with fishing rods like the other vacationers.

But now her youthful fancies were behind her, Kate told herself. Now, she could clearly remember how many hours her father had closeted himself in his hotel room, reading book after book that he brought with him from the mainland library. He'd been researching even then. She was sure he'd continued that research in the following summers when she had refused to go back. Refused to go back, Kate remembered, because of Ky Silver.

Ky had asked her to believe in fairy tales. He asked her to give him the impossible. When she refused, frightened, he shrugged and walked away without a second look. She had never gone back to the white sand and gulls since then.

Kate looked down again at her father's papers. She had to go back now—go back and finish what her father had started. Perhaps, more than the house, the trust fund, the antique jewelry that had been her mother's, this was her father's legacy to her. If she filed those papers neatly away, they'd haunt her for the rest of her life.

She had to go back, Kate reaffirmed as she took off her glasses and folded them neatly on the blotter. And it was Ky Silver she'd have to go to. Her father's aspirations had drawn her away from Ky once; now, four years later, they were drawing her back.

But Dr. Kathleen Hardesty knew the difference between fairy tales and reality. Reaching in her father's desk drawer, she drew out a sheet of thick creamy stationery and began to write.

Ky let the wind buffet him as he opened the throttle. He liked speed in much the same way he liked a lazy afternoon in the hammock. They were two of the things that made life worthwhile. He was used to the smell of salt spray, but he still inhaled deeply. He was well accustomed to the vibration of the deck under his feet, but he still felt it. He wasn't a man to let anything go unnoticed or unappreciated.

He grew up in this quiet, remote little coastal town, and though he'd traveled and intended to travel more, he didn't plan to live anywhere else. It suited him— the freedom of the sea, and the coziness of a small community.

He didn't resent the tourists because he knew they helped keep the village alive, but he preferred the island in winter. Then the storms blew wild and cold, and only the hearty would brave the ferry across Hatteras Inlet.

He fished, but unlike the majority of his neighbors, he rarely sold what he caught. What he pulled out of the sea, he ate. He dove, occasionally collecting shells, but again, this was for his own pleasure. Often he took tourists out on his boat to fish or to scuba dive, because there were times he enjoyed the company. But there were afternoons, like this sparkling one, when he simply wanted the sea to himself.

He had always been restless. His mother had said that he came into the world two weeks early because he grew impatient waiting. Ky turned thirty-two that spring, but was far from settled. He knew what he wanted—to live as he chose. The trouble was that he wasn't certain just what he wanted to choose.

At the moment, he chose the open sky and the endless sea. There were other moments when he knew that that wouldn't be enough.

But the sun was hot, the breeze cool and the shoreline was drawing near. The boat's motor was purring smoothly and in the small cooler was a tidy catch of fish he'd cook up for his supper that night. On a crystal, sparkling afternoon, perhaps it was enough.

From the shore he looked like a pirate might if there were pirates in the twentieth century. His hair was long enough to curl over his ears and well over the collar of a shirt had he worn one. It was black, a rich, true black that might have come from his Arapaho or Sicilian blood. His eyes were the deep, dark green of the sea on a cloudy day. His skin was bronzed from years in the sun, taut from the years of swimming and pulling in nets. His bone structure was also part of his heritage, sculpted, hard, defined.

When he smiled as he did now, racing the wind to shore, his face took on that reckless freedom women found irresistible. When he didn't smile, his eyes could turn as cold as a lion's before a leap. He discovered long ago that women found that equally irresistible.

Ky drew back on the throttle so that the boat slowed, rocked, then glided into its slip in Silver Lake Harbor. With the quick, efficient movements of one born to the sea, he leaped onto the dock to secure the lines.

"Catch anything?"

Ky straightened and turned. He smiled, but absently, as one does at a brother seen almost every day of one's life. "Enough. Things slow at the Roost?"

Marsh smiled, and there was a brief flicker of family resemblance, but his eyes were a calm light brown and his hair was carefully styled. "Worried about your investment?"

Ky gave a half-shrug. "With you running things?"

Marsh didn't comment. They knew each other as intimately as men ever know each other. One was restless, the other calm. The opposition never seemed to matter. "Linda wants you to come up for dinner. She worries about you."

She would, Ky thought, amused. His sister-in-law loved to mother and fuss, even though she was five years younger than Ky. That was one of the reasons the restaurant she ran with Marsh was such a success—that, plus Marsh's business sense and the hefty investment and shrewd renovations Ky had made. Ky left the managing up to his brother and his sister-in-law. He didn't mind owning a restaurant, even keeping half an eye on the profit and loss, but he certainly had no interest in running one.

After the lines were secure, he wiped his palms down the hips of his cut-offs. "What's the special tonight?"

Marsh dipped his hands into his front pockets and rocked back on his heels. "Bluefish."

Grinning, Ky tossed back the lid of his cooler revealing his catch. "Tell Linda not to worry. I'll eat."

"That's not going to satisfy her." Marsh glanced at his brother as Ky looked out to sea. "She thinks you're alone too much."

"You're only alone too much if you don't like being alone." Ky glanced back over his shoulder. He didn't want to debate now, when the exhilaration of the speed and the sea were still upon him. But he'd never been a man to placate. "Maybe you two should think about having another baby, then Linda would be too busy to worry about big brothers."

"Give me a break. Hope's only eighteen months old."

"You've got to add nine to that," Ky reminded him carelessly. He was fond of his niece, despite—no, because she was a demon. "Anyway, it looks like the family lineage is in your hands."

"Yeah." Marsh shifted his feet, cleared his throat

and fell silent. It was a habit he'd carried since childhood, one that could annoy or amuse Ky depending on his mood. At the moment, it was only mildly distracting.

Something was in the air. He could smell it, but he couldn't quite identify it. A storm brewing, he wondered? One of those hot, patient storms that seemed capable of brewing for weeks. He was certain he could smell it.

"Why don't you tell me what else is on your mind?" Ky suggested. "I want to get back to the house and clean these."

"You had a letter. It was put in our box by mistake."

It was a common enough occurrence, but by his brother's expression Ky knew there was more. His sense of an impending storm grew sharper. Saying nothing, he held out his hand.

"Ky…" Marsh began. There was nothing he could say, just as there'd been nothing to say four years before. Reaching in his back pocket, he drew out the letter.

The envelope was made from heavy cream-colored paper. Ky didn't have to look at the return address. The handwriting and the memories it brought leaped out at him. For a moment, he felt his breath catch in his lungs as it might if someone had caught him with a blow to the solar plexus. Deliberately, he expelled it. "Thanks," he said, as if it meant nothing. He stuck the letter in his pocket before he picked up his cooler and gear.

"Ky—" Again Marsh broke off. His brother had turned his head, and the cool, half-impatient stare said very clearly—back off. "If you change your mind about dinner," Marsh said.

"I'll let you know." Ky went down the length of the dock without looking back.

He was grateful he hadn't bothered to bring his car down to the harbor. He needed to walk. He needed the fresh air and the exercise to keep his mind clear while he remembered what he didn't want to remember. What he never really forgot.

Kate. Four years ago she'd walked out of his life with the same sort of cool precision with which she'd walked into it. She had reminded him of a Victorian doll—a little prim, a little aloof. He'd never had much patience with neatly folded hands or haughty manners, yet almost from the first instant he'd wanted her.

At first, he thought it was the fact that she was so different. A challenge—something for Ky Silver to conquer. He enjoyed teaching her to dive, and watching the precise step-by-step way she learned. It hadn't been any hardship to look at her in a snug scuba suit, although she didn't have voluptuous curves. She had a trim, neat, almost boylike figure and what seemed like yards of thick, soft hair.

He could still remember the first time she took it down from its pristine knot. It left him breathless, hurting, fascinated. Ky would have touched it—touched her then and there if her father hadn't been standing beside her. But if a man was clever, if a man was determined, he could find a way to be alone with a woman.

Ky had found ways. Kate had taken to diving as though she'd been born to it. While her father had buried himself in his books, Ky had taken Kate out on the water—under the water, to the silent, dreamlike world that had attracted her just as it had always attracted him.

He could remember the first time he kissed her. They had been wet and cool from a dive, standing on the deck of his boat. He was able to see the lighthouse behind her and the vague line of the coast. Her hair had flowed down her back, sleek from the water, dripping with it. He'd reached out and gathered it in his hand.

"What are you doing?"

Four years later, he could hear that low, cultured, eastern voice, the curiosity in it. It took no effort for him to see the curiosity that had been in her eyes.

"I'm going to kiss you."

The curiosity had remained in her eyes, fascinating him. "Why?"

"Because I want to."

It was as simple as that for him. He wanted to. Her body had stiffened as he'd drawn her against him. When her lips parted in protest, he closed his over them. In the time it takes a heart to beat, the rigidity had melted from her body. She'd kissed him with all the young, stored-up passion that had been in her— passion mixed with innocence. He was experienced enough to recognize her innocence, and that too had fascinated him. Ky had, foolishly, youthfully and completely, fallen in love.

Kate had remained an enigma to him, though they shared impassioned hours of laughter and long, lazy talks. He admired her thirst for learning and she had a predilection for putting knowledge into neat slots that baffled him. She was enthusiastic about diving, but it hadn't been enough for her simply to be able to swim freely underwater, taking her air from tanks. She had to know how the tanks worked, why they were fashioned a certain way. Ky watched her absorb what he told her, and knew she'd retain it.

They had taken walks along the shoreline at night and she had recited poetry from memory. Beautiful words, Byron, Shelley, Keats. And he, who'd never been overly impressed by such things, had eaten it up because her voice had made the words somehow personal. Then she'd begin to talk about syntax, iambic pentameters, and Ky would find new ways to divert her.

For three months, he did little but think of her. For the first time, Ky had considered changing his lifestyle. His little cottage near the beach needed work. It needed furniture. Kate would need more than milk crates and the hammock that had been his style. Because he'd been young and had never been in love before, Ky had taken his own plans for granted.

She'd walked out on him. She'd had her own plans, and he hadn't been part of them.

Her father came back to the island the following summer, and every summer thereafter. Kate never came back. Ky knew she had completed her doctorate and was teaching in a prestigious ivy league school where her father was all but a cornerstone. She had what she wanted. So, he told himself as he swung open the screen door of his cottage, did he. He went where he wanted, when he wanted. He called his own shots. His responsibilities extended only as far as he chose to extend them. To his way of thinking, that itself was a mark of success.

Setting the cooler on the kitchen floor, Ky opened the refrigerator. He twisted the top off a beer and drank half of it in one icy cold swallow. It washed some of the bitterness out of his mouth.

Calm now, and curious, he pulled the letter out of his pocket. Ripping it open, he drew out the single neatly written sheet.

Dear Ky,
You may or may not be aware that my father suffered a fatal heart attack two weeks ago. It was very sudden, and I'm currently trying to tie up the many details this involves.

In going through my father's papers, I find that he had again made arrangements to come to the island this summer, and engage your services. I now find it necessary to take his place. For reasons which I'd rather explain in person, I need your help. You have my father's deposit. When I arrive in Ocracoke on the fifteenth, we can discuss terms.

If possible, contact me at the hotel, or leave a message. I hope we'll be able to come to a mutually agreeable arrangement. Please give my best to Marsh. Perhaps I'll see him during my stay.

Best,
Kathleen Hardesty

So the old man was dead. Ky set down the letter and lifted his beer again. He couldn't say he'd had any liking for Edwin Hardesty. Kate's father had been a stringent, humorless man. Still, he hadn't disliked him. Ky had, in an odd way, gotten used to his company over the past few summers. But this summer, it would be Kate.

Ky glanced at the letter again, then jogged his memory until he remembered the date. Two days, he mused. She'd be there in two days...to discuss terms. A smile played around the corners of his mouth but it didn't have anything to do with humor. They'd discuss terms, he agreed silently as he scanned Kate's letter again.

She wanted to take her father's place. Ky wondered if she'd realized, when she wrote that, just how ironic it was. Kathleen Hardesty had been obediently dogging her father's footsteps all her life. Why should that change after his death?

Had she changed? Ky wondered briefly. Would that fascinating aura of innocence and aloofness still cling to her? Or perhaps that had faded with the years. Would that rather sweet primness have developed into a rigidity? He'd see for himself in a couple of days, he realized, but tossed the letter onto the counter rather than into the trash.

So, she wanted to engage his services, he mused. Leaning both hands on either side of the sink, he looked out the window in the direction of the water he could smell, but not quite see. She wanted a business arrangement—the rental of his boat, his gear and his time. He felt the bitterness well up and swallowed it as cleanly as he had the beer. She'd have her business arrangement. And she'd pay. He'd see to that.

Ky left the kitchen with his catch still in the cooler. The appetite he'd worked up with salt spray and speed had vanished.

Kate pulled her car onto the ferry to Ocracoke and set the brake. The morning was cool and very clear. Even so, she was tempted to simply lean her head back and close her eyes. She wasn't certain what impulse had pushed her to drive from Connecticut rather than fly, but now that she'd all but reached her destination, she was too weary to analyze.

In the bucket seat beside her was her briefcase, and inside, all the papers she'd collected from her father's desk. Perhaps once she was in the hotel on the island, she could go through them again, understand them better. Perhaps the feeling that she was doing the right thing would come back. Over the past few days she'd lost that sense.

The closer she came to the island, the more she began to think she was making a mistake. Not to the island, Kate corrected ruthlessly—the closer she came to Ky. It was a fact, and Kate knew it was imperative to face facts so that they could be dealt with logically.

She had a little time left, a little time to calm the feelings that had somehow gotten stirred up during the drive south. It was foolish, and somehow it helped Kate to remind herself of that. She wasn't a woman returning to a lover, but a woman hoping to engage a diver in a very specific venture. Past personal feelings wouldn't enter into it because they were just that. Past.

The Kate Hardesty who'd arrived on Ocracoke four years ago had little to do with the Dr. Kathleen Hardesty who was going there now. She wasn't young, inexperienced or impressionable. Those reckless, wild traits of Ky's wouldn't appeal to her now. They wouldn't frighten her. They would be, if Ky agreed to her terms, business partners.

Kate felt the ferry move beneath her as she stared through the windshield. Yes, she thought, unless Ky had changed a great deal, the prospect of diving for treasure would appeal to his sense of adventure.

She knew enough about diving in the technical sense to be sure she'd find no one better equipped for the job. It was always advisable to have the best. More relaxed and less weary, Kate stepped out of her car to stand at the rail. From there she could watch the gulls swoop and the tiny uninhabited islands pass by. She felt a sense of homecoming, but pushed it away. Connecticut was home. Once Kate did what she came for, she'd go back.

The water swirled behind the boat. She couldn't hear it over the motor, but looking down she could watch the wake. One island was nearly imperceptible under a flock of big, brown pelicans. It made her smile, pleased to see the odd, awkward-looking birds again. They passed the long spit of land, where fishermen parked trucks and tried their luck, near the point where bay met sea. She could watch the waves crash and foam where there was no shore, just a turbulent marriage of waters. That was something she hadn't forgotten, though she hadn't seen it since she left the island. Nor had she forgotten just how treacherous the current was along that verge.

Excitement. She breathed deeply before she turned back to her car. The treacherous was always exciting.

When the ferry docked, she had only a short wait before she could drive her car onto the narrow blacktop. The trip to town wouldn't take long, and it wasn't possible to lose your way if you stayed on the one long road. The sea battered on one side, the sound flowed smoothly on the other—both were deep blue in the late morning light.

Her nerves were gone, at least that's what she told herself. It had just been a case of last-minute jitters—

very normal. She was prepared to see Ky again, speak to him, work with him if they could agree on the terms.

With the windows down, the soft, moist air blew around her. It was soothing. She'd almost forgotten just how soothing air could be, or the sound of water lapping constantly against sand. It was right to come. When she saw the first faded buildings of the village, she felt a wave of relief. She was here. There was no turning back now.

The hotel where she had stayed that summer with her father was on the sound side of the island. It was small and quiet. If the service was a bit slow by northern standards, the view made up for it.

Kate pulled up in front and turned off the ignition. Self-satisfaction made her sigh. She'd taken the first step and was completely prepared for the next.

Then as she stepped out of the car, she saw him. For an instant, the confident professor of English literature vanished. She was only a woman, vulnerable to her own emotions.

Oh God, he hasn't changed. Not at all. As Ky came closer, she could remember every kiss, every murmur, every crazed storm of their loving. The breeze blew his hair back from his face so that every familiar angle and plane was clear to her. With the sun warm on her skin, bright in her eyes, she felt the years spin back, then forward again. He hadn't changed.

He hadn't expected to see her yet. Somehow he thought she'd arrive that afternoon. Yet he found it necessary to go by the Roost that morning knowing the restaurant was directly across from the hotel where she'd be staying.

She was here, looking neat and a bit too thin in her

tailored slacks and blouse. Her hair was pinned up so that the soft femininity of her neck and throat were revealed. Her eyes seemed too dark against her pale skin—skin Ky knew would turn golden slowly under the summer sun.

She looked the same. Soft, prim, calm. Lovely. He ignored the thud in the pit of his stomach as he stepped in front of her. He looked her up and down with the arrogance that was so much a part of him. Then he grinned because he had an overwhelming urge to strangle her.

"Kate. Looks like my timing's good."

She was almost certain she couldn't speak and was therefore determined to speak calmly. "Ky, it's nice to see you again."

"Is it?"

Ignoring the sarcasm, Kate walked around to her trunk and released it. "I'd like to get together with you as soon as possible. There are some things I want to show you, and some business I'd like to discuss."

"Sure, always open for business."

He watched her pull two cases from her trunk, but didn't offer to help. He saw there was no ring on her hand—but it wouldn't have mattered.

"Perhaps we can meet this afternoon then, after I've settled in." The sooner the better, she told herself. They would establish the purpose, the ground rules and the payment. "We could have lunch in the hotel."

"No, thanks," he said easily, leaning against the side of her car while she set her cases down. "You want me, you know where to find me. It's a small island."

With his hands in the pockets of his jeans, he walked away from her. Though she didn't want to, Kate remembered that the last time he'd walked away, they'd stood in almost the same spot.

Picking up her cases, she headed for the hotel, perhaps a bit too quickly.

Chapter 2

She knew where to find him. If the island had been double in size, she'd still have known where to find him. Kate acknowledged that Ky hadn't changed. That meant if he wasn't out on his boat, he would be at home, in the small, slightly dilapidated cottage he owned near the beach. Because she felt it would be a strategic error to go after him too soon, she dawdled over her unpacking.

But there were memories even here, where she'd spent one giddy, whirlwind night of love with Ky. It had been the only time they were able to sleep together through the night, embracing each other in the crisp hotel sheets until the first light of dawn crept around the edges of the window shades. She remembered how reckless she'd felt during those few stolen hours, and how dull the morning had seemed because it brought them to an end.

Now she could look out the same window she had stood by then, staring out in the same direction she'd stared out then when she watched Ky walk away. She remembered the sky had been streaked with a rose color before it had brightened to a pure, pale blue.

Then, with her skin still warm from her lover's touch and her mind glazed with lack of sleep and passion, Kate had believed such things could go on forever. But of course they couldn't. She had seen that only weeks later. Passion and reckless nights of loving had to give way to responsibilities, obligations.

Staring out the same window, in the same direction, Kate could feel the sense of loss she'd felt that long ago dawn without the underlying hope that they'd be together again. And again.

They wouldn't be together again, and there'd been no one else since that one heady summer. She had her career, her vocation, her books. She had had her taste of passion.

Turning away, she busied herself by rearranging everything she'd just arranged in her drawers and closet. When she decided she'd stalled in her hotel room long enough, Kate started out. She didn't take her car. She walked, just as she always walked to Ky's home.

She told herself she was over the shock of seeing him again. It was only natural that there be some strain, some discomfort. She was honest enough to admit that it would have been easier if there'd been only strain and discomfort, and not that one sharp quiver of pleasure. Kate acknowledged it, now that it had passed.

No, Ky Silver hadn't changed, she reminded herself. He was still arrogant, self-absorbed and cocky. Those traits might have appealed to her once, but she'd been very young. If she were wise, she could use those same traits to persuade Ky to help her. Yes, those traits, she thought, and the tempting offer of a treasure hunt. Even at her most pessimistic, she couldn't believe Ky would refuse. It was his nature to take chances.

This time she'd be in charge. Kate drew in a deep breath of warm air that tasted of sea. Somehow she felt it would steady her. Ky was going to find she was no longer naive, or susceptible to a few careless words of affection.

With her briefcase in hand, Kate walked through the village. This too was the same, she thought. She was glad of it. The simplicity and solitude still appealed to her. She enjoyed the dozens of little shops, the restaurants and small inns tucked here and there, all somehow using the harbor as a central point, the lighthouse as a landmark. The villagers still made the most of their notorious one-time resident and permanent ghost, Blackbeard. His name or face was lavishly displayed on store signs.

She passed the harbor, unconsciously scanning for Ky's boat. It was there, in the same slip he'd always used—clean lines, scrubbed deck, shining hardware. The flying bridge gleamed in the afternoon light and looked the same as she remembered. Reckless, challenging. The paint was fresh and there was no film of salt spray on the bridge windows. However careless Ky had been about his own appearance or his home, he'd always pampered his boat.

The *Vortex*. Kate studied the flamboyant lettering on the stern. He could pamper, she thought again, but he also expected a lot in return. She knew the speed he could urge out of the secondhand cabin cruiser he'd lovingly reconstructed himself. Nothing could block the image of the days she'd stood beside him at the helm. The wind had whipped her hair as he'd laughed and pushed for speed, and more speed. Her heart thudded, her pulse raced until she was certain nothing and no one could catch them. She'd been afraid, of him, of the rush of wind—but she'd stayed with both. In the end, she'd left both.

He enjoyed the demanding, the thrilling, the frightening. Kate gripped the handle of her briefcase tighter. Isn't that why she came to him? There were dozens of other experienced divers, many, many other experts on the coastal waters of the Outer Banks. There was only one Ky Silver.

"Kate? Kate Hardesty?"

At the sound of her name, Kate turned and felt the years tumble back again. "Linda!" This time there was no restraint. With an openness she showed to very few, Kate embraced the woman who dashed up to her. "It's wonderful to see you." With a laugh, she drew Linda away to study her. The same chestnut hair cut short and pert, the same frank, brown eyes. It seemed very little had changed on the island. "You look wonderful."

"When I looked out the window and saw you, I could hardly believe it. Kate, you've barely changed at all." With her usual candor and lack of pretension, Linda took a quick, thorough survey. It was quick only because she did things quickly, but it wasn't subtle. "You're too thin," she decided. "But that might be jealousy."

"You still look like a college freshman," Kate returned. "That is jealousy."

As swiftly as the laugh had come, Linda sobered.

"I'm sorry about your father, Kate. These past weeks must've been difficult for you."

Kate heard the sincerity, but she'd already tied up her grief and stored it away. "Ky told you?"

"Ky never tells me anything," Linda said with a sniff. In an unconscious move, she glanced in the direction of his boat. It was in its slip and Kate had been walking north—in the direction of Ky's cottage. There could be only one place she could have been going. "Marsh did. How long are you going to stay?"

"I'm not sure yet." She felt the weight of her briefcase. Dreams held the same weight as responsibilities. "There are some things I have to do."

"One of the things you have to do is have dinner at the Roost tonight. It's the restaurant right across from your hotel."

Kate looked back at the rough wooden sign. "Yes, I noticed it. Is it new?"

Linda glanced over her shoulder with a self-satisfied nod. "By Ocracoke standards. We run it."

"We?"

"Marsh and I." With a beaming smile, Linda held out her left hand. "We've been married for three years." Then she rolled her eyes in a habit Kate remembered. "It only took me fifteen years to convince him he couldn't live without me."

"I'm happy for you." She was, and if she felt a pang, she ignored it. "Married and running a restaurant. My father never filled me in on island gossip."

"We have a daughter too. Hope. She's a year and a half old and a terror. For some reason, she takes after Ky." Linda sobered again, laying a hand lightly on Kate's arm. "You're going to see him now." It wasn't a question; she didn't bother to disguise it as one.

"Yes." *Keep it casual,* Kate ordered herself. Don't let the questions and concern in Linda's eyes weaken you. There were ties between Linda and Ky, not only newly formed family ones, but the older tie of the island. "My father was working on something. I need Ky's help with it."

Linda studied Kate's calm face. "You know what you're doing?"

"Yes." She didn't show a flicker of unease. Her stomach slowly wrapped itself in knots. "I know what I'm doing."

"Okay." Accepting Kate's answer, but not satisfied, Linda dropped her hand. "Please come by—the restaurant or the house. We live just down the road from Ky. Marsh'll want to see you, and I'd like to show off Hope—and our menu," she added with a grin. "Both are outstanding."

"Of course I'll come by." On impulse, she took both of Linda's hands. "It's really good to see you again. I know I didn't keep in touch, but—"

"I understand." Linda gave her hands a quick squeeze. "That was yesterday. I've got to get back, the lunch crowd's pretty heavy during the season." She let out a little sigh, wondering if Kate was as calm as she seemed. And if Ky were as big a fool as ever. "Good luck," she murmured, then dashed across the street again.

"Thanks," Kate said under her breath. She was going to need it.

The walk was as beautiful as she remembered. She passed the little shops with their display windows showing handmade crafts or antiques. She passed the blue-and-white clapboard houses and the neat little streets on the outskirts of town with their bleached green lawns and leafy trees.

A dog raced back and forth on the length of his chain as she wandered by, barking at her as if he knew he was supposed to but didn't have much interest in it. She could see the tower of the white lighthouse. There'd been a keeper there once, but those days were over. Then she was on the narrow path that led to Ky's cottage.

Her palms were damp. She cursed herself. If she had to remember, she'd remember later, when she was alone. When she was safe.

The path was as it had been, just wide enough for a car, sparsely graveled, lined with bushes that always grew out a bit too far. The bushes and trees had always had a wild, overgrown look that suited the spot. That suited him.

Ky had told her he didn't care much for visitors. If he wanted company, all he had to do was go into town where he knew everyone. That was typical of Ky Silver, Kate mused. If I want you, I'll let you know. Otherwise, back off.

He'd wanted her once… Nervous, Kate shifted the briefcase to her other hand. Whatever he wanted now, he'd have to hear her out. She needed him for what he was best at—diving and taking chances.

When the house came into view, she stopped, staring. It was still small, still primitive. But it no longer looked as though it would keel over on its side in a brisk wind.

The roof had been redone. Obviously Ky wouldn't

need to set out pots and pans during a rain any longer. The porch he'd once talked vaguely about building now ran the length of the front, sturdy and wide. The screen door that had once been patched in a half a dozen places had been replaced by a new one. Yet nothing looked new, she observed. It just looked right. The cedar had weathered to silver, the windows were untrimmed but gleaming. There was, much to her surprise, a spill of impatiens in a long wooden planter.

She'd been wrong, Kate decided as she walked closer. Ky Silver had changed. Precisely how, and precisely how much, she had yet to find out.

She was nearly to the first step when she heard sounds coming from the rear of the house. There was a shed back there, she remembered, full of boards and tools and salvage. Grateful that she didn't have to meet him in the house, Kate walked around the side to the tiny backyard. She could hear the sea and knew it was less than a two-minute walk through high grass and sand dunes.

Did he still go down there in the evenings? she wondered. Just to look, he'd said. Just to smell. Sometimes he'd pick up driftwood or shells or whatever small treasures the sea gave up to the sand. Once he'd given her a small smooth shell that fit into the palm of her hand— very white with a delicate pink center. A woman with her first gift of diamonds could not have been more thrilled.

Shaking the memories away, she went into the shed. It was as tall as the cottage and half as wide. The last time she'd been there, it'd been crowded with planks and boards and boxes of hardware. Now she saw the hull of a boat. At a worktable with his back to her, Ky sanded the mast.

"You've built it." The words came out before she could stop them, full of astonished pleasure. How many times had he told her about the boat he'd build one day? It had seemed to Kate it had been his only concrete ambition. Mahogany on oak, he'd said. A seventeen-foot sloop that would cut through the water like a dream. He'd have bronze fastenings and teak on the deck. One day he'd sail the inner coastal waters from Ocracoke to New England. He'd described the boat so minutely that she'd seen it then just as clearly as she saw it now.

"I told you I would." Ky turned away from the mast and faced her. She, in the doorway, had the sun at her back. He was half in shadow.

"Yes." Feeling foolish, Kate tightened her grip on the briefcase. "You did."

"But you didn't believe me." Ky tossed aside the sandpaper. Did she have to look so neat and cool, and impossibly lovely? A trickle of sweat ran down his back. "You always had a problem seeing beyond the moment."

Reckless, impatient, compelling. Would he always bring those words to her mind? "You always had a problem dealing with the moment," she said.

His brow lifted, whether in surprise or derision she couldn't be sure. "Then it might be said *we* always had a problem." He walked to her, so that the sun slanting through the small windows fell over him, then behind him. "But it didn't always seem to matter." To satisfy himself that he still could, Ky reached out and touched her face. She didn't move, and her skin was as soft and cool as he remembered. "You look tired Kate."

The muscles in her stomach quivered, but not her voice. "It was a long trip."

His thumb brushed along her cheekbone. "You need some sun."

This time she backed away. "I intend to get some."

"So I gathered from your letter." Pleased that she'd retreated first, Ky leaned against the open door. "You wrote that you wanted to talk to me in person. You're here. Why don't you tell me what you want?"

The cocky grin might have made her melt once. Now it stiffened her spine. "My father was researching a project. I intend to finish it."

"So?"

"I need your help."

Ky laughed and stepped past her into the sunlight. He needed the air, the distance. He needed to touch her again. "From your tone, there's nothing you hate more than asking me for it."

"No." She stood firm, feeling suddenly strong and bitter. "Nothing."

There was no humor in his eyes as he faced her again. The expression in them was cold and flat. She'd seen it before. "Then let's understand each other before we start. You left the island and me, and took what I wanted."

He couldn't make her cringe now as he once had with only that look. "What happened four years ago has nothing to do with today."

"The hell it doesn't." He came toward her again so that she took an involuntary step backward. "Still afraid of me?" he asked softly.

As it had a moment ago, the question turned the fear to anger. "No," she told him, and meant it. "I'm not afraid of you, Ky. I've no intention of discussing the past, but I will agree that I left the island and you. I'm here now on business. I'd like you to hear me out. If you're interested, we'll discuss terms, nothing else."

"I'm not one of your students, professor." The drawl crept into his voice, as it did when he let it. "Don't instruct."

She curled her fingers tighter around the handle of her briefcase. "In business, there are always ground rules."

"Nobody agreed to let you make them."

"I made a mistake," Kate said quietly as she fought for control. "I'll find someone else."

She'd taken only two steps away when Ky grabbed her arm. "No, you won't." The stormy look in his eyes made her throat dry. She knew what he meant. She'd never find anyone else that could make her feel as he made her feel, or want as he made her want. Deliberately, Kate removed his hand from her arm.

"I came here on business. I've no intention of fighting with you over something that doesn't exist any longer."

"We'll see about that." How long could he hold on? Ky wondered. It hurt just to look at her and to feel her withdrawing with every second that went by. "But for now, why don't you tell me what you have in that businesslike briefcase, professor."

Kate took a deep breath. She should have known it wouldn't be easy. Nothing was ever easy with Ky. "Charts," she said precisely. "Notebooks full of research, maps, carefully documented facts and precise theories. In my opinion, my father was very close to pinpointing the exact location of the *Liberty,* an English merchant vessel that sank, stores intact, off the North Carolina coast two hundred and fifty years ago."

He listened without a comment or a change of expression from beginning to end. When she finished, Ky studied her face for one long moment. "Come inside," he said and turned toward the house. "Show me what you've got."

His arrogance made her want to turn away and go back to town exactly as she'd come. There were other divers, others who knew the coast and the waters as well as Ky did. Kate forced herself to calm down, forced herself to think. There were others, but if it was a choice between the devil she knew and the unknown, she had no choice. Kate followed him into the house.

This, too, had changed. The kitchen she remembered had had a paint splattered floor, with the only usable counter space being a tottering picnic table. The floor had been stripped and varnished, the cabinets redone, and scrubbed butcher block counters lined the sink. He had put in a skylight so that the sun spilled down over the picnic table, now re-worked and re-painted, with benches along either side.

"Did you do all of this yourself?"

"Yeah. Surprised?"

So he didn't want to make polite conversation. Kate set her briefcase on the table. "Yes. You always seemed content that the walls were about to cave in on you."

"I was content with a lot of things, once. Want a beer?"

"No." Kate sat down and drew the first of her father's notebooks out of her briefcase. "You'll want to read these. It would be unnecessary and time-consuming for you to read every page, but if you'd look over the ones I've marked, I think you'll have enough to go by."

"All right." Ky turned from the refrigerator, beer in hand. He sat, watching her over the rim as he took the first swallow, then he opened the notebook.

Edwin Hardesty's handwriting was very clear and precise. He wrote down his facts in didactic, unromantic terms. What could have been exciting was as dry as a thesis, but it was accurate. Ky had no doubt of that.

The *Liberty* had been lost, with its stores of sugar, tea, silks, wine and other imports for the colonies. Hardesty had listed the manifest down to the last piece of hardtack. When it had left England, the ship had also been carrying gold. Twenty-five thousand in coins of the realm. Ky glanced up from the notebook to see Kate watching him.

"Interesting," he said simply, and turned to the next page she marked.

There'd been only three survivors who'd washed up on the island. One of the crew had described the storm that had sunk the *Liberty,* giving details on the height of the waves, the splintering wood, the water gushing into the hole. It was a grim, grisly story which Hardesty had recounted in his pragmatic style, complete with footnotes. The crewman had also given the last known location of the ship before it had gone down. Ky didn't require Hardesty's calculations to figure the ship had sunk two-and-a-half miles off the coast of Ocracoke.

Going from one notebook to another, Ky read through Hardesty's well-drafted theories, his clear to-the-point documentations, corroborated and recorroborated. He scanned the charts, then studied them with more care. He remembered the man's avid interest in diving, which had always seemed inconsistent with his precise lifestyle.

So he'd been looking for gold, Ky mused. All these years the man had been digging in books and looking for gold. If it had been anyone else, Ky might have dismissed it as another fable. Little towns along the coast were full of stories about buried treasure. Edward Teach had used the shallow waters of the inlets to frustrate and outwit the crown until his last battle off the shores of Ocracoke. That alone kept the dreams of finding sunken treasures alive.

But it was Dr. Edwin J. Hardesty, Yale professor, an unimaginative, humorless man who didn't believe there was time to be wasted on the frivolous, who'd written these notebooks.

Ky might still have dismissed it, but Kate was sitting across from him. He had enough adventurous blood in him to believe in destinies.

Setting the last notebook aside, he picked up his beer again. "So, you want to treasure hunt."

She ignored the humor in his voice. With her hands folded on the table, she leaned forward. "I intend to follow through with what my father was working on."

"Do you believe it?"

Did she? Kate opened her mouth and closed it again. She had no idea. "I don't believe that all of my father's time and research should go for nothing. I want to try. As it happens, I need you to help me do it. You'll be compensated."

"Will I?" He studied the liquid left in the beer bottle with a half smile. "Will I indeed?"

"I need you, your boat and your equipment for a month, maybe two. I can't dive alone because I just don't know the waters well enough to risk it, and I don't have the time to waste. I have to be back in Connecticut by the end of August."

"To get more chalk dust under your fingernails."

She sat back slowly. "You have no right to criticize my profession."

"I'm sure the chalk's very exclusive at Yale," Ky commented. "So you're giving yourself six weeks or so to find a pot of gold."

"If my father's calculations are viable, it won't take that long."

"If," Ky repeated. Setting down his bottle, he leaned forward. "I've got no timetable. You want six weeks of my time, you can have it. For a price."

"Which is?"

"A hundred dollars a day and fifty percent of whatever we find."

Kate gave him a cool look as she slipped the notebooks back into her briefcase. "Whatever I was four years ago, Ky, I'm not a fool now. A hundred dollars a day is outrageous when we're dealing with monthly rates. And fifty percent is out of the question." It gave her a certain satisfaction to bargain with him. This made it business, pure and simple. "I'll give you fifty dollars a day and ten percent."

With the maddening half grin on his face he swirled the beer in the bottle. "I don't turn my boat on for fifty a day."

She tilted her head a bit to study him. Something tore inside him. She'd often done that whenever he said something she wanted to think over. "You're more mercenary than you once were."

"We've all got to make a living, professor." Didn't

she feel anything? he thought furiously. Wasn't she suffering just a little, being in the house where they'd made love their first and last time? "You want a service," he said quietly, "you pay for it. Nothing's free. Seventy-five a day and twenty-five percent. We'll say it's for old-times' sake."

"No, we'll say it's for business' sake." She made herself extend her hand, but when his closed over it, she regretted the gesture. It was calloused, hard, strong. Kate knew how his hand felt skimming over her skin, driving her to desperation, soothing, teasing, seducing.

"We have a deal." Ky thought he could see a flash of remembrance in her eyes. He kept her hand in his knowing she didn't welcome his touch. Because she didn't. "There's no guarantee you'll find your treasure."

"That's understood."

"Fine. I'll deduct your father's deposit from the total."

"All right." With her free hand, she clutched at her briefcase. "When do we start?"

"Meet me at the harbor at eight tomorrow." Deliberately, he placed his other free hand over hers on the leather case. "Leave this with me. I want to look over the papers some more."

"There's no need for you to have them," Kate began, but his hands tightened on hers.

"If you don't trust me with them, you take them along." His voice was very smooth and very quiet. At its most dangerous. "And find yourself another diver."

Their gazes locked. Her hands were trapped and so was she. Kate knew there would be sacrifices she'd have to make. "I'll meet you at eight."

"Fine." He released her hands and sat back. "Nice doing business with you, Kate."

Dismissed, she rose. Just how much had she sacrificed already? she wondered. "Goodbye."

He lifted and drained his half-finished beer when the screen shut behind her. Then he made himself sit there until he was certain that when he rose and walked to the window she'd be out of sight. He made himself sit there until the air flowing through the screens had carried her scent away.

Sunken ships and deep-sea treasure. It would have excited him, captured his imagination, enthusiasm and interest if he hadn't had an overwhelming urge to just get in his boat and head toward the horizon. He hadn't believed she could still affect him that way, that much, that completely. He'd forgotten that just being within touching distance of her tied his stomach in knots.

He'd never gotten over her. No matter what he filled his life with over the past four years, he'd never gotten over the slim, intellectual woman with the haughty face and doe's eyes.

Ky sat, staring at the briefcase with her initials stamped discreetly near the handle. He'd never expected her to come back, but he'd just discovered he'd never accepted the fact that she'd left him. Somehow, he'd managed to deceive himself through the years. Now, seeing her again, he knew it had just been a matter of pure survival and nothing to do with truth. He'd had to go on, to pretend that that part of his life was behind him, or he would have gone mad.

She was back now, but she hadn't come back to him. A business arrangement. Ky ran his hand over the smooth leather of the case. She simply wanted the best diver she knew and was willing to pay for him. Fee for services, nothing more, nothing less. The past meant little or nothing to her.

Fury grew until his knuckles whitened around the bottle. He'd give her what she paid for, he promised himself. And maybe a bit extra.

This time when she went away, he wouldn't be left feeling like an inadequate fool. She'd be the one who would have to go on pretending for the rest of her life. This time when she went away, he'd be done with her. God, he'd have to be.

Rising quickly, he went out to the shed. If he stayed inside, he'd give in to the need to get very, very drunk.

Chapter 3

Kate had the water in the tub so hot that the mirror over the white pedestal sink was fogged. Oil floated on the surface, subtly fragrant and soothing. She'd lost track of how long she lay there—soaking, recharging. The next irrevocable step had been taken. She'd survived. Somehow during her discussion with Ky in his kitchen she had fought back the memories of laughter and passion. She couldn't count how many meals they'd shared there, cooking their catch, sipping wine.

Somehow during the walk back to her hotel, she'd overcome the need to weep. Tomorrow would be just a little easier. Tomorrow, and every day that followed. She had to believe it.

His animosity would help. His derision toward her kept Kate from romanticizing what she had to tell herself had never been more than a youthful summer fling.

Perspective. She'd always been able to stand back and align everything in its proper perspective.

Perhaps her feelings for Ky weren't as dead as she had hoped or pretended they were. But her emotions were tinged with bitterness. Only a fool asked for more sorrow. Only a romantic believed that bitterness could ever be sweet. It had been a long time since Kate had been a romantic fool. Even so, they would work together because both had an interest in what might be lying on the sea floor.

Think of it. Two hundred and fifty years. Kate closed her eyes and let her mind drift. The silks and sugar would be gone, but would they find brass fittings deep in corrosion after two-and-a-half centuries? The hull would be covered with fungus and barnacles, but how much of the oak would still be intact? Might the log have been secured in a waterproof hold and still be legible? It could be donated to a museum in her father's name. It would be something—the last something she could do for him. Perhaps then she'd be able to lay all her ambiguous feelings to rest.

The gold, Kate thought as she rose from the tub, the gold would survive. She wasn't immune to the lure of it. Yet she knew it would be the hunt that would be exciting, and somehow fulfilling. If she found it...

What would she do? Kate wondered. She dropped the hotel towel over the rod before she wrapped herself in her robe. Behind her, the mirror was still fogged with steam from the water that drained slowly from the tub. Would she put her share tidily in some conservative investments? Would she take a leisurely trip to the Greek islands to see what Byron had seen and fallen in love with there? With a laugh, Kate walked through to the other room to pick up her brush. Strange, she hadn't thought beyond the search yet. Perhaps that was for the best, it wasn't wise to plan too far ahead.

You always had a problem seeing beyond the moment.

Damn him! With a sudden fury, Kate slammed the brush onto the dresser. She'd seen beyond the moment. She'd seen that he'd offered her no more than a tentative affair in a run-down beach shack. No guarantees, no commitment, no future. She only thanked God she'd had enough of her senses left to understand it and to walk away from what was essentially nothing at all. She'd never let Ky know just how horribly it had hurt to walk away from nothing at all.

Her father had been right to quietly point out the weaknesses in Ky, and her obligation to herself and her chosen profession. Ky's lack of ambition, his careless attitude toward the future weren't qualities, but flaws. She'd had a responsibility, and by accepting it had given herself independence and satisfaction.

Calmer, she picked up her brush again. She was dwelling on the past too much. It was time to stop. With the deft movements of habit, she secured her hair into a sleek twist. From this time on, she'd think only of what was to come, not what had, or might have been.

She needed to get out.

With panic just under the surface, Kate pulled a dress out of her closet. It no longer mattered that she was tired, that all she really wanted to do was to crawl into bed and let her mind and body rest. Nerves wouldn't permit it. She'd go across the street, have a drink with Linda and Marsh. She'd see their baby, have a long, extravagant dinner. When she came back to the hotel, alone, she'd make certain she'd be too tired for dreams.

Tomorrow, she had work to do.

Because she dressed quickly, Kate arrived at the Roost just past six. What she saw, she immediately approved of. It wasn't elegant, but it was comfortable. It didn't have the dimly lit, cathedral feel of so many of the restaurants she'd dined in with her father, with colleagues, back in Connecticut. It was relaxed, welcoming, cozy.

There were paintings of ships and boats along the stuccoed walls, of armadas and cutters. Throughout the dining room was other sailing paraphernalia—a ship's compass with its brass gleaming, a colorful spinnaker draped behind the bar with the stools in front of it shaped like wooden kegs. There was a crow's nest spearing toward the ceiling with ferns spilling out and down the mast.

The room was already half full of couples and families, the bulk of whom Kate identified as tourists. She could hear the comforting sound of cutlery scraping lightly over plates. There was the smell of good food and the hum of mixed conversations.

Comfortable, she thought again, but definitely well organized. Waiters and waitresses in sailor's denims moved smoothly, making every second count without looking rushed. The window opened out to a full evening view of Silver Lake Harbor. Kate turned her back on it because she knew her gaze would fall on the *Vortex* or its empty slip.

Tomorrow was soon enough for that. She wanted one night without memories.

"Kate."

She felt the hands on her shoulders and recognized the voice. There was a smile on her face when she turned around. "Marsh, I'm so glad to see you."

In his quiet way, he studied her, measured her and saw both the strain and the relief. In the same way, he'd had a crush on her that had faded into admiration and respect before the end of that one summer. "Beautiful as ever. Linda said you were, but it's nice to see for myself."

She laughed, because he'd always been able to make her feel as though life could be honed down to the most simple of terms. She'd never questioned why that trait had made her relax with Marsh and tingle with Ky.

"Several congratulations are in order, I hear. On your marriage, your daughter and your business."

"I'll take them all. How about the best table in the house?"

"No less than I expected." She linked her arm through his. "Your life agrees with you," she decided as he led her to a table by the window. "You look happy."

"Look and am." He lifted a hand to brush hers. "We were sorry to hear about your father, Kate."

"I know. Thank you."

Marsh sat across from her and fixed her with eyes so much calmer, so much softer than his brother's. She'd always wondered why the man with the dreamer's eyes had been so practical while Ky had been the real dreamer. "It's tragic, but I can't say I'm sorry it brought you back to the island. We've missed you." He paused, just long enough for effect. "All of us."

Kate picked up the square carmine-colored napkin and ran it through her hands. "Things change," she said deliberately. "You and Linda are certainly proof of that. When I left, you thought she was a bit of a nuisance."

"That hasn't changed," he claimed and grinned. He glanced up at the young, ponytailed waitress. "This is Cindy, she'll take good care of you, Miss Hardesty—" He looked back at Kate with a grin. "I guess I should say Dr. Hardesty."

"Miss'll do," Kate told him. "I've taken the summer off."

"Miss Hardesty's a guest, a special one," he added, giving the waitress a smile. "How about a drink before you order? Or a bottle of wine?"

"Piesporter," the reply came from a deep, masculine voice.

Kate's fingers tightened on the linen, but she forced herself to look up calmly to meet Ky's amused eyes.

"The professor has a fondness for it."

"Yes, Mr. Silver."

Before Kate could agree or disagree, the waitress had dashed off.

"Well, Ky," Marsh commented easily. "You have a way of making the help come to attention."

With a shrug, Ky leaned against his brother's chair. If the three of them felt the air was suddenly tighter, each concealed it in their own way. "I had an urge for scampi."

"I can recommend it," Marsh told Kate. "Linda and the chef debated the recipe, then babied it until they reached perfection."

Kate smiled at Marsh as though there were no dark, brooding man looking down at her. "I'll try it. Are you going to join me?"

"I wish I could. Linda had to run home and deal

with some crisis—Hope has a way of creating them and browbeating the babysitter—but I'll try to get back for coffee. Enjoy your dinner." Rising, he sent his brother a cool, knowing look, then walked away.

"Marsh never completely got over that first case of adulation," Ky commented, then took his brother's seat without invitation.

"Marsh has always been a good friend." Kate draped the napkin over her lap with great care. "Though I realize this is your brother's restaurant, Ky, I'm sure you don't want my company for dinner any more than I want yours."

"That's where you're wrong." He sent a quick, dashing smile at the waitress as she brought the wine. He didn't bother to correct Kate's assumption on the Roost's ownership. Kate sat stone-faced, her manners too good to allow her to argue, while Cindy opened the bottle and poured the first sip for Ky to taste.

"It's fine," he told her. "I'll pour." Taking the bottle, he filled Kate's glass to within half an inch of the rim. "Since we've both chosen the Roost tonight, why don't we have a little test?"

Kate lifted her glass and sipped. The wine was cool and dry. She remembered the first bottle they'd shared—sitting on the floor of his cottage the night she gave him her innocence. Deliberately, she took another swallow. "What kind of test?"

"We can see if the two of us can share a civilized meal in public. That was something we never got around to before."

Kate frowned as he lifted his glass. She'd never seen Ky drink from a wineglass. The few times they had indulged in wine, it had been drunk out of one of the half a dozen water glasses he'd owned. The stemware seemed too delicate for his hand, the wine too mellow for the look in his eye.

No, they'd never eaten dinner in public before. Her father would have exuded disapproval for socializing with someone he'd considered an employee. Kate had known it, and hadn't risked it.

Things were different now, she told herself as she lifted her own glass. In a sense, Ky was now her employee. She could make her own judgments. Recklessly, she toasted him. "To a profitable arrangement then."

"I couldn't have said it better myself." He touched the rim of his glass to hers, but his gaze was direct and uncomfortable. "Blue suits you," he said, referring to her dress, but not taking his eyes off hers. "The deep midnight blue that makes your skin look like something that should be tasted very, very carefully."

She stared at him, stunned at how easily his voice could take on that low, intimate tone that had always made the blood rush out of her brain. He'd always been able to make words seem something dark and secret. That had been one of his greatest skills, one she had never been prepared for. She was no more prepared for it now.

"Would you care to order now?" The waitress stopped beside the table, cheerful, eager to please.

Ky smiled when Kate remained silent. "We're having scampi. The house dressing on the salads will be fine." He leaned back, glass in hand, still smiling. But the smile on his lips didn't connect with his eyes. "You're not drinking your wine. Maybe I should've asked if your taste has changed over the years."

"It's fine." Deliberately she sipped, then kept the

glass in her hand as though it would anchor her. "Marsh looks well," she commented. "I was happy to hear about him and Linda. I always pictured them together."

"Did you?" Ky lifted his glass toward the lowering evening light slanting through the window. He watched the colors spear through the wine and glass and onto Kate's hand. "He didn't. But then…" Shifting his gaze, he met her eyes again. "Marsh always took more time to make up his mind than me."

"Recklessness," she continued as she struggled just to breathe evenly, "was always more your style than your brother's."

"But you didn't come to my brother with your charts and notes, did you?"

"No." With an effort she kept her voice and her eyes level. "I didn't. Perhaps I decided a certain amount of recklessness had its uses."

"Find me useful, do you, Kate?"

The waitress served the salads but didn't speak this time. She saw the look in Ky's eyes.

So had Kate. "When I'm having a job done, I've found that it saves a considerable amount of time and trouble to find the most suitable person." With forced calm, she set down her wine and picked up her fork. "I wouldn't have come back to Ocracoke for any other reason." She tilted her head, surprised by the quick surge of challenge that rushed through her. "Things will be simpler for both of us if that's clear up front."

Anger moved through him, but he controlled it. If they were playing word games, he had to keep his wits. She'd always been clever, but now it appeared the cleverness was glossed over with sophistication. He remembered the innocent, curious Kate with a pang. "As

I recall, you were always one for complicating rather than simplifying. I had to explain the purpose, history and mechanics of every piece of equipment before you'd take the first dive."

"That's called caution, not complication."

"You'd know more about caution than I would. Some people spend half their lives testing the wind." He drank deeply of the wine. "I'd rather ride with it."

"Yes." This time it was she who smiled with her lips only. "I remember very well. No plans, no ties, tomorrow the wind might change."

"If you're anchored in one spot too long, you can become like those trees out there." He gestured out the window where a line of sparse junipers bent away from the sea. "Stunted."

"Yet you're still here, where you were born, where you grew up."

Slowly Ky poured her more wine. "The island's too isolated, the life a bit too basic for some. I prefer it to those structured little communities with their parties and country clubs."

Kate looked like she belonged in such a place, Ky thought as he fought against the frustrated desire that ebbed and flowed inside him. She belonged in an elegant silk suit, holding a Dresden cup and discussing an obscure eighteenth-century English poet. Was that why she could still make him feel rough and awkward and too full of longings?

If they could be swept back in time, he'd have stolen her, taken her out to open sea and kept her there. They would have traveled from port to exotic port. If having her meant he could never go home again, then he'd have sailed until his time was up. But he would have had her. Ky's fingers tightened around his glass. By God, he would have had her.

The main course was slipped in front of him discreetly. Ky brought himself back to the moment. It wasn't the eighteenth century, but today. Still, she had brought him the past with the papers and maps. Perhaps they'd both find more than they'd bargained for.

"I looked over the things you left with me."

"Oh?" She felt a quick tingle of excitement but speared the first delicate shrimp as though it were all that concerned her.

"Your father's research is very thorough."

"Of course."

Ky let out a quick laugh. "Of course," he repeated, toasting her. "In any case, I think he might have been on the right track. You do realize that the section he narrowed it down to goes into a dangerous area."

Her brows drew together, but she continued to eat. "Sharks?"

"Sharks are a little difficult to confine to an area," he said easily. "A lot of people forget that the war came this close in the forties. There are still mines all along the coast of the Outer Banks. If we're going down to the bottom, it'd be smart to keep that in mind."

"I've no intention of being careless."

"No, but sometimes people look so far ahead they don't see what's under their feet."

Though he'd eaten barely half of his meal, Ky picked up his wine again. How could he eat when his whole system was aware of her? He couldn't stop himself from wondering what it would be like to pull those confining pins out of her hair as he'd done so often in the past. He couldn't prevent the memory from springing up about what it had been like to bundle her into his arms and just hold her there with her body fitting so neatly against his. He could picture those long, serious looks she'd give him just before passion would start to take over, then the freedom he could feel racing through her in those last heady moments of lovemaking.

How could it have been so right once and so wrong now? Wouldn't her body still fit against his? Wouldn't her hair flow through his hands as it fell—that quiet brown that took on such fascinating lights in the sun. She'd always murmur his name after passion was spent, as if the sound alone sustained her. He wanted to hear her say it, just once more, soft and breathless while they were tangled together, bodies still warm and pulsing. He wasn't sure he could resist it.

Absently Ky signaled for coffee. Perhaps he didn't want to resist it. He needed her. He'd forgotten just how sharp and sure a need could be. Perhaps he'd take her. He didn't believe she was indifferent to him—certain things never fade completely. In his own time, in his own way, he'd take what he once had from her. And pray it would be enough this time.

When he looked back at her, Kate felt the warning signals shiver through her. Ky was a difficult man to understand. She knew only that he'd come to some decision and that it involved her. Grateful for the warming effects of the coffee, she drank. She was in charge this time, she reminded herself, every step of the way and she'd make him aware of it. There was no time like the present to begin.

"I'll be at the harbor at eight," she said briskly. "I'll require tanks, of course, but I brought my own wet suit. I'd appreciate it if you'd have my briefcase and its contents on board. I believe we'd be wise to spend between six and eight hours out a day."

"Have you kept up with your diving?"

"I know what to do."

"I'd be the last to argue that you had the best teacher." He tilted his cup back in a quick, impatient gesture Kate found typical of him. "But if you're rusty, we'll take it slow for a day or two."

"I'm a perfectly competent diver."

"I want more than competence in a partner."

He saw the flare in her eyes and his need sharpened. It was a rare and arousing thing to watch her controlled and reasonable temperament heat up. "We're not partners. You're working for me."

"A matter of viewpoint," Ky said easily. He rose, deliberately blocking her in. "We'll be putting in a full day tomorrow, so you'd better go catch up on all the sleep you've been missing lately."

"I don't need you to worry about my health, Ky."

"I worry about my own," he said curtly. "You don't go under with me unless you're rested and alert. You come to the harbor in the morning with shadows under your eyes, you won't make the first dive." Furiously she squashed the urge to argue with the reasonable. "If you're sluggish, you make mistakes," Ky said briefly. "A mistake you make can cost me. That logical enough for you, professor?"

"It's perfectly clear." Bracing herself for the brush of bodies, Kate rose. But bracing herself didn't stop the jolt, not for either of them.

"I'll walk you back."

"It's not necessary."

His hand curled over her wrist, strong and stubborn. "It's civilized," he said lazily. "You were always big on being civilized."

Until you'd touch me, she thought. No, she wouldn't remember that, not if she wanted to sleep tonight. Kate merely inclined her head in cool agreement. "I want to thank Marsh."

"You can thank him tomorrow." Ky dropped the waitress's tip on the table. "He's busy."

She started to protest, then saw Marsh disappear into what must have been the kitchen. "All right." Kate moved by him and out into the balmy evening air.

The sun was low, though it wouldn't set for nearly an hour. The clouds to the west were just touched with mauve and rose. When she stepped outside, Kate decided there were more people in the restaurant than there were on the streets.

A charter fishing boat glided into the harbor. Some of the tourists would be staying on the island, others would be riding back across Hatteras Inlet on one of the last ferries of the day.

She'd like to go out on the water now, while the light was softening and the breeze was quiet. Now, she thought, while others were coming in and the sea would stretch for mile after endless empty mile.

Shaking off the mood, she headed for the hotel. What she needed wasn't a sunset sail but a good solid night's sleep. Daydreaming was foolish, and tomorrow too important.

The same hotel. Ky glanced up at her window. He already knew she had the same room. He'd walked her there before, but then she'd have had her arm through his in that sweet way she had of joining them together.

She'd have looked up and laughed at him over something that had happened that day. And she'd have kissed
him, warm, long and lingeringly before the door would
close behind her.

Because her thoughts had run the same gamut, Kate
turned to him while they were still outside the hotel.
"Thank you, Ky." She made a business out of shifting
her purse strap on her arm. "There's no need for you
to go any further out of your way."

"No, there isn't." He'd have something to take home
with him that night, he thought with sudden, fierce impatience. And he'd leave her something to take up to
the room where they'd had one long, glorious night.
"But then we've always looked at needs from different
angles." He cupped his hand around the back of her
neck, holding firm as he felt her stiffen.

"Don't." She didn't back away. Kate told herself
she didn't back away because to do so would make her
seem vulnerable. And she was, feeling those long hard
fingers play against her skin again.

"I think this is something you owe me," he told her
in a voice so quiet it shivered on the air. "Maybe something I owe myself."

He wasn't gentle. That was deliberate. Somewhere
inside him was a need to punish for what hadn't been—
or perhaps what had. The mouth he crushed on hers
hungered, the arms he wrapped around her demanded.
If she'd forgotten, he thought grimly, this would remind
her. And remind him.

With her arms trapped between them, he could feel
her hands ball into tight fists. Let her hate him, loathe
him. He'd rather that than cool politeness.

But God she was sweet. Sweet and as delicate as one

of the frothy waves that lapped and spread along the shoreline. Dimly, distantly, he knew he could drown in her without a murmur or complaint.

She wanted it to be different. Oh, how she wanted it to be different so that she'd feel nothing. But she felt everything.

The hard, impatient mouth that had always thrilled and bemused her—it was the same. The lean restless body that fit so unerringly against her—no different. The scent that clung to him, sea and salt—hadn't changed. Always when he kissed her, there'd been the sounds of water or wind or gulls. That, too, remained constant. Behind them boats rocked gently in their slips, water against wood. A gull resting on pilings let out a long, lonely call. The light dimmed as the sun dropped closer to the sea. The flood of past feelings rose up to merge and mingle with the moment.

She didn't resist him. Kate had told herself she wouldn't give him the satisfaction of a struggle. But the command to her brain not to respond was lost in the thin clouds of dusk. She gave because she had to. She took because she had no choice.

His tongue played over hers and her fists uncurled until Kate's palms rested against his chest. So warm, so hard, so familiar. He kissed as he always had, with complete concentration, no inhibitions and little patience.

Time tumbled back and she was young and in love and foolish. Why, she wondered while her head swam, should that make her want to weep?

He had to let her go or he'd beg. Ky could feel it rising in him. He wasn't fool enough to plead for what was already gone. He wasn't strong enough to accept that he had to let go again. The tug-of-war going on inside him was fierce enough to make him moan. On the sound he pulled away from her, frustrated, infuriated, bewitched.

Taking a moment, he stared down at her. Her look was the same, he realized—that half surprised, half speculative look she'd given him after their first kiss. It disoriented him. Whatever he'd sought to prove, Ky knew now he'd only proven that he was still as much enchanted with her as he'd ever been. He bit back an oath, instead, giving her a half salute as he walked away.

"Get eight hours of sleep," he ordered without turning around.

Chapter 4

Some mornings the sun seemed to rise more slowly than others, as if nature wanted to show off her particular majesty just a bit longer. When she'd gone to bed, Kate had left her shades up knowing that the morning light would awaken her before the travel alarm beside her bed rang.

She took the dawn as a gift to herself, something individual and personal. Standing at the window, she watched it bloom. The first quiet breeze of morning drifted through the screen to run over her hair and face, through the thin material of her nightshirt, cool and promising. While she stood, Kate absorbed the colors, the light and the silent thunder of day breaking over water.

The lazy contemplation was far different from her structured routine of the past months and years. Mornings had been a time to dress, a time to run over her schedule and notes for the day's classes over two cups of coffee and a quick breakfast. She never had time to give herself the dawn, so she took it now.

She slept better than she'd expected, lulled by the quiet, exhausted by the days of traveling and the strain on her emotions. There'd been no dreams to haunt her from the time she'd turned back the sheets until the first light had fallen over her face. Then she rose quickly. There'd be no dreams now.

Kate let the morning wash over her with all its new promises, its beginnings. Today was the start. Everything, from the moment she'd taken out her father's papers until she'd seen Ky again, had been a prelude. Even the brief, torrid embrace of the night before had been no more than a ghost of the past. Today was the real beginning.

She dressed and went out into the morning.

Breakfast was impossible. The excitement she'd so meticulously held off was beginning to strain for freedom. The feeling that what she was doing was right was back with her. Whatever it took, whatever it cost her, she'd look for the gold her father had dreamed of. She'd follow his directions. If she found nothing, she'd have looked anyway.

In looking, Kate had come to believe she'd lay all her personal ghosts to rest.

Ky's kiss. It had been aching, disturbing as it had always been. She'd been absorbed, just as she'd always been. Though she knew she had to face both Ky and the past, she hadn't known it would be so frighteningly easy to go back—back to that dark, dreamy world where only he had taken her.

Now that she knew, now that she'd faced even that, Kate had to prepare to fight the wind.

He'd never forgiven her, she realized, for saying no. For bruising his pride. She'd gone back to her world when he'd asked her to stay in his. Asked her to stay, Kate remembered, without offering anything, not even a promise. If he'd given her that, no matter how casual or airy the promise might have been, she wouldn't have gone. She wondered if he knew that.

Perhaps he thought if he could make her lose herself to him again, the scales would be even. She wouldn't lose. Kate stuck her hands into the pockets of her brief pleated shorts. No, she didn't intend to lose. If he had pressed her last night, if he'd known just how weakened she'd been by that one kiss...

But he wouldn't know, she told herself. She wouldn't weaken again. For the summer, she'd make the treasure her goal and her one ambition. She wouldn't leave the island empty-handed this time.

He was already on board the *Vortex*. Kate could see him stowing gear, his hair tousled by the breeze that flowed in from the sea. With only cut-offs and a sleeveless T-shirt between him and the sun she could see the muscles coil and relax, the skin gleam.

Magnificent. She felt the dull ache deep in her stomach and tried to rationalize it away. After all, a well-honed masculine build should make a woman respond. It was natural. One could even call it impersonal, Kate decided. As she started down the dock she wished she could believe it.

He didn't see her. A fishing boat already well out on the water had caught his attention. For a moment, she stopped, just watching him. Why was it she could always sense the restlessness in him? There was movement in him even when he was still, sound even when he was silent. What was it he saw when he looked out over the sea? Challenge? Romance?

He was a man who always seemed poised for action, for doing. Yet he could sit quietly and watch the waves as if there were nothing more important than that endless battle between earth and water.

Just now he stood on the deck of his boat, hands on hips, watching the tubby fishing vessel putt toward the horizon. It was something he'd seen countless times, yet he stopped to take it in again. Kate looked where Ky looked and wished she could see what he was seeing.

Quietly she went forward, her deck shoes making no sound, but he turned, eyes still intense. "You're early," he said, and with no more greeting reached out a hand to help her on board.

"I thought you might be as anxious to start as I am."

Palm met palm, rough against smooth. Both of them broke contact as soon as possible.

"It should be an easy ride." He looked back to sea, toward the boat, but this time he didn't focus on it. "The wind's coming in from the north, no more than ten knots."

"Good." Though it wouldn't have mattered to her nor, she thought, to him, if the wind had been twice as fast. This was the morning to begin.

She could sense the impatience in him, the desire to be gone and doing. Wanting to make things as simple as possible Kate helped Ky cast off, then walked to the stern. That would keep the maximum distance between them. They didn't speak. The engine roared to life, shattering the calm. Smoothly, Ky maneuvered the small cruiser out of the harbor, setting up a small wake that caused the water to lap against pilings. He kept the same steady even speed while they sailed through the shallows of Ocracoke Inlet. Looking back, Kate watched the distance between the boat and the village grow.

The dreamy quality remained. The last thing she saw was a child walking down a pier with a rod cocked rakishly over his shoulder. Then she turned her face to the sea.

Warm wind, glaring sun. Excitement. Kate hadn't been sure the feelings would be the same. But when she closed her eyes, letting the dull red light glow behind her lids, the salty mist touch her face, she knew this was a love that had remained constant, one that had waited for her.

Sitting perfectly still, she could feel Ky increase the speed until the boat was eating its way through the water as sleekly as a cat moves through the jungle. With her eyes closed, she enjoyed the movement, the speed, the sun. This was a thrill that had never faded. Tasting it again, she understood that it never would.

She'd been right, Kate realized, the hunt would be much more exciting than the final goal. The hunt, and no matter how cautious she was, the man at the helm.

He'd told himself he wouldn't look back at her. But he had to—just once. Eyes closed, a smile playing around her mouth, hair dancing around her face where the wind nudged it from the pins. It brought back a flash of memory—to the first time he'd seen her like that and realized he had to have her. She looked calm, totally at peace. He felt there was a war raging inside him that he had no control over.

Even when he turned back to sea again Ky could see her, leaning back against the stern, absorbing what wind and water offered. In defense, he tried to picture her in a classroom, patiently explaining the intricacies of *Don Juan* or *Henry IV*. It didn't help. He could only imagine her sitting behind him, soaking up sun and wind as if she'd been starved for it.

Perhaps she had been. Though she didn't know what direction Ky's thoughts had taken, Kate realized she'd never been further away from the classroom or the demands she placed on herself there than she was at this moment. She was part teacher, there was no question of that, but she was also, no matter how she'd tried to banish it, part dreamer.

With the sun and the wind on her skin, she was too exhilarated to be frightened by the knowledge, too content to worry. It was a wild, free sensation to experience again something known, loved, then lost.

Perhaps... Perhaps it was too much like the one frenzied kiss she'd shared with Ky the night before, but she needed it. It might be a foolish need, even a dangerous one. Just once, only this once, she told herself, she wouldn't question it.

Steady, strong, she opened her eyes again. Now she could watch the sun toss its diamonds on the surface of the water. They rippled, enticing, enchanting. The fishing boat Ky had watched move away from the island before them was anchored, casting its nets. A purse seiner, she remembered. Ky had explained the wide, weighted net to her once and how it was often used to haul in menhaden.

She wondered why he'd never chosen that life, where he could work and live on the water day after day. But not alone, she recalled with a ghost of a smile. Fisher-men were their own community, on the sea and off it. It wasn't often Ky chose to share himself or his time with anyone. There were times, like this one, when she understood that perfectly.

Whether it was the freedom or the strength that was in her, Kate approached him without nerves. "It's as beautiful as I remember."

He dreaded having her stand beside him again. Now, however, he discovered the tension at the base of his neck had eased. "It doesn't change much." Together they watched the gulls swoop around the fishing boat, hoping for easy pickings. "Fishing's been good this year."

"Have you been doing much?"

"Off and on."

"Clamming?"

He had to smile when he remembered how she'd looked, jeans rolled up to her knees, bare feet full of sand as he'd taught her how to dig. "Yeah."

She, too, remembered, but her only memories were of warm days, warm nights. "I've often wondered what it's like on the island in winter."

"Quiet."

She took the single careless answer with a nod. "I've often wondered why you preferred that."

He turned to her, measuring. "Have you?"

Perhaps that had been a mistake. Since it had al-ready been made, Kate shrugged. "It would be fool-ish of me to say I hadn't thought of the island or you at all during the last four years. You've always made me curious."

He laughed. It was so typical of her to put things

that way. "Because all your tidy questions weren't answered. You think too much like a teacher, Kate."

"Isn't life a multiple choice?" she countered. "Maybe two or three answers would fit, but only one's ultimately right."

"No, only one's ultimately wrong." He saw her eyes take on that thoughtful, considering expression. She was, he knew, weighing the pros and cons of his statement. Whether she agreed or not, she'd consider all the angles. "You haven't changed either," he murmured.

"I thought the same of you. We're both wrong. Neither of us have stayed the same. That's as it should be." Kate looked away from him, further east, then gave a quick cry of pleasure. "Oh, look!" Without thinking, she put her hand on his arm, slender fingers gripping taut muscle. "Dolphins."

She watched them, a dozen, perhaps more, leap and dive in their musical pattern. Pleasure was touched with envy. To move like that, she thought, from water to air and back to water again. It was a freedom that might drive a man mad with the glory of it. But what a madness...

"Fantastic, isn't it?" she murmured. "To be part of the air and the sea. I'd nearly forgotten."

"How much?" Ky studied her profile until he could have etched the shape of it on the wind. "How much have you nearly forgotten?"

Kate turned her head, only then realizing just how close they stood. Unconsciously, she'd moved nearer to him when she'd seen the dolphins. Now she could see nothing but his face, inches from hers, feel nothing but the warm skin beneath her hand. His question, the depth of it, seemed to echo off the surface of the water to haunt her.

She stepped back. The drop before her was very deep and torn with riptides. "All that was necessary," she said simply. "I'd like to look over my father's charts. Did you bring them on board?"

"Your briefcase is in the cabin." His hands gripped the wheel tightly, as though he were fighting against a storm. Perhaps he was. "You should be able to find your way below."

Without answering, Kate walked around him to the short steep steps that led belowdecks.

There were two narrow bunks with the spreads taut enough to bounce a coin if one was dropped. The galley just beyond would have all the essentials, she knew, in small, efficient scale. Everything would be in its place, as tidy as a monk's cell.

Kate could remember lying with Ky on one of the pristine bunks, flushed with passion while the boat swayed gently in the current and the music from his radio played jazz.

She gripped the leather of her case as if the pain in her fingers would help fight off the memories. To fight everything off entirely was too much to expect, but the intensity eased. Carefully she unfolded one of her father's charts and spread it on the bunk.

Like everything her father had done, the chart was precise and without frills. Though it had certainly not been his field, Hardesty had drawn a chart any sailor would have trusted.

It showed the coast of North Carolina, Pamlico Sound and the Outer Banks, from Manteo to Cape Lookout. As well as the lines of latitude and longitude, the chart also had the thin crisscrossing lines that marked depth.

Seventy-six degrees north by thirty-five degrees east. From the markings, that was the area her father had decided the *Liberty* had gone down. That was southeast of Ocracoke by no more than a few miles. And the depth… Yes, she decided as she frowned over the chart, the depth would still be considered shallow diving. She and Ky would have the relative freedom of wet suits and tanks rather than the leaded boots and helmets required for deep-sea explorations.

X marks the spot, she thought, a bit giddy, but made herself fold the chart with the same care she'd used to open it. She felt the boat slow then heard the resounding silence when the engines shut off. A fresh tremor of anticipation went through her as she climbed the steps into the sunlight again.

Ky was already checking the tanks though she knew he would have gone over all the equipment thoroughly before setting out. "We'll go down here," he said as he rose from his crouched position. "We're about half a mile from the last place your father went in last summer."

In one easy motion he pulled off his shirt. Kate knew he was self-aware, but he'd never been self-conscious. Ky had already stripped down to brief bikini trunks before she turned away for her own gear.

If her heart was pounding, it was possible to tell herself it was in anticipation of the dive. If her throat was dry, she could almost believe it was nerves at the thought of giving herself to the sea again. His body was hard and brown and lean, but she was only concerned with his skill and his knowledge. And he, she told herself, was only concerned with his fee and his twenty-five percent of the find.

She wore a snug tank suit under her shorts that clung to subtle curves and revealed long, slender legs that Ky knew were soft as water, strong as a runner's. He began to pull on the thin rubber wet suit. They were here to look for gold, to find a treasure that had been lost. Some treasures, he knew, could never be recovered.

As he thought of it, Ky glanced up to see Kate draw the pins from her hair. It fell, soft and slow, over, then past her shoulders. If she'd shot a dart into his chest, she couldn't have pierced his heart more accurately. Swearing under his breath, Ky lifted the first set of tanks.

"We'll go down for an hour today."

"But—"

"An hour's more than enough," he interrupted without sparing her a glance. "You haven't worn tanks in four years."

Kate slipped into the set he offered her, securing the straps until they were snug, but not tight. "I didn't tell you that."

"No, but you'd sure as hell have told me if you had." The corner of his mouth lifted when she remained silent. After attaching his own tanks, Ky climbed over the side onto the ladder. She could either argue, he figured, or she could follow.

To clear his mask, he spat into it, rubbed, then reached down to rinse it in salt water. Pulling it over his eyes and nose, Ky dropped into the sea. It took less than ten seconds before Kate plunged into the water beside him. He paused a moment, to make certain she didn't flounder or forget to breathe, then he headed for greater depth.

No, she wouldn't forget to breathe, but the first breath was almost a sigh as her body submerged. It was as thrilling to her as it had been the first time, this incredible ability to stay beneath the ocean's surface and breathe air.

Kate looked up to see the sun spearing through the water, and held out a hand to watch the watery light play on her skin. She could have stayed there, she realized, just reveling in it. But with a curl of her body and a kick, she followed Ky into depth and dimness.

Ky saw a school of menhaden and wondered if they'd end up in the net of the fishing boat he'd watched that morning. When the fish swerved in a mass and rushed past him, he turned to Kate again. She'd been right when she'd told him she knew what to do. She swam as cleanly and as competently as ever.

He expected her to ask him how he intended to look for the *Liberty,* what plan he'd outlined. When she hadn't, Ky had figured it was for one of two reasons. Either she didn't want to have any in-depth conversation with him at the moment, or she'd already reasoned it out for herself. It seemed more likely to be the latter, as her mind was also as clean and competent as ever.

The most logical method of searching seemed to be a semi-circular route around Hardesty's previous dives. Slowly and methodically, they would widen the circle. If Hardesty had been right, they'd find the *Liberty* eventually. If he'd been wrong...they'd have spent the summer treasure hunting.

Though the tanks on her back reminded Kate not to take the weightless freedom for granted, she thought she could stay down forever. She wanted to touch— the water, the sea grass, the soft, sandy bottom. Reaching out toward a school of bluefish she watched them scatter defensively then regroup. She knew there were times when, as a diver moved through the dim, liquid world, he could forget the need for the sun. Perhaps Ky had been right in limiting the dive. She had to be careful not to take what she found again for granted.

The flattened disklike shape caught Ky's attention. Automatically, he reached for Kate's arm to stop her forward progress. The stingray that scuttled along the bottom looking for tasty crustaceans might be amusing to watch, but it was deadly. He gauged this one to be as long as he was tall with a tail as sharp and cruel as a razor. They'd give it a wide berth.

Seeing the ray reminded Kate that the sea wasn't all beauty and dreams. It was also pain and death. Even as she watched, the stingray struck out with its whiplike tail and caught a small, hapless bluefish. Once, then twice. It was nature, it was life. But she turned away. Through the protective masks, her eyes met Ky's.

She expected to see derision for an obvious weakness, or worse, amusement. She saw neither. His eyes were gentle, as they were very rarely. Lifting a hand, he ran his knuckles down her cheek, as he'd done years before when he'd chosen to offer comfort or affection. She felt the warmth, it reflected in her eyes. Then, as quickly as the moment had come, it was over. Turning, Ky swam away, gesturing for her to follow.

He couldn't afford to be distracted by those glimpses of vulnerability, those flashes of sweetness. They had already done him in once. Top priority was the job they'd set out to do. Whatever other plans he had, Ky intended to be in full control. When the time was right, he'd have his fill of Kate. That he promised himself.

He'd take exactly what he felt she owed him. But she wouldn't touch his emotions again. When he took her to bed, it would be with cold calculation.

That was something else he promised himself.

Though they found no sign of the *Liberty*, Ky saw wreckage from other ships—pieces of metal, rusted, covered with barnacles. They might have been from a sub or a battleship from World War II. The sea absorbed what remained in her.

He was tempted to swim farther out, but knew it would take twenty minutes to return to the boat. Circling around, he headed back, overlapping, double-checking the area they'd just covered.

Not quite a needle in a haystack, Ky mused, but close. Two centuries of storms and currents and sea quakes. Even if they had the exact location where the *Liberty* had sunk, rather than the last known location, it took calculation and guesswork, then luck to narrow the field down to a radius of twenty miles.

Ky believed in luck much the same way he imagined Hardesty had believed in calculation. Perhaps with a mixture of the two, he and Kate would find what was left of the *Liberty*.

Glancing over, he watched Kate gliding beside him. She was looking everywhere at once, but Ky didn't think her mind was on treasure or sunken ships. She was, as she'd been that summer before, completely enchanted with the sea and the life it held. He wondered if she still remembered all the information she'd demanded of him before the first dive. What about the physiological adjustments to the body? How was the CO_2 absorbed? What about the change in external pressure?

Ky felt a flash of humor as they started to ascend. He was dead sure Kate remembered every answer he'd given her, right down to the decimal point in pounds of pressure per square inch.

The sun caught her as she rose toward the surface, slowly. It shone around and through her hair, giving her an ethereal appearance as she swam straight up, legs kicking gently, face tilted toward sun and surface. If there were mermaids, Ky knew they'd look as she did—slim, long, with pale loose hair free in the water. A man could only hold on to a mermaid if he accepted the world she lived in as his own. Reaching out, he caught the tip of her hair in his fingers just before they broke the surface together.

Kate came up laughing, letting her mouthpiece fall and pushing her mask up. "Oh, it's wonderful! Just as I remembered." Treading water, she laughed again and Ky realized it was a sound he hadn't heard in four years. But he remembered it exactly.

"You looked like you wanted to play more than you wanted to look for sunken ships." He grinned at her, enjoying her pleasure and the ease of a smile he'd never expected to see again.

"I did." Almost reluctant, she reached out for the ladder to climb on board. "I never expected to find anything the first time down, and it was so wonderful just to dive again." She stripped off her tanks then checked the valves herself before she set them down. "Whenever I go down I begin to believe I don't need the sun anymore. Then when I come up it's warmer and brighter than I remember."

With the adrenaline still flowing, she peeled off her

flippers, then her mask, to stand, face lifted toward the sun. "There's nothing else exactly like it."

"Skin diving." Ky tugged down the zipper of his wet suit. "I tried some in Tahiti last year. It's incredible being in that clear water with no equipment but a mask and flippers, and your own lungs."

"Tahiti?" Surprised and interested, Kate looked back as Ky stripped off the wet suit. "You went there?"

"Couple of weeks late last year." He dropped the wet suit in the big plastic can he used for storing equipment before rinsing.

"Because of your affection for islands?"

"And grass skirts."

The laughter bubbled out again. "I'm sure you'd look great in one."

He'd forgotten just how quick she could be when she relaxed. Because the gesture appealed, Ky reached over and gave her hair a quick tug. "I wish I'd taken snapshots." Turning, he jogged down the steps into the cabin.

"Too busy ogling the natives to put them on film for posterity?" Kate called out as she dropped down on the narrow bench on the starboard side.

"Something like that. And, of course, trying to pretend I didn't notice the natives ogling me."

She grinned. "People in grass skirts," she began then let out a muffled shout as he tossed a peach in her direction. Catching it cleanly, Kate smiled at him before she bit into the fruit.

"Still have good reflexes," Ky commented as he came up the last step.

"Especially when I'm hungry." She touched her

tongue to her palm where juice dribbled. "I couldn't eat this morning, I was too keyed up."

He held out one of two bottles of cold soda he'd taken from the refrigerator. "About the dive?"

"That and…" Kate broke off, surprised that she was talking to him as if it had been four years before.

"And?" Ky prompted. Though his tone was casual, his gaze had sharpened.

Aware of it, Kate rose, turning away to look back over the stern. She saw nothing there but sky and water. "It was the morning," she murmured. "The way the sun came up over the water. All that color." She shook her head and water dripped from the ends of her hair onto the deck. "I haven't watched a sunrise in a very long time."

Making himself relax again, Ky leaned back, biting into his own peach as he watched her. "Why?"

"No time. No need."

"Do they both mean the same thing to you?"

Restless, she moved her shoulders. "When your life revolves around schedules and classes, I suppose one equals the other."

"That's what you want? A daily timetable?"

Kate looked back over her shoulder, meeting his eyes levelly. How could they ever understand each other? she wondered. Her world was as foreign to him as his to her. "It's what I've chosen."

"One of your multiple choices of life?" Ky countered, giving a short laugh before he tilted his bottle back again.

"Maybe, or maybe some parts of life only have one choice." She turned completely around, determined not to lose the euphoria that had come to her with the dive. "Tell me about Tahiti, Ky. What's it like?"

"Soft air, soft water. Blue, green, white. Those are the colors that come to mind, then outrageous splashes of red and orange and yellow."

"Like a Gauguin painting."

The length of the deck separated them. Perhaps that made it easier for him to smile. "I suppose, but I don't think he'd have appreciated all the hotels and resorts. It isn't an island that's been left to itself."

"Things rarely are."

"Whether they should be or not."

Something in the way he said it, in the way he looked at her, made Kate think he wasn't speaking of an island now, but of something more personal. She drank, cooling her throat, moistening her lips. "Did you scuba?"

"Some. Shells and coral so thick I could've filled a boat with them if I'd wanted. Fish that looked like they should've been in an aquarium. And sharks." He remembered one that had nearly caught him half a mile out. Remembering made him grin. "The waters off Tahiti are anything but boring."

Kate recognized the look, the recklessness that would always surface just under his skill. Perhaps he didn't look for trouble, but she thought he'd rarely sidestep it. No, she doubted they'd ever fully understand each other, if they had a lifetime.

"Did you bring back a shark's tooth necklace?"

"I gave it to Hope." He grinned again. "Linda won't let her have it yet."

"I should think not. Does it feel odd, being an uncle?"

"No. She looks like me."

"Ah, the male ego."

Ky shrugged, aware that he had a healthy share and was comfortable with it. "I get a kick out of watching her run Marsh and Linda in circles. There's not much entertainment on the island."

She tried to imagine Ky being entertained by something as tame as a baby girl. She failed. "It's strange," Kate said after a moment. "Coming back to find Marsh and Linda married and parents. When I left Marsh treated Linda like his little sister."

"Didn't your father keep you up on progress on the island?"

The smile left her eyes. "No."

Ky lifted a brow. "Did you ask?"

"No."

He tossed his empty bottle into a small barrel. "He hadn't told you anything about the ship either, about why he kept coming back to the island year after year."

She tossed her drying hair back from her face. It hadn't been put in the tone of a question. Still, she answered because it was simpler that way. "No, he never mentioned the *Liberty* to me."

"That doesn't bother you?"

The ache came, but she pushed it aside. "Why should it?" she countered. "He was entitled to his own life, his privacy."

"But you weren't."

She felt the chill come and go. Crossing the deck, Kate dropped her bottle beside Ky's before reaching for her shirt. "I don't know what you mean."

"You know exactly what I mean." He closed his hand over hers before she could pull the shirt on. Because it would've been cowardly to do otherwise, she lifted her head and faced him. "You know," he said again, quietly. "You just aren't ready to say it out loud yet."

"Leave it alone, Ky." Her voice trembled, and though it infuriated her, she couldn't prevent it. "Just leave it."

He wanted to shake her, to make her admit, so that he could hear, that she'd left him because her father had preferred it. He wanted her to say, perhaps sob, that she hadn't had the strength to stand up to the man who had shaped and molded her life to suit his values and wants.

With an effort, he relaxed his fingers. As he had before, Ky turned away with something like a shrug. "For now," he said easily as he went back to the helm. "Summer's just beginning." He started the engine before turning around for one last look. "We both know what can happen during a summer."

Chapter 5

"The first thing you have to understand about Hope," Linda began, steadying a vase the toddler had jostled, "is that she has a mind of her own."

Kate watched the chubby black-haired Hope climb onto a wing-backed chair to examine herself in an ornamental mirror. In the fifteen minutes Kate had been in Linda's home, Hope hadn't been still a moment. She was quick, surprisingly agile, with a look in her eyes that made Kate believe she knew exactly what she wanted and intended to get it, one way or the other. Ky had been right. His niece looked like him, in more ways than one.

"I can see that. Where do you find the energy to run a restaurant, keep a home and manage a fireball?"

"Vitamins." Linda sighed. "Lots and lots of vitamins. Hope, don't put your fingers on the glass."

"Hope!" the toddler cried out, making faces at herself in the mirror. "Pretty, pretty, pretty."

"The Silver ego," Linda commented. "It never tarnishes."

With a chuckle, Kate watched Hope crawl backward out of the chair, land on her diaper-padded bottom and begin to systematically destroy the tower of blocks she'd built a short time before. "Well, she is pretty. It only shows she's smart enough to know it."

"It's hard for me to argue that point, except when she's spread toothpaste all over the bathroom floor." With a contented sigh, Linda sat back on the couch. She enjoyed having Monday afternoons off to play with Hope and catch up on the dozens of things that went by the wayside when the restaurant demanded her time. "You've been here over a week now, and this is the first time we've been able to talk."

Kate bent over to ruffle Hope's hair. "You're a busy woman."

"So are you."

Kate heard the question, not so subtly submerged in the statement, and smiled. "You know I didn't come back to the island to fish and wade, Linda."

"All right, all right, the heck with being tactful." With a mother's skill, she kept her antenna honed on her active toddler and leaned toward Kate. "What *are* you and Ky doing out on his boat every day?"

With Linda, evasions were neither necessary nor advisable. "Looking for treasure," Kate said simply.

"Oh." Expressing only mild surprise, Linda saved a budding African violet from her daughter's curious fingers. "Blackbeard's treasure." She handed Hope a rubber duck in lieu of the plant. "My grandfather still tells stories about it. Pieces of eight, a king's ransom and bottles of rum. I always figured that it was buried on land."

Amused at the way Linda could handle the toddler without breaking rhythm, Kate shook her head. "No, not Blackbeard's."

There were dozens of theories and myths about where the infamous pirate had hidden his booty, and fantastic speculation on just how rich the trove was. Kate had never considered them any more than stories. Yet, she supposed, in her own way, she was following a similar fantasy.

"My father'd been researching the whereabouts of an English merchant ship that sank off the coast here in the eighteenth century."

"Your father?" Instantly Linda's attention sharpened. She couldn't conceive of the Edwin Hardesty she remembered from summers past as a treasure searcher. "That's why he kept coming to the island every summer? I could never figure out why..." She broke off, grimaced, then plunged ahead. "I'm sorry, Kate, but he never seemed the type to take up scuba diving as a hobby, and I never once saw him with a fish. He certainly managed to keep what he was doing a secret."

"Yes, even from me."

"You didn't know?" Linda glanced over idly as Hope began to beat on a plastic bucket with a wooden puzzle piece.

"Not until I went through his papers a few weeks ago. I decided to follow through on what he'd started."

"And you came to Ky."

"I came to Ky." Kate smoothed the material of her thin summer skirt over her knees. "I needed a boat, a diver, preferably an islander. He's the best."

Linda's attention shifted from her daughter to Kate. There was simple understanding there, but it didn't completely mask impatience. "Is that the only reason you came to Ky?"

Needs rose up to taunt her. Memories washed up in one warm wave. "Yes, that's the only reason."

Linda wondered why Kate should want her to believe what Kate didn't believe herself. "What if I told you he's never forgotten you?"

Kate shook her head quickly, almost frantically. "Don't."

"I love him." Linda rose to distract Hope who'd discovered tossing blocks was more interesting than stacking them. "Even though he's a frustrating, difficult man. He's Marsh's brother." She set Hope in front of a small army of stuffed animals before she turned and smiled. "He's my brother. And you were the first mainlander I was ever really close to. It's hard for me to be objective."

It was tempting to pour out her heart, her doubts. Too tempting. "I appreciate that, Linda. Believe me, what was between Ky and me was over a long time ago. Lives change."

Making a neutral sound, Linda sat again. There were some people you didn't press. Ky and Kate were both the same in that area, however diverse they were otherwise. "All right. You know what I've been doing the past four years." She sent a long-suffering look in Hope's direction. "Tell me what your life's been like."

"Quieter."

Linda laughed. "A small border war would be quieter than life in this house."

"Earning my doctorate as early as I did took a lot of

concentrated effort." She'd needed that one goal to keep herself level, to keep herself...calm. "When you're teaching as well it doesn't leave much time for anything else." Shrugging, she rose. It sounded so staid, she realized. So dull. She'd wanted to learn, she'd wanted to teach, but in and of itself, it sounded hollow.

There were toys spread all over the living room, tiny pieces of childhood. A tie was tossed carelessly over the back of a chair next to a table where Linda had dropped her purse. Small pieces of a marriage. Family. She wondered, with a panic that came and went quickly, how she would ever survive the empty house back in Connecticut.

"This past year at Yale has been fascinating and difficult." Was she defending or explaining? Kate wondered impatiently. "Strange, even though my father taught, I didn't realize that being a teacher is just as hard and demanding as being a student."

"Harder," Linda declared after a moment. "You have to have the answers."

"Yes." Kate crouched down to look at Hope's collection of stuffed animals. "I suppose that's part of the appeal, though. The challenge of either knowing the answer or reasoning it out, then watching it sink in."

"Hoping it sinks in?" Linda ventured.

Kate laughed again. "Yes, I suppose that's it. When it does, that's the most rewarding aspect. Being a mother can't be that much different. You're teaching every day."

"Or trying to," Linda said dryly.

"The same thing."

"You're happy?"

Hope squeezed a bright pink dragon then held it out

for Kate. Was she happy? Kate wondered as she obliged by cuddling the dragon in turn. She'd been aiming for achievement, she supposed, not happiness. Her father had never asked that very simple, very basic question. She'd never taken the time to ask herself. "I want to teach," she answered at length. "I'd be unhappy if I couldn't."

"That's a roundabout way of answering without answering at all."

"Sometimes there isn't any yes or no."

"Ky!" Hope shouted so that Kate jolted, whipping her head around to the front door.

"No." Linda noted the reaction, but said nothing. "She means the dragon. He gave it to her, so it's Ky."

"Oh." She wanted to swear but managed to smile as she handed the baby back her treasured dragon. It wasn't reasonable that just his name should make her hands unsteady, her pulse unsteady, her thoughts unsteady. "He wouldn't pick the usual, would he?" she asked carelessly as she rose.

"No." She gave Kate a very direct, very level look. "His tastes have always run to the unique."

Amusement helped to relax her. Kate's brow rose as she met the look. "You don't give up, do you?"

"Not on something I believe in." A trace of stubbornness came through. The stubbornness, Kate mused, that had kept her determinedly waiting for Marsh to fall in love with her. "I believe in you and Ky," Linda continued. "You two can make a mess of it for as long as you want, but I'll still believe in you."

"You haven't changed," Kate said on a sigh. "I came back to find you a wife, a mother and the owner of a restaurant, but you haven't changed at all."

"Being a wife and mother only makes me more certain that what I believe is right." She had her share of arrogance, too, and used it. "We don't own the restaurant," she added as an afterthought.

"No?" Surprised, Kate looked up again. "But I thought you said the Roost was yours and Marsh's."

"We run it," Linda corrected. "And we do have a twenty percent interest." Sitting back, she gave Kate a pleased smile. There was nothing she liked better than to drop small bombs in calm water and watch the ripples. "Ky owns the Roost."

"Ky?" Kate couldn't have disguised the astonishment if she'd tried. The Ky Silver she thought she knew hadn't owned anything but a boat and a shaky beach cottage. He hadn't wanted to. Buying a restaurant, even a small one on a remote island took more than capital. It took ambition.

"Apparently he didn't bother to mention it."

"No." He'd had several opportunities, Kate recalled, the night they'd had dinner. "No, he didn't. It doesn't seem characteristic," she murmured. "I can picture him buying another boat, a bigger boat or a faster boat, but I can't imagine him buying a restaurant."

"I guess it surprised everyone except Marsh—but then Marsh knows Ky better than anyone. A couple of weeks before we were married, Ky told us he'd bought the place and intended to remodel. Marsh was ferrying over to Hatteras every day to work, I was helping out in my aunt's craft shop during the season. When Ky asked if we wanted to buy in for twenty percent and take over as managers, we jumped at it." She smiled, pleased, and perhaps relieved. "It wasn't a mistake for any of us."

Kate remembered the homey atmosphere, the excellent seafood, the fast service. No, it hadn't been a mistake, but Ky... "I just can't picture Ky in business, not on land anyway."

"Ky knows the island," Linda said simply. "And he knows what he wants. To my way of thinking, he just doesn't always know how to get it."

Kate was going to avoid that area of speculation. "I'm going to take a walk down to the beach," she decided. "Would you like to come?"

"I'd love to, but—" With a gesture of her hand Linda indicated why Hope had been quiet for the last few minutes. With her arm hooked around her dragon, she was sprawled over the rest of the animals, sound asleep.

"It's either stop or go with her, isn't it?" Kate observed with a laugh.

"The nice thing is that when she stops, so can I." Expertly Linda gathered up Hope, cradling her daughter on her shoulder. "Have a nice walk, and stop into the Roost tonight if you have the chance."

"I will." Kate touched Hope's head, the thick, dark, disordered hair that was so much like her uncle's. "She's beautiful, Linda. You're very lucky."

"I know. It's something I don't ever forget."

Kate let herself out of the house and walked along the quiet street. Clouds were low, making the light gloomy, but the rain held off. She could taste it in the breeze, the clean freshness of it, mixed with the faintest hint of the sea. It was in that direction she walked.

On an island, she'd discovered, you were much more drawn to the water than to the land. It was the one thing she'd understood completely about Ky, the one thing she'd never questioned.

It had been easier to avoid going to the beach in Connecticut, though she'd always loved the rocky, windy New England coast. She'd been able to resist it, knowing what memories it would bring back. Pain. Kate had learned there were ways of avoiding pain. But here, knowing you could reach the edge of land by walking in any direction, she couldn't resist. It might have been wiser to walk to the sound, or the inlet. She walked to the sea.

It was warm enough that she needed no more than the sheer skirt and blouse, breezy enough so that the material fluttered around her. She saw two men, caps low over foreheads, their rods secured in the sand, talking together while they sat on buckets and waited for a strike. Their voices didn't carry above the roar and thunder of surf, but she knew their conversation would deal with bait and lures and yesterday's catch. She wouldn't disturb them, nor they her. It was the way of the islander to be friendly enough, but not intrusive.

The water was as gray as the sky, but she didn't mind. Kate had learned not just to accept its moods but to appreciate the contrasts of each one. When the sea was like this, brooding, with threats of violence on the surface, that meant a storm. She found it appealed to a restlessness in herself she rarely acknowledged.

Whitecaps tossed with systematic fever. The spray rose high and wide. The cry of gulls didn't seem lonely or plaintive now, but challenging. No, a gray gloomy sky meeting a gray sea was anything but dull. It teamed with energy. It boiled with life.

The wind tugged at her hair, loosening pins. She didn't notice. Standing just away from the edge of the surf, Kate faced wind and sea with her eyes wide. She had to think about what she'd just discovered about Ky. Perhaps what she had been determined not to discover about herself.

Thinking there, alone in the gray threatening light before a storm, was what Kate felt she needed. The constant wind blowing in from the east would keep her head clear. Maybe the smells and sounds of the sea would remind her of what she'd had and rejected, and what she'd chosen to have.

Once she'd had a powerful force that had held her swirling, breathless. That force was Ky, a man who could pull on your emotions, your senses, by simply being. The recklessness had attracted her once, the tough arrogance combined with unexpected gentleness. What she saw as his irresponsibility had disturbed her. Kate sensed that he was a man who would drift through life when she'd been taught from birth to seek out a goal and work for it to the exclusion of all else. It was that very different outlook on life that set them poles apart.

Perhaps he had decided to take on some responsibility in his life with the restaurant, Kate decided. If he had she was glad of it. But it couldn't make any difference. They were still poles apart.

She chose the calm, the ordered. Success was satisfaction in itself when success came from something loved. Teaching was vital to her, not just a job, not even a profession. The giving of knowledge fed her. Perhaps for a moment in Linda's cozy, cluttered home it hadn't seemed like enough. Not quite enough. Still, Kate knew if you wished for too much, you often received nothing at all.

With the wind whipping at her face she watched the

rain begin far out to sea in a dark curtain. If the past had been a treasure she'd lost, no chart could take her back. In her life, she'd been taught only one direction.

Ky never questioned his impulses to walk on the beach. He was a man who was comfortable with his own mood swings, so comfortable, he rarely noticed them. He hadn't deliberately decided to stop work on his boat at a certain time. He simply felt the temptation of sea and storm and surrendered to it.

Ky watched the seas as he made his way up and over the hill of sand. He could have found his way without faltering in the dark, with no moon. He'd stood on shore and watched the rain at sea before, but repetition didn't lessen the pleasure. The wind would bring it to the island, but there was still time to seek shelter if shelter were desired. More often than not, Ky would let the rain flow over him while the waves rose and fell wildly.

He'd seen his share of tropical storms and hurricanes. While he might find them exhilarating, he appreciated the relative peace of a summer rain. Today he was grateful for it. It had given him a day away from Kate.

They had somehow reached a shaky, tense coexistence that made it possible for them to be together day after day in a relatively small space. The tension was making him nervy; nervy enough to make a mistake when no diver could afford to make one.

Seeing her, being with her, knowing she'd withdrawn from him as a person was infinitely more difficult than being apart from her. To Kate, he was only a means to an end, a tool she used in the same way he imagined she used a textbook. If that was a bitter pill, he felt he had only himself to blame. He'd accepted her terms. Now all he had to do was live with them.

He hadn't heard her laugh again since the first dive. He missed that, Ky discovered, every bit as much as he missed the taste of her lips, the feel of her in his arms. She wouldn't give him any of it willingly, and he'd nearly convinced himself he didn't want her any other way.

But at night, alone, with the sound of the surf in his head, he wasn't sure he'd survive another hour. Yet he had to. It was the fierce drive for survival that had gotten him through the past years. Her rejection had eaten away at him, then it had pushed him to prove something to himself. Kate had been the reason for his risking every penny he'd had to buy the Roost. He'd needed something tangible. The Roost had given him that, in much the same way the charter boat he'd recently bought gave him a sense of worth he once thought was unnecessary.

So he owned a restaurant that made a profit, and a boat that was beginning to justify his investment. It had given his innate love of risk an outlet. It wasn't money that mattered, but the dealing, the speculation, the possibilities. A search for sunken treasure wasn't much different.

What was she looking for really? Ky wondered. Was the gold her objective? Was she simply looking for an unusual way to spend her holiday? Was she still trying to give her father the blind devotion he'd expected all her life? Was it the hunt? Watching the wall of rain move slowly closer, Ky found of all the possibilities he wanted it to be the last.

With perhaps a hundred yards between them, both Kate and Ky looked out to the sea and the rain without being aware of each other. He thought of her and she of him, but the rain crept closer and time slipped by. The wind grew bolder. Both of them could admit to the restlessness that churned inside them, but neither could acknowledge simple loneliness.

Then they turned to walk back up the dunes and saw each other.

Kate wondered how long he'd been there, and how, when she could feel the waves of tension and need, she hadn't known the moment he'd stepped onto the beach. Her mind, her body—always so calm and co-operative—sprang to fevered life when she saw him. Kate knew she couldn't fight that, only the outcome. Still, she wanted him. She told herself that just wanting was asking for disaster, but that didn't stop the need. If she ran from him now she'd admit defeat. Instead, Kate took the first step across the sand toward him.

The thin white cotton of her skirt flapped around her, billowing, then clinging to the slender body he already knew. Her skin seemed very pale, her eyes very dark. Again Ky thought of mermaids, of illusions and of foolish dreams.

"You always liked the beach before a storm," Kate said when she reached him. She couldn't smile though she told herself she would. She wanted, though she told herself she wouldn't.

"It won't be much longer." He hooked his thumbs into the front pockets of his jeans. "If you didn't bring your car, you're going to get wet."

"I was visiting Linda." Kate turned her head to look back at the rain. No, it wouldn't be much longer. "It doesn't matter," she murmured. "Storms like this are over just as quickly as they begin." Storms like this, she thought, and like others. "I met Hope. You were right."

"About what?"

"She looks like you." This time she did manage to smile, though the tension was balled at the base of her neck. "Did you know she named a doll after you?"

"A dragon's not a doll," Ky corrected. His lips curved. He could resist a great deal, be apathetic about a great deal more, but he found it virtually impossible to do either when it came to his niece. "She's a great kid. Hell of a sailor."

"You take her out on your boat?"

He heard the astonishment and shrugged it away. "Why not? She likes the water."

"I just can't picture you…" Breaking off, Kate turned back to the sea again. No, she couldn't picture him entertaining a child with toy dragons and boat rides, just as she couldn't picture him in the business world with ledgers and accountants. "You surprise me," she said a bit more casually. "About a lot of things."

He wanted to reach out and touch her hair, wrap those loose blowing ends around his finger. He kept his hands in his pockets. "Such as?"

"Linda told me you own the Roost."

He didn't have to see her face to know it would hold that thoughtful, considering expression. "That's right, or most of it anyway."

"You didn't mention it when we were having dinner there."

"Why should I?" She didn't have to see him to know he shrugged. "Most people don't care who owns a place as long as the food's good and the service is quick."

"I guess I'm not most people." She said it quietly, so quietly the words barely carried over the sound of the waves. Even so, Ky tensed.

"Why would it matter to you?"

Before she could think, she turned back, her eyes full of emotion. "Because it all matters. The whys, the hows. Because so much has changed and so much is the same. Because I want…" Breaking off, she took a step back. The look in her eyes turned to panic just before she started to dash away.

"What?" Ky demanded, grabbing her arm. "What do you want?"

"I don't know!" she shouted, unaware that it was the first time she'd done so in years. "I don't know what I want. I don't understand why I don't."

"Forget about understanding." He pulled her closer, holding her tighter when she resisted—or tried to. "Forget everything that's not here and now." The nights of restlessness and frustration already had his mercurial temperament on edge. Seeing her when he hadn't expected to made his emotions teeter. "You walked away from me once, but I won't crawl for you again. And you," he added with his eyes suddenly dark, his face suddenly close, "you damn well won't walk away as easily this time, Kate. Not this time."

With his arms wrapped around her he held her against him. His lips hovered above hers, threatening, promising. She couldn't tell. She didn't care. It was their taste she wanted, their pressure, no matter how harsh, how demanding. No matter what the consequence. Intellect and emotion might battle, and the battle might be eternal. Yet as she stood there crushed against him, feeling the wind whip at both of them, she already knew what the inevitable outcome would be.

"Tell me what you want, Kate." His voice was low, but as demanding as a shout. "Tell me what you want— now."

Now, she thought. If there could only be just now. She started to shake her head, but his breath feathered over her skin. That alone made future and past fade into insignificance.

"You," she heard herself murmur. "Just you." Reaching up she drew his face down to hers.

A wild passionate wind, a thunderous surf, the threat of rain just moments away. She felt his body—hard and confident against hers. She tasted his lips—soft, urgent. Over the thunder in her head and the thunder to the east, she heard her own moan. She wanted, as long as the moment lasted.

His tongue tempted; she surrendered to it. He dove deep and took all, then more. It might never be enough. With no hesitation, Kate met demand with demand, heat with heat. While mouth sought mouth, her hands roamed his face, teaching what she hadn't forgotten, reacquainting her with the familiar.

His skin was rough with a day's beard, the angle of cheek and jaw, hard and defined. As her fingers inched up she felt the soft brush of his hair blown by the wind. The contrast made her tremble before she dove her fingers deeper.

She could make him blind and deaf with needs. Knowing it, Ky couldn't stop it. The way she touched him, so sure, so sweet while her mouth was molten fire. Desire boiled in him, rising so quickly he was weak with it before his mind accepted what his body couldn't deny. He held her closer, hard against soft, rough against smooth, flame against flame.

Through the thin barrier of her blouse he felt her flesh warm to his touch. He knew the skin here would be delicate, as fragile as the underside of a rose. The scent would be as sweet, the taste as honeyed. Memories, the moment, the dream of more, all these combined to make him half mad. He knew what it would be like to have her, and knowing alone aroused. He felt her now, and feeling made him irrational.

He wanted to take her right there, next to the sea, while the sky opened up and poured over them.

"I want you." With his face buried against her neck he searched for all the places he remembered. "You know how much. You always knew."

"Yes." Her head was spinning. Every touch, every taste added speed to the whirl. Whatever doubts she'd had, Kate had never doubted the want. She hadn't always understood it, the intensity of it, but she'd never doubted it. It was pulling at her now—his, hers—the mutual, mindless passion they'd always been able to ignite in one another. She knew where it would lead—to dark, secret places full of sound and velocity. Not the eye of the hurricane, never the calm with him, but full fury from beginning to end. She knew where it would lead, and knew there'd be glory and freedom. But Ky had spoken no less than the truth when he'd said she wouldn't walk away so easily this time. It was that truth that made her reach for reason, when it would have been so simple to reach for madness.

"We can't." Breathless, she tried to turn in his arms. "Ky, *I* can't." This time when she took his face in her hands it was to draw it away from hers. "This isn't right for me."

Fury mixed with passion. It showed in his eyes, in the press of his fingers on her arms. "It's right for you. It's never been anything but right for you."

"No." She had to deny it, she had to mean it, because he was so persuasive. "No, it's not. I've always been attracted to you. It'd be ridiculous for me to try to pretend otherwise, but this isn't what I want for myself."

His fingers tightened. If they brought her pain neither of them acknowledged it. "I told you to tell me what you wanted. You did."

As he spoke the sky opened, just as he'd imagined. Rain swept in from the sea, tasting of salt, the damp wind and mystery. Instantly drenched, they stood just as they were, close, distant, with his hands firm on her arms and hers light on his face. She felt the water wash over her body, watched it run over his. It stirred her. She couldn't say why, she wouldn't give in to it.

"At that moment I did want you, I can't deny it."

"And now?" he demanded.

"I'm going back to the village."

"Damn it, Kate, what else do you want?"

She stared at him through the rain. His eyes were dark, stormy as the sea that raged behind him. Somehow he was more difficult to resist when he was like this, volatile, on edge, not quite controlled. She felt desire knot in her stomach, and swim in her head. That was all, Kate told herself. That was all it had ever been. Desire without understanding. Passion without future. Emotion without reason.

"Nothing you can give me," she whispered, knowing she'd have to dig for the strength to walk away, dig for it even to take the first step. "Nothing we can give to each other." Dropping her hands she stepped back. "I'm going back."

"You'll come back to me," Ky said as she took the first steps from him. "And if you don't," he added in a tone that made her hesitate, "it won't make any difference. We'll finish what's been started again."

She shivered, but continued to walk. *Finish what's been started again.* That was what she most feared.

Chapter 6

The storm passed. In the morning the sea was calm and blue, sprinkled with diamonds of sunlight from a sky where all clouds had been whisked away. It was true that rain freshened things—the air, grass, even the wood and stone of buildings.

The day was perfect, the wind calm. Kate's nerves rolled and jumped.

She'd committed herself to the project. It was her agreement with Ky that forced her to go to the harbor as she'd been doing every other morning. It made her climb on deck when she wanted nothing more than to pack and leave the island the way she'd come. If Ky could complete the agreement after what had passed between them on the beach, so could she.

Perhaps he sensed the fatigue she was feeling, but he made no comment on it. They spoke only when necessary as he headed out to open sea. Ky stood at the helm, Kate at the stern. Still, even the roar of the engine didn't disguise the strained silence. Ky checked the boat's compass, then cut the engines. Silence continued, thunderously.

With the deck separating them, each began to don their equipment—wet suits, the weight belts that would give them neutral buoyancy in the water, headlamps to light the sea's dimness, masks for sight. Ky checked his depth gauge and compass on his right wrist, then the luminous dial of the watch on his left while Kate attached the scabbard for her diver's knife onto her leg just below the knee.

Without speaking, they checked the valves and gaskets on the tanks, then strapped them on, securing buckles. As was his habit, Ky went into the water first, waiting until Kate joined him. Together they jackknifed below the surface.

The familiar euphoria reached out for her. Each time she dived, Kate expected the underwater world to become more commonplace. Each time it was still magic. She acknowledged what made it possible for her to join creatures of the sea—the regulator with its mouthpiece and hose that brought her air from the tanks on her back, the mask that gave her visibility. She knew the importance of every gauge. She acknowledged the technology, then put it in the practical side of her brain while she simply enjoyed.

They swam deeper, keeping in constant visual contact. Kate knew Ky often dived alone, and that doing so was always a risk. She also knew that no matter how much anger and resentment he felt toward her, she could trust him with her life.

She relied on Ky's instincts as much as his ability. It was his expertise that guided her now, perhaps more than her father's careful research and calculations. They were combing the very edge of the territory her father had mapped out, but Kate felt no discouragement. If she hadn't trusted Ky's skill and instincts, she would never have come back to Ocracoke.

They were going deeper now than they had on their other dives. Kate equalized by letting a tiny bit of air into her suit. Feeling the "squeeze" on her eardrums at the change in pressure, she relieved it carefully. A damaged eardrum could mean weeks without being able to dive.

When Ky signaled for her to switch on her headlamp she obeyed without question. Excitement began to rise.

The sunlight was fathoms above them. The world here never saw it. Sea grass swayed in the current. Now and then a fish, curious and brave enough, would swim along beside them only to vanish in the blink of an eye at a sudden movement.

Ky swam smoothly through the water, using his feet to propel him at a steady pace. Their lamps cut through the murk, surprising more fish, illuminating rock formations that had existed under the sea for centuries. Kate discovered shapes and faces in them.

No, she could never dive alone, Kate decided as Ky slowed his pace to keep rhythm with her more meandering one. It was so easy for her to lose her sense of time and direction. Air came into her lungs with a simple drawing of breath as long as the tanks held oxygen, but the gauges on her wrist only worked if she remembered to look at them.

Even mortality could be forgotten in enchantment.

And enchantment could too easily lead to a mistake. It was a lesson she knew, but one that could slip away from her. The timelessness, the freedom was seductive. The feeling was somehow as sensual as the timeless freedom felt in a lover's arms. Kate knew this pleasure could be as dangerous as a lover, but found it as difficult to resist.

There was so much to see, to touch. Crustaceans of different shapes, sizes and hues. They were alive here in their own milieu, so different from when they washed up helplessly on the beach for children to collect in buckets. Fish swam in and out of waving grass that would be limp and lifeless on land. Unlike dolphins or man, some creatures would never know the thrill of both air and water.

Her beam passed over another formation, crusted with barnacles and sea life. She nearly passed it, but curiosity made her turn back so that the light skimmed over it a second time. Odd, she thought, how structured some of the shapes could be. It almost looked like...

Hesitating, using her arms to reverse her progress, Kate turned in the water to play her light over the shape from end to end. Excitement rose so quickly she grabbed Ky's arm in a grip strong enough to make him stop to search for a defect in her equipment. With a shake of her head Kate warded him off, then pointed.

When their twin lights illuminated the form on the ocean floor, Kate nearly shouted with the discovery. It wasn't a shelf of rock. The closer they swam toward it the more apparent that became. Though it was heavily corroded and covered with crustaceans, the shape of the cannon remained recognizable.

Ky swam around the barrel. When he removed his

knife and struck the cannon with the hilt the metallic sound rang out strangely. Kate was certain she'd never heard anything more musical. Her laughter came out in a string of bubbles that made Ky look in her direction and grin.

They'd found a corroded cannon, he thought, and she was as thrilled as if they'd found a chest full of doubloons. And he understood it. They'd found something perhaps no one had seen for two centuries. That in itself was a treasure.

With a movement of his hand he indicated for her to follow, then they began to swim slowly east. If they'd found a cannon, it was likely they'd find more.

Reluctant to leave her initial discovery, Kate swam with him, looking back as often as she looked ahead. She hadn't realized the excitement would be this intense. How could she explain what it felt like to discover something that had lain untouched on the sea floor for more than two centuries? Who would understand more clearly, she wondered, her colleagues at Yale or Ky? Somehow she felt her colleagues would understand intellectually, but they would never understand the exhilaration. Intellectual pleasure didn't make you giddy enough to want to turn somersaults.

How would her father have felt if he'd found it? She wished she knew. She wished she could have given him that one instant of exultation, perhaps shared it with him as they'd so rarely shared anything. He'd only known the planning, the theorizing, the bookwork. With one long look at that ancient weapon, she'd known so much more.

When Ky stopped and touched her shoulders, her emotions were as mixed as her thoughts. If she could have spoken she'd have told him to hold her, though she wouldn't have known why. She was thrilled, yet running through the joy was a thin shaft of sorrow— for what was lost, she thought. For what she'd never be able to find again.

Perhaps he knew something of what moved her. They couldn't communicate with words, but he touched her cheek—just a brush of his finger over her skin. It was more comforting to her than a dozen soft speeches.

She understood then that she'd never stopped loving him. No matter how many years, how many miles had separated them, what life she had she'd left with him. The time in between had been little more than existence. It was possible to live with emptiness, even to be content with it until you had that heady taste of life again.

She might have panicked. She might have run if she hadn't been trapped there, fathoms deep in the midst of a discovery. Instead, she accepted the knowledge, hoping that time would tell her what to do.

He wanted to ask her what was going through her mind. Her eyes were full of so many emotions. Words would have to wait. Their time in the sea was almost up. He touched her face again and waited for the smile. When she gave it to him, Ky pointed at something behind her that he had just noticed moments before.

An oaken plank, old, splintered and bumpy with parasites. For the second time Ky removed his knife and began to pry the board from its bed. Silt floated up thinly, cutting visibility before it settled again. Replacing his knife, Ky gave the thumbs-up signal that meant they'd surface. Kate shook her head indicating that they should continue to search, but Ky merely pointed to his watch, then again to the surface.

Frustrated with the technology that allowed her to dive, but also forced her to seek air again, Kate nodded.

They swam west, back toward the boat. When she passed the cannon again, Kate felt a quick thrill of pride. She'd found it. And the discoveries were only beginning.

The moment her head was above water, she started to laugh. "We found it!" She grabbed the ladder with one hand as Ky began to climb up, placing his find and his tanks on the deck first. "I can't believe it, after hardly more than a week. It's incredible, that cannon lying down there all these years." Water ran down her face but she didn't notice. "We have to find the hull, Ky." Impatient, she released her tanks and handed them up to him before she climbed aboard.

"The chances are good—eventually."

"Eventually?" Kate tossed her wet hair out of her eyes. "We found this in just over a week." She indicated the board on the deck. She crouched over it, just wanting to touch. "We found the *Liberty.*"

"We found a wreck," he corrected. "It doesn't have to be the *Liberty.*"

"It is," she said with a determination that caused his brow to lift. "We found the cannon and this just on the edge of the area my father had charted. It all fits too well."

"Regardless of what wreck it is, it's undocumented. You'll get your name in the books, professor."

Annoyed, she rose. They stood facing each other on either side of the plank they'd lifted out of the sea. "I don't care about having my name in the books."

"Your father's name then." He unzipped his wet suit to let his skin dry.

She remembered her feelings after spotting the cannon, how Ky had seemed to understand them. Could they only be kind to each other, only be close to each other, fathoms under the surface? "Is there something wrong with that?"

"Only if it's an obsession. You always had a problem with your father."

"Because he didn't approve of you?" she shot back.

His eyes took on that eerily calm, almost flat expression that meant his anger was lethal. "Because it mattered too much to you what he approved of."

That stung. The truth often did. "I came here to finish my father's project," she said evenly. "I made that clear from the beginning. You're still getting your fee."

"You're still following directions. His directions." Before she could retort, he turned toward the cabin. "We'll eat and rest before we go back under."

With an effort, she held on to her temper. She wanted to dive again, badly. She wanted to find more. Not for her father's approval, Kate thought fiercely. Certainly not for Ky's. She wanted this for herself. Pulling down the zipper of her wet suit, she went down the cabin steps.

She'd eat because strength and energy were vital to a diver. She'd rest for the same reason. Then, she determined, she'd go back to the wreck and find proof that it was the *Liberty*.

Calmer, she watched Ky go through a small cupboard. "Peanut butter?" she asked when she saw the jar he pulled out.

"Protein."

Her laugh helped her to relax again. "Do you still eat it with bananas?"

"It's still good for you."

Though she wrinkled her nose at the combination, she reminded herself that beggars couldn't be choosers. "When we find the treasure," she said recklessly, "I'll buy you a bottle of champagne."

Their fingers brushed as he handed her the first sandwich. "I'll hold you to it." He picked up his own sandwich and a quart of milk. "Let's eat on deck."

He wasn't certain if he wanted the sun or the space, but it wasn't any easier to be with her in that tiny cabin than it had been the first time, or the last. Taking her assent for granted, Ky went up the stairs again, without looking back. Kate followed.

"It might be good for you," Kate commented as she took the first bite, "but it still tastes like something you give five-year-olds when they scrape their knees."

"Five-year-olds require a lot of protein."

Giving up, Kate sat cross-legged on the deck. The sun was bright, the movement of the boat gentle. She wouldn't let his digs get to her, nor would she dig back. They were in this together, she reminded herself. Tension and sniping wouldn't help them find what they sought.

"It's the *Liberty,* Ky," she murmured, looking at the plank again. "I know it is."

"It's possible." He stretched out with his back against the port side. "But there are a lot of wrecks, unidentified and otherwise, all through these waters. Diamond Shoals is a graveyard."

"Diamond Shoals is fifty miles north."

"And the entire coastline along these barrier islands

is full of littoral currents, rip currents and shifting sand ridges. Two hundred years ago they didn't have modern navigational devices. Hell, they didn't even have the lighthouses until the nineteenth century. I couldn't even give you an educated guess as to how many ships went down from the time Columbus set out until World War II."

Kate took another bite. "We're only concerned with one ship."

"Finding one's no big problem," he returned. "Finding a specific one's something else. Last year, after a couple of hurricanes breezed through, they found wrecks uncovered on the beach on Hatteras. There are plenty of houses on the island that were built from pieces of wreckage like that." He pointed to the plank with the remains of his sandwich.

Kate frowned at the board again. "It could be the *Liberty* just as easily as it couldn't."

"All right." Appreciating her stubbornness, Ky grinned. "But whatever it is, there might be treasure. Anything lost for more than two hundred years is pretty much finders keepers."

She didn't want to say that it wasn't any treasure she wanted. Just the *Liberty*'s. From what he said before, Kate was aware he already understood that. It was simply different for him. She took a long drink of cold milk. "What do you plan to do with your share?"

With his eyes half closed, he shrugged. He could do as he pleased now, a cache of gold wouldn't change that. "Buy another boat, I imagine."

"With what two-hundred-year-old gold would be worth today, you'd be able to buy a hell of a boat."

He grinned, but kept his eyes shaded. "I intend to. What about you?"

"I'm not sure." She wished she had some tangible goal for the money, something exciting, even fanciful. It just didn't seem possible to think beyond the hunt yet. "I thought I might travel a bit."

"Where?"

"Greece maybe. The islands."

"Alone?"

The food and the motion of the boat lulled her. She made a neutral sound as she shut her eyes.

"Isn't there some dedicated teacher you'd take with you? Someone you could discuss the Trojan War with?"

"Mmm, I don't want to go to Greece with a dedicated teacher."

"Someone else?"

"There's no one."

Sitting on the deck with her face lifted, her hair blowing, she looked like a finely crafted piece of porcelain. Something a man might look at, admire, but not touch. When her eyes were open, hot, her skin flushed with passion, he burned for her. When she was like this, calm, distant, he ached. He let the needs run through him because he knew there was no stopping them.

"Why?"

"Hmm?"

"Why isn't there anyone?"

Lazily she opened her eyes. "Anyone?"

"Why don't you have a lover?"

The sleepy haze cleared from her eyes instantly. He saw her fingers tense on the dark blue material that stretched snugly over her knees. "It's none of your business whether I do or not."

"You've just told me you don't."

"I told you there's no one I'd travel with," she corrected, but when she started to rise, he put a hand on her shoulder.

"It's the same thing."

"No, it's not, but it's still none of your business, Ky, any more than your personal life is mine."

"I've had women," he said easily. "But I haven't had a lover since you left the island."

She felt the pain and the pleasure sweep up through her. It was dangerous to dwell on the sensation. As dangerous as it was to lose yourself deep under the ocean. "Don't." She lifted her hand to remove his from her shoulder. "This isn't good for either of us."

"Why?" His fingers linked with hers. "We want each other. We both know the rules this time around."

Rules. No commitment, no promises. Yes, she understood them this time, but like mortality during a dive, they could easily be forgotten. Even now, with his eyes on hers, her fingers caught in his, the structure of those rules became dimmer and dimmer. He would hurt her again. There was never any question of that. Somehow, in the past twenty-four hours, it had become a matter of *how* she would deal with the pain, not *if.*

"Ky, I'm not ready." Her voice was low, not pleading, but plainly vulnerable. Though she wasn't aware of it, there was no defense she could put to better use.

He drew her up so that they were both standing, touching only hand to hand. Though she was tall, her slimness made her appear utterly fragile. It was that and the way she looked at him, with her head tilted back so their eyes could meet, that prevented him from taking what he was determined to have, without questions, without her willingness. Ruthlessly, that was how he told himself he wanted to take her, even though he knew he couldn't.

"I'm not a patient man."

"No."

He nodded, then released her hand while he still could. "Remember it," he warned before he turned to go to the helm. "We'll take the boat east, over the wreck and dive again."

An hour later they found a piece of rigging, broken and corroded, less than three yards from the cannon. By hand signals, Ky indicated that they'd start a stockpile of the salvage. Later they'd come back with the means of bringing it up. There were more planks, some too big for a man to carry up, some small enough for Kate to hold in one hand.

When she found a pottery bowl, miraculously unbroken, she realized just what an archaeologist must feel after hours of digging when he unearths a fragment of another era. Here it was, cupped in her hand, a simple bowl, covered with silt, covered with age. Someone had eaten from it once, a seaman, relaxing briefly below deck, perhaps on his first voyage across the Atlantic to the New World. His last journey in any event, Kate mused as she turned the bowl over in her hand.

The rigging, the cannon, the planks equaled ship. The bowl equaled man.

Though she put the bowl with the other pieces of their find, she intended to take it up with her on this dive. Whatever other artifacts they found could go to a museum, but the first, she'd keep.

They found pieces of glass that might have come from bottles that held whiskey, chunks of crockery that hadn't survived intact like the bowl. Bits of cups, bowls, plates littered the sea floor.

The galley, she decided. They must have found the galley. Over the years, the water pressure would have simply disintegrated the ship until it was all pieces spread on and under the floor of the ocean. It would, in essence, have become part of the sea, a home for the creatures and plant life that dwelt there.

But they'd found the galley. If they could find something, just one thing with the ship's name inscribed on it, they'd be certain.

Diligently, using her knife as a digging tool, Kate worked at the floor of the sea. It wasn't a practical way to search, but she saw no harm in trying her luck. They'd found crockery, glass, the unbroken bowl. Even as she glanced up she saw Ky examining what might have been half a dinner plate.

When she unearthed a long wooden ladle, Kate found that her excitement increased. They *had* found the galley, and in time, she'd prove to Ky that they'd found the *Liberty*.

Engrossed in her find, she turned to signal to Ky and moved directly into the path of a stingray.

He saw it. Ky was no more than a yard from Kate when the movement of the ray unearthing itself from its layer of sand and silt had caught his eye. His movement was pure reflex, done without thought or plan. He was quick. But even as he grabbed Kate's hand to swing her back behind him, out of range, the wicked, saw-toothed tail lashed out.

Her scream was muffled by the water, but the sound went through Ky just as surely as the stingray's poison went through Kate. Her body went stiff against his, rigid in pain and shock. The ladle she'd found floated down, out of her grip, until it landed silently on the bottom.

He knew what to do. No rational diver goes down unless he has a knowledge of how to handle an emergency. Still, Ky felt a moment of panic. This wasn't just another diver, it was Kate. Before his mind could clear, her stiffened body went limp against him. Then he acted.

Cool, almost mechanically, he tilted her head back with the chin carry to keep her air passage open. He held her securely, pressing his chest into her tanks, keeping his hand against her rib cage. It ran through his mind that it was best she'd fainted. Unconscious she wouldn't struggle as she might had she been awake and in pain. It was best she'd fainted because he couldn't bear to think of her in pain. He kicked off for the surface.

On the rise he squeezed her, hard, forcing expanding air out of her lungs. There was always the risk of embolism. They were going up faster than safety allowed. Even while he ventilated his own lungs, Ky kept a lookout. She would bleed, and blood brought sharks.

The minute they surfaced, Ky released her weight belt. Supporting her with his arm wrapped around her, his hand grasping the ladder, Ky unhooked his tanks, slipped them over the side of the boat, then removed Kate's. Her face was waxy, but as he pulled the mask from her face she moaned. With that slight sound of life some of the blood came back to his own body. With her draped limply over his shoulder, he climbed the ladder onto the *Vortex*.

He laid her down on the deck, and with hands that

didn't hesitate, began to pull the wet suit from her. She moaned again when he drew the snug material over the wound just above her ankle, but she didn't reach the surface of consciousness. Grimly, Ky examined the laceration the ray had caused. Even through the protection of her suit, the tail had penetrated deep into her skin. If Ky had only been quicker...

Cursing himself, Ky hurried to the cabin for the first-aid kit.

As consciousness began to return, Kate felt the ache swimming up from her ankle to her head. Spears of pain shot through her, sharp enough to make her gasp and struggle, as if she could move away from it and find ease again.

"Try to lie still."

The voice was gentle and calm. Kate balled her hands into fists and obeyed it. Opening her eyes, she stared up at the pure blue sky. Her mind whirled with confusion, but she stared at the sky as though it were the only tangible thing in her life. If she concentrated, she could rise above the hurt. The ladle. Opening her hand she found it empty, she'd lost the ladle. For some reason it seemed vital that she have it.

"We found the galley." Her voice was hoarse with anguish, but her one hand remained open and limp. "I found a ladle. They'd have used it for spooning soup into that bowl. The bowl—it wasn't even broken. Ky..." Her voice weakened with a new flood of sensation as memory began to return. "It was a stingray. I wasn't watching for it, it just seemed to be there. Am I going to die?"

"No!" His answer was sharp, almost angry. Bending over her, he placed both hands on her shoulders so that she'd look directly into his face. He had to be sure she understood everything he said. "It was a stingray," he confirmed, not adding that it had been a good ten feet long. "Part of the spine's broken off, lodged just above your ankle."

He watched her eyes cloud further, part pain, part fear. His hands tightened on her shoulders. "It's not in deep. I can get it out, but it'll hurt like hell."

She knew what he was saying. She could stay as she was until he got her back to the doctor on the island, or she could trust him to treat her now. Though her lips trembled, she kept her eyes on his and spoke clearly.

"Do it now."

"Okay." He continued to stare at her, into the eyes that were glazed with shock. "Hang on. Don't try to be brave. Scream as much as you want but try not to move. I'll be quick." Bending farther, he kissed her hard. "I promise."

Kate nodded, then concentrating on the feeling of his lips against hers, shut her eyes. He was quick. Within seconds she felt the hurt rip through her, over the threshold she thought she could bear and beyond... She pulled in air to scream, but went back under the surface into liquid dimness.

Ky let the blood flow freely onto the deck for a moment, knowing it would wash away some of the poison. His hands had been rock steady when he'd pulled the spine from her flesh. His mind had been cold. Now with her blood on his hands, they began to shake. Ignoring them, and the icy fear of seeing Kate's smooth skin ripped and raw, Ky washed the wound, cleansed it, bound it. Within the hour, he'd have her to a doctor.

With unsteady fingers, he checked the pulse at the

base of her neck. It wasn't strong, but it was steady. Lifting an eyelid with his thumb, he checked her pupils. He didn't believe she was in shock, she'd simply escaped from the pain. He thanked God for that.

On a long breath he let his forehead rest against hers, only for a moment. He prayed that she'd remain unconscious until she was safely under a doctor's care.

He didn't take the time to wash her blood from his hands before he took the helm. Ky whipped the boat around in a quick circle and headed full throttle back to Ocracoke.

Chapter 7

As she started to float toward consciousness, Kate focused, drifted, then focused again. She saw the whirl of a white ceiling rather than the pure blue arc of sky. Even when the mist returned she remembered the hurt and thrashed out against it. She couldn't face it a second time. Yet she found as she rose closer to the surface that she didn't have the will to fight against it. That brought fear. If she'd had the strength, she might have wept.

Then she felt a cool hand on her cheek. Ky's voice pierced the last layers of fog, low and gentle. "Take it easy, Kate. You're all right now. It's all over."

Though her breath hitched as she inhaled, Kate opened her eyes. The pain didn't come. All she felt was his hand on her cheek, all she saw was his face. "Ky." When she said his name, Kate reached for his hand, the one solid thing she was sure of. Her own voice frightened her. It was hardly more than a wisp of air.

"You're going to be fine. The doctor took care of you." As he spoke, Ky rubbed his thumb over her knuckles, establishing a point of concentration, and kept his other hand lightly on her cheek, knowing that contact was important. He'd nearly gone mad waiting for her to open her eyes again. "Dr. Bailey, you remember. You met him before."

It seemed vital that she should remember so she forced her mind to search back. She had a vague picture of a tough, weathered old man who looked more suited to the sea than the examining room. "Yes. He likes…likes ale and flounder."

He might have laughed at her memory if her voice had been stronger. "You're going to be fine, but he wants you to rest for a few more days."

"I feel…strange." She lifted a hand to her own head as if to assure herself it was still there.

"You're on medication, that's why you're groggy. Understand?"

"Yes." Slowly she turned her head and focused on her surroundings. The walls were a warm ivory, not the sterile white of a hospital. The dark oak trim gleamed dully. On the hardwood floor lay a single rug, its muted Indian design fading with age. It was the only thing Kate recognized. The last time she'd been in Ky's bedroom only half the drywall had been in place and one of the windows had had a long, thin crack in the bottom pane. "Not the hospital," she managed.

"No." He stroked her head, needing to touch as much as to check for her fever that had finally broken near dawn. "It was easier to bring you here after Bailey took care of you. You didn't need a hospital, but neither of us liked the idea of your being in a hotel right now."

"Your house," she murmured, struggling to concentrate her strength. "This is your bedroom, I remember the rug."

They'd made love on it once. That's what Ky remembered. With an effort, he kept his hands light. "Are you hungry?"

"I don't know." Basically, she felt nothing. When she tried to sit up, the drug spun in her head, making both the room and reality reel away. That would have to stop, Kate decided while she waited for the dizziness to pass. She'd rather have some pain than that helpless, weighted sensation.

Without fuss, Ky moved the pillows and shifted her to a sitting position. "The doctor said you should eat when you woke up. Just some soup." Rising he looked down on her, in much the same way, Kate thought, as he'd looked at a cracked mast he was considering mending. "I'll fix it. Don't get up," he added as he walked to the door. "You're not strong enough yet."

As he went into the hall he began to swear in a low, steady stream.

Of course she wasn't strong enough, he thought with a last vicious curse. She was pale enough to fade into the sheets she lay on. No resistance, that's what Bailey had said. Not enough food, not enough sleep, too much strain. If he could do nothing else, Ky determined as he pulled open a kitchen cupboard, he could do something about that. She was going to eat, and lie flat on her back until the doctor said otherwise.

He'd known she was weak, that was the worst of it. Ky dumped the contents of a can into a pot then hurled the empty container into the trash. He'd seen the strain on her face, the shadows under her eyes, he'd heard the traces of fatigue come and go in her voice, but he'd been too wrapped up in his own needs to do anything about it.

With a flick of the wrist, he turned on the burner under the soup, then the burner under the coffee. God, he needed coffee. For a moment he simply stood with his fingers pressed against his eyes waiting for his system to settle.

He couldn't remember ever spending a more frantic twenty-four hours. Even after the doctor had checked and treated her, even when Ky had brought her home and she'd been fathoms deep under the drug, his nerves hadn't eased. He'd been terrified to leave the room for more than five minutes at a time. The fever had raged through her, though she'd been unaware. Most of the night he'd sat beside her, bathing away the sweat and talking to her, though she couldn't hear.

Through the night he'd existed on coffee and nerves. With a half laugh he reached for a cup. It looked like that wasn't going to change for a while yet.

He knew he still wanted her, knew he still felt something for her, under the bitterness and anger. But until he'd seen her lying unconscious on the deck of his boat, with her blood on his hands, he hadn't realized that he still loved her.

He'd known what to do about the want, even the bitterness, but now, faced with love, Ky hadn't a clue. It didn't seem possible for him to love someone so frail, so calm, so…different than he. Yet the emotion he'd once felt for her had grown and ripened into something so solid he couldn't see any way around it. For now, he'd concentrate on getting her on her feet again. He poured the soup into a bowl and carried it upstairs.

It would have been an easy matter to close her eyes and slide under again. Too easy. Willing herself to stay awake, Kate concentrated on Ky's room. There were a number of changes here as well, she mused. He'd trimmed the windows in oak, giving them a wide sill where he'd scattered the best of his shells. A piece of satiny driftwood stood, beautiful as a piece of sculpture. There was a paneled closet door with a faceted glass knob where there'd once been a rod, a round-backed rattan chair where there'd been packing crates.

Only the bed was the same, she mused. The wide four-poster had been his mother's. She knew he'd given the rest of his family's furniture to Marsh. Ky had told her once he'd felt no need or desire for it, but he kept the bed. He was born there, unexpectedly, during a night in which the island had been racked by a storm.

And they'd made love there, Kate remembered as she ran her fingers over the sheets. The first time, and the last.

Stopping the movement of her fingers, she looked over as Ky came back into the room. Memories had to be pushed aside. "You've done a lot of work in here."

"A bit." He set the tray over her lap as he sat on the edge of the bed.

As the scent of the soup reached her, Kate shut her eyes. Just the aroma seemed to be enough. "It smells wonderful."

"The smell won't put any meat on you."

She smiled, and opened her eyes again. Then before she'd realized it, Ky had spoon-fed her the first bite. "It tastes wonderful too." Though she reached for the spoon, he dipped it into the bowl himself then held it to her lips. "I can do it," she began, then was forced to swallow more broth.

"Just eat." Fighting off waves of emotion he spoke briskly. "You look like hell."

"I'm sure I do," she said easily. "Most people don't look their best a couple of hours after being stung by a stingray."

"Twenty-four," Ky corrected as he fed her another spoon of soup.

"Twenty-four what?"

"Hours." Ky slipped in another spoonful when her eyes widened.

"I've been unconscious for twenty-four hours?" She looked to the window and the sunlight as if she could find some means of disproving it.

"You slipped in and out quite a bit before Bailey gave you the shot. He said you probably wouldn't remember." *Thank God,* Ky added silently. Whenever she'd fought her way back to consciousness, she'd been in agony. He could still hear her moans, feel the way she'd clutched him. He never knew a person could suffer physically for another's pain the way he'd suffered for hers. Even now it made his muscles clench.

"That must've been some shot he gave me."

"He gave you what you needed." His eyes met hers. For the first time Kate saw the fatigue in them, and the anger.

"You've been up all night," she murmured. "Haven't you had any rest at all?"

"You needed to be watched," he said briefly. "Bailey wanted you to stay under, so you'd sleep through the worst of the pain, and so you'd just sleep period."

His voice changed as he lost control over the anger. He couldn't prevent the edge of accusation from showing, partly for her, partly for himself. "The wound wasn't that bad, do you understand? But you weren't in any shape to handle it. Bailey said you've been well on the way to working yourself into exhaustion."

"That's ridiculous. I don't—"

Ky swore at her, filling her mouth with more soup. "Don't tell me it's ridiculous. I had to listen to him. I had to look at you. You don't eat, you don't sleep, you're going to fall down on your face."

There was too much of the drug in her system to allow her temper to bite. Instead of annoyance, her words came out like a sigh. "I didn't fall on my face."

"Only a matter of time." Fury was coming too quickly. Though his fingers tightened on the spoon, Ky held it back. "I don't care how much you want to find the treasure, you can't enjoy it if you're flat on your back."

The soup was warming her. As much as her pride urged her to refuse, her system craved the food. "I won't be," she told him, not even aware that her words were beginning to slur. "We'll dive again tomorrow, and I'll prove it's the *Liberty*."

He started to swear at her, but one look at the heavy eyes and the pale cheeks had him swallowing the words. "Sure." He spooned in more soup knowing she'd be asleep again within moments.

"I'll give the ladle and the rigging and the rest to a museum." Her eyes closed. "For my father."

Ky set the tray on the floor. "Yes, I know."

"It was important to him. I need...I just need to give him something." Her eyes fluttered open briefly.

"I didn't know he was ill. He never told me about his heart, about the pills. If I'd known…"

"You couldn't have done any more than you did." His voice was gentle again as he shifted the pillows down.

"I loved him."

"I know you did."

"I could never seem to make the people I love understand what I need. I don't know why."

"Rest now. When you're well, we'll find the treasure."

She felt herself sinking into warmth, softness, the dark. "Ky." Kate reached out and felt his fingers wrap around hers. With her eyes closed, it was all the reality she needed.

"I'll stay," he murmured, brushing the hair from her cheek. "Just rest."

"All those years…" He could feel her fingers relaxing in his as she slipped deeper. "I never forgot you. I never stopped wanting you. Not ever…"

He stared down at her as she slept. Her face was utterly peaceful, pale as marble, soft as silk. Unable to resist, he lifted her fingers to his own cheek, just to feel her flesh against his. He wouldn't think about what she'd said now. He couldn't. The strain of the last day had taken a toll on him as well. If he didn't get some rest, he wouldn't be able to care for her when she woke again.

Rising, Ky pulled down the shades, and took off his shirt. Then he lay down next to Kate in the big four-poster bed and slept for the first time in thirty-six hours.

The pain was a dull, consistent throb, not the silvery sharp flash she remembered, but a gnawing ache that wouldn't pass. When it woke her, Kate lay still, trying to orient herself. Her mind was clearer now. She was grateful for that, even though with the drug out of her system she was well aware of the wound. It was dark, but the moonlight slipped around the edges of the shades Ky had drawn. She was grateful for that too. It seemed she'd been a prisoner of the dark for too long.

It was night. She prayed it was only hours after she'd last awoken, not another full day later. She didn't want that quick panic at the thought of losing time again. Because she needed to be certain she was in control this time, she went over everything she remembered.

The pottery bowl, the ladle, then the stingray. She closed her eyes a moment, knowing it would be a very long time before she forgot what it had felt like to be struck with that whiplike tail. She remembered waking up on the deck of the *Vortex*, the pure blue sky overhead, and the strong, calm way Ky had spoken to her before he'd pulled out the spine. That pain, the horror of that one instant was very clear. Then, there was nothing else.

She remembered nothing of the journey back to the island, or of Dr. Bailey's ministrations or of being transported to Ky's home. Her next clear image was of waking in his bedroom, of dark oak trim on the windows, wide sills with shells set on them.

He'd fed her soup—yes, that was clear, but then things started to become hazy again. She knew he'd been angry, though she couldn't remember why. At the moment, it was more important to her that she could put events in some sort of sequence.

As she lay in the dark, fully awake and finally aware, she heard the sound of quiet, steady breathing beside her. Turning her head, Kate saw Ky beside her, hardly more than a silhouette with the moonlight just touching the skin of his chest so that she could see it rise and fall.

He'd said he would stay, she remembered. And he'd been tired. Abruptly Kate remembered there'd been fatigue in his eyes as well as temper. He'd been caring for her.

A mellow warmth moved through her, one she hadn't felt in a very long time. He had taken care of her, and though it had made him angry, he'd done it. And he'd stayed. Reaching out, she touched his cheek.

Though the gesture was whisper light, Ky awoke immediately. His sleep had been little more than a half doze so that he could recharge his system yet be aware of any sign that Kate needed attention. Sitting up, he shook his head to clear it.

He looked like a boy caught napping. For some reason the gesture moved Kate unbearably. "I didn't mean to wake you," she murmured.

He reached for the lamp beside the bed and turned it on low. Though his body revolted against the interruption, his mind was fully awake. "Pain?"

"No."

He studied her face carefully. The glazed look from the drug had left her eyes, but the color hadn't returned. "Kate."

"All right. Some."

"Bailey left some pills."

As he started to rise, Kate reached for him again. "No, I don't want anything. It makes me groggy."

"It takes away the pain."

"Not now, Ky, please. I promise I'll tell you if it gets bad."

Because her voice was close to desperate he made himself content with that. At the moment, she looked too fragile to argue with. "Are you hungry?"

She smiled, shaking her head. "No. It must be the middle of the night. I was only trying to orient myself." She touched him again, in gratitude, in comfort. "You should sleep."

"I've had enough. Anyway, you're the patient."

Automatically, he put his hand to her forehead to check for fever. Touched, Kate laid hers over it. She felt the quick reflexive tensing of his fingers.

"Thank you." When he would have removed his hand, she linked her fingers with his. "You've been taking good care of me."

"You needed it," he said simply and much too swiftly. He couldn't allow her to stir him now, not when they were in that big, soft bed surrounded by memories.

"You haven't left me since it happened."

"I had no place to go."

His answer made her smile. Kate reached up her free hand to touch his cheek. There had been changes, she thought, many changes. But so many things had stayed the same. "You were angry with me."

"You haven't been taking care of yourself." He told himself he should move away from the bed, from Kate, from everything that weakened him there.

He stayed, leaning over her, one hand caught in hers. Her eyes were dark, soft in the dim light, full of the sweetness and innocence he remembered. He wanted to hold her until there was no more pain for either of them, but he knew, if he pressed his body against hers now, he wouldn't stop. Again he started to move, pulling away the hand that held hers. Again Kate stopped him.

"I would've died if you hadn't gotten me up."

"That's why it's smarter to dive with a partner."

"I might still have died if you hadn't done everything you did."

He shrugged this off, too aware that the fingers on his face were stroking lightly, something she had done in the past. Sometimes before they'd made love, and often afterward, when they'd talked in quiet voices, she'd stroke his face, tracing the shape of it as though she'd needed to memorize it. Perhaps she, too, sometimes awoke in the middle of the night and remembered too much.

Unable to bear it, Ky put his hand around her wrist and drew it away. "The wound wasn't that bad," he said simply.

"I've never seen a stingray that large." She shivered and his hand tightened on her wrist.

"Don't think about it now. It's over."

Was it? she wondered as she lifted her head and looked into his eyes. Was anything ever really over? For four years she'd told herself there were joys and pains that could be forgotten, absorbed into the routine that was life as it had to be lived. Now, she was no longer sure. She needed to be. More than anything else, she needed to be sure.

"Hold me," she murmured.

Was she trying to make him crazy? Ky wondered. Did she want him to cross the border, that edge he was trying so desperately to avoid? It took most of the strength he had left just to keep his voice even. "Kate, you need to sleep now. In the morning—"

"I don't want to think about the morning," she murmured. "Only now. And now I need you to hold me."
Before he could refuse, she slipped her arms around his waist and rested her head on his shoulder.

She felt his hesitation, but not his one vivid flash of longing before his arms came around her. On a long breath Kate closed her eyes. Too much time had passed since she'd had this, the gentleness, the sweetness she'd experienced only with Ky. No one else had ever held her with such kindness, such simple compassion. Somehow, she never found it odd that a man could be so reckless and arrogant, yet kind and compassionate at the same time.

Perhaps she'd been attracted to the recklessness, but it had been the kindness she had fallen in love with. Until now, in the quiet of the deep night, she hadn't understood. Until now, in the security of his arms, she hadn't accepted what she wanted.

Life as it had to be lived, she thought again. Was taking what she so desperately needed part of that?

She was so slender, so soft beneath the thin nightshirt. Her hair lay over his skin, loose and free, its color muted in the dim light. He could feel her palms against his back, those elegant hands that had always made him think more of an artist than a teacher. Her breathing was quiet, serene, as he knew it was when she slept. The light scent of woman clung to the material of the nightshirt.

Holding her didn't bring the pain he'd expected but a contentment he'd been aching for without realizing it. The tension in his muscles eased, the knot in his stomach vanished. With his eyes closed, he rested his cheek on her hair. It seemed like a lifetime since he'd known the pleasure of quiet satisfaction. She'd asked him to hold her, but had she known he needed to be held just as badly?

Kate felt him relax degree by degree and wondered if it had been she who'd caused the tension in him, and she who'd ultimately released it. Had she hurt him more than she'd realized? Had he cared more than she'd dared to believe? Or was it simply that the physical need never completely faded? It didn't matter, not tonight.

Ky was right. She knew the rules this time around. She wouldn't expect more than he offered. Whatever he offered was much, much more than she'd had in the long, dry years without him. In turn, she could give what she ached to give. Her love.

"It's the same for me as it always was," she murmured. Then, tilting her head back, she looked at him. Her hair streamed down her back, her eyes were wide and honest. He felt the need slam into him like a fist.

"Kate—"

"I never expected to feel the same way when I came back," she interrupted. "I don't think I'd have come. I wouldn't have had the courage."

"Kate, you're not well." He said it very slowly, as if he had to explain to them both. "You've lost blood, had a fever. It's taken a lot out of you. It'd be best, I think, if you tried to sleep now."

She felt no fever now. She felt cool and light and full of needs. "That day on the beach during the storm, you said I'd come to you." Kate brought her hands up his back until they reached his shoulders. "Even then

I knew you were right. I'm coming to you now. Make love with me, Ky, here, in the bed where you loved me that first time."

And the last, he remembered, fighting back a torrent of desire. "You're not well," he managed a second time.

"Well enough to know what I want." She brushed her lips over his chin where his beard grew rough with neglect. So long...that was all that would come clearly to her. It had been so long. Too long. "Well enough to know what I need. It's always been you." Her fingers tightened on his shoulders, her lips inches from his. "It's only been you."

Perhaps moving away from her was the answer. But some answers were impossible. "Tomorrow you may be sorry."

She smiled in her calm, quiet way that always moved him. "Then we'll have tonight."

He couldn't resist her. The warmth. He didn't want to hurt her. The softness. The need building inside him threatened to send them both raging even though he knew she was still weak, still fragile. He remembered how it had been the first time, when she'd been innocent. He'd been so careful, though he had never felt the need to care before, and hadn't since. Remembering that, he laid her back.

"We'll have tonight," he repeated and touched his lips to hers.

Sweet, fresh, clean. Those words went through his head, those sensations went through his system as her lips parted for his. So he lingered over her kiss, enjoying with tenderness what he'd once promised himself to take ruthlessly. His mouth caressed, without haste, without pressure. Tasting, just tasting, while the hunger grew.

Her hands reached for his face, fingers stroking, the rough, the smooth. She could hear her own heart beat in her head, feel the slow, easy pleasure that came in liquid waves. He murmured to her, lovely, quiet words that made her thrill when she felt them formed against her mouth. With his tongue he teased hers in long, lazy sweeps until she felt her mind cloud as it had under the drug. Then when she felt the first twinge of desperation, he kissed her with an absorbed patience that left her weak.

He felt it—that initial change from equality to submission that had always excited him. The aggression would come later, knocking the breath from him, taking him to the edge. He knew that too. But for the moment, she was soft, yielding.

He slid his hands over the nightshirt, stroking, lingering. The material between his flesh and hers teased them both. She moved to his rhythm, glorying in the steady loss of control. He took her deeper with a touch, still deeper with a taste. She dove, knowing the full pleasure of ultimate trust. Wherever he took her, she wanted to go.

With a whispering movement he took his hand over the slender curve of her breast. She was soft, the material smooth, making her hardening nipple a sensuous contrast. He loitered there while her breathing grew unsteady, reveling in the changes of her body. Lingering over each separate button of her nightshirt, Ky unfastened them, then slowly parted the material, as if he were unveiling a priceless treasure.

He'd never forgotten how lovely she was, how exciting delicacy could be. Now that he had her again, he
allowed himself the time to look, to touch carefully,
all the while watching the contact of his lean, tanned
hand against her pale skin. With tenderness he felt seldom and demonstrated rarely, he lowered his mouth,
letting his lips follow the progress his fingers had already begun.

She was coming to life under him. Kate felt her
blood begin to boil as though it had lain dormant in
her veins for years. She felt her heart begin to thump
as though it had been frozen in ice until that moment.
She heard her name as only he said it. As only he could.

Sensations? Could there be so many of them? Could
she have known them all once, experienced them all
once, then lived without them? A whisper, a sigh, the
brush of a fingertip along her skin. The scent of a man
touched by the sea, the taste of her lover lingering on
her lips. The glow of soft lights against closed lids.
Time faded. No yesterday. No tomorrow.

She could feel the slick material of the nightshirt
slide away, then the warm, smooth sheets beneath her
back. The skim of his tongue along her rib cage incited a thrill that began in her core and exploded inside her head.

She remembered the dawn breaking slowly over
the sea. Now she knew the same magnificence inside
her own body. Light and warmth spread through her,
gradually, patiently, until she was glowing with a new
beginning.

He hadn't known he could hold such raging desire
in check and still feel such complete pleasure, such

whirling excitement. He was aware of every heightening degree of passion that worked through her. He understood the changing, rippling thrill she felt if he used more pressure here, a longer taste there. It brought him a wild sense of power, made only more acute by the knowledge that he must harness it. She was fluid. She was silk. And then with a suddenness that sent him reeling, she was fire.

Her body arched on the first tumultuous crest. It ripped through her like a madness. Greedy, ravenous for more, she began to demand what he'd only hinted at. Her hands ran over him, nearly destroying his control in a matter of seconds. Her mouth was hot, hungry, and sought his with an urgency he couldn't resist. Then she rained kisses over his face, down his throat until he gripped the sheets with his hands for fear of crushing her too tightly and bruising her skin.

She touched him with those slender, elegant fingers so that the blood rushed fast and furious into his head. "You make me crazy," he murmured.

"Yes." She could do no more than whisper, but her eyes opened. "Yes."

"I want to watch you go up," he said softly as he slid into her. "I want to see what making love with me does to you."

She arched again, the moan inching out of her as she experienced a second wild peak. He saw her eyes darken, cloud as he took her slowly, steadily toward the verge between passion and madness. He watched the color come into her cheeks, saw her lips tremble as she spoke his name. Her hands gripped his shoulders, but neither of them knew her short, tapered nails dug into his skin.

They moved together, neither able to lead, both able to follow. As pleasure built, he never took his eyes from her face.

All sensation focused into one. They were only one. With a freedom that reaches perfection only rarely, they gave perfection to each other.

Chapter 8

She was sleeping soundly when Ky woke. Ky observed a hint of color in her cheeks and was determined to see that it stayed there. The touch of his hand to her hair was gentle but proprietary. Her skin was cool and dry, her breathing quiet but steady.

What she'd given him the night before had been offered with complete freedom, without shadows of the past, with none of the bitter taste of regret. It was something else he intended to keep constant.

No, he wasn't going to allow her to withdraw from him again. Not an inch. He'd lost her four years ago, or perhaps he'd never really had her—not in the way he'd believed, not in the way he'd taken for granted. But this time, Ky determined, it would be different.

In his own way, he needed to take care of her. Her fragility drew that from him. In another way, he needed a partner on equal terms. Her strength offered him that. For reasons he never completely understood, Kate was exactly what he'd always wanted.

Clumsiness, arrogance, inexperience, or perhaps a combination of all three made him lose her once. Now that he had a second chance, he was going to make sure it worked. With a little more time, he might figure out how.

Rising, he dressed in the shaded light of the bedroom, then left her to sleep.

When she woke slowly, Kate was reluctant to surface from the simple pleasure of a dream. The room was dim, her mind was hazy with sleep and fantasy. The throb in her leg came as a surprise. How could there be pain when everything was so perfect? With a sigh, she reached for Ky and found the bed empty.

The haze vanished immediately, as did all traces of sleep and the pretty edge of fantasy. Kate sat up, and though the movement jolted the pain in her leg, she stared at the empty space beside her.

Had that been a dream as well? she wondered. Tentatively, she reached out and found the sheets cool. All a fantasy brought on by medication and confusion? Unsure, unsteady, she pushed the hair away from her face. Was it possible that she'd imagined it all—the gentleness, the sweetness, the passion?

She'd needed Ky. That hadn't been a dream. Even now she could feel the dull ache in her stomach that came from need. Had the need caused her to fantasize all that strange, stirring beauty during the night? The bed beside her was empty, the sheets cool. She was alone.

The pleasure she awoke with drained, leaving her

empty, leaving her grateful for the pain that was her only grip on reality. She wanted to weep, but found she hadn't the energy for tears.

"So you're up."

Ky's voice made her whip her head around. Her nerves were strung tight. He walked into the bedroom carrying a tray, wearing an easy smile.

"That saves me from having to wake you up to get some food into you." Before he approached the bed, he went to both windows and drew up the shades. Light poured into the room and the warm breeze that had been trapped behind the shades rushed in to ruffle the sheets. Feeling it, she had to control a shudder. "How'd you sleep?"

"Fine." The awkwardness was unexpected. Kate folded her hands and sat perfectly still. "I want to thank you for everything you've done."

"You've already thanked me once. It wasn't necessary then or now." Because her tone had put him on guard, Ky stopped next to the bed to take a good long look at her. "You're hurting."

"It's not bad."

"This time you take a pill." After setting the tray on her lap, he walked to the dresser and picked up a small bottle. "No arguments," he said, anticipating her refusal.

"Ky, it's really not bad." When had he offered her a pill before? The struggle to remember brought only more frustration. "There's barely any pain."

"Any pain's too much." He sat on the bed, and putting the pill into her palm curled her hand over it with his own. "When it's you."

With her fingers curled warmly under his, she knew.

Elation came so quietly she was afraid to move and chase it away. "I didn't dream it, did I?" she whispered.

"Dream what?" He kissed the back of her hand before he handed her the glass of juice.

"Last night. When I woke up, I was afraid it had all been a dream."

He smiled and, bending, touched his lips to hers. "If it was, I had the same dream." He kissed her again, with humor in his eyes. "It was wonderful."

"Then it doesn't matter whether it was a dream or not."

"Oh, no, I prefer reality."

With a laugh, she started to drop the pill on the tray, but he stopped her. "Ky—"

"You're hurting," he said again. "I can see it in your eyes. Your medication wore off hours ago, Kate."

"And kept me unconscious for an entire day."

"This is mild, just to take the edge off. Listen—" His hand tightened on hers. "I had to watch you in agony."

"Ky, don't."

"No, you'll do it for me if not for yourself. I had to watch you bleed and faint and drift in and out of consciousness." He ran his hand down her hair, then cupped her face so she'd look directly into his eyes. "I can't tell you what it did to me because I don't know how to describe it. I know I can't watch you in pain anymore."

In silence, she took the pill and drained the glass of juice. For him, as he said, not for herself. When she swallowed the medication, Ky tugged at her hair. "It hardly has more punch than an aspirin, Kate. Bailey said he'd give you something stronger if you needed it, but he'd rather you go with this."

"It'll be fine. It's really more uncomfortable than painful." It wasn't quite the truth, nor did he believe her, but they both let it lie for the moment. Each of them moved cautiously, afraid to spoil what might have begun to bloom again. Kate glanced down at the empty juice glass. The cold, fresh flavor still lingered on her tongue. "Did Dr. Bailey say when I could dive again?"

"Dive?" Ky's brows rose as he uncovered the plate of bacon, eggs and toast. "Kate, you're not even getting up out of bed for the rest of the week."

"Out of bed?" she repeated. "A week?" She ignored the overloaded plate of food as she gaped at him. "Ky, I was stung by a stingray, not attacked by a shark."

"You were stung by a stingray," he agreed. "And your system was so depleted Bailey almost sent you to a hospital. I realize things might've been rough on you since your father died, but you haven't helped anything by not taking care of yourself."

It was the first time he'd mentioned her father's death, and Kate noted he still expressed no sympathy. "Doctors tend to fuss," she began.

"Bailey doesn't," he interrupted. The anger came back and ran along the edge of his words. "He's a tough, cynical old goat, but he knows his business. He told me that you'd apparently worked yourself right to the edge of exhaustion, that your resistance was nil and that you were a good ten pounds underweight." He held out the fork. "We're going to do something about that, professor. Starting now."

Kate looked down at what had to be four large eggs,

scrambled, six slices of bacon and four pieces of toast. "I can see you intend to," she murmured.

"I'm not having you sick." He took her hand again and his grip was firm. "I'm going to take care of you, Kate, whether you like it or not."

She looked back at him in her calm, considering way. "I don't know if I do like it," she decided. "But I suppose we'll both find out."

Ky dipped the fork into the eggs. "Eat."

A smile played at the corners of her mouth. She'd never been pampered in her life and thought it might be entirely too easy to get used to it. "All right, but this time I'll feed myself."

She already knew she'd never finish the entire meal, but for his sake, and the sake of peace, she was determined to deal with half of it. That had been precisely his strategy. If he'd have brought her a smaller portion, she'd have eaten half of that, and have eaten less. He knew her better than either one of them fully realized.

"You're still a wonderful cook," she commented, breaking a piece of bacon in half. "Much better than I."

"If you're good, I might broil up some flounder tonight."

She remembered just how exquisitely he prepared fish. "How good?"

"As good as it takes." He accepted the slice of toast she offered him but dumped on a generous slab of jam. "Maybe I'll beg some of the hot fudge cake from the Roost."

"Looks like I'll have to be on my best behavior."

"That's the idea."

"Ky…" She was already beginning to poke at her

eggs. Had eating always been quite such an effort? "About last night, what happened—"

"Should never have stopped," he finished.

Her lashes swept up, and her eyes were quiet and candid. "I'm not sure."

"I am," he countered. Taking her face in his hands, he kissed her, softly, with only a hint of passion. But the hint was a promise of much more. "Let it be enough for now, Kate. If it has to get complicated, let's wait until other things are a little more settled."

Complicated. Were commitments complicated, the future, promises? She looked down at her plate knowing she simply didn't have the strength to ask or to answer. Not now. "In a way I feel as though I'm slipping back—to that summer four years ago. And yet..."

"It's like a step forward."

Kate looked at him again, but this time reached out. He'd always understood. Though he said little, though his way was sometimes rough, he'd always understood. "Yes. Either way it's a little unnerving."

"I've never liked smooth water. You get a better ride with a few waves."

"Perhaps." She shook her head. Slipping back, stepping forward, it hardly mattered. Either way, she was moving toward him. "Ky, I can't eat any more."

"I figured." Easily, he picked up an extra fork from the tray and began eating the cooling eggs himself. "It's still probably more than you eat for breakfast in a week."

"Probably," she agreed in a murmur, realizing just how well he'd maneuvered her. Kate lay back against the propped-up pillows, annoyed that she was growing sleepy again. No more medication, she decided silently as Ky polished off their joint breakfast. If she could just avoid that, and go out for a little while, she'd be fine. The trick would be to convince Ky.

Kate looked toward the window, and the sunshine. "I don't want to lose a week's time going over the wreck."

He didn't have to follow the direction of her gaze to follow the direction of her thoughts. "I'll be going down," he said easily. "Tomorrow, the next day anyway." Sooner, he thought to himself, depending on how Kate mended.

"Alone?"

He caught the tone as he bit into the last piece of bacon. "I've gone down alone before."

She would have protested, stating how dangerous it was, if she'd believed it would have done any good. Ky did a great deal alone because that was how he preferred it. Instead, Kate chose another route.

"We're looking for the *Liberty* together, Ky. It isn't a one-man operation."

He sent her a long, quiet look before he picked up the coffee she hadn't touched. "Afraid I'll take off with the treasure?"

"Of course not." She wouldn't allow her emotions to get in the way. "If I hadn't trusted your integrity," she said evenly, "I wouldn't have shown you the chart in the first place."

"Fair enough," he allowed with a nod. "So if I continue to dive while you're recuperating, we won't lose time."

"I don't want to lose you either." It was out before she could stop it. Swearing lightly, Kate looked toward the window again. The sky was the pale blue sometimes seen on summer mornings.

Ky merely sat for a moment while the pleasure of her words rippled through him. "You'd worry about me?"

Angry, Kate turned back. He looked so smug, so infuriatingly content. "No, I wouldn't worry. God usually makes a point of looking after fools."

Grinning, he set the tray on the floor beside the bed. "Maybe I'd like you to worry, a little."

"Sorry I can't oblige you."

"Your voice gets very prim when you're annoyed," he commented. "I like it."

"I'm not prim."

He ran a hand down her loosened hair. No, she looked anything but prim at the moment. Soft and feminine, but not prim. "Your voice is. Like one of those pretty, lacy ladies who used to sit in parlors eating finger sandwiches."

She pushed his hand aside. He wouldn't get around her with charm. "Perhaps I should shout instead."

"Like that too, but more..." He kissed one cheek, then the other. "I like to see you smile at me. The way you smile at nobody else."

Her skin was already beginning to warm. No, he might not get around her with charm, but...he'd distract her from her point if she wasn't careful. "I'd be bored, that's all. If I have to sit here, hour after hour with nothing to do."

"I've got lots of books." He slipped her nightshirt down her shoulder then kissed her bare skin with the lightest of touches. "Probably lay my hands on some crossword puzzles, too."

"Thanks a lot."

"There's a copy of Byron downstairs."

Despite her determination not to, Kate looked toward him again. "Byron?"

"I bought it after you left. The words are wonderful." He had the three buttons undone with such quick expertise, she never noticed. "But I could always hear the way you'd say them. I remember one night on the beach, when the moon was full on the water. I don't remember the name of the poem, but I remember how it started, and how it sounded when you said it. 'It is the hour'," he began, then smiled at her.

"'It is the hour'," Kate continued, "'when from the boughs the nightingale is heard/It is the hour when lovers' vows seem sweet in every whisper'd word/And gentle winds, and waters near make music to the lonely ear'…" She trailed off, remembering even the scent of that night. "You were never very interested in Byron's technique."

"No matter how hard you tried to explain it to me."

Yes, he was distracting her. Kate was already finding it difficult to remember what point she'd been trying to make. "He was one of the leading poets of his day."

"Hmm." Ky caught the lobe of her ear between his teeth.

"He had a fascination for war and conflict, and yet he had more love affairs in his poems than Shelley or Keats."

"How about out of his poems?"

"There too." She closed her eyes as his tongue began to do outrageous things to her nervous system. "He used humor, satire as well as a pure lyrical style. If he'd ever completed *Don Juan*…" She trailed off with a sigh that edged toward a moan.

"Did I interrupt you?" Ky brushed his fingers down her thigh. "I really love to hear you lecture."

"Yes."

"Good." He traced her lips with his tongue. "I just thought maybe I could give you something to do for a while." He skimmed his hand over her hip then up to the side of her breast. "So you won't be bored by staying in bed. Want to tell me more about Byron?"

With a long quiet breath, she wound her arms around his neck. The point she'd been trying to make didn't seem important any longer. "No, but I might like staying in bed after all, even without the crossword puzzles."

"You'll relax." He said it softly, but the command was unmistakable. She might have argued, but the kiss was long and lingering, leaving her slow and helplessly yielding.

"I don't have a choice," she murmured. "Between the medication and you."

"That's the idea." He'd love her, Ky thought, but so gently she'd have nothing to do but feel. Then she'd sleep. "There are things I want from you." He lifted his head until their eyes met. "Things I need from you."

"You never tell me what they are."

"Maybe not." He laid his forehead on hers. Maybe he just didn't know how to tell her. Or how to ask. "For now, what I want is to see you well." Again he lifted his head, and his eyes focused on hers. "I'm not an unselfish man, Kate. I want that just as much for myself as I want it for you. I fully intended to have you back in my bed, but I didn't want it for you. I fully intended to have you back in my bed, but I didn't care to have you unconscious here first."

"Whatever you intended, I make my own choices." Her hands slid up his shoulders to touch his face. "I chose to make love with you then. I choose to make love with you now."

He laughed and pressed her palm to his lips. "Professor, you think I'd have given you a choice? Maybe we don't know each other as well as we should at this point, but you should know that much."

Thoughtfully, she ran her thumb down his cheekbone. It was hard, elegantly defined. Somehow it suited him in the same way the unshaven face suited him. But did she? Kate wondered. Were they, despite all their differences, right for each other?

It seemed when they were like this, there was no question of suitability, no question of what was right or wrong. Each completed the other. Yet there had to be more. No matter how much each of them denied it on the surface, there had to be more. And ultimately, there had to be a choice.

"When you take what isn't offered freely, you have nothing." She felt the rough scrape of his unshaven face on her palm and the thrill went through her system. "If I give, you have whatever you need without asking."

"Do I?" he murmured before he touched his lips to hers again. "And you? What do you have?"

She closed her eyes as her body drifted on a calm, quiet plane of pleasure. "What I need."

For how long? The question ran through his mind, prodding against his contentment. But he didn't ask. There'd be a time, he knew, for more questions, for the hundreds of demands he wanted to make. For ultimatums. Now she was sleepy, relaxed in the way he wanted her to be.

With no more words he let her body drift, stroking gently, letting her system steep in the pleasure he could give. With no one else could he remember asking so little for himself and receiving so much. She was the hinge that could open or close the door on the better part of him.

He listened to her sigh as he touched her. The second was a kind of pure contentment that mirrored his own feelings. It seemed neither of them required any more.

Kate knew it shouldn't be so simple. It had never been simple with anyone else, so that in the end she'd never given herself to anyone else. Only with Ky had she ever known that full excitement that left her free. Only with Ky had she ever known the pure ease that felt so right.

They'd been apart four years, yet if it had been forty, she would have recognized his touch in an instant. That touch was all she needed to make her want him.

She remembered the demands and fire that had always been threaded through their lovemaking before. It had been the excitement she'd craved even while it had baffled her. Now there was patience touched with a consideration she didn't know he was capable of.

Perhaps if she hadn't loved him already, she would have fallen in love at that moment when the sun filtered through the windows and his hands were on her skin. She wanted to give him the fire, but his hands kept it banked. She wanted to meet any demands, but he made none. Instead, she floated on the clouds he brought to her.

Though the heat smoldered inside him, she kept him sane. Just by her pliancy. Though passion began to take over, she kept him calm. Just by her serenity.

He'd never looked for serenity in his life. It had simply come to him, as Kate had. He'd never understood what it meant to be calm, but he had known the emptiness and the chaos of living without it.

Without urgency or force, he slipped inside her. Slowly, with a sweetness that made her weak, he gave her the ultimate gift. Passion, fulfillment, with the softer emotions covering a need that seemed insatiable.

Then she slept, and he left her to her dreams.

When she awoke again, Kate wasn't groggy, but weak. Even as sleep cleared, a sense of helpless annoyance went though her. It was midafternoon. She didn't need a clock, the angle of the sunlight that slanted through the window across from the bed told her what time it was. More hours had been lost without her knowledge. And where was Ky?

Kate groped for her nightshirt and slipped into it. If he followed his pattern, he'd be popping through the door with a loaded lunch tray and a pill. Not this time, Kate determined as she eased herself out of bed. Nothing else was going into her system that made her lose time.

But as she stood, the dregs of the medication swam in her head. Reflexively, she nearly sat again before she stopped herself. Infuriated, she gripped the bedpost, breathed deeply then put her weight on her injured foot. It took the pain to clear her head.

Pain had its uses, she thought grimly. After she'd given the hurt a moment to subside, it eased into a throb. That could be tolerated, she told herself and walked to the mirror over Ky's dresser.

She didn't like what she saw. Her hair was listless,

her face washed-out and her eyes dull. Swearing, she put her hands to her cheeks and rubbed as though she could force color into them. What she needed, Kate decided, was a hot shower, a shampoo and some fresh air. Regardless of what Ky thought, she was going to have them.

Taking a deep breath, she headed for the door. Even as she reached for the knob, it opened.

"What're you doing up?"

Though they were precisely the words she'd expected, Kate had expected them from Ky, not Linda. "I was just—"

"Do you want Ky to skin me alive?" Linda demanded, backing Kate toward the bed with a tray of steaming soup in her hand. "Listen, you're supposed to rest and eat, then eat and rest. Orders."

Realizing abruptly that she was retreating, Kate held her ground. "Whose?"

"Ky's. And," she continued before Kate could retort, "Dr. Bailey's."

"I don't have to take orders from either of them."

"Maybe you don't," Linda agreed dryly. "But I don't argue with a man who's protecting his woman, or with the man who poked a needle into my bottom when I was three. Both of them can be nasty. Now lie down."

"Linda…" Though she knew the sigh sounded long suffering, Kate couldn't prevent it. "I've a cut on my leg. I've been in bed for something like forty-eight hours straight. If I don't have a shower and a breath of air soon, I'm going to go crazy."

A smile tugged at Linda's mouth that she partially concealed by nibbling on her lower lip. "A bit grumpy, are we?"

"I can be more than a bit." This time the sigh was simply bad tempered. "Look at me!" Kate demanded, tugging on her hair. "I feel as though I've just crawled out from under a rock."

"Okay. I know how I felt after I'd delivered Hope. After I'd had my cuddle with her I wanted a shower and shampoo so bad I was close to tears." She set the tray on the table beside the bed. "You can have ten minutes in the shower, then you can eat while I change your bandage. But Ky made me swear I'd make you eat every bite." She put her hands on her hips. "So that's the deal."

"He's overreacting," Kate began. "It's absurd. I don't need to be babied this way."

"Tell me that when you don't look like I could blow you over. Now come on, I'll give you a hand in the shower."

"No, damn it, I'm perfectly capable of taking a shower by myself." Ignoring the pain in her leg, she stormed out of the room, slamming the door at her back. Linda swallowed a laugh and sat down on the bed to wait.

Fifteen minutes later, refreshed and thoroughly ashamed of herself, Kate came back in. Wrapped in Ky's robe, she rubbed a towel over her hair. "Linda—"

"Don't apologize. If I'd been stuck in bed for two days, I'd snap at the first person who gave me trouble. Besides—" Linda knew how to play her cards "—if you're really sorry you'll eat all your soup, so Ky won't yell at me."

"All right." Resigned, Kate sat back in the bed and took the tray on her lap. She swallowed the first bite of soup and stifled her objection as Linda began to fiddle with her bandage. "It's wonderful."

"The seafood chowder's one of our specialties. Oh, honey." Linda's eyes darkened with concern after she removed the gauze. "This must've hurt like hell. No wonder Ky's been frantic."

Drumming up her courage, Kate leaned over enough to look at the wound. There was no inflammation as she'd feared, no puffiness. Though the slice was six inches in length, it was clean. Her stomach muscles unknotted. "It's not so bad," she murmured. "There's no infection."

"Look, I've been caught by a stingray, a small one. I probably had a cut half an inch across and I cried like a baby. Don't tell me it's not so bad."

"Well, I slept through most of it." She winced, then deliberately relaxed her muscles.

Linda narrowed her eyes as she studied Kate's face. "Ky said you should have a pill if there was any pain when you woke."

"If you want to do me a favor, you can dump them out." Calmly, Kate ate another spoonful of soup. "I really hate to argue with him, or with you, but I'm not taking any more pills and losing any more time. I appreciate the fact that he wants to pamper me. It's unexpectedly sweet, but I can only take it so far."

"He's worried about you. He feels responsible."

"For my carelessness?" With a shake of her head, Kate concentrated on finishing the soup. "It was an accident, and if there's blame, it's mine. I was so wrapped up in looking for salvage I didn't take basic precautions. I practically bumped into the ray." With an effort, she controlled a shudder. "Ky acted much more quickly than I. He'd already started to pull me out of range. If he hadn't, things would have been much more serious."

"He loves you."

Kate's fingers tightened on the spoon. With exaggerated care, she set it back on the tray. "Linda, there's a vast difference between concern, attraction, even affection and love."

Linda simply nodded in agreement. "Yes. I said Ky loves you."

She managed to smile and pick up the tea that had been cooling beside the soup. "*You* said," Kate returned simply. "*Ky* hasn't."

"Well neither did Marsh until I was ready to strangle him, but that didn't stop me."

"I'm not you." Kate lay back against the pillows, grateful that most of the weakness and the weariness had passed. "And Ky isn't Marsh."

Impatient, Linda rose and swirled around the room. "People who complicate simple things make me so mad!"

Smiling, Kate sipped her tea. "Others simplify the complicated."

With a sniff, Linda turned back. "I've known Ky Silver all my life. I watched him bounce around from one cute girl to the next, then one attractive woman to another until I lost count. Then you came along." Stopping, she leaned against the bedpost. "It was as if someone had hit him over the head with a blunt instrument. You dazed him, Kate, almost from the first minute. You fascinated him."

"Dazing, fascinating." Kate shrugged while she tried to ignore the ache in her heart. "Flattering, I suppose, but neither of those things equals love."

The stubborn line came and went between Linda's brows. "I don't believe love comes in an instant, it grows. If you could have seen the way Ky was after you left four years ago, you'd know—"

"Don't tell me about four years ago," Kate interrupted. "What happened four years ago is over. Ky and I are two different people today, with different expectations. This time..." She took a deep breath. "This time when it ends, I won't be hurt because I know the limits."

"You've just gotten back together and you're already talking about endings and limitations!" Dragging a hand through her hair, Linda came forward to sit on the edge of the bed. "What's wrong with you? Don't you know how to wish anymore? How to dream?"

"I was never very good at either. Linda..." She hesitated, wanting to choose her phrasing carefully. "I don't want to expect any more from Ky than what he can easily give. After August, I know we'll each go back to our separate worlds—there's no bridge between them. Maybe I was meant to come back so we could make up for whatever pain we caused each other before. This time I want to leave still being friends. He's..." She hesitated again because this phrasing was even more important. "He's always been a very important part of my life."

Linda waited a moment, then narrowed her eyes. "That's about the dumbest thing I've ever heard."

Despite herself, Kate laughed. "Linda—"

Holding up her hands, she shook her head and cut Kate off. "No, I can't talk about it anymore, I get too mad and I'm supposed to be taking care of you." She let out her breath on a huff as she removed Kate's tray.

"I just can't understand how anyone so smart could be so stupid, but the more I think about it the more I can see that you and Ky deserve each other."

"That sounds more like an insult than a compliment."

"It was."

Kate pushed her tongue against her teeth to hold back a smile. "I see."

"Don't look so smug just because you've made me so angry I don't want to talk about it anymore." She drew her shoulders back. "I might just give Ky a piece of my mind when he gets home."

"That's his problem," Kate said cheerfully. "Where'd he go?"

"Diving."

Amusement faded. "Alone?"

"There's no use worrying about it." Linda spoke briskly as she cursed herself for not thinking of a simple lie. "He dives alone ninety percent of the time."

"I know." But Kate folded her hands, preparing to worry until he returned.

Chapter 9

"I'm going with you."

The sunlight was strong, the scent of the ocean pure. Through the screen the sound of gulls from a quarter of a mile away could be heard clearly. Ky turned from the stove where he poured the last cup of coffee and eyed Kate as she stood in the doorway.

She'd pinned her hair up and had dressed in thin cotton pants and a shirt, both of which were baggy and cool. It occured to him that she looked more like a student than a college professor.

He knew enough of women and their illusions to see that she'd added color to her cheeks. She hadn't needed blusher the evening before when he'd returned from the wreck. Then she had been angry, and passionate. He nearly smiled as he lifted his cup.

"You wasted your time getting dressed," he said easily. "You're going back to bed."

Kate disliked stubborn people, people who demanded their own way flatly and unreasonably. At that moment, she decided they were *both* stubborn. "No." On the surface she remained as calm as he was while she walked into the kitchen. "I'm going with you."

Unlike Kate, Ky never minded a good argument. Preparing for one, he leaned back against the stove. "I don't take down a diver against doctor's orders."

She'd expected that. With a shrug, she opened the refrigerator and took out a bottle of juice. She knew she was being bad tempered, and though it was completely out of character, she was enjoying the experience. The simple truth was that she had to do something or go mad.

As far as she could remember, she'd never spent two more listless days. She had to move, think, feel the sun. It might have been satisfying to stomp her feet and demand, but, she thought, fruitless. If she had to compromise to get her way, then compromise she would.

"I can rent a boat and equipment and go down on my own." With the glass in hand, she turned, challenging. "You can't stop me."

"Try me."

It was said simply, quietly, but she'd seen the flare of anger in his eyes. *Better,* she thought. *Much better.* "I've a right to do precisely as I choose. We both know it." Perhaps her leg was uncomfortable, but as to the rest of her body, it was charged up and ready to move. Nor was there anything wrong with her mind. Kate had plotted her strategy very well. After all, she thought grimly, there'd certainly been enough time to think it through.

"We both know you're not in any shape to dive." His

first urge was to carry her back to bed, his second to shake her until she rattled. Ky did neither, only drank his coffee and watched her over the rim. A power struggle wasn't something he'd expected, but he wouldn't back away from it. "You're not stupid, Kate. You know you can't go down yet, and you know I won't let you."

"I've rested for two days. I feel fine." As she walked toward him she was pleased to see him frown. He understood she had a mind of her own, and that he had to deal with it. The truth was, she was stronger than either of them had expected her to be. "As far as diving goes, I'm willing to leave that to you for the next couple of days, but…" She paused, wanting to be certain he knew she was negotiating, not conceding. "I'm going out on the *Vortex* with you. And I'm going out this morning."

He lifted a brow. She'd never intended to dive, but she'd used it as a pressure point to get what she wanted. He couldn't blame her. Ky remembered recovering from a broken leg when he was fourteen. The pain was vague in his mind now, but the boredom was still perfectly clear. "You'll lie down in the cabin when you're told."

She smiled and shook her head. "I'll lie down in the cabin if I need to."

He took her chin in his hand and squeezed. "Damn right you will. Okay, let's go. I want an early start."

Once he was resigned, Ky moved quickly. She could either keep up, or be left behind. Within minutes he parked his car near his slip at Silver Lake Harbor and was boarding the *Vortex*. Content, Kate took a seat beside him at the helm and prepared to enjoy the sun and the wind. Already she felt the energy begin to churn.

"I've done a chart of the wreck as of yesterday's dive," he told her as he maneuvered out of the harbor.

"A chart?" Automatically she pushed at her hair as she turned toward him. "You didn't show me."

"Because you were asleep when I finished it."

"I've been asleep ninety percent of the time," she mumbled.

As he headed out to sea, Ky laid a hand on her shoulder. "You look better, Kate, no shadows. No strain. That's more important."

For a moment, just a moment, she pressed her cheek against his hand. Few women could resist such soft concern, and yet…she didn't want his concern to cloud their reason for being together. Concern could turn to pity. She needed him to see her as a partner, as equal. As long as she was his lover, it was vital that they meet on the same ground. Then when she left… When she left there'd be no regrets.

"I don't need to be pampered anymore, Ky."

His shoulders moved as he glanced at the compass. "I enjoyed it."

She was resisting being cared for. He understood it, appreciated it and regretted it. There had been something appealing about seeing to her needs, about having her depend on him. He didn't know how to tell her he wanted her to be well and strong just as much as he wanted her to turn to him in times of need.

Somehow, he felt their time together had been too short for him to speak. He didn't deal well with caution. As a diver, he knew its importance, but as a man… As a man he fretted to go with his instincts, with his impulses.

His fingers brushed her neck briefly before he

turned to the wheel. He'd already decided he'd have to approach his relationship with Kate as he'd approach a very deep, very dangerous dive—with an eye on currents, pressure and the unexpected.

"That chart's in the cabin," he told her as he cut the engine. "You might want to look it over while I'm down."

She agreed with a nod, but the restlessness was already on her as Ky began to don his equipment. She didn't want to make an issue of his diving alone. He wouldn't listen to her in any case; if anything came of it, it would only be an argument. In silence she watched him check his tanks. He'd be down for an hour. Kate was already marking time.

"There are cold drinks in the galley." He adjusted the strap of his mask before climbing over the side. "Don't sit in the sun too long."

"Be careful," she blurted out before she could stop herself.

Ky grinned, then was gone with a quiet splash.

Though she ran over to the side, Kate was too late to watch him dive. For a long time after, she simply leaned over the boat, staring at the water's surface. She imagined Ky going deeper, deeper, adjusting his pressure, moving out with power until he'd reached the bottom and the wreck.

He'd brought back the bowl and ladle the evening before. They sat on the dresser in his bedroom while the broken rigging and pieces of crockery were stored downstairs. Thus far he'd done no more than gather what they'd already found together, but today, Kate thought with a twinge of impatience, he'd extend the search. Whatever he found, he'd find alone.

She turned away from the water, frustrated that she was excluded. It occurred to her that all her life she'd been an onlooker, someone who analyzed and explained the action rather than causing it. This search had been her first opportunity to change that, and now she was back to square one.

Stuffing her hands in her pockets, Kate looked up at the sky. There were clouds to the west, but they were thin and white. Harmless. She felt too much like that herself at the moment—something unsubstantial. Sighing, she went below deck. There was nothing to do now but wait.

Ky found two more cannons and sent up buoys to mark their position. It would be possible, if he didn't find something more concrete, to salvage the cannons and have them dated by an expert. Though he swam from end to end, searching carefully, he knew it was unlikely he'd find a date stamp through the layers of corrosion. But in time... Satisfied, he swam north.

If he accomplished nothing else on this dive, he wanted to establish the size of the site. With luck it would be fairly small, perhaps no bigger than a football field. However, there was always the chance that the wreckage could be scattered over several square miles. Before they brought in a salvage ship, he wanted to take a great deal of care with the preliminary work.

They would need tools. A metal detector would be invaluable. Thus far, they'd done no more than find a wreck, no matter how certain Kate was that it was the *Liberty*. For the moment he had no way to determine the origin of the ship, he had to find cargo. Once he'd found that, perhaps treasure would follow.

Once he'd found the treasure... Would she leave?

Would she take her share of the gold and the artifacts and drive home?

Not if he could help it, Ky determined as he shone his headlamp over the sea floor. When the search was over and they'd salvaged what could be salvaged from the sea, it would be time to salvage what they'd once had—what had perhaps never truly been lost. If they could find what had been buried for centuries, they could find what had been buried for four years.

He couldn't find much without tools. Most of the ship—or what remained of it—was buried under silt. On another dive, he'd use the prop-wash, the excavation device he'd constructed in his shop. With that he could blow away inches of sediment at a time—a slow but safe way to uncover artifacts. But someone would have to stay on board to run it.

He thought of Kate and rejected the idea immediately. Though he had no doubt she could handle the technical aspect—it would only have to be explained to her once—she'd never go for it. Ky began to think it was time they enlisted Marsh.

He knew his air time was almost up and he'd have to surface for fresh tanks. Still, he lingered near the bottom, searching, prodding. He wanted to take something up for Kate, something tangible that would put the enthusiasm back in her eyes.

It took him more than half of his allotted time to find it, but when Ky held the unbroken bottle in his hand, he knew Kate's reaction would be worth the effort. It was a common bottle, not priceless crystal, but he could see no mold marks, which meant it had been hand blown. Crust was weathered over it in layers, but Ky took the time to carefully chip some away, from the bottom only. If the date wasn't on the bottom, he'd need the crust to have the bottle dated. Already he was thinking of the Corning Glass Museum and their rate of success.

Then he saw the date, and with a satisfied grin placed the find in the goodie bag on his belt. With his air supply running short, he started toward the surface.

His hour was up. Or so nearly up, Kate thought, that he should have surfaced already if he'd allowed himself any safety factor. She paced from port to starboard and back again. Would he always risk his own welfare to the limit?

She'd long since given up sitting quietly in the cabin, going over the makeshift chart Ky had begun. She'd found a book on shipwrecks that Ky had obviously purchased recently, and though it had also been among her father's research books, she'd skimmed through it again.

It gave a detailed guide to identifying and excavating a wreck, listed common mistakes and hazards. She found it difficult to read about hazards while Ky was alone beneath the surface. Still, even the simple language of the book couldn't disguise the adventure. For perhaps half the time Ky had been gone, she'd lost herself in it. Spanish galleons, Dutch merchant ships, English frigates.

She'd found the list of wrecks off North Carolina alone extensive. But these, she'd thought, had already been located, documented. The adventure there was over. One day, because of the chain her father had started and she'd continued, the *Liberty* would be among them.

Fretfully, Kate waited for Ky to surface. She thought

of her father. He'd pored over this same book as well—planning, calculating. Yet his calculations hadn't taken him beyond the initial stage. If he'd shared his goal with her, would he have taken her on his summer quests? She'd never know, because she'd never been given the choice.

She was making her own choices now, Kate mused. Her first had been to return to Ocracoke, accepting the consequences. Her next had been to give herself to Ky without conditions. Her last, she thought as she stared down at the quiet water, would be to leave him again. Yet, in reality, perhaps she'd still been given no choice. It was all a matter of currents. She could only swim against them for so long.

Relief washed over her when she spotted the flow of bubbles. Ky grabbed the bottom rung of the ladder as he pushed up his mask. "Waiting for me?"

Relief mixed with annoyance for the time she'd spent worrying about him. "You cut it close."

"Yeah, a little." He passed up his tanks. "I had to stop and get you a present."

"It's not a joke, Ky." Kate watched him come over the side, agile, lean and energetic. "You'd be furious with me if I'd cut my time that close."

"Leave it up to Linda to fuss," he advised as he pulled down the zipper of his wet suit. "She was born that way." Then he grabbed her, crushing her against him so that she felt the excitement he'd brought up with him. His mouth closed over hers, tasting of salt from the sea. Because he was wet, her clothes clung to him, binding them together for the brief instant he held her. But when he would have released her, she held fast, drawing the kiss out into something that warmed his cool skin.

"I worry about you, Ky." For one last moment, she held on fiercely. "Damn it, is that what you want to hear?"

"No." He took her face in his hands and shook his head. "No."

Kate broke away, afraid she'd say too much, afraid she'd say things neither of them were ready to hear. She knew the rules this time. She groped for something calm, something simple. "I suppose I got a bit frantic waiting up here. It's different when you're down."

"Yeah." What did she want from him? he wondered. Why was it that every time she started to show her concern for him, she clammed up? "I've got some more things to add to the chart."

"I saw the buoys you sent up." Kate moistened her lips and relaxed, muscle by muscle.

"Two more cannons. From the size of them, I'd say she was a fairly small ship. It's unlikely she was constructed for battle."

"She was a merchant ship."

"Maybe. I'm going to take the metal detector down and see what I come up with. From the stuff we've found, I don't think she's buried too deep."

Kate nodded. Delve into business, keep the personal aspect light. "I'd like to send off a piece of the planking and some of the glass to be analyzed. I think we'll have more luck with the glass, but it doesn't hurt to cover all the angles."

"No, it doesn't. Don't you want your present?"

At ease again, she smiled. "I thought you were joking. Did you bring me a shell?"

"I thought you'd like this better." Reaching into his bag, Ky brought out the bottle. "It's too bad it's not still corked. We could've had wine with peanut butter."

"Oh, Ky, it's not damaged!" Thrilled, she reached out for it, but he pulled it back out of reach and grinned.

"Bottoms up," he told her and turned the bottle up-side down.

Kate stared at the smeared bottom of the bottle. "Oh, God," she whispered. "It's dated. 1749." Gingerly, she took the bottle in both hands. "The year before the *Liberty* sank."

"It's another ship, maybe," Ky reminded her. "But it does narrow down the time element."

"Over two hundred years," she murmured. "Glass, it's so breakable, so vulnerable, and yet it survived two centuries." Her eyes lit with enthusiasm as she looked back at him. "Ky, we should be able to find out where the bottle was made."

"Probably, but most glass bottles found on wrecks from the seventeenth and eighteenth century were man-ufactured in England anyway. It wouldn't prove the ship was English."

She let out a huff of breath, but her energy hadn't dimmed. "You've been doing your research."

"I don't go into any project until I know the angles." Ky knelt down to check the fresh tanks.

"You're going back down now?"

"I want to get as much mapped out as I can before we start dealing with too much equipment."

She'd done enough homework herself to know that the most common mistake of the modern-day salvor was in failing to map out a site. Yet she couldn't stem her impatience. It seemed so time-consuming when they could be concentrating on getting under the layers of silt.

It seemed to her that she and Ky had changed positions somehow. She'd always been the cautious one, proceeding step by logical step, while he'd taken the risks. Struggling with the impotence of having to wait and watch, she stood back while he strapped on the fresh tanks. As she watched, Ky picked up a brass rod.

"What's that for?"

"It's the base for this." He held out a device that resembled a compass. "It's called an azimuth circle. It's a cheap, effective way to map out the site. I drive this into the approximate center of the wreck so that it becomes the datum point, align the circle with the magnetic north, then I use a length of chain to measure the distance to the cannons, or whatever I need to map. After I get it set, I'll be back up for the metal detector."

Frustration built again. He was doing all the work while she simply stood still. "Ky, I feel fine. I could help if—"

"No." He didn't bother to argue or list reasons. He simply went over the side and under.

It was midafternoon when they started back. Ky spent the last hour at sea adding to the chart, putting in the information he'd gathered that day. He'd brought more up in his goodie bag—a tankard, spoons and forks that might have been made of iron. It seemed they had indeed found the galley. Kate decided she'd begin a detailed list of their finds that evening. If it was all she could do at the moment, she'd do it with pleasure.

Her mood had lifted a bit since she'd caught three good-size bluefish while Ky had been down at the wreck the second time. No matter how much Ky argued, she fully intended to cook them herself and eat them sitting at the table, not lying in bed.

"Pretty pleased with yourself, aren't you?"

She gave him a cool smile. They were cruising back toward Silver Lake Harbor and though she felt a weariness, it was a pleasant feeling, not the dragging fatigue of the past days. "Three bluefish in that amount of time's a very respectable haul."

"No argument there. Especially since I intend to eat half of them."

"I'm going to grill them."

"Are you?"

She met his lifted brow with a neutral look. "I caught, I cook."

Ky kept the boat at an even speed as he studied her. She looked a bit tired, but he thought he could convince her to take a nap if he claimed he wanted one himself. She was healing quickly. And she was right. He couldn't pamper her. "I could probably bring myself to start the charcoal for you."

"Fair enough. I'll even let you clean them."

He laughed at the bland tone and ruffled her hair until the pins fell out.

"Ky!" Automatically, Kate reached up to repair the damage.

"Wear it up in the school room," he advised, tossing some of the pins overboard. "I find it difficult to resist you when your hair's down and just a bit mussed."

"Is that so?" She debated being annoyed, then decided there were more productive ways to pass the time. Kate let the wind toss her hair as she moved closer to him so that their bodies touched. She smiled at the quick look of surprise in his eyes as she slipped both hands under his T-shirt. "Why don't you turn off the engine and show me what happens when you stop resisting?"

For all her generosity and freedom in lovemaking, she'd never been the initiator. Ky found himself both baffled and aroused as she smiled up at him, her hands stroking slowly over his chest. "You know what happens when I stop resisting," he murmured.

She gave a low, quiet laugh. "Refresh my memory." Without waiting for an answer, she drew back on the throttle herself until the boat was simply idling. "You didn't make love with me last night." Her hands slid around and up his back.

"You were sleeping." She was seducing him in the middle of the afternoon, in the middle of the ocean. He found he wanted to savor the new experience as much as he wanted to bring it to fruition.

"I'm not sleeping now." Rising on her toes, she brushed her lips over his, lightly, temptingly. She felt his heartbeat race against her body and reveled in a sense of power she'd never explored. "Or perhaps you're in a hurry to get back, and uh, clean fish."

She was taunting him. Why had he never seen the witch in her before? Ky felt his stomach knot with need, but when he drew her closer, she resisted. Just slightly. Just enough to torment. "If I make love with you now, I won't be gentle."

She kept her lips inches from his. "Is that a warning?" she whispered. "Or a promise?"

He felt the first tremor move through him and was astonished. Not even for her had he ever trembled. Not even for her. The need grew, stretching restlessly, recklessly. "I'm not sure you know what you're doing, Kate."

Nor did she, but she smiled because it no longer mattered. Only the outcome mattered. "Come down to the cabin with me and we'll both find out." She slipped away from him and without a word disappeared below deck.

His hand wasn't steady when he reached for the key to turn off the engines. He needed a moment, perhaps a bit more, to regain the control he'd held so carefully since they'd become lovers again. Ever since he'd had her blood on his hands, he had a tremendous fear of hurting her. Since he'd had a taste of her again, he had an equal fear of driving her away. Caution was a strain, but he'd kept it in focus with sheer will. As Ky started down the steps, he told himself he'd continue to be cautious.

She'd unbuttoned her blouse but hadn't removed it. When he came into the narrow cabin with her, Kate smiled. She was afraid, though she hardly knew why. But over the fear was a heady sense of power and strength that fought for full release. She wanted to take him to the edge, to push him to the limits of passion. At that moment, she was certain she could.

When he came no closer to her, Kate stepped forward and pulled his shirt over his head. "Your skin's gold," she murmured. "It's always excited me." Taking her pleasure slowly, she ran her hands up his sides, feeling the quiver she caused. "You've always excited me."

Her hands were steady, her pulse throbbed as she unsnapped his cut-offs. With her eyes on his, she slowly, slowly, undressed him. "No one's ever made me want the way you make me want."

He had to stop her and take control again. She couldn't know the effect of those long, fragile fingers when they brushed easily over his skin, or how her calm eyes made him rage inside.

"Kate..." He took her hands in his and bent to kiss her. But she turned her head, meeting his neck with warm lips that sent a spear of fire up his spine.

Then her body was pressed against his, flesh meeting flesh where her blouse parted. Her mouth trailed over his chest, her hands down his back to his hips. He felt the fury of desire whip through him as though it had sharp, hungry teeth.

So he forgot control, gentleness, vulnerability. She drove him to forget. She intended to.

They were tangled on the narrow bunk, her blouse halfway down her back and parted so that her breasts pushed into his chest, driving him mad with their firm, subtle curves. She nipped at his lips, demanding, pushing for more, still more. Waves of passion overtook them.

His need was incendiary. She was like a flame, impossible to hold, searing here, singeing there until his body was burning with needs and fierce fantasies.

Her hands were swift, sending sharp gasping pleasure everywhere at once until he wasn't sure he could take it anymore. Yet he no longer thought of stopping her. Less of stopping himself.

His hands gripped her with an urgency that made her moan from the sheer strength in them. She wanted his strength now—mindless strength that would carry them both to a place they'd never gone before. And she was leading. The knowledge made her laugh aloud as she tasted his skin, his lips, his tongue.

She slid down his body, feeling each jolt of pleasure as it shot through him. There could be no slow, lingering loving now. They'd pushed each other beyond reason. The air here was dark and thin and whirling with sound. Kate drank it in.

When he found her moist, hot and ready she let him take her over peak after shuddering peak, knowing as he drove her, she drove him. Her body was filled with sensations that came and went like comets, slipped away and burst on her again, and again. Through the thunder in her head she heard herself say his name, clear and quick.

On the sound, she took him into her and welcomed the madness.

Chapter 10

She was wrong.

Kate had thought she'd be ready, even anxious to dive again. There hadn't been a day during her recuperation that she hadn't thought of going down. Every time Ky had brought back an artifact, she was thrilled with the discovery and frustrated with her own lack of participation. Like a schoolgirl approaching summer, she'd begun to count the days.

Now, a week after the accident, Kate stood on the deck of the *Vortex* with her mouth dry and her hands trembling as she pulled on her wet suit. She could only be grateful that Ky was already over the side, hooking up his home-rigged prop-wash to the boat's propeller. Drafted to the crew, Marsh stood at the stern watching his brother. With Linda's eager support, he'd agreed to give Ky a few hours a day of his precious free time while he was needed.

Kate took the moment she had alone to gather her thoughts and her nerve.

It was only natural to be anxious about diving after the experience she'd had. Kate told herself that was logical. But it didn't stop her hands from trembling as she zipped up her suit. She could equate it with falling off a horse and having to mount again. It was psychological. But it didn't ease the painful tension in her stomach.

Trembling hands and nerves. With or without them, she told herself as she hooked on her weight belt, she was going down. Nothing, not even her own fears, was going to stop her from finishing what she'd begun.

"He's got it," Marsh called out when Ky signaled him.

"I'll be ready." Kate picked up the cloth bag she'd use to bring up small artifacts. With luck, and if the prop-wash did its job, she knew they'd soon need more sophisticated methods to bring up the salvage.

"Kate."

She didn't look up, but continued to hook on the goodie bag. "Yes?"

"You know it's only natural that you'd be nervous going down." Marsh touched a hand to her shoulder, but she busied herself by strapping on her diving knife. "If you want a little more time, I'll work with Ky and you can run the wash."

"No." She said it too quickly, then cursed herself. "It's all right, Marsh." With forced calm she hung the underwater camera she'd purchased only the day before around her neck. "I have to take the first dive sometime."

"It doesn't have to be now."

She smiled at him again thinking how calm, how steady he appeared when compared to Ky. This was the sort of man it would have made sense for her to be attracted to. Confused emotions made no sense. "Yes, it does. Please." She put her hand on his arm before he could speak again. "Don't say anything to Ky."

Did she think he'd have to? Marsh wondered as he inclined his head in agreement. Unless he was way off the mark, Marsh was certain Ky knew every expression, every gesture, every intonation of her voice.

"Let's run it a couple of minutes at full throttle." Ky climbed over the side, dripping and eager. "With the depth and the size of the prop, we're going to have to test the effect. There might not be enough power to do us any good."

In agreement, Marsh went to the helm. "Are you thinking about using an air lift?"

Ky's only answer was a noncommittal grunt. He had thought of it. The metal tube with its stream of compressed air was a quick, efficient way to excavate on silty bottoms. They might get away with the use of a small air lift, if it became necessary. But perhaps the prop-wash would do the job well enough. Either way, he was thinking more seriously about a bigger ship, with more sophisticated equipment and more power. As he saw it, it all depended on what they found today.

He picked up one last piece of equipment—a small powerful spear gun. He'd take no more chances with Kate.

"Okay, slow it down to the minimum," he ordered. "And keep it there. Once Kate and I are down, we don't want the prop-wash shooting cannonballs around."

Kate stopped the deep breathing she was using to

ease tension. Her voice was cool and steady. "Would it have that kind of power?"

"Not at this speed." Ky adjusted his mask then took her hand. "Ready?"

"Yes."

Then he kissed her, hard. "You've got guts, professor," he murmured. His eyes were dark, intense as they passed over her face. "It's one of the sexiest things about you." With this he was over the side.

He knew. Kate gave a quiet unsteady sigh as she started down the ladder. He knew she was afraid, and that had been his way of giving her support. She looked up once and saw Marsh. He lifted his hand in salute. Throat dry, nerves jumping, Kate let the sea take her.

She felt a moment's panic, a complete disorientation the moment she was submerged. It ran through her head that down here, she was helpless. The deeper she went, the more vulnerable she became. Choking for air, she kicked back toward the surface and the light.

Then Ky had her hands, holding her to him, holding her under. His grip was firm, stilling the first panic. Feeling the wild race of her pulse, he held on during her first resistance.

Then he touched her cheek, waiting until she'd calmed enough to look at him. In his eyes she saw strength and challenge. Pride alone forced her to fight her way beyond the fear and meet him, equal to equal.

When she'd regulated her breathing, accepting that her air came through the tanks on her back, he kissed the back of her hand. Kate felt the tension give. She wouldn't be helpless, she reminded herself. She'd be careful.

With a nod, she pointed down, indicating she was

ready to dive. Keeping hands linked, they started toward the bottom.

The whirlpool action created by the wash of the prop had already blasted away some of the sediment. At first glance Ky could see that if the wreck was buried under more than a few feet, they'd need something stronger than his homemade apparatus and single prop engine. But for now, it would do. Patience, which came to him only with deliberate effort, was more important at this stage than speed. With the wreck, he thought, and—he glanced over at the woman beside him—with a great deal more. He had to take care not to hurry.

It was still working, blowing away some of the overburden at a rate Ky figured would equal an inch per minute. He and Kate alone couldn't deal with any more speed. He watched the swirl of water and sediment while she swam a few feet away to catalog one of the cannons on film. When she came closer, he grinned as she placed the camera in front of her face again. She was relaxed, her initial fear forgotten. He could see it simply in the way she moved. Then she let the camera fall so they could begin the search again.

Kate saw something solid wash away from the hole being created by the whirl of water. Grabbing it up, she found herself holding a candlestick. In her excitement, she turned it over and over in her hand.

Silver? she wondered with a rush of adrenaline. Had they found their first real treasure? It was black with oxidation, so it was impossible to be certain what it was made of. Still, it thrilled her. After days and days of only waiting, she was again pursuing the dream.

When she looked up, Ky was already gathering the uncovered items and laying them in the mesh basket.

There were more candleholders, more tableware, but not the plain unglazed pottery they'd found before. Kate's pulse began to drum with excitement while she meticulously snapped pictures. They'd be able to find a hallmark, she was certain of it. Then they'd know if they had indeed found a British ship. Ordinary seamen didn't use silver, or even pewter table service. They'd uncovered more than the galley now. And they were just beginning.

When Ky found the first piece of porcelain he signaled to her. True, the vase—if that's what it once had been—had suffered under the water pressure and the years. It was broken so that only half of the shell remained, but so did the manufacturer's mark.

When Kate read it, she gripped Ky's arm. *Whieldon.* English. The master potter who'd trained the likes of Wedgwood. Kate cupped the broken fragment in her hands as though it were alive. When she lifted her eyes to Ky's they were filled with triumph.

Fretting against her inability to speak, Kate pointed to the mark again. Ky merely nodded and indicated the basket. Though she was loath to part with it, Kate found herself even more eager to discover more. She settled the porcelain in the mesh. When she swam back, Ky's hands were filled with other pieces. Some were hardly more than shards, others were identifiable as pieces left from bowls or lids.

No, it didn't prove it was a merchant ship, Kate told herself as she gathered what she could herself. So far, it only proved that the officers and perhaps some passengers had eaten elegantly on their way to the New World. English officers, she reminded herself. In her mind they'd taken the identification that far.

The force of the wash sent an object shooting up. Ky reached out for it and found a crusted, filthy pot he guessed would have been used for tea or coffee. Perhaps it was cracked under the layers, but it held together in his hands. He tapped on his tank to get Kate's attention.

She knew it was priceless the moment she saw it. Stemming impatience, she signaled for Ky to hold it out as she lifted the camera again. Obliging, he crossed his legs like a genie and posed.

It made her giggle. They'd perhaps just found something worth thousands of dollars, but he could still act silly. Nothing was too serious for Ky. As she brought him into frame, Kate felt the same foolish pleasure. She'd known the hunt would be exciting, perhaps rewarding, but she'd never known it would be fun. She swam forward and reached for the pot herself.

Running her fingers over it, she could detect some kind of design under the crust. Not ordinary pottery, she was sure. Not utility-ware. She held something elegant, something well crafted.

He understood its worth as well as she. Taking it from her, Ky indicated they would bring it and the rest of the morning's salvage to the surface. Pointing to his watch he showed her that their tanks were running low.

She didn't argue. They'd come back. The *Liberty* would wait for them. Each took a handle of the mesh basket and swam leisurely toward the surface.

"Do you know how I feel?" Kate demanded the moment she could speak.

"Yes." Ky gripped the ladder with one hand and waited for her to unstrap her tanks and slip them over onto the deck. "I know just how you feel."

"The teapot." Breathing fast, she hauled herself up the ladder. "Ky, it's priceless. It's like finding a perfectly formed rose inside a mass of briars." Before he could answer, she was laughing and calling out to Marsh. "It's fabulous! Absolutely fabulous."

Marsh cut the engine then walked over to help them. "You two work fast." Bending he touched a tentative finger to the pot. "God, it's all in one piece."

"We'll be able to date it as soon as it's cleaned. But look." Kate drew out the broken vase. "This is the mark of an English potter. English," she repeated, turning to Ky. "He trained Wedgwood, and Wedgwood didn't begin manufacturing until the 1760s, so—"

"So this piece more than likely came from the era we're looking for," Ky finished. "*Liberty* or not," he continued, crouching down beside her. "It looks like you've found yourself an eighteenth-century wreck that's probably of English origin and certainly hasn't been recorded before." He took one of her hands between both of his. "Your father would've been proud of you."

Stunned, she stared at him. Emotions raced through her with such velocity she had no way of controlling or channeling them. The hand holding the broken vase began to tremble. Quickly, she set it down in the basket again and rose.

"I'm going below," she managed and fled.

Proud of her. Kate put a hand over her mouth as she stumbled into the cabin. His pride, his love. Wasn't it all she'd really ever wanted from her father? Was it possible she could only gain it after his death?

She drank in deep gulps of air and struggled to level her emotions. No, she wanted to find the *Liberty,* she wanted to bring her father's dream to reality, have his name on a plaque in a museum with the artifacts they'd found. She owed him that. But she'd promised herself she'd find the *Liberty* for herself as well. For herself.

It was her choice, her first real decision to come in from the sidelines and act on her own. For herself, Kate thought again as she brought the first surge of emotion under control.

"Kate?"

She turned, and though she thought she was perfectly calm, Ky could see the turmoil in her eyes. Unsure how to handle it, he spoke practically.

"You'd better get out of that suit."

"But we're going back down."

"Not today." To prove his point he began to strip out of his own suit just as Marsh started the engines.

Automatically, she balanced herself as the boat turned. "Ky, we've got two more sets of tanks. There's no reason for us to go back when we're just getting started."

"Your first dive took most of the strength you've built up. If you want to dive tomorrow, you've got to take it slow today."

Her anger erupted so quickly, it left them both astonished. "The hell with that!" she exploded. "I'm sick to death of being treated as if I don't know my own limitations or my own mind and body."

Ky walked into the galley and picked up a can of beer. With a flick of his wrist, air hissed out. "I don't know what you're talking about."

"I lay in bed for the better part of a week because

of pressure from you and Linda and anyone else who came around me. I'm not tolerating this any longer."

With one hand, he pushed dripping hair from his forehead as he lifted the can. "You're tolerating exactly what's necessary until I say differently."

"You say?" she tossed back. Cheeks flaming, she strode over to him. "I don't have to do what you say, or what anyone says. Not anymore. It's about time you remember just who's in charge of this salvage operation."

His eyes narrowed. "In charge?"

"I hired you. Seventy-five a day and twenty-five percent. Those were the terms. There was nothing in there about you running my life."

He abruptly went still. For a moment, all that could be heard over the engines was her angry breathing. *Dollars and percents,* he thought with a deadly sort of calm. *Just dollars and percents.* "So that's what it comes down to?"

Too overwrought to see beyond her own anger, she continued to lash out. "We made an agreement. I fully intend to see that you get everything we arranged, but I won't have you telling me when I can go down. I won't have you judging when I'm well and when I'm not. I'm sick to death of being dictated to. And I won't be—not by you, not by anyone. Not any longer."

The metal of the can gave under his fingers. "Fine. You do exactly what you want, professor. But while you're about it, get yourself another diver. I'll send you a bill." Ky went up the cabin steps the way he came down. Quickly and without a sound.

With her hands gripped together, Kate sat down on the bunk and waited until she heard the engines stop again. She refused to think. Thinking hurt. She refused to feel. There was too much to feel. When she was certain she was in control, she stood and went up on deck.

Everything was exactly as she'd left it—the wire basket filled with bits of porcelain and tableware, her nearly depleted tanks. Ky was gone. Marsh walked over from the stern where he'd been waiting for her.

"You're going to need a hand with these."

Kate nodded and pulled a thigh length T-shirt over her tank suit. "Yes. I want to take everything back to my room at the hotel. I have to arrange for shipping."

"Okay." But instead of reaching down for the basket, he took her arm. "Kate, I don't like to give advice."

"Good." Then she swore at her own rudeness. "I'm sorry, Marsh. I'm feeling a little rough at the moment."

"I can see that, and I know things aren't always smooth for you and Ky. Look, he has a habit of closing himself up, of not saying everything that's on his mind. Or worse," Marsh added. "Of saying the first thing that comes to mind."

"He's perfectly free to do so. I came here for the specific purpose of finding and excavating the *Liberty*. If Ky and I can't deal together on a business level, I have to do without his help."

"Listen, he has a few blind spots."

"Marsh, you're his brother. Your allegiance is with him as it should be."

"I care about both of you."

She took a deep breath, refusing to let the emotion surface and carry her with it. "I appreciate that. The best thing you can do for me now, perhaps for both of us, is to tell me where I can rent a boat and some equipment. I'm going back out this afternoon."

"Kate."

"I'm going back out this afternoon," she repeated. "With or without your help."

Resigned, Marsh picked up the mesh basket. "All right, you can use mine."

It took the rest of the morning for Kate to arrange everything, including the resolution of a lengthy argument with Marsh. She refused to let him come with her, ending by saying she'd simply rent a boat and do without his assistance altogether. In the end, she stood at the helm of his boat alone and headed out to sea.

She craved the solitude. Almost in defiance, she pushed the throttle forward. If it was defiance, she didn't care, any more than she cared whom she was defying. It was vital to do this one act for herself.

She refused to think about Ky, about why she'd exploded at him. If her words had been harsh, they'd also been necessary. She comforted herself with that. For too long, for a lifetime, she'd been influenced by someone else's opinion, someone else's expectations.

Mechanically, she stopped the engines and put on her equipment, checking and rechecking as she went. She'd never gone down alone before. Even that seemed suddenly a vital thing to do.

With a last look at her compass, she took the mesh basket over the side.

As she went deep, a thrill went through her. She was alone. In acres and acres of sea, she was alone. The water parted for her like silk. She was in control, and her destiny was her own.

She didn't rush. Kate found she wanted that euphoric feeling of being isolated under the sea where only curious fish bothered to give her a passing glance. Ultimately, her only responsibility here was to herself. Briefly, she closed her eyes and floated. At last, only to herself.

When she reached the site, she felt a new surge of pride. This was something she'd done without her father. She wouldn't think of the whys or the hows now, but simply the triumph. For two centuries, it had waited. And now, *she'd* found it. She circled the hole the prop-wash had created and began to fan using her hand.

Her first find was a dinner plate with a flamboyant floral pattern around the rim. She found one, then half a dozen, two of which were intact. On the back was the mark of an English potter. There were cups as well, dainty, exquisite English china that might have graced the table of a wealthy colonist, might have become a beloved heirloom, if nature hadn't interfered. Now they looked like something out of a horror show— crusted, misshapen with sea life. They couldn't have been more beautiful to her.

As she continued to fan, Kate nearly missed what appeared to be a dark sea shell. On closer examination she saw it was a silver coin. She couldn't make out the currency, but knew it didn't matter. It could just as easily be Spanish, as she'd read that Spanish currency had been used by all European nations with settlements in the New World.

The point was, it was a coin. The first coin. Though it was silver, not gold, and unidentifiable at the moment, she'd found it by herself.

Kate started to slip it into her goodie bag when her arm was jerked back.

The thrill of fear went wildly from her toes to her throat. The spear gun was on board the *Vortex*. She had no weapon. Before she could do more than turn in defense, she was caught by the shoulders with Ky's furious hands.

Terror died, but the anger in his eyes only incited her own. Damn him for frightening her, for interfering. Shaking him away, Kate signaled for him to leave. With one arm, he encircled her waist and started for the surface.

Only once did she even come close to breaking away from him. Ky simply banded his arm around her again, more tightly, until she had a choice between submitting or cutting off her own air.

When they broke the surface, Kate drew in breath to shout, but even in this, she was out-maneuvered.

"Idiot!" he shouted at her, dragging her to the ladder. "One day off your back and you jump into forty feet of water by yourself. I don't know why in hell I ever thought you had any brains."

Breathless, she heaved her tanks over the side. When she was on solid ground again, she intended to have her say. For now, she'd let him have his.

"I take my eyes off you for a couple hours and you go off half-cocked. If I'd murdered Marsh, it would have been on your head."

To her further fury, Kate saw that she'd boarded the *Vortex*. Marsh's boat was nowhere in sight.

"Where's the *Gull?*" she demanded.

"Marsh had the sense to tell me what you were doing." The words came out like bullets as he stripped off his gear. "I didn't kill him because I needed him to come out with me and take the *Gull* back." He stood in front of her, dripping, and as furious as she'd ever seen him. "Don't you have any more sense than to dive out here alone?"

She tossed her head back. "Don't you?"

Infuriated, he grabbed her and started to peel the wet suit from her himself. "We're not talking about me, damn it. I've been diving since I was six. I know the currents."

"*I* know the currents."

"And I haven't been flat on my back for a week."

"I was flat on my back for a week because you were overreacting." She struggled away from him, and because the wet suit was already down to her waist, peeled it off. "You've no right to tell me when and where I can dive, Ky. Superior strength gives you no right to drag me up when I'm in the middle of salvaging."

"The hell with what I have a right to do." Grabbing her again, he shook her with more violence than he'd ever shown her. A dozen things might have happened to her in the thirty minutes she'd been down. A dozen things he knew too well. "I make my own rights. You're not going down alone if I have to chain you up to stop it."

"You told me to get another diver," she said between her teeth. "Until I do, I dive alone."

"You threw that damn business arrangement in my face. Percentages. Lousy percentages and a daily rate. Do you know how that made me feel?"

"No!" she shouted, pushing him away. "No, I don't know how that made you feel. I don't know how anything makes you feel. You don't tell me." Dragging both hands through her dripping hair she walked away. "We agreed to the terms. That's all I know."

"That was before."

"Before what?" she demanded. Tears brimmed for no reason she could name, but she blinked them back again. "Before I slept with you?"

"Damn it, Kate." He was across the deck, backing her into the rail before she could take a breath. "Are you trying to get at me for something I did or didn't do four years ago? I don't even know what it is. I don't know what you want from me or what you don't want and I'm sick of trying to outguess you."

"I don't want to be pushed into a corner," she told him fiercely. "That's what I don't want. I don't want to be expected to fall in passively with someone else's plans for me. That's what I don't want. I don't want it assumed that I simply don't have any personal goals or wishes of my own. Or any basic competence of my own. *That's* what I don't want!"

"Fine." They were both losing control, but he no longer gave a damn. Ky ripped off his wet suit and tossed it aside. "You just remember something, lady. I don't expect anything of you and I don't assume. Once maybe, but not anymore. There was only one person who ever pushed you into a corner and it wasn't me." He hurled his mask across the deck where it bounced and smacked into the side. "I'm the one who let you go."

She stiffened. Even with the distance between them he could see her eyes frost over. "I won't discuss my father with you."

"You caught on real quick though, didn't you?"

"You resented him. You—"

"I?" Ky interrupted. "Maybe you better look at yourself, Kate."

"I loved him," she said passionately. "All my life I tried to show him. You don't understand."

"How do you know that I don't understand?" he exploded. "Don't you know I can see what you're feeling every time we find something down there? Do you think I'm so blind I don't see that you're hurting because *you* found it, not him? Don't you think it tears me apart to see that you punish yourself for not being what you think he wanted you to be? And I'm tired," he continued as her breath started to hitch. "Damn tired of being compared to and measured by a man you loved without ever being close to him."

"I don't." She covered her face, hating the weakness but powerless against it. "I don't do that. I only want…"

"What?" he demanded. "What do you want?"

"I didn't cry when he died," she said into her hands. "I didn't cry, not even at the funeral. I owed him tears, Ky. I owed him something."

"You don't owe him anything you didn't already give him over and over again." Frustrated, he dragged a hand through his hair before he went to her. "Kate." Because words seemed useless, he simply gathered her close.

"I didn't cry."

"Cry now," he murmured. He pressed his lips to the top of her head. "Cry now."

So she did, desperately, for what she'd never been able to quite touch, for what she'd never been able to quite hold. She'd ached for love, for the simple companionship of understanding. She wept because it was too late for that now from her father. She wept because she wasn't certain she could ask for love again from anyone else.

Ky held her, lowering her onto the bench as he cradled her in his lap. He couldn't offer her words of comfort. They were the most difficult words for him to come by. He could only offer her a place to weep, and silence.

As the tears began to pass, she kept her face against his shoulder. There was such simplicity there, though it came from a man of complications. Such gentleness, though it sprang from a restless nature. "I couldn't mourn for him before," she murmured. "I'm not sure why."

"You don't have to cry to mourn."

"Maybe not," she said wearily. "I don't know. But it's true, what you said. I've wanted to do all this for him because he'll never have the chance to finish what he started. I don't know if you can understand, but I feel if I do this I'll have done everything I could. For him, and for myself."

"Kate." Ky tipped back her head so he could see her face. Her eyes were puffy, rimmed with red. "I don't have to understand. I just have to love you."

He felt her stiffen in his arms and immediately cursed himself. Why was it he never said things to her the way they should be said? Sweetly, calmly, softly. She was a woman who needed soft words, and he was a man who always struggled with them.

She didn't move, and for a long, long moment, they stayed precisely as they were.

"Do you?" she managed after a moment.

"Do I what?"

Would he make her drag it from him? "Love me?"

"Kate." Frustrated, he drew away from her. "I don't know how else to show you. You want bouquets of flowers, bottles of French champagne, poems? Damn it, I'm not made that way."

"I want a straight answer."

He let out a short breath. Sometimes her very calmness drove him to distraction. "I've always loved you. I've never stopped."

That went through her, sharp, hot, with a mixture of pain and pleasure she wasn't quite sure how to deal with. Slowly, she rose out of his arms, and walking across the deck, looked out to sea. The buoys that marked the site bobbed gently. Why were there no buoys in life to show you the way?

"You never told me."

"Look, I can't even count the number of women I've said it to." When she turned back with her brow raised, he rose, uncomfortable. "It was easy to say it to them because it didn't mean anything. It's a hell of a lot harder to get the words out when you mean them, and when you're afraid someone's going to back away from you the minute you do."

"I wouldn't have done that."

"You backed away, you went away for four years, when I asked you to stay."

"You asked me to stay," she reminded him. "You asked me not to go back to Connecticut, but to move in with you. Just like that. No promises, no commitment, no sign that you had any intention of building a life with me. I had responsibilities."

"To do what your father wanted you to do."

She swallowed that. It was true in its way. "All right, yes. But you never said you loved me."

He came closer. "I'm telling you now."

She nodded, but her heart was in her throat. "And

I'm not backing away. I'm just not sure I can take the next step. I'm not sure you can either."

"You want a promise."

She shook her head, not certain what she'd do if indeed he gave her one. "I want time, for both of us. It seems we both have a lot of thinking to do."

"Kate." Impatient, he came to her, taking her hands. They trembled. "Some things you don't have to think about. Some things you can think about too much."

"You've lived your life a certain way a long time, and I mine," she said quickly. "Ky, I've just begun to change—to feel the change. I don't want to make a mistake, not with you. It's too important. With time—"

"We've lost four years," he interrupted. He needed to resolve something, he discovered, and quickly. "I can't wait any longer to hear it if it's inside you."

Kate let out the breath she'd been holding. If he could ask, she could give. It would be enough. "I love you, Ky. I never stopped either. I never told you when I should have."

He felt the weight drain from his body as he cupped her face. "You're telling me now."

It was enough.

Chapter 11

Love. Kate had read hundreds of poems about that one phenomenon. She'd read, analyzed and taught from countless novels where love was the catalyst to all action, all emotion. With her students, she'd dissected innumerable lines from books, plays and verse that all led back to that one word.

Now, for perhaps the first time in her life, it was offered to her. She found it had more power than could possibly be taught. She found she didn't understand it.

Ky hadn't Byron's way with words, or Keat's romantic phrasing. What he'd said, he'd said simply. It meant everything. She still didn't understand it.

She could, in her own way, understand her feelings. She'd loved Ky for years, since that first revelation one summer when she'd come to know what it meant to want to fully share oneself with another.

But what, she wondered, did Ky find in her to love? It wasn't modesty that caused her to ask herself this question, but the basic practicality she'd grown up with. Where there was an effect, there was a cause. Where there was reaction, there was action. The world ran on this principle. She'd won Ky's love—but how?

Kate had no insecurity about her own intelligence. Perhaps, if anything, she overrated her mind, and it was this that caused her to underrate her other attributes.

He was a man of action, of restless and mercurial nature. She, on the other hand, considered herself almost blandly level. While she thrived on routine, Ky thrived on the unexpected. Why should he love her? Yet he did.

If she accepted that, it was vital to come to a resolution. Love led to commitment. It was there that she found the wall solid, without footholds.

He lived on a remote island because he was basically a loner, because he preferred moving at his own pace, in his own time. She was a teacher who lived by a day-to-day schedule. Without the satisfaction of giving knowledge, she'd stagnate. In the structured routine of a college town, Ky would go mad.

Because she could find no compromise, Kate opted to do what she'd decided to do in the beginning. She'd ride with the current until the summer was over. Perhaps by then, an answer would come.

They spoke no more of percentages. Kate quietly dropped the notion of keeping her hotel room. These, she told herself, were small matters when so much more hung in the balance during her second summer with Ky.

The days went quickly with her and Ky working together with the prop-wash or by hand. Slowly, painstakingly, they uncovered more salvage. The candlesticks had turned out to be pewter, but the coin had been Spanish silver. Its date had been 1748.

In the next two-week period, they uncovered much more—a heavy intricately carved silver platter, more china and porcelain, and in another area dozens of nails and tools.

Kate documented each find on film, for practical and personal reasons. She needed the neat, orderly way of keeping track of the salvage. She wanted to be able to look back on those pictures and remember how she felt when Ky held up a crusted teacup or an oxidized tankard. She'd be able to look and remember how he'd played an outstaring game with a large lazy bluefish. And lost.

More than once Ky had suggested the use of a larger ship equipped for salvage. They discussed it, and its advantages, but they never acted on it. Somehow, they both felt they wanted to move slowly, working basically with their own hands until there came a time when they had to make a decision.

The cannons and the heavier pieces of ship's planking couldn't be brought up without help, so these they left to the sea for the time being. They continued to use tanks, rather than changing to a surface-supplied source of air, so they had to surface and change gear every hour or so. A diving rig would have saved time— but that wasn't their goal.

Their methods weren't efficient by professional salvor standards, but they had an unspoken agreement. Stretch time. Make it last.

The nights they spent together in the big four-poster,

talking of the day's finds, or of tomorrow's, making love, marking time. They didn't speak of the future that loomed after the summer's end. They never talked of what they'd do the day after the treasure was found.

The treasure became their focus, something that kept them from reaching out when the other wasn't ready.

The day was fiercely hot as they prepared to dive. The sun was baking. It was mid-July. She'd been in Ocracoke for a month. For all her practicality, Kate told herself it was an omen. Today was the turning point of summer.

Even as she pulled the wet suit up to her waist, sweat beaded on her back. She could almost taste the cool freshness of the water. The sun glared on her tanks as she lifted them, bouncing off to spear her eyes.

"Here." Taking them from her, Ky strapped them onto her back, checking the gauges himself. "The water's going to feel like heaven."

"Yeah." Marsh tipped up a quart bottle of juice. "Think of me baking up here while you're having all the fun."

"Keep the throttle low, brother," Ky said with a grin as he climbed over the side. "We'll bring you a reward."

"Make it something round and shiny with a date stamped on it," Marsh called back, then winked at Kate as she started down the ladder. "Good luck."

She felt the excitement as the water lapped over her ankles. "Today, I don't think I need it."

The noise of the prop-wash disturbed the silence of the water, but not the mystery. Even with technology and equipment, the water remained an enigma, part beauty, part danger. They went deeper and deeper until they reached the site with the scoops in the silt caused by their earlier explorations.

They'd already found what they thought had been the officers' and passengers' quarters, identifying it by the discovery of a snuff box, a silver bedside candle-holder and Ky's personal favorite—a decorated sword. The few pieces of jewelry they'd found indicated a personal cache rather than cargo.

Though they fully intended to excavate in the area of the cache, it was the cargo they sought. Using the passengers' quarters and the galley as points of reference, they concentrated on what should have been the stern of the ship.

There were ballast rocks to deal with. This entailed a slow, menial process that required moving them by hand to an area they'd already excavated. It was time consuming, unrewarding and necessary. Still, Kate found something peaceful in the mindless work, and something fascinating about the ability to do it under fathoms of water with basically little effort. She could move a ballast pile as easily as Ky, whereas on land, she would have tired quickly.

Reaching down to clear another area, Ky's fingers brushed something small and hard. Curious, he fanned aside a thin layer of silt and picked up what at first looked like a tab on a can of beer. As he brought it closer, he saw it was much more refined, and though there were layers of crust on the knob of the circle, he felt his heart give a quick jerk.

He'd heard of diamonds in the rough, but he'd never thought to find one by simply reaching for it. He was no expert, but as he painstakingly cleaned what he could from the stone, he judged it to be at least two carats. With a tap on Kate's shoulder, he got her attention.

It gave him a great deal of pleasure to see her eyes widen and to hear the muffled sound of her surprise. Together, they turned it over and over again. It was dull and dirty, but the gem was there.

They were finding bits and pieces of civilization. Perhaps a woman had worn the ring while dining with the captain on her way to America. Perhaps some British officer had carried it in his vest pocket, waiting to give it to the woman he'd hoped to marry. It might have belonged to an elderly widow, or a young bride. The mystery of it, and its tangibility, were more precious than the stone itself. It was...lasting.

Ky held it out to her, offering. Their routine had fallen into a finders-keepers arrangement, in that whoever found a particular piece carried it in their own bag to the surface where everything was carefully cataloged on film and paper. Kate looked at the small, water-dulled piece of the past in Ky's fingers.

Was he offering her the ring because it was a woman's fancy, or was he offering her something else? Unsure, she shook her head, pointing to the bag on his belt. If he were asking her something, she needed it to be done with words.

Ky dropped the ring into his bag, secured it, then went back to work.

He thought he understood her, in some ways. In other ways, Ky found she was as much a mystery as the sea. What did she want from him? If it was love, he'd given her that. If it was time, they were both running out of it. He wanted to demand, was accustomed to demanding, yet she blocked his ability with a look.

She said she'd changed—that she was just beginning to feel in control of her life. He thought he understood that, as well as her fierce need for independence. And yet... He'd never known anything but independence. He, too, had changed. He needed her to give him the boundaries and the borders that came with dependence. His for her, and hers for him. Was the timing wrong again? Would it ever be right?

Damn it, he wanted her, he thought as he heaved another rock out of his way. Not just for today, but for tomorrow. Not tied against him, but bound to him. Why couldn't she understand that?

She loved him. It was something she murmured in the night when she was sleepy and caught close against him. She wasn't a woman to use words unless they had meaning. Yet with the love he offered and the love she returned, she'd begun to hold something back from him, as though he could have only a portion of her, but not all. Edged with frustration, he cleared more ballast. He needed, and would have, all.

Marriage? Was he thinking of marriage? Kate found herself flustered and uneasy. She'd never expected Ky to look for that kind of commitment, that kind of permanency. Perhaps she'd misread him. After all, it was difficult to be certain of someone's intention, yet she knew just how clearly Ky and she had been able to communicate underwater.

There was so much to consider, so many things to weigh. He wouldn't understand that, Kate mused. Ky was a man who made decisions in an instant and took the consequences. He wouldn't think about all the variables, all the what-ifs, all the maybes. She had to think about them all. She simply knew no other way.

Kate watched the silt and sand blowing away, causing a cuplike indentation to form on the ocean floor. Outside influences, she mused. They could eat away at the layers and uncover the core, but sometimes what was beneath couldn't stand up to the pressure.

Is that what would happen between her and Ky? How would their relationship hold up under the pressure of variant lifestyles—the demands of her profession and the free-wheeling tone of his? Would it stay intact, or would it begin to sift away, layer by layer? How much of herself would he ask her to give? And in loving, how much of herself would she lose?

It was a possibility she couldn't ignore, a threat she needed to build a solid defense against. Time. Perhaps time was the answer. But summer was waning.

The force of the wash made a small object spin up, out of the layer of silt and into the water. Kate grabbed at it and the sharp edge scraped her palm. Curious, she turned it over for examination. A buckle? she wondered. The shape seemed to indicate it, and she could just make out a fastening. Even as she started to hold it out for Ky another, then another was pushed off the ocean bed.

Shoe buckles, Kate realized, astonished. Dozens of them. No, she realized as more and more began to twist up in the water's spin and reel away. Hundreds. With a quick frenzy, she began to gather what she could. More than hundreds, she discovered as her heart thudded. There were thousands of them, literally thousands.

She held a buckle in her hand and looked at Ky in triumph. They'd found the cargo. There'd been shoe buckles on the manifest of the *Liberty*. Five thousand of them. Nothing but a merchantman carried something like that in bulk.

Proof. She waved the buckle, her arm sweeping out in slow motion to take in the swarm of them swirling away from the wash and dropping again. Proof, her mind shouted out. The cargo-hold was beneath them. And the treasure. They had only to reach it.

Ky took her hands and nodded, knowing what was in her mind. Beneath his fingers he could feel the race of her pulse. He wanted that for her, the excitement, the thrill that came from discovering something only half believed in. She brought the back of his hand to her cheek, her eyes laughing, buckles spinning around them. Kate wanted to laugh until she was too weak to stand. Five thousand shoe buckles would guide them to a chest of gold.

Kate saw the humor in his eyes and knew Ky's thoughts ran along the same path as hers. He pointed to himself, then thumbs up. With a minimum of signaling, he told Kate that he would surface to tell Marsh to shut off the engines. It was time to work by hand.

Excited, she nodded. She wanted only to begin. Resting near the bottom, Kate watched Ky go up and out of sight. Oddly, she found she needed time alone. She'd shared the heady instant of discovery with Ky, and now she needed to absorb it.

The *Liberty* was beneath her, the ship her father had searched for. The dream he'd kept close, carefully researching, meticulously calculating, but never finding.

Joy and sorrow mixed as she gathered a handful of the buckles and placed them carefully in her bag. For him. In that moment she felt she'd given him everything she'd always needed to.

Carefully, and this time for personal reasons rather than the catalog, she began to shoot pictures. Years from now, she thought. Years and years from now, she'd look at a snapshot of swirling silt and drifting pieces of metal, and she'd remember. Nothing could ever take that moment of quiet satisfaction from her.

She glanced up at the sudden silence. The wash had stilled. Ky had reached the surface. Silt and the pieces of crusted, decorated metal began to settle again without the agitation of the wash. The sea was a world without sound, without movement.

Kate looked down at the scoop in the ocean floor. They were nearly there. For a moment she was tempted to begin to fan and search by herself, but she'd wait for Ky. They began together, and they'd finish together. Content, she watched for his return.

When Kate saw the movement above her, she started to signal. Her hand froze in place, then her arm, her shoulder and the rest of her body, degree by degree. It came smoothly through the water, sleek and silent. Deadly.

The noise of the prop-wash had kept the sea life away. Now the abrupt quiet brought out the curious. Among the schools of harmless fish glided the long bulletlike shape of a shark.

Kate was still, hardly daring to breathe as she feared even the trail of bubbles might attract him. He moved without haste, apparently not interested in her. Perhaps he'd already hunted successfully that day. But even with a full belly, a shark would attack what annoyed his uncertain temper.

She gauged him to be ten feet in length. Part of her mind registered that he was fairly small for what she recognized as a tiger shark. They could easily double that length. But she knew the jaws, those large sickle-shaped teeth, would be strong, merciless and fatal.

If she remained still, the chances were good that he would simply go in search of more interesting waters. Isn't that what she'd read sitting cozily under lamplight at her own desk? Isn't that what Ky had told her once when they'd shared a quiet lunch on his boat? All that seemed so remote, so unreal now, as she looked above and saw the predator between herself and the surface.

It was movement that attracted them, she reminded herself as she forced her mind to function. The movement a swimmer made with kicking feet and sweeping arms.

Don't panic. She forced herself to breathe slowly. No sudden moves. She forced her nervous hands to form tight, still fists.

He was no more than ten feet away. Kate could see the small black eyes and the gentle movement of his gills. Breathing shallowly, she never took her eyes from his. She had only to be perfectly still and wait for him to swim on.

But Ky. Kate's mouth went dry as she looked toward the direction where Ky had disappeared moments before. He'd be coming back, any minute, unaware of what was lurking near the bottom. Waiting. Cruising.

The shark would sense the disturbance in the water with the uncanny ability the hunter had. The kick of Ky's feet, the swing of his arms would attract the shark long before Kate would have a chance to warn him of any danger.

He'd be unaware, helpless, and then... Her blood seemed to freeze. She'd heard of the sensation but now she experienced it. Cold seemed to envelop her. Terror made her head light. Kate bit down on her lip until pain cleared her thoughts. She wouldn't stand by idly while Ky came blindly into a death trap.

Glancing down, she saw the spear gun. It was over five feet away and unloaded for safety. Safety, she thought hysterically. She'd never loaded one, much less shot one. And first, she'd have to get to it. There'd only be one chance. Knowing she'd have no time to settle her nerves, Kate made her move.

She kept her eyes on the shark as she inched slowly toward the gun. At the moment, he seemed to be merely cruising, not particularly interested in anything. He never even glanced her way. Perhaps he would move on before Ky came back, but she needed the weapon. Fingers shaking, she gripped the butt of the gun. Time seemed to crawl. Her movements were so slow, so measured, she hardly seemed to move at all. But her mind whirled.

Even as she gripped the spear she saw the shape that glided down from the surface. The shark turned lazily to the left. To Ky.

No! her mind screamed as she rammed the spear into position. Her only thought that of protecting what she loved. Kate swam forward without hesitation, taking a path between Ky and the shark. She had to get close.

Her mind was cold now, with fear, with purpose. For the second time, she saw those small, deadly eyes. This time, they focused on her. If she'd never seen true evil before, Kate knew she faced it now. This was cruelty, and a death that wouldn't come easily.

The shark moved toward her with a speed that made

her heart stop. His jaws opened. There was a black, black cave behind them.

Ky dove quickly, wanting to get back to Kate, wanting to search for what had brought them back together. If it was the treasure she needed to settle her mind, he'd find it. With it, they could open whatever doors they needed to open, lock whatever needed to be locked. Excitement drummed through him as he dove deeper.

When he spotted the shark, he pulled up short. He'd felt that deep primitive fear before, but never so sharply. Though it was less than useless against such a predator, he reached for his diver's knife. He'd left Kate alone. Cold-bloodedly, he set for the attack.

Like a rocket, Kate shot up between himself and the shark. Terror such as he'd never known washed over him. Was she mad? Was she simply unaware? Giving no time to thought, Ky barreled through the water toward her.

He was too far away. He knew it even as the panic hammered into him. The shark would be on her before he was close enough to sink the knife in.

When he saw what she held in her hand, and realized her purpose he somehow doubled his speed. Everything was in slow motion, and yet it seemed to happen in the blink of an eye. He saw the gaping hole in the shark's mouth as it closed in on Kate. For the first time in his life, prayers ran through him like water.

The spear shot out, sinking deep through the shark's flesh. Instinctively, Kate let herself drop as the shark came forward full of anger and pain. He would follow her now, she knew. If the spear didn't work, he would be on her in moments.

Ky saw blood gush from the wound. It wouldn't

be enough. The shark jerked as if to reject the spear, and slowed his pace. Just enough. Teeth bared, Ky fell on its back, hacking with the knife as quickly as the water would allow. The shark turned, furious. Using all his strength, Ky turned with it, forcing the knife into the underbelly and ripping down. It ran through his mind that he was holding death, and it was as cold as the poets said.

From a few feet away, Kate watched the battle. She was numb, body and mind. Blood spurted out to dissipate in the water. Letting the empty gun fall, she too reached for her knife and swam forward.

But it was over. One instant the fish and Ky were as one form, locked together. Then they were separate as the body of the shark sank lifelessly toward the bottom. She saw the eyes one last time.

Her arm was gripped painfully. Limp, Kate allowed herself to be dragged to the surface. Safe. It was the only clear thought her mind could form. He was safe.

Too breathless to speak, Ky pulled her toward the ladder, tanks and all. He saw her slip near the top and roll onto the deck. Even as he swung over himself, he saw two fins slice through the water and disappear below where the blood drew them.

"What the hell—" Jumping up from his seat, Marsh ran across the deck to where Kate still lay, gasping for air.

"Sharks." Ky cut off the word as he knelt beside her. "I had to bring her up fast. Kate." Ky reached a hand beneath her neck, lifting her up as he began to take off her tanks. "Are you dizzy? Do you have any pain— your knees, elbows?"

Though she was still gasping for air, she shook her

head. "No, no, I'm all right." She knew he worried about decompression sickness and tried to steady herself to reassure him. "Ky, we weren't that deep after—when we came up."

He nodded, grimly acknowledging that she was winded, not incoherent. Standing, he pulled off his mask and heaved it across the deck. Temper helped alleviate the helpless shaking. Kate merely drew her knees up and rested her forehead on them.

"Somebody want to fill me in?" Marsh asked, glancing from one to the other. "I left off when Ky came up raving about shoe buckles."

"Cargo-hold," Kate murmured. "We found it."

"So Ky said." Marsh glanced at his brother whose knuckles were whitening against the rail as he looked out to sea. "Run into some company down there?"

"There was a shark. A tiger."

"She nearly got herself killed," Ky explained. Fury was a direct result of fear, and just as deadly. "She swam right in front of him." Before Marsh could make any comment, Ky turned on Kate. "Did you forget everything I taught you?" he demanded. "You manage to get a doctorate but you can't remember that you're supposed to minimize your movements when a shark's cruising? You know that arm and leg swings attract them, but you swim in front of him, flailing around as though you wanted to shake hands—holding a damn spear gun that's just as likely to annoy him as do any real damage. If I hadn't been coming down just then, he'd have torn you to pieces."

Kate lifted her head slowly. Whatever emotion she'd felt up to that moment was replaced by an anger so deep it overshadowed everything. Meticulously she removed her flippers, her mask and her weight belt before she rose. "If you hadn't been coming down just then," she said precisely, "there'd have been no reason for me to swim in front of him." Turning, she walked to the steps and down into the cabin.

For a full minute there was utter silence on deck. Above, a gull screeched, then swerved west. Knowing there'd be no more dives that day, Marsh went to the helm. As he glanced over he saw the deep stain of blood on the water's surface.

"It's customary," he began with his back to his brother, "to thank someone when they save your life." Without waiting for a comment, he switched on the engine.

Shaken, Ky ran a hand through his hair. Some of the shark's blood had stained his fingers. Standing still, he stared at it.

Not through carelessness, he thought with a jolt. It had been deliberate. Kate had deliberately put herself in the path of the shark. For him. She'd risked her life to save him. He ran both hands over his face before he started below deck.

He saw her sitting on a bunk with a glass in her hand. A bottle of brandy sat at her feet. When she lifted the glass to her lips her hand shook lightly. Beneath the tan the sun had given her, her face was drawn and pale. No one had ever put him first so completely, so unselfishly. It left him without any idea of what to say.

"Kate…"

"I'm not in the mood to be shouted at right now,"

she told him before she drank again. "If you need to vent your temper, you'll have to save it."

"I'm not going to shout." Because he felt every bit as unsteady as she did, he sat beside her and lifted the bottle, drinking straight from it. The brandy ran hot and strong through him. "You scared the hell out of me."

"I'm not going to apologize for what I did."

"I should thank you." He drank again and felt the nerves in his stomach ease. "The point is, you had no business doing what you did. Nothing but blind luck kept you from being torn up down there."

Turning her head, she stared at him. "I should've stayed safe and sound on the bottom while you dealt with the shark—with your diver's knife."

He met the look levelly. "Yes."

"And you'd have done that, if it'd been me?"

"That's different."

"Oh." Glass in hand, she rose. She took a moment to study him, that raw-boned, dark face, the dripping hair that needed a trim, the eyes that reflected the sea. "Would you care to explain that little piece of logic to me?"

"I don't have to explain it, it just is." He tipped the bottle back again. It helped to cloud his imagination which kept bringing images of what might have happened to her.

"No, it just isn't, and that's one of your major problems."

"Kate, have you any idea what could have happened if you hadn't lucked out and hit a vital spot with that spear?"

"Yes." She drained her glass and felt some of the edge dull. The fear might come back again unexpectedly, but she felt she was strong enough to deal with it. And the anger. No matter how it slashed at her, she would put herself between him and danger again. "I understand perfectly. Now, I'm going up with Marsh."

"Wait a minute." He stood to block her way. "Can't you see that I couldn't stand it if anything happened to you? I want to take care of you. I need to keep you safe."

"While you take all the risks?" she countered. "Is that supposed to be the balance of our relationship, Ky? You man, me woman? I bake bread, you hunt the meat?"

"Damn it, Kate, it's not as basic as that."

"It's just as basic as that," she tossed back. The color had come back to her face. Her legs were steady again. And she would be heard. "You want me to be quiet and content—and amenable to the way you choose to live. You want me to do as you say, bend to your will, and yet I know how you felt about my father."

It didn't seem she had the energy to be angry any longer. She was just weary, bone weary from slamming herself up against a wall that didn't seem ready to budge.

"I spent all my life doing what it pleased him to have me do," she continued in calmer tones. "No waves, no problems, no rebellion. He gave me a nod of approval, but no true respect and certainly no true affection. Now, you're asking me to do the same thing again with you." She felt no tears, only that weariness of spirit. "Why do you suppose the only two men I've ever loved should want me to be so utterly pliant to their will? Why do you suppose I lost both of them because I tried so hard to do just that?"

"No." He put his hands on her shoulders. "No, that's

not true. It's not what I want from you or for you. I just want to take care of you."

She shook her head. "What's the difference, Ky?" she whispered. "What the hell's the difference?" Pushing past him, Kate went out on deck.

Chapter 12

Because in her quiet, immovable way Kate had demanded it, Ky left her alone. Perhaps it was for the best as it gave him time to think and to reassess what he wanted.

He realized that because of his fear for her, because of his need to care for her, he'd hurt her and damaged their already tenuous relationship.

On a certain level, she'd hit the mark in her accusations. He did want her to be safe and cared for while he sweated and took the risks. It was his nature to protect what he loved—in Kate's case, perhaps too much. It was also his nature to want other wills bent to his. He wanted Kate, and was honest enough to admit that he'd already outlined the terms in his own mind.

Her father's quiet manipulating had infuriated Ky and yet, he found himself doing the same thing. Not so quietly, he admitted, not nearly as subtly, but he was doing the same thing. Still, it wasn't for the same reasons. He wanted Kate to be with him, to align herself to him. It was as simple as that. He was certain, if she'd just let him, that he could make her happy.

But he never fully considered that she'd have demands or terms of her own. Until now, Ky hadn't thought how he'd adjust to them.

The light of dawn was quiet as Ky added the finishing touches to the lettering on his sailboat. For most of the night, he'd worked in the shed, giving Kate her time alone, and himself the time to think. Now that the night was over, only one thing remained clear. He loved her. But it had come home to him that it might not be enough. Though impatience continued to push at him, he reined it in. Perhaps he had to leave it to her to show him what would be.

For the next few days, they would concentrate on excavating the cargo that had sunk two centuries before. The longer they searched, the more the treasure became a symbol for him. If he could give it to her, it would be the end of the quest for both of them. Once it was over, they'd both have what they wanted. She, the fulfillment of her father's dream, and he, the satisfaction of seeing her freed from it.

Ky closed the shed doors behind him and headed back for the house. In a few days, he thought with a glance over his shoulder, he'd have something else to give her. Something else to ask her.

He was still some feet away from the house when he smelled the morning scents of bacon and coffee drifting through the kitchen windows. When he entered,

Kate was standing at the stove, a long T-shirt over her tank suit, her feet bare, her hair loose. He could see the light dusting of freckles over the bridge of her nose, and the pale soft curve of her lips.

His need to gather her close rammed into him with such power, he had to stop and catch his breath. "Kate—"

"I thought since we'd be putting in a long day we should have a full breakfast." She'd heard him come in, sensed it. Because it made her knees weak, she spoke briskly. "I'd like to get an early start."

He watched her drop eggs into the skillet where the white began to sizzle and solidify around the edges. "Kate, I'd like to talk to you."

"I've been thinking we might consider renting a salvage ship after all," she interrupted, "and perhaps hiring another couple of divers. Excavating the cargo's going to be very slow work with just the two of us. It's certainly time we looked into lifting bags and lines."

Long days in the sun had lightened her hair. There were shades upon shades of variation so that as it flowed it reminded him of the smooth soft pelt of a deer. "I don't want to talk business now."

"It's not something we can put off too much longer." Efficiently, she scooped up the eggs and slid them onto plates. "I'm beginning to think we should expedite the excavation rather than dragging it out for what may very well be several more weeks. Then, of course, if we're talking about excavating the entire site, it would be months."

"Not now." Ky turned off the burner under the skillet. Taking both plates from Kate, he set them on the table. "Look, I have to do something, and I'm not sure I'll do it very well."

Turning, Kate took silverware from the drawer and went to the table. "What?"

"Apologize." When she looked back at him in her cool, quiet way, he swore. "No, I won't do it well."

"It isn't necessary."

"Yes, it's necessary. Sit down." He let out a long breath as she remained standing. "Please," he added, then took a chair himself. Without a word, Kate sat across from him. "You saved my life yesterday." Even saying it aloud, he felt uneasy about it. "It was no less than that. I never could have taken that shark with my diver's knife. The only reason I did was because you'd weakened and distracted him."

Kate lifted her coffee and drank as though they were discussing the weather. It was the only way she had of blocking out images of what might have been. "Yes."

With a frustrated laugh, Ky stabbed at his eggs. "Not going to make it easy on me, are you?"

"No, I don't think I am."

"I've never been that scared," he said quietly. "Not for myself, certainly not for anyone else. I thought he had you." He looked up and met her calm, patient eyes. "I was still too far away to do anything about it. If…"

"Sometimes it's best not to think about the ifs."

"All right." He nodded and reached for her hand. "Kate, realizing you put yourself in danger to protect me only made it worse somehow. The possibility of anything happening to you was bad enough, but the idea of it happening because of me was unbearable."

"You would've protected me."

"Yes, but—"

"There shouldn't be any buts, Ky."

"Maybe there shouldn't be," he agreed, "but I can't promise there won't be."

"I've changed." The fact filled her with an odd sense of power and unease. "For too many years I've channeled my own desires because I thought somehow that approval could be equated with love. I know better now."

"I'm not your father, Kate."

"No, but you also have a way of imposing your will on me. My fault to a point." Her voice was calm, level, as it was when she lectured her students. She hadn't slept while Ky had spent his hours in the shed. Like him, she'd spent her time in thought, in search for the right answers. "Four years ago, I had to give to one of you and deny the other. It broke my heart. Today, I know I have to answer to myself first." With her breakfast hardly touched, she took her plate to the sink. "I love you, Ky," she murmured. "But I have to answer to myself first."

Rising, he went to her and laid his hands on her shoulders. Somehow the strength that suddenly seemed so powerful in her both attracted him yet left him uneasy. "Okay." When she turned into his arms, he felt the world settle a bit. "Just let me know what the answer is."

"When I can." She closed her eyes and held tight. "When I can."

For three long days they dove, working away the silt to find new discoveries. With a small air lift and their own hands, they found the practical, the beautiful and the ordinary. They came upon more than eight thousand of the ten thousand decorated pipes on the *Liberty*'s manifest. At least half of them, to Kate's delight, had their bowls intact. They were clay, long-stemmed pipes with the bowls decorated with oak leaves or bunches of grapes and flowers. In a heady moment of pleasure, she snapped Ky's picture as he held one up to his lips.

She knew that at auction, they would more than pay for the investment she'd made. And, with them, the donation she'd make to a museum in her father's name was steadily growing. But more than this, the discovery of so many pipes on a wreck added force to their claim that the ship was English.

There were also snuff boxes, again thousands, leaving literally no doubt in her mind that they'd found the merchantman *Liberty*. They found tableware, some of it elegant, some basic utility-ware, but again in quantity. Their list of salvage grew beyond anything Kate had imagined, but they found no chest of gold.

They took turns hauling their finds to the surface, using an inverted plastic trash can filled with air to help them lift. Even with this, they stored the bulk of it on the sea floor. They were working alone again, without a need for Marsh to man the prop-wash. As it had been in the beginning, the project became a personal chore for only the two of them. What they found became a personal triumph. What they didn't find, a personal disappointment.

Kate delegated herself to deal with the snuff boxes, transporting them to the mesh baskets. Already, she was planning to clean several of them herself as part of the discovery. Beneath the layers of time there might be something elegant, ornate or ugly. She didn't believe it mattered what she found, as long as she found it.

Tea, sugar and other perishables the merchant ship

had carried were long since gone without a trace. What she and Ky found now were the solid pieces of civilization that had survived centuries in the sea. A pipe meant for an eighteenth-century man had never reached the New World. It should have made her sad but, because it had survived, because she could hold it in her hand more than two hundred years later, Kate felt a quiet triumph. Some things last, whatever the odds.

Reaching down, she disturbed something that lay among the jumbled snuff boxes. Automatically, she jerked her hand back. Memories of the stingray and other dangers were still very fresh. When the small round object clinked against the side of a box and lay still, her heart began to pound. Almost afraid to touch, Kate reached for it. Between her fingers, she held a gold coin from another era.

Though she had read it was likely, she hadn't expected it to be as bright and shiny as the day it was minted. The pieces of silver they'd found had blackened, and other metal pieces had corroded, some of them crystalized almost beyond recognition. Yet, the gold, the small coin she'd plucked from the sea floor, winked back at her.

Its origin was English. The long-dead king stared out at her. The date was 1750.

"Ky!" Foolishly, she said his name. Though the sound was muffled and indistinguishable, he turned. Unable to wait, Kate swam toward him, clutching the coin. When she reached him, she took his hand and pressed the gold into his palm.

He knew at the moment of contact. He had only to look into her eyes. Taking her hand, he brought it to his lips. She'd found what she wanted. For no reason he could name, he felt empty. He pressed the coin back into her hand, closing her fingers over it tightly. The gold was hers.

Swimming beside her, Ky moved to the spot where Kate had found the coin. Together, they fanned, using all the patience each of them had stored. In the twenty minutes of bottom time they had left, they uncovered only five more coins. As if they were as fragile as glass, Kate placed them in her bag. Each took a mesh basket filled with salvage and surfaced.

"It's there, Ky." Kate let her mouthpiece drop as Ky hauled the first basket over the rail. "It's the *Liberty,* we've proven it."

"It's the *Liberty,*" he agreed, taking the second basket from her. "You've finished what your father started."

"Yes." She unhooked her tanks, but it was more than their weight she felt lifted from her shoulders. "I've finished." Digging into her bag, she pulled out the six bright coins. "These were loose. We still haven't found the chest. If it still exists."

He'd already thought of that, but not how he'd tell her his own theory. "They might have taken the chest to another part of the boat when the storm hit." It was a possibility; it had given them hope that the chest was still there.

Kate looked down. The glittery metal seemed to mock her. "It's possible they put the gold in one of the lifeboats when they manned them. The survivor's story wasn't clear after the ship began to break up."

"A lot of things are possible." He touched her cheek briefly before he started to strip off his gear. "With a little luck and a little more time, we might find it all."

She smiled as she dropped the coins back into her bag. "Then you could buy your boat."

"And you could go to Greece." Stripped down to his bathing trunks, Ky went to the helm. "We need to give ourselves the full twelve hours before we dive again, Kate. We've been calling it close as it is."

"That's fine." She made a business of removing her own suit. She needed the twelve hours, she discovered, for more than the practical reason of residual nitrogen.

They spoke little on the trip back. They should've been ecstatic. Kate knew it, and though she tried, she couldn't recapture that quick boost she'd felt when she picked up the first coin.

She discovered that if she'd had a choice she would have gone back weeks, to the time when the gold was a distant goal and the search was everything.

It took the rest of the day to transport the salvage from the *Vortex* to Ky's house, to separate and catalog it. She'd already decided to contact the Park Service. Their advice in placing many of the artifacts would be invaluable. After taxes, she'd give her father his memorial. And, she mused, she'd give Ky whatever he wanted out of the salvage.

Their original agreement no longer mattered to her. If he wanted half, she'd give it. All she wanted, Kate realized, was the first bowl she'd found, the blackened silver coin and the gold one that had led her to the five other coins.

"We might think about investing in a small electrolytic reduction bath," Ky murmured as he turned what he guessed was a silver snuff box in his palm. "We could treat a lot of this salvage ourselves." Coming to a decision, he set the box down. "We're going to have to think about a bigger ship and equipment. It might be best to stop diving for the next couple of days while we arrange for it. It's been six weeks, and we've barely scratched the surface of what's down there."

She nodded, not entirely sure why she wanted to weep. He was right. It was time to move on, to expand. How could she explain to him, when she couldn't explain to herself, that she wanted nothing else from the sea? While the sun set, she watched him meticulously list the salvage.

"Ky…" She broke off because she couldn't find the words to tell him what moved through her. Sadness, emptiness, needs.

"What's wrong?"

"Nothing." But she took his hands as she rose. "Come upstairs now," she said quietly. "Make love with me before the sun goes down."

Questions ran through him, but he told himself they could wait. The need he felt from her touched off his own. He wanted to give her, and to take from her, what couldn't be found anywhere else.

When they entered the bedroom it was washed with the warm, lingering light of the sun. The sky was slowly turning red as he lay beside her. Her arms reached out to gather him close. Her lips parted. Refusing to rush, they undressed each other. No boundaries. Flesh against flesh they lay. Mouth against mouth they touched.

Kisses—long and deep—took them both beyond the ordinary world of place and time. Here, there were dozens of sensations to be felt, and no questions to be asked. Here, there was no past, no tomorrow, only the moment. Her body went limp under his, but her mouth hungered and sought.

No one else... No one else had ever taken her beyond herself so effortlessly. Never before had anyone made her so completely aware of her own body. A feathery touch along her skin drove pleasure through her with inescapable force.

The scent of sea still clung to both of them. As pleasure became liquid, they might have been fathoms under the ocean, moving freely without the strict rules of gravity. There were no rules here.

As his hands brought their emotions rising to the surface, so did hers for him. She explored the rippling muscles of his back, near the shoulders. Lingering there, she enjoyed just the feel of one of the subtle differences between them. His skin was smooth, but muscles bunched under it. His hands were gentle, but the palms were hard. He was lean, but there was no softness there.

Again and again she touched and tasted, needing to absorb him. Above all else, she needed to experience everything they'd ever had together this one time. They made love here, she remembered, that first time. The first time...and the last. Whenever she thought of him, she'd remember the quieting light of dusk and the distant sound of surf.

He didn't understand why he felt such restrained urgency from her, but he knew she needed everything he could give her. He loved her, perhaps not as gently as he could, but more thoroughly than ever before.

He touched. "Here," Ky murmured, using his fingertips to drive her up. As she gasped and arched, he watched her. "You're soft and hot."

He tasted. "And here..." With his tongue, he pushed her to the edge. As her hands gripped his, he groaned.

Pleasure heaped upon pleasure. "You taste like temptation—sweet and forbidden. Tell me you want more."

"Yes." The word came out on a moan. "I want more."

So he gave her more.

Again and again, he took her up, watching the astonished pleasure on her face, feeling it in the arch of her body, hearing it in her quick breaths. She was helpless, mindless, his. He drove his tongue into her and felt her explode, wave after wave.

As she shuddered, he moved up her body, hands fast, mouth hot and open. Suddenly, on a surge of strength, she rolled on top of him. Within seconds, she'd devastated his claim to leadership. All fire, all speed, all woman, she took control.

Heedless, greedy, they moved over the bed. Murmurs were incoherent, care was forgotten. They took with only one goal in mind. Pleasure—sweet, forbidden pleasure.

Shaking, locked tight, they reached the goal together.

Dawn was breaking, clear and calm as Kate lay still, watching Ky sleep. She knew what she had to do for both of them, to both of them. Fate had brought them together a second time. It wouldn't bring them together again.

She'd bargained with Ky, offering him a share of gold for his skill. In the beginning, she'd believed that she wanted the treasure, needed it to give her all the options she'd never had before. That choice. Now, she knew she didn't want it at all. A hundred times more gold wouldn't change what was between her and Ky—what drew them to each other, and what kept them apart.

She loved him. She understood that, in his way, he

loved her. Did that change the differences between them? Did that make her able and willing to give up her own life to suit his, or able and willing to demand that he do the same?

Their worlds were no closer together now than they'd been four years ago. Their desires no more in tune. With the gold she'd leave for him, he'd be able to do what he wanted with his life. She needed no treasure for that.

If she stayed... Unable to stop herself, Kate reached out to touch his cheek. If she stayed she'd bury herself for him. Eventually, she'd despise herself for it, and he'd resent her. Better that they take what they'd had for a few weeks than cover it with years of disappoinments.

The treasure was important to him. He'd taken risks for it, worked for it. She'd give her father his memorial. Ky would have the rest.

Quietly, still watching him sleep, she dressed.

It didn't take Kate long to gather what she'd come with. Taking her suitcase downstairs, she carefully packed what she'd take with her from the *Liberty*. In a box, she placed the pottery bowl wrapped in layers of newspaper. The coins, the blackened silver and the shiny gold, she zipped into a small pouch. With equal care, she packed the film she'd taken during their days under the ocean.

What she'd designated for the museum she'd already marked. Leaving the list on the table, she left the house.

She told herself it would be cleaner if she left no note, yet she found herself hesitating. How could she make him understand? After putting her suitcase in her car, she went back into the house. Quietly, she took the five gold coins upstairs and placed them on Ky's

dresser. With a last look at him as he slept, she went
back out again.

She'd have a final moment with the sea. In the quiet
air of morning, Kate walked over the dunes.

She'd remember it this way—empty, endless and
full of sound. Surf foamed against the sand, white on
white. What was beneath the surface would always call
her—the memories of peace, of excitement, of sharing
both with Ky. Only a summer, she thought. Life was
made of four seasons, not one.

Day was strengthening, and her time was up. Turning, she scanned the island until she saw the tip of
the lighthouse. Some things lasted, she thought with a
smile. She'd learned a great deal in a few short weeks.
She was her own woman at last. She could make her
own way. As a teacher, she told herself that knowledge
was precious. But it made her ache with loneliness. She
left the empty sea behind her.

Though she wanted to, Kate deliberately kept herself
from looking at the house as she walked back to her
car. She didn't need to see it again to remember it. If
things had been different... Kate reached for the door
handle of her car. Her fingers were still inches from it
when she was spun around.

"What the hell're you doing?"

Facing Ky, she felt her resolve crumble, then re-
build. He was barely awake, and barely dressed. His
eyes were heavy with sleep, his hair disheveled from
it. All he wore was a pair of ragged cut-offs. She folded
her hands in front of her and hoped her voice would
be strong and clear.

"I had hoped to be gone before you woke."

"Gone?" His eyes locked on hers. "Where?"

"I'm going back to Connecticut."

"Oh?" He swore he wouldn't lose his temper. Not this time. This time, it might be fatal for both of them. "Why?"

Her nerves skipped. The question had been quiet enough, but she knew that cold, flat expression in his eyes. The wrong move, and he'd leap. "You said it yourself yesterday, Ky, when we came up from the last dive. I've done what I came for."

He opened his hand. Five coins shone in the morning sun. "What about this?"

"I left them for you." She swallowed, no longer certain how long she could speak without showing she was breaking in two. "The treasure isn't important to me. It's yours."

"Damn generous of you." Turning over his hand, he dropped the coins into the sand. "That's how much the gold means to me, professor."

She stared at the gold on the ground in front of her. "I don't understand you."

"*You* wanted the treasure," he tossed at her. "It never mattered to me."

"But you said," she began, then shook her head. "When I first came to you, you took the job because of the treasure."

"I took the job because of you. You wanted the gold, Kate."

"It wasn't the money." Dragging a hand through her hair, she turned away. "It was never the money."

"Maybe not. It was your father."

She nodded because it was true, but it no longer hurt. "I finished what he started, and I gave myself something. I don't want any more coins, Ky."

"Why are you running away from me again?"

Slowly, she turned back. "We're four years older than we were before, but we're the same people."

"So?"

"Ky, when I went away before, it was partially because of my father, because I felt I owed him my loyalty. But if I'd thought you'd wanted me. *Me*," she repeated, placing her palm over her heart, "not what you wanted me to be. If I'd thought that, and if I'd thought you and I could make a future together, I wouldn't have gone. I wouldn't be leaving now."

"What the hell gives you the right to decide what I want, what I feel?" He whirled away from her, too furious to remain close. "Maybe I made mistakes, maybe I just assumed too much four years ago. Damn it, I paid for it, Kate, every day from the time you left until you came back. I've done everything I could to be careful this time around, not to push, not to assume. Then I wake up and find you leaving without a word."

"There aren't any words, Ky. I've always given you too many of them, and you've never given me enough."

"You're better with words than I am."

"All right, then I'll use them. I love you." She waited until he turned back to her. The restlessness was on him again. He was holding it off with sheer will. "I've always loved you, but I think I know my own limitations. Maybe I know yours too."

"No, you think too much about limitations, Kate, and not enough about possibilities. I let you walk away from me before. It's not going to be so easy this time."

"I have to be my own person, Ky. I won't live the rest of my life as I've lived it up to now."

"Who the hell wants you to?" he exploded. "Who

the hell wants you to be anything but what you are? It's about time you stopped equating love with responsibility and started looking at the other side of it. It's sharing, giving and taking and laughing. If I ask you to give part of yourself to me, I'm going to give part of myself right back."

Unable to stop himself he took her arms in his hands, just holding, as if through the contact he could make his words sink in.

"I don't want your constant devotion. I don't want you to be obliged to me. I don't want to go through life thinking that whatever you do, you do because you want to please me. Damn it, I don't want that kind of responsibility."

Without words, she stared at him. He'd never said anything to her so simply, so free of half meanings. Hope rose in her. Yet still, he was telling her only what he didn't want. Once he gave her the flip side of that coin hope could vanish.

"Tell me what you do want."

He had only one answer. "Come with me a minute." Taking her hand, he drew her toward the shed. "When I started this, it was because I'd always promised myself I would. Before long, the reasons changed." Turning the latch, he pulled the shed doors open.

For a moment, she saw nothing. Gradually, her eyes adjusted to the dimness and she stepped inside. The boat was nearly finished. The hull was sanded and sealed and painted, waiting for Ky to take it outside and attach the mast. It was lovely, clean and simple. Just looking at it, Kate could imagine the way it would flow with the wind. Free, light and clever.

"It's beautiful, Ky. I always wondered…" She broke off as she read the name printed boldly on the stern. *Second Chance*.

"That's all I want from you," Ky told her, pointing to the two words. "The boat's yours. When I started it, I thought I was building it for me. But I built it for you, because I knew it was one dream you'd share with me. I only want what's printed on it, Kate. For both of us." Speechless, she watched him lean over the starboard side and open a small compartment. He drew out a tiny box.

"I had this cleaned. You wouldn't take it from me before." Opening the lid, he revealed the diamond he'd found, sparkling now in a simple gold setting. "It didn't cost me anything and it wasn't made especially for you. It's just something I found among a bunch of rocks."

When she started to speak, he held up a hand. "Hold on. You wanted words, I haven't finished with them yet. I know you have to teach, I'm not asking you to give it up. I am asking that you give me one year here on the island. There's a school here, not Yale, but people still have to be taught. A year, Kate. If it isn't what you want after that, I'll go back with you."

Her brows drew together. "Back? To Connecticut? You'd live in Connecticut?"

"If that's what it takes."

A compromise…she thought, baffled. Was he offering to adjust his life for hers? "And if that isn't right for you?"

"Then we'll try someplace else, damn it. We'll find someplace in between. Maybe we'll move half a dozen times in the next few years. What does it matter?"

What did it matter? she wondered as she studied

him. He was offering her what she'd waited for all of her life. Love without chains.

"I want you to marry me." He wondered if that simple statement shook her as much as it did him. "Tomorrow isn't soon enough, but if you'll give me the year, I can wait."

She nearly smiled. He'd never wait. Once he had her promise of the year, he'd subtly and not so subtly work on her until she found herself at the altar. It was nearly tempting to make him go through the effort.

Limitations? Had she spoken of limitations? Love had none.

"No," she decided aloud. "You only get the year if I get the ring. And what goes with it."

"Deal." He took her hand quickly as though she might change her mind. "Once it's on, you're stuck, professor." Pulling the ring from the box he slipped it onto her finger. Swearing lightly, he shook his head. "It's too big."

"It's all right. I'll keep my hand closed for the next fifty years or so." With a laugh, she went into his arms. All doubts vanished. They'd make it, she told herself. South, north or anywhere in between.

"We'll have it sized," he murmured, nuzzling into her neck.

"Only if they can do it while it's on my finger." Kate closed her eyes. She'd just found everything. Did he know it? "Ky, about the *Liberty,* the rest of the treasure."

He tilted her face up to kiss her. "We've already found it."

* * * * *

RISKY BUSINESS

For Michael and Darlene,
good friends.

Chapter 1

"Watch your step, please. Please, watch your step. Thank you." Liz took a ticket from a sunburned man with palm trees on his shirt, then waited patiently for a woman with two bulging straw baskets to dig out another one.

"I hope you haven't lost it, Mabel. I told you to let me hold it."

"I haven't lost it," the woman said testily before she pulled out the little piece of blue cardboard.

"Thank you. Please take your seats." It was several more minutes before everyone was settled and she could take her own. "Welcome aboard the *Fantasy,* ladies and gentlemen."

With her mind on a half dozen other things, Liz began her opening monologue. She gave an absent-minded nod to the man on the dock who cast off the ropes before she started the engine. Her voice was pleasant and easy as she took another look at her watch. They were already fifteen minutes behind schedule. She gave one last scan of the beach, skimming by lounge chairs, over bodies already stretched and oiled slick, like offerings to the sun. She couldn't hold the tour any longer.

The boat swayed a bit as she backed it from the dock and took an eastern course. Though her thoughts were scattered, she made the turn from the coast expertly. She could have navigated the boat with her eyes closed. The air that ruffled around her face was soft and already warming, though the hour was early. Harmless and powder-puff white, clouds dotted the horizon. The water, churned by the engine, was as blue as the guidebooks promised. Even after ten years, Liz took none of it for granted—especially her livelihood. Part of that depended on an atmosphere that made muscles relax and problems disappear.

Behind her in the long, bullet-shaped craft were eighteen people seated on padded benches. They were already murmuring about the fish and formations they saw through the glass bottom. She doubted if any of them thought of the worries they'd left behind at home.

"We'll be passing Paraiso Reef North," Liz began in a low, flowing voice. "Diving depths range from thirty to fifty feet. Visibility is excellent, so you'll be able to see star and brain corals, sea fans and sponges, as well as schools of sergeant majors, groupers and parrot fish. The grouper isn't one of your prettier fish, but it's versatile. They're all born female and produce eggs before they change sex and become functioning males."

Liz set her course and kept the speed steady. She

went on to describe the elegantly colored angelfish, the shy, silvery smallmouth grunts, and the intriguing and dangerous sea urchin. Her clients would find the information useful when she stopped for two hours of snorkeling at Palancar Reef.

She'd made the run before, too many times to count. It might have become routine, but it was never monotonous. She felt now, as she always did, the freedom of open water, blue sky and the hum of engine with her at the controls. The boat was hers, as were three others, and the little concrete block dive shop close to shore. She'd worked for all of it, sweating through months when the bills were steep and the cash flow slight. She'd made it. Ten years of struggle had been a small price to pay for having something of her own. Turning her back on her country, leaving behind the familiar, had been a small price to pay for peace of mind.

The tiny, rustic island of Cozumel in the Mexican Caribbean promoted peace of mind. It was her home now, the only one that mattered. She was accepted there, respected. No one on the island knew of the humiliation and pain she'd gone through before she'd fled to Mexico. Liz rarely thought of it, though she had a vivid reminder.

Faith. Just the thought of her daughter made her smile. Faith was small and bright and precious, and so far away. Just six weeks, Liz thought, and she'd be home from school for the summer.

Sending her to Houston to her grandparents had been for the best, Liz reminded herself whenever the ache of loneliness became acute. Faith's education was more important than a mother's needs. Liz had worked, gambled, struggled so that Faith could have everything she was entitled to, everything she would have had if her father...

Determined, Liz set her mind on other things. She'd promised herself a decade before that she would cut Faith's father from her mind, just as he had cut her from his life. It had been a mistake, one made in naïveté and passion, one that had changed the course of her life forever. But she'd won something precious from it: Faith.

"Below, you see the wreck of a forty-passenger Convair airliner lying upside down." She slowed the boat so that her passengers could examine the wreck and the divers out for early explorations. Bubbles rose from air tanks like small silver disks. "The wreck's no tragedy," she continued. "It was sunk for a scene in a movie and provides divers with easy entertainment."

Her job was to do the same for her passengers, she reminded herself. It was simple enough when she had a mate on board. Alone, she had to captain the boat, keep up the light, informative banter, deal with snorkel equipment, serve lunch and count heads. It just hadn't been possible to wait any longer for Jerry.

She muttered to herself a bit as she increased speed. It wasn't so much that she minded the extra work, but she felt her paying customers were entitled to the best she could offer. She should have known better than to depend on him. She could have easily arranged for someone else to come along. As it was, she had two men on the dive boat and two more in the shop. Because her second dive boat was due to launch at noon, no one could be spared to mate the glass bottom on a day trip. And Jerry had come through before, she reminded herself. With him on board, the women passengers were so charmed that Liz didn't think they even noticed the watery world the boat passed over.

Who could blame them? she thought with a half smile. If she hadn't been immune to men in general, Jerry might have had her falling over her own feet. Most women had a difficult time resisting dark, cocky looks, a cleft chin and smoky gray eyes. Add to that a lean, muscular build and a glib tongue, and no female was safe.

But that hadn't been why Liz had agreed to rent him a room, or give him a part-time job. She'd needed the extra income, as well as the extra help, and she was shrewd enough to recognize an operator when she saw one. Previous experience had taught her that it made good business sense to have an operator on your side. She told herself he'd better have a good excuse for leaving her without a crew, then forgot him.

The ride, the sun, the breeze relaxed her. Liz continued to speak of the sea life below, twining facts she'd learned while studying marine biology in college with facts she'd learned firsthand in the waters of the Mexican Caribbean. Occasionally one of her passengers would ask a question or call out in excitement over something that skimmed beneath them. She answered, commented and instructed while keeping the flow light. Because three of her passengers were Mexican, she repeated all her information in Spanish. Because there were several children on board, she made certain the facts were fun.

If things had been different, she would have been a teacher. Liz had long since pushed that early dream from her mind, telling herself she was more suited to the business world. Her business world. She glanced over where the clouds floated lazily over the horizon. The sun danced white and sharp on the surface of blue water. Below, coral rose like castles or waved like fans. Yes, she'd chosen her world and had no regrets.

When a woman screamed behind her, Liz let off the throttle. Before she could turn, the scream was joined by another. Her first thought was that perhaps they'd seen one of the sharks that occasionally visited the reefs. Set to calm and soothe, Liz let the boat drift in the current. A woman was weeping in her husband's arms, another held her child's face protectively against her shoulder. The rest were staring down through the clear glass. Liz took off her sunglasses as she walked down the two steps into the cabin.

"Please try to stay calm. I promise you, there's nothing down there that can hurt you in here."

A man with a Nikon around his neck and an orange sun visor over a balding dome gave her a steady look.

"Miss, you'd better radio the police."

Liz looked down through the clear glass, through the crystal blue water. Her heart rose to her throat. She saw now why Jerry had stood her up. He was lying on the white sandy bottom with an anchor chain wrapped around his chest.

The moment the plane finished its taxi, Jonas gathered his garment bag and waited impatiently for the door to be opened. When it did, there was a whoosh of hot air and the drone of engines. With a quick nod to the flight attendant he strode down the steep metal stairs. He didn't have the time or the inclination to appreciate the palm trees, the bursts of flowers or the dreamy blue sky. He walked purposefully, eyes straight ahead and narrowed against the sun. In his dark suit and trim tie he could have been a businessman, one who'd come to Cozumel to work, not to play. Whatever grief, whatever anger he felt were carefully masked by a calm, unapproachable expression.

The terminal was small and noisy. Americans on vacation stood in groups laughing or wandered in confusion. Though he knew no Spanish, Jonas passed quickly through customs then into a small, hot alcove where men waited at podiums to rent cars and Jeeps. Fifteen minutes after landing, Jonas was backing a compact out of a parking space and heading toward town with a map stuck in the sun visor. The heat baked right through the windshield.

Twenty-four hours before, Jonas had been sitting in his large, elegantly furnished, air-conditioned office. He'd just won a long, tough case that had taken all his skill and mountains of research. His client was a free man, acquitted of a felony charge that carried a minimum sentence of ten years. He'd accepted his fee, accepted the gratitude and avoided as much publicity as possible.

Jonas had been preparing to take his first vacation in eighteen months. He'd felt satisfied, vaguely tired and optimistic. Two weeks in Paris seemed like the perfect reward for so many months of ten-hour days. Paris, with its ageless sophistication and cool parks, its stunning museums and incomparable food was precisely what suited Jonas Sharpe.

When the call had come through from Mexico, it had taken him several moments to understand. When he'd answered that he did indeed have a brother Jeremiah, Jonas's predominant thought had been that Jerry had gotten himself into trouble again, and he was going to have to bail him out.

By the time he'd hung up the phone, Jonas couldn't think at all. Numb, he'd given his secretary instructions to cancel his Paris arrangements and to make new ones for a flight to Cozumel the next day. Then Jonas had picked up the phone to call his parents and tell them their son was dead.

He'd come to Mexico to identify the body and take his brother home to bury. With a fresh wave of grief, Jonas experienced a sense of inevitability. Jerry had always lived on the edge of disaster. This time he'd stepped over. Since childhood Jerry had courted trouble—charmingly. He'd once joked that Jonas had taken to law so he could find the most efficient way to get his brother out of jams. Perhaps in a sense it had been true.

Jerry had been a dreamer. Jonas was a realist. Jerry had been unapologetically lazy, Jonas a workaholic. They were—had been—two sides of a coin. As Jonas drew up to the police station in San Miguel it was with the knowledge that part of himself had been erased.

The scene at port should have been painted. There were small fishing boats pulled up on the grass. Huge gray ships sat complacently at dock while tourists in flowered shirts or skimpy shorts strolled along the sea wall. Water lapped and scented the air.

Jonas got out of the car and walked to the police station to begin to wade through the morass of paperwork that accompanied a violent death.

Captain Moralas was a brisk, no-nonsense man who had been born on the island and was passionately dedicated to protecting it. He was approaching forty and awaiting the birth of his fifth child. He was proud of his position, his education and his family, though the order often varied. Basically, he was a quiet man who enjoyed classical music and a movie on Saturday nights.

Because San Miguel was a port, and ships brought sailors on leave, tourists on holiday, Moralas was no stranger to trouble or the darker side of human nature. He did, however, pride himself on the low percentage of violent crime on his island. The murder of the American bothered him in the way a pesky fly bothered a man sitting contentedly on his porch swing. A cop didn't have to work in a big city to recognize a professional hit. There was no room for organized crime on Cozumel.

But he was also a family man. He understood love, and he understood grief, just as he understood certain men were compelled to conceal both. In the cool, flat air of the morgue, he waited beside Jonas. The American stood a head taller, rigid and pale.

"This is your brother, Mr. Sharpe?" Though he didn't have to ask.

Jonas looked down at the other side of the coin. "Yes."

In silence, he backed away to give Jonas the time he needed.

It didn't seem possible. Jonas knew he could have stood for hours staring down at his brother's face and it would never seem possible. Jerry had always looked for the easy way, the biggest deal, and he hadn't always been an admirable man. But he'd always been so full of life. Slowly, Jonas laid his hand on his brother's. There was no life there now, and nothing he could do; no amount of maneuvering or pulling of strings would bring it back. Just as slowly he removed his hand. It didn't seem possible, but it was.

Moralas nodded to the attendant. "I'm sorry."

Jonas shook his head. Pain was like a dull-edged knife through the base of his skull. He coated it with ice. "Who killed my brother, Captain?"

"I don't know. We're investigating."

"You have leads?"

Moralas gestured and started down the corridor. "Your brother had been in Cozumel only three weeks, Mr. Sharpe. At the moment, we are interviewing everyone who had contact with him during that time." He opened a door and stepped out into the air, breathing deeply of the fresh air and the flowers. The man beside him didn't seem to notice the change. "I promise you, we will do everything possible to find your brother's killer."

The rage Jonas had controlled for so many hours bubbled toward the surface. "I don't know you." With a steady hand he drew out a cigarette, watching the captain with narrowed eyes as he lit it. "You didn't know Jerry."

"This is my island." Moralas's gaze remained locked with Jonas's. "If there's a murderer on it, I'll find him."

"A professional." Jonas blew out smoke that hung in the air with no breeze to brush it away. "We both know that, don't we?"

Moralas said nothing for a moment. He was still waiting to receive information on Jeremiah Sharpe. "Your brother was shot, Mr. Sharpe, so we're investigating to find out why, how and who. You could help me by giving me some information."

Jonas stared at the door a moment—the door that led down the stairs, down the corridor and to his brother's body. "I've got to walk," he murmured.

Moralas waited until they'd crossed the grass, then the road. For a moment, they walked near the sea wall in silence. "Why did your brother come to Cozumel?"

"I don't know." Jonas drew deeply on the cigarette until it burned into the filter. "Jerry liked palm trees."

"His business? His work?"

With a half laugh Jonas ground the smoldering filter underfoot. Sunlight danced in diamonds on the water. "Jerry liked to call himself a freelancer. He was a drifter." And he'd brought complications to Jonas's life as often as he'd brought pleasure. Jonas stared hard at the water, remembering shared lives, diverse opinions. "For Jerry, it was always the next town and the next deal. The last I heard—two weeks ago—he was giving diving lessons to tourists."

"The Black Coral Dive Shop," Moralas confirmed. "Elizabeth Palmer hired him on a part-time basis."

"Palmer." Jonas's attention shifted away from the water. "That's the woman he was living with."

"Miss Palmer rented your brother a room," Moralas corrected, abruptly proper. "She was also among the group to discover your brother's body. She's given my department her complete cooperation."

Jonas's mouth thinned. How had Jerry described this Liz Palmer in their brief phone conversation weeks before? A sexy little number who made great tortillas. She sounded like another one of Jerry's tough ladies on the lookout for a good time and the main chance. "I'll need her address." At the captain's quiet look he only raised a brow. "I assume my brother's things are still there."

"They are. I have some of your brother's personal effects, those that he had on him, in my office. You're welcome to collect them and what remains at Miss Palmer's. We've already been through them."

Jonas felt the rage build again and smothered it. "When can I take my brother home?"

"I'll do my best to complete the paperwork today. I'll need you to make a statement. Of course, there are forms." He looked at Jonas's set profile and felt a new tug of pity. "Again, I'm sorry."

He only nodded. "Let's get it done."

Liz let herself into the house. While the door slammed behind her, she flicked switches, sending two ceiling fans whirling. The sound, for the moment, was company enough. The headache she'd lived with for over twenty-four hours was a dull, nagging thud just under her right temple. Going into the bathroom, she washed down two aspirin before turning on the shower.

She'd taken the glass bottom out again. Though it was off season, she'd had to turn a dozen people away. It wasn't every day a body was found off the coast, and the curious had come in force. Morbid, she thought, then stripped and stepped under the cold spray of the shower. How long would it take, she wondered, before she stopped seeing Jerry on the sand beneath the water?

True, she'd barely known him, but he'd been fun and interesting and good company. He'd slept in her daughter's bed and eaten in her kitchen. Closing her eyes, she let the water sluice over her, willing the headache away. She'd be better, she thought, when the police finished the investigation. It had been hard, very hard, when they'd come to her house and searched through Jerry's things. And the questions.

How much had she known about Jerry Sharpe? He'd

been American, an operator, a womanizer. She'd been able to use all three to her benefit when he'd given diving lessons or acted as mate on one of her boats. She'd thought him harmless—sexy, attractive and basically lazy. He'd boasted of making it big, of wheeling a deal that would set him up in style. Liz had considered it so much hot air. As far as she was concerned, nothing set you up in style but years of hard work—or inherited wealth.

But Jerry's eyes had lit up when he'd talked of it, and his grin had been appealing. If she'd been a woman who allowed herself dreams, she would have believed him. But dreams were for the young and foolish. With a little tug of regret, she realized Jerry Sharpe had been both.

Now he was gone, and what he had left was still scattered in her daughter's room. She'd have to box it up, Liz decided as she turned off the taps. It was something, at least. She'd box up Jerry's things and ask that Captain Moralas what to do about them. Certainly his family would want whatever he'd left behind. Jerry had spoken of a brother, whom he'd affectionately referred to as "the stuffed shirt." Jerry Sharpe had been anything but stuffy.

As she walked to the bedroom, Liz wrapped her hair in the towel. She remembered the way Jerry had tried to talk his way between her sheets a few days after he'd moved in. Smooth talk, smooth hands. Though he'd had her backed into the doorway, kissing her before she'd evaded it, Liz had easily brushed him off. He'd taken her refusal good-naturedly, she recalled, and they'd remained on comfortable terms. Liz pulled on an oversized shirt that skimmed her thighs.

The truth was, Jerry Sharpe had been a good-natured, comfortable man with big dreams. She wondered, not for the first time, if his dreams had had something to do with his death.

She couldn't go on thinking about it. The best thing to do was to pack what had belonged to Jerry back into his suitcase and take it to the police.

It made her feel gruesome. She discovered that after only five minutes. Privacy, for a time, had been all but her only possession. To invade someone else's made her uneasy. Liz folded a faded brown T-shirt that boasted the wearer had hiked the Grand Canyon and tried not to think at all. But she kept seeing him there, joking about sleeping with one of Faith's collection of dolls. He'd fixed the window that had stuck and had cooked paella to celebrate his first paycheck.

Without warning, Liz felt the first tears flow. He'd been so alive, so young, so full of that cocky sense of confidence. She'd hardly had time to consider him a friend, but he'd slept in her daughter's bed and left clothes in her closet.

She wished now she'd listened to him more, been friendlier, more approachable. He'd asked her to have drinks with him and she'd brushed him off because she'd had paperwork to do. It seemed petty now, cold. If she'd given him an hour of her life, she might have learned who he was, where he'd come from, why he'd died.

When the knock at the door sounded, she pressed her hands against her cheeks. Silly to cry, she told herself, when tears never solved anything. Jerry Sharpe was gone, and it had nothing to do with her.

She brushed away the tears as she walked to the

door. The headache was easing. Liz decided it would be best if she called Moralas right away and arranged to have the clothes picked up. She was telling herself she really wasn't involved at all when she opened the door.

For a moment she could only stare. The T-shirt she hadn't been aware of still holding slipped from her fingers. She took one stumbling step back as she felt a rushing sound fill her head. Because her vision dimmed, she blinked to clear it. The man in the doorway stared back at her accusingly.

"Jer-Jerry," she managed and nearly screamed when he took a step forward.

"Elizabeth Palmer?"

She shook her head, numb and terrified. She had no superstitions. She believed in action and reaction on a purely practical level. When someone died, they couldn't come back. And yet she stood in her living room with the fans whirling and watched Jerry Sharpe step over her threshold. She heard him speak to her again.

"Are you Liz Palmer?"

"I saw you." She heard her own voice rise with nerves but couldn't take her eyes from his face. The cocky good looks, the cleft chin, the smoky eyes under thick dark brows. It was a face that appealed to a woman's need to risk, or to her dreams of risking. "Who are you?"

"Jonas Sharpe. Jerry was my brother. My twin brother."

When she discovered her knees were shaking, she sat down quickly. No, not Jerry, she told herself as her heartbeat leveled. The hair was just as dark, just as full, but it lacked Jerry's unkempt shagginess. The face was just as attractive, just as ruggedly hewn, but she'd never seen Jerry's eyes so hard, so cold. And this man wore a suit as though he'd been born in one. His stance was one of restrained passion and impatience. It took her a moment, only a moment, before anger struck.

"You did that on purpose." Because her palms were damp she rubbed them against her knees. "It was a hideous thing to do. You knew what I'd think when I opened the door."

"I needed a reaction."

She sat back and took a deep, steadying breath. "You're a bastard, Mr. Sharpe."

For the first time in hours, his mouth curved…only slightly. "May I sit down?"

She gestured to a chair. "What do you want?"

"I came to get Jerry's things. And to talk to you."

As he sat, Jonas took a long look around. His was not the polite, casual glance a stranger indulges himself in when he walks into someone else's home, but a sharp-eyed, intense study of what belonged to Liz Palmer. It was a small living area, hardly bigger than his office. While he preferred muted colors and clean lines, Liz chose bright, contrasting shades and odd knickknacks. Several Mayan masks hung on the walls, and rugs of different sizes and hues were scattered over the floor. The sunlight, fading now, came in slats through red window blinds. There was a big blue pottery vase on a woven mat on the table, but the butter-yellow flowers in it were losing their petals. The table itself didn't gleam with polish, but was covered with a thin layer of dust.

The shock that had had her stomach muscles jumping had eased. She said nothing as he looked around the room because she was looking at him. A mirror image of Jerry, she thought. And weren't mirror im-

ages something like negatives? She didn't think he'd
be fun to have around. She had a frantic need to order
him out, to pitch him out quickly and finally. Ridiculous, she told herself. He was just a man, and nothing
to her. And he had lost his brother.

"I'm sorry, Mr. Sharpe. This is a very difficult time
for you."

His gaze locked on hers so quickly that she tensed
again. She'd barely been aware of his inch-by-inch
study of her room, but she couldn't remain unmoved
by his study of her.

She wasn't what he'd expected. Her face was all angles—wide cheekbones, a long narrow nose and a chin
that came to a suggestion of a point. She wasn't beautiful, but stunning in an almost uncomfortable way. It
might have been the eyes, a deep haunted brown, that
rose a bit exotically at the outer edge. It might have
been the mouth, full and vulnerable. The shirt overwhelmed her body with its yards of material, leaving
only long, tanned legs bare. Her hands, resting on the
arms of her chair, were small, narrow and ringless.
Jonas had thought he knew his brother's taste as well
as his own. Liz Palmer didn't suit Jerry's penchant for
the loud and flamboyant, or his own for the discreet
sophisticate.

Still, Jerry had lived with her. Jonas thought grimly
that she was taking the murder of her lover very well.
"And a difficult time for you."

His long study had left her shaken. It had gone beyond natural curiosity and made her feel like a speci-
men, filed and labeled for further research. She tried
to remember that grief took different forms in different people. "Jerry was a nice man. It isn't easy to—"

"How did you meet him?"

Words of sympathy cut off, Liz straightened in her chair. She never extended friendliness where it wasn't likely to be accepted. If he wanted facts only, she'd give him facts. "He came by my shop a few weeks ago. He was interested in diving."

Jonas's brow lifted as in polite interest but his eyes remained cold. "In diving."

"I own a dive shop on the beach—rent equipment, boat rides, lessons, day trips. Jerry was looking for work. Since he knew what he was doing, I gave it to him. He crewed on the dive boat, gave some of the tourists lessons, that sort of thing."

Showing tourists how to use a regulator didn't fit with Jonas's last conversation with his brother. Jerry had talked about cooking up a big deal. Big money, big time. "He didn't buy in as your partner?"

Something came into her face—pride, disdain, amusement. Jonas couldn't be sure. "I don't take partners, Mr. Sharpe. Jerry worked for me, that's all."

"All?" The brow came up again. "He was living here."

She caught the meaning, had dealt with it from the police. Liz decided she'd answered all the questions she cared to and that she'd given Jonas Sharpe more than enough of her time. "Jerry's things are in here." Rising, she walked out of the room. Liz waited at the doorway to her daughter's room until Jonas joined her. "I was just beginning to pack his clothes. You'd probably prefer to do that yourself. Take as much time as you need."

When she started to turn away, Jonas took her arm. He wasn't looking at her, but into the room with the shelves of dolls, the pink walls and lacy curtains. And at his brother's clothes tossed negligently over the back of a painted white chair and onto a flowered spread. It hurt, Jonas discovered, all over again.

"Is this all?" It seemed so little.

"I haven't been through the drawers or the closet yet. The police have." Suddenly weary, she pulled the towel from her head. Dark blond hair, still damp, tumbled around her face and shoulders. Somehow her face seemed even more vulnerable. "I don't know anything about Jerry's personal life, his personal belongings. This is my daughter's room." She turned her head until their eyes met. "She's away at school. This is where Jerry slept." She left him alone.

Twenty minutes was all he needed. His brother had traveled light. Leaving the suitcase in the living room, Jonas walked through the house. It wasn't large. The next bedroom was dim in the early evening light, but he could see a splash of orange over a rattan bed and a desk cluttered with files and papers. It smelled lightly of spice and talcum powder. Turning away, he walked toward the back and found the kitchen. And Liz.

It was when he smelled the coffee that Jonas remembered he hadn't eaten since morning. Without turning around, Liz poured a second cup. She didn't need him to speak to know he was there. She doubted he was a man who ever had to announce his presence. "Cream?"

Jonas ran a hand through his hair. He felt as though he were walking through someone else's dream. "No, black."

When Liz turned to offer the cup, he saw the quick jolt. "I'm sorry," she murmured, taking up her own cup. "You look so much like him."

"Does that bother you?"

"It unnerves me."

He sipped the coffee, finding it cleared some of the mists of unreality. "You weren't in love with Jerry."

Liz sent him a look of mild surprise. She realized he'd thought she'd been his brother's lover, but she hadn't thought he'd have taken the next step. "I only knew him a few weeks." Then she laughed, remembering another time, another life. "No, I wasn't in love with him. We had a business relationship, but I liked him. He was cocky and well aware of his own charms. I had a lot of repeat female customers over the past couple of weeks. Jerry was quite an operator," she murmured, then looked up, horrified. "I'm sorry."

"No." Interested, Jonas stepped closer. She was a tall woman, so their eyes stayed level easily. She smelled of the talcum powder and wore no cosmetics. Not Jerry's type, he thought again. But there was something about the eyes. "That's what he was, only most people never caught on."

"I've known others." And her voice was flat. "Not so harmless, not so kind. Your brother was a nice man, Mr. Sharpe. And I hope whoever… I hope they're found."

She watched the gray eyes ice over. The little tremor in her stomach reminded her that cold was often more dangerous than heat. "They will be. I may need to talk with you again."

It seemed a simple enough request, but she backed away from it. She didn't want to talk to him again, she didn't want to be involved in any way. "There's nothing else I can tell you."

"Jerry was living in your house, working for you."

"I don't know anything." Her voice rose as she spun away to stare out the window. She was tired of the questions, tired of people pointing her out on the beach as the woman who'd found the body. She was tired of having her life turned upside down by the death of a man she had hardly known. And she was nervous, she admitted, because Jonas Sharpe struck her as a man who could keep her life turned upside down as long as it suited him. "I've talked to the police again and again. He worked for me. I saw him a few hours out of the day. I don't know where he went at night, who he saw, what he did. It wasn't my business as long as he paid for the room and showed up to work." When she looked back, her face was set. "I'm sorry for your brother, I'm sorry for you. But it's not my business."

He saw the nerves as her hands unclenched but interpreted them in his own way. "We disagree, Mrs. Palmer."

"Miss Palmer," she said deliberately, and watched his slow, acknowledging nod. "I can't help you."

"You don't know that until we talk."

"All right. I won't help you."

He inclined his head and reached for his wallet. "Did Jerry owe you anything on the room?"

She felt the insult like a slap. Her eyes, usually soft, usually sad, blazed. "He owed me nothing, and neither do you. If you've finished your coffee…"

Jonas set the cup on the table. "I've finished. For now." He gave her a final study. Not Jerry's type, he thought again, or his. But she had to know something. If he had to use her to find out, he would. "Good night."

Liz stayed where she was until the sound of the front door closing echoed back at her. Then she shut her eyes. None of her business, she reminded herself. But she could still see Jerry under her boat. And now, she could see Jonas Sharpe with grief hard in his eyes.

Chapter 2

Liz considered working in the dive shop the next thing to taking a day off. Taking a day off, actually staying away from the shop and the boats, was a luxury she allowed herself rarely, and only when Faith was home on holiday. Today, she'd indulged herself by sending the boats out without her so that she could manage the shop alone. Be alone. By noon, all the serious divers had already rented their tanks so that business at the shop would be sporadic. It gave Liz a chance to spend a few hours checking equipment and listing inventory.

The shop was a basic cinder-block unit. Now and again, she toyed with the idea of having the outside painted, but could never justify the extra expense. There was a cubbyhole she wryly referred to as an office, where she'd crammed an old gray steel desk and one swivel chair. The rest of the room was crowded with equipment that lined the floor, was stacked on shelves or hung from hooks. Her desk had a dent in it the size of a man's foot, but her equipment was top grade and flawless.

Masks, flippers, tanks, snorkels could be rented individually or in any number of combinations. Liz had learned that the wider the choice, the easier it was to move items out and draw the customer back. The equipment was the backbone of her business. Prominent next to the wide square opening that was only closed at night with a heavy wooden shutter was a list, in English and Spanish, of her equipment, her services and the price.

When she'd started eight years before, Liz had stocked enough tanks and gear to outfit twelve divers. It had taken every penny she'd saved—every penny Marcus had given a young, dewy-eyed girl pregnant with his child. The girl had become a woman quickly, and that woman now had a business that could accommodate fifty divers from the skin out, dozens of snorkelers, underwater photographers, tourists who wanted an easy day on the water or gung-ho deep-sea fishermen.

The first boat she'd gambled on, a dive boat, had been christened *Faith,* for her daughter. She'd made a vow when she'd been eighteen, alone and frightened, that the child she carried would have the best. Ten years later, Liz could look around her shop and know she'd kept her promise.

More, the island she'd fled to for escape had become home. She was settled there, respected, depended on. She no longer looked over the expanses of white sand, blue water, longing for Houston or a pretty house with a flowing green lawn. She no longer looked back at the education she'd barely begun, or what she might have been. She'd stopped pining for a man who didn't want her or the child they'd made. She'd never go back. But Faith could. Faith could learn how to speak French, wear silk dresses and discuss wine and music. One day Faith would go back and mingle unknowingly with her cousins on their own level.

That was her dream, Liz thought as she carefully filled tanks. To see her daughter accepted as easily as she herself had been rejected. Not for revenge, Liz mused, but for justice.

"Howdy there, missy."

Crouched near the back wall, Liz turned and squinted against the sun. She saw a portly figure stuffed into a black-and-red wet suit, topped by a chubby face with a fat cigar stuck in the mouth.

"Mr. Ambuckle. I didn't know you were still on the island."

"Scooted over to Cancun for a few days. Diving's better here."

With a smile, she rose to go to her side of the opening. Ambuckle was a steady client who came to Cozumel two or three times a year and always rented plenty of tanks. "I could've told you that. See any of the ruins?"

"Wife dragged me to Tulum." He shrugged and grinned at her with popping blue eyes. "Rather be thirty feet down than climbing over rocks all day. Did get some snorkeling in. But a man doesn't fly all the way from Dallas just to paddle around. Thought I'd do some night diving."

Her smile came easily, adding something soft and

approachable to eyes that were usually wary. "Fix you right up. How much longer are you staying?" she asked as she checked an underwater flash.

"Two more weeks. Man's got to get away from his desk."

"Absolutely." Liz had often been grateful so many people from Texas, Louisiana and Florida felt the need to get away.

"Heard you had some excitement while we were on the other side."

Liz supposed she should be used to the comment by now, but a shiver ran up her spine. The smile faded, leaving her face remote. "You mean the American who was murdered?"

"Put the wife in a spin. Almost couldn't talk her into coming back over. Did you know him?"

No, she thought, not as well as she should have. To keep her hands busy, she reached for a rental form and began to fill it out. "As a matter of fact, he worked here a little while."

"You don't say?" Ambuckle's small blue eyes sparkled a bit. But Liz supposed she should be used to that, as well.

"You might remember him. He crewed the dive boat the last time you and your wife went out."

"No kidding?" Ambuckle's brow creased as he chewed on the cigar. "Not that good-looking young man—Johnny, Jerry," he remembered. "Had the wife in stitches."

"Yes, that was him."

"Shame," Ambuckle murmured, but looked rather pleased to have known the victim. "Had a lot of zip."

"Yes, I thought so, too." Liz lugged the tanks

through the door and set them on the stoop. "That should take care of it, Mr. Ambuckle."

"Add a camera on, missy. Want to get me a picture of one of those squids. Ugly things."

Amazed, Liz plucked one from the shelf and added it to the list on a printed form. She checked her watch, noted down the time and turned the form for Ambuckle's signature. After signing, he handed her bills for the deposit. She appreciated the fact that Ambuckle always paid in cash, American. "Thanks. Glad to see you back, Mr. Ambuckle."

"Can't keep me away, missy." With a whoosh and a grunt, he hefted the tanks on his shoulders. Liz watched him cross to the walkway before she filed the receipt. Unlocking her cash box, she stored the money.

"Business is good."

She jolted at the voice and looking up again stared at Jonas Sharpe.

She'd never again mistake him for Jerry, though his eyes were almost hidden this time with tinted glasses, and he wore shorts and an open shirt in lieu of a suit. There was a long gold chain around his neck with a small coin dangling. She recalled Jerry had worn one. But something in the way Jonas stood, something in the set of his mouth made him look taller and tougher than the man she'd known.

Because she didn't believe in polite fencing, Liz finished relocking the cash box and began to check the straps and fasteners on a shelf of masks. No faulty equipment went out of her shop. "I didn't expect to see you again."

"You should have." Jonas watched her move down the shelf. She seemed stronger, less vulnerable than she had when he'd seen her a week ago. Her eyes were cool, her voice remote. It made it easier to do what he'd come for. "You have quite a reputation on the island."

She paused long enough to look over her shoulder. "Really?"

"I checked," he said easily. "You've lived here for ten years. Built this place from the first brick and have one of the most successful businesses on the island."

She examined the mask in her hand meticulously. "Are you interested in renting some equipment, Mr. Sharpe? I can recommend the snorkeling right off this reef."

"Maybe. But I think I'd prefer to scuba."

"Fine. I can give you whatever you need." She set the mask down and chose another. "It isn't necessary to be certified to dive in Mexico; however, I'd recommend a few basic lessons before you go down. We offer two different courses—individual or group."

He smiled at her for the first time, a slow, appealing curving of lips that softened the toughness around his mouth. "I might take you up on that. Meantime, when do you close?"

"When I'm ready to." The smile made a difference, she realized, and she couldn't let it. In defense, she shifted her weight on one hip and sent him a look of mild insolence. "This is Cozumel, Mr. Sharpe. We don't run nine to five here. Unless you want to rent some equipment or sign up for a tour, you'll have to excuse me."

He reached in to close his hand over hers. "I didn't come back to tour. Have dinner with me tonight. We can talk."

She didn't attempt to free her hand but stared at him.

Running a business had taught her to be scrupulously polite in any circumstances. "No, thank you."

"Drinks, then."

"No."

"Miss Palmer…" Normally, Jonas was known for his deadly, interminable patience. It was a weapon, he'd learned, in the courtroom and out of it. With Liz, he found it difficult to wield it. "I don't have a great deal to go on at this point, and the police haven't made any progress at all. I need your help."

This time Liz did pull away. She wouldn't be sucked in, that she promised herself, not by quiet words or intense eyes. She had her life to lead, a business to run and, most important, a daughter coming home in a matter of weeks. "I won't get involved. I'm sorry, even if I wanted to, there'd be nothing I could do to help."

"Then it won't hurt to talk to me."

"Mr. Sharpe." Liz wasn't known for her patience. "I have very little free time. Running this business isn't a whim or a lark, but a great deal of work. If I have a couple of hours to myself in the evening, I'm not going to spend them being grilled by you. Now—"

She started to brush him off again when a young boy came running up to the window. He was dressed in a bathing suit and slick with suntan lotion. With a twenty-dollar bill crumpled in his hand, he babbled a request for snorkeling equipment for himself and his brother. He spoke in quick, excited Spanish as Liz checked out the equipment, asking if she thought they'd see a shark.

She answered him in all seriousness as she exchanged money for equipment. "Sharks don't live in the reef, but they do visit now and again." She saw the light of adventure in his eyes. "You'll see parrot fish." She held her hands apart to show him how big. "And if you take some bread crumbs or crackers, the sergeant majors will follow you, lots of them, close enough to touch."

"Will they bite?"

She grinned. "Only the bread crumbs. Adios."

He dashed away, kicking up sand.

"You speak Spanish like a native," Jonas observed, and thought it might come in handy. He'd also noticed the pleasure that had come into her eyes when she'd talked with the boy. There'd been nothing remote then, nothing sad or haunted. Strange, he mused, he'd never noticed just how much a barometer of feeling the eyes could be.

"I live here," she said simply. "Now, Mr. Sharpe—"

"How many boats?"

"What?"

"How many do you have?"

She sucked in a deep breath and decided she could humor him for another five minutes. "I have four. The glass bottom, two dive boats and one for deep-sea fishing."

"Deep-sea fishing." That was the one, Jonas decided. A fishing boat would be private and isolated. "I haven't done any in five or six years. Tomorrow." He reached in his wallet. "How much?"

"It's fifty dollars a person a day, but I don't take the boat out for one man, Mr. Sharpe." She gave him an easy smile. "It doesn't make good business sense."

"What's your minimum?"

"Three. And I'm afraid I don't have anyone else lined up. So—"

He set four fifty-dollar bills on the counter. "The extra fifty's to make sure you're driving the boat." Liz looked down at the money. An extra two hundred would help buy the aqua bikes she'd been thinking about. Several of the other dive shops already had them and she kept a constant eye on competition. Aqua biking and wind surfing were becoming increasingly popular, and if she wanted to keep up... She looked back at Jonas Sharpe's dark, determined eyes and decided it wasn't worth it.

"My schedule for tomorrow's already set. I'm afraid I—"

"It doesn't make good business sense to turn down a profit, Miss Palmer." When she only moved her shoulders, he smiled again, but this time it wasn't so pleasant. "I'd hate to mention at the hotel that I couldn't get satisfaction at The Black Coral. It's funny how word of mouth can help or damage a small business."

Liz picked up the money, one bill at a time. "What business are you in, Mr. Sharpe?"

"Law."

She made a sound that might have been a laugh as she pulled out a form. "I should've guessed. I knew someone studying law once." She thought of Marcus with his glib, calculating tongue. "He always got what he wanted, too. Sign here. We leave at eight," she said briskly. "The price includes a lunch on board. If you want beer or liquor, you bring your own. The sun's pretty intense on the water, so you'd better buy some sunscreen." She glanced beyond him. "One of my dive boats is coming back. You'll have to excuse me."

"Miss Palmer..." He wasn't sure what he wanted to say to her, or why he was uncomfortable having completed a successful maneuver. In the end, he pocketed his receipt. "If you change your mind about dinner—"

"I won't."

"I'm at the El Presidente."

"An excellent choice." She walked through the doorway and onto the dock to wait for her crew and clients.

By seven-fifteen, the sun was up and already burning off a low ground mist. What clouds there were, were thin and shaggy and good-natured.

"Damn!" Liz kicked the starter on her motorbike and turned in a little U toward the street. She'd been hoping for rain.

He was going to try to get her involved. Even now, Liz could imagine those dark, patient gray eyes staring into hers, hear the quietly insistent voice. Jonas Sharpe was the kind of man who took no for an answer but was dogged enough to wait however long it took for the yes. Under other circumstances, she'd have admired that. Being stubborn had helped her start and succeed in a business when so many people had shaken their heads and warned her against it. But she couldn't afford to admire Jonas Sharpe. Budgeting her feelings was every bit as important as budgeting her accounts.

She couldn't help him, Liz thought again, as the soft air began to play around her face. Everything she'd known about Jerry had been said at least twice. Of course she was sorry, and had grieved a bit herself for a man she'd hardly known, but murder was a police matter. Jonas Sharpe was out of his element.

She was in hers, Liz thought as her muscles began to relax with the ride. The street was bumpy, patched in a good many places. She knew when to weave and sway. There were houses along the street with deep green grass and trailing vines. Already clothes were waving out on lines. She could hear an early newscast buzzing through someone's open window and the sound of children finishing chores or breakfast before school. She turned a corner and kept her speed steady.

There were a few shops here, closed up tight. At the door of a market, Señor Pessado fumbled with his keys. Liz tooted her horn and exchanged waves. A cab passed her, speeding down the road to the airport to wait for the early arrivals. In a matter of moments, Liz caught the first scent of the sea. It was always fresh. As she took the last turn, she glanced idly in her rearview mirror. Odd, she thought—hadn't she seen that little blue car yesterday? But when she swung into the hotel's parking lot, it chugged past.

Liz's arrangement with the hotel had been of mutual benefit. Her shop bordered the hotel's beach and encouraged business on both sides. Still, whenever she went inside, as she did today to collect the lunch for the fishing trip, she always remembered the two years she'd spent scrubbing floors and making beds.

"Buenos días, Margarita."

The young woman with a bucket and mop started to smile. *"Buenos días,* Liz. *¿Cómo està?"*

"Bien. How's Ricardo?"

"Growing out of his pants." Margarita pushed the button of the service elevator as they spoke of her son. "Faith comes home soon. He'll be glad."

"So will I." They parted, but Liz remembered the months they'd worked together, changing linen, hauling towels, washing floors. Margarita had been a friend, like so many others she'd met on the island who'd shown kindness to a young woman who'd carried a child but had no wedding ring.

She could have lied. Even at eighteen Liz had been aware she could have bought a ten-dollar gold band and had an easy story of divorce or widowhood. She'd been too stubborn. The baby that had been growing inside her belonged to her. Only to her. She'd feel no shame and tell no lies.

By seven forty-five, she was crossing the beach to her shop, lugging a large cooler packed with two lunches and a smaller one filled with bait. She could already see a few tubes bobbing on the water's surface. The water would be warm and clear and uncrowded. She'd like to have had an hour for snorkeling herself.

"Liz!" The trim, small-statured man who walked toward her was shaking his head. There was a faint, pencil-thin mustache above his lip and a smile in his dark eyes. "You're too skinny to carry that thing."

She caught her breath and studied him up and down. He wore nothing but a skimpy pair of snug trunks. She knew he enjoyed the frank or surreptitious stares of women on the beach. "So're you, Luis. But don't let me stop you."

"So you take the fishing boat today?" He hefted the larger cooler and walked with her toward the shop. "I changed the schedule for you. Thirteen signed up for the glass bottom for the morning. We got both dive boats going out, so I told my cousin Miguel to help fill in today. Okay?"

"Terrific." Luis was young, fickle with women and fond of his tequila, but he could be counted on in a pinch. "I guess I'm going to have to hire someone on, at least part-time."

Luis looked at her, then at the ground. He'd worked closest with Jerry. "Miguel, he's not dependable. Here one day, gone the next. I got a nephew, a good boy. But he can't work until he's out of school."

"I'll keep that in mind," Liz said absently. "Let's just put this right on the boat. I want to check the gear."

On board, Liz went through a routine check on the tackle and line. As she looked over the big reels and massive rods, she wondered, with a little smirk, if the lawyer had ever done any big-game fishing. Probably wouldn't know a tuna if it jumped up and bit his toe, she decided.

The decks were clean, the equipment organized, as she insisted. Luis had been with her the longest, but anyone who worked for Liz understood the hard and fast rule about giving the clients the efficiency they paid for.

The boat was small by serious sport fishing standards, but her clients rarely went away dissatisfied. She knew the waters all along the Yucatan Peninsula and the habits of the game that teemed below the surface. Her boat might not have sonar and fish finders and complicated equipment, but she determined to give Jonas Sharpe the ride of his life. She'd keep him so busy, strapped in a fighting chair, that he wouldn't have time to bother her. By the time they docked again, his arms would ache, his back would hurt and the only thing he'd be interested in would be a hot bath and bed. And if he wasn't a complete fool, she'd see to it that he had a trophy to take back to wherever he'd come from.

Just where was that? she wondered as she checked the gauges on the bridge. She'd never thought to ask Jerry. It hadn't seemed important. Yet now she found herself wondering where Jonas came from, what kind of life he led there. Was he the type who frequented elegant restaurants with an equally elegant woman on his arm? Did he watch foreign films and play bridge? Or did he prefer noisy clubs and hot jazz? She hadn't been able to find his slot as easily as she did with most people she met, so she wondered, perhaps too much. Not my business, she reminded herself and turned to call to Luis.

"I'll take care of everything here. Go ahead and open the shop. The glass bottom should be ready to leave in half an hour."

But he wasn't listening. Standing on the deck, he stared back at the narrow dock. She saw him raise a shaky hand to cross himself. *"Madre de Dios."*

"Luis?" She came down the short flight of stairs to join him. "What—"

Then she saw Jonas, a straw hat covering his head, sunglasses shading his eyes. He hadn't bothered to shave, so that the light growth of beard gave him a lazy, vagrant look accented by a faded T-shirt and brief black trunks. He didn't, she realized, look like a man who'd play bridge. Knowing what was going through Luis's mind, Liz shook his arm and spoke quickly.

"It's his brother, Luis. I told you they were twins."

"Back from the dead," Luis whispered.

"Don't be ridiculous." She shook off the shudder his words brought her. "His name is Jonas and he's nothing like Jerry at all, really. You'll see when you talk to him. You're prompt, Mr. Sharpe," she called out, hoping to jolt Luis out of his shock. "Need help coming aboard?"

"I can manage." Hefting a small cooler, Jonas stepped lightly on deck. "The *Expatriate.*" He referred to the careful lettering on the side of the boat. "Is that what you are?"

"Apparently." It was something she was neither proud nor ashamed of. "This is Luis—he works for me. You gave him a jolt just now."

"Sorry." Jonas glanced at the slim man hovering by Liz's side. There was sweat beading on his lip. "You knew my brother?"

"We worked together," Luis answered in his slow, precise English. "With the divers. Jerry, he liked best to take out the dive boat. I'll cast off." Giving Jonas a wide berth, Luis jumped onto the dock.

"I seem to affect everyone the same way," Jonas observed. "How about you?" He turned dark, direct eyes to her. Though he no longer made her think of Jerry, he unnerved her just the same. "Still want to keep me at arm's length?"

"We pride ourselves in being friendly to all our clients. You've hired the *Expatriate* for the day, Mr. Sharpe. Make yourself comfortable." She gestured toward a deck chair before climbing the steps to the bridge and calling out to Luis. "Tell Miguel he gets paid only if he finishes out the day." With a final wave to Luis, she started the engine, then cruised sedately toward the open sea.

The wind was calm, barely stirring the water. Liz could see the dark patches that meant reefs and kept the speed easy. Once they were in deeper water, she'd open it up a bit. By midday the sun would be stunningly hot. She wanted Jonas strapped in his chair and fighting two hundred pounds of fish by then.

"You handle a wheel as smoothly as you do a customer."

A shadow of annoyance moved in her eyes, but she kept them straight ahead. "It's my business. You'd be more comfortable on the deck in a chair, Mr. Sharpe."

"Jonas. And I'm perfectly comfortable here." He gave her a casual study as he stood beside her. She wore a fielder's cap over her hair with white lettering promoting her shop. On her T-shirt, the same lettering was faded from the sun and frequent washings. He wondered, idly, what she wore under it. "How long have you had this boat?"

"Almost eight years. She's sound." Liz pushed the throttle forward. "The waters are warm, so you'll find tuna, marlin, swordfish. Once we're out you can start chumming."

"Chumming?"

She sent him a quick look. So she'd been right—he didn't know a line from a pole. "Bait the water," she began. "I'll keep the speed slow and you bait the water, attract the fish."

"Seems like taking unfair advantage. Isn't fishing supposed to be luck and skill?"

"For some people it's a matter of whether they'll eat or not." She turned the wheel a fraction, scanning the water for unwary snorkelers. "For others, it's a matter of another trophy for the wall."

"I'm not interested in trophies."

She shifted to face him. No, he wouldn't be, she decided, not in trophies or in anything else without a purpose. "What are you interested in?"

"At the moment, you." He put his hand over hers and let off the throttle. "I'm in no hurry."

"You paid to fish." She flexed her hand under his.

"I paid for your time," he corrected.

He was close enough that she could see his eyes beyond the tinted lenses. They were steady, always steady, as if he knew he could afford to wait. The hand still over hers wasn't smooth as she'd expected, but hard and worked. No, he wouldn't play bridge, she thought again. Tennis, perhaps, or hand ball, or something else that took sweat and effort. For the first time in years she felt a quick thrill race through her—a thrill she'd been certain she was immune to. The wind tossed the hair back from her face as she studied him.

"Then you wasted your money."

Her hand moved under his again. Strong, he thought, though her looks were fragile. Stubborn. He could judge that by the way the slightly pointed chin stayed up. But there was a look in her eyes that said *I've been hurt, I won't be hurt again.* That alone was intriguing, but added to it was a quietly simmering sexuality that left him wondering how it was his brother hadn't been her lover. Not, Jonas was sure, for lack of trying.

"If I've wasted my money, it won't be the first time. But somehow I don't think I have."

"There's nothing I can tell you." Her hand jerked and pushed the throttle up again.

"Maybe not. Or maybe there's something you know without realizing it. I've dealt in criminal law for over ten years. You'd be surprised how important small bits of information can be. Talk to me." His hand tightened briefly on hers. "Please."

She thought she'd hardened her heart, but she could feel herself weakening. Why was it she could haggle for hours over the price of scuba gear and could never refuse a softly spoken request? He was going to cause her nothing but trouble. Because she already knew it, she sighed.

"We'll talk." She cut the throttle so the boat would drift. "While you fish." She managed to smile a bit as she stepped away. "No chum."

With easy efficiency, Liz secured the butt of a rod into the socket attached to a chair. "For now, you sit and relax," she told him. "Sometimes a fish is hot enough to take the hook without bait. If you get one, you strap yourself in and work."

Jonas settled himself in the chair and tipped back his hat. "And you?"

"I go back to the wheel and keep the speed steady so we tire him out without losing him." She gathered her hair in one hand and tossed it back. "There're better spots than this, but I'm not wasting my gas when you don't care whether you catch a fish or not."

His lips twitched as he leaned back in the chair. "Sensible. I thought you would be."

"Have to be."

"Why did you come to Cozumel?" Jonas ignored the rod in front of him and took out a cigarette.

"You've been here for a few days," she countered. "You shouldn't have to ask."

"Parts of your own country are beautiful. If you've been here ten years, you'd have been a child when you left the States."

"No, I wasn't a child." Something in the way she said it had him watching her again, looking for the secret she held just beyond her eyes. "I came because it seemed like the right thing to do. It was the right thing. When I was a girl, my parents would come here almost every year. They love to dive."

"You moved here with your parents?"

"No, I came alone." This time her voice was flat. "You didn't pay two hundred dollars to talk about me, Mr. Sharpe."

"It helps to have some background. You said you had a daughter. Where is she?"

"She goes to school in Houston—that's where my parents live."

Toss a child, and the responsibility, onto grandparents and live on a tropical island. It might leave a bad taste in his mouth, but it wasn't something that would surprise him. Jonas took a deep drag as he studied Liz's profile. It just didn't fit. "You miss her."

"Horribly," Liz murmured. "She'll be home in a few weeks, and we'll spend the summer together. September always comes too soon." Her gaze drifted off as she spoke, almost to herself. "It's for the best. My parents take wonderful care of her and she's getting an excellent education—taking piano lessons and ballet. They sent me pictures from a recital, and..." Her eyes filled with tears so quickly that she hadn't any warning. She shifted into the wind and fought them back, but he'd seen them. He sat smoking silently to give her time to recover.

"Ever get back to the States?"

"No." Liz swallowed and called herself a fool. It had been the pictures, she told herself, the pictures that had come in yesterday's mail of her little girl wearing a pink dress.

"Hiding from something?"

She whirled back, tears replaced with fury. Her body was arched like a bow ready to launch. Jonas held up a hand.

"Sorry. I have a habit of poking into secrets."

She forced herself to relax, to strap back passion as she'd taught herself so long ago. "It's a good way to lose your fingers, Mr. Sharpe."

He chuckled. "That's a possibility. I've always considered it worth the risk. They call you Liz, don't they?"

Her brow lifted under the fringe that blew around her brow. "My friends do."

"It suits you, except when you try to be aloof. Then it should be Elizabeth."

She sent him a smoldering look, certain he was trying to annoy her. "No one calls me Elizabeth."

He merely grinned at her. "Why weren't you sleeping with Jerry?"

"I beg your pardon?"

"Yes, definitely Elizabeth. You're a beautiful woman in an odd sort of way." He tossed out the compliment as casually as he tossed the cigarette into the water. "Jerry had a…fondness for beautiful women. I can't figure out why you weren't lovers."

For a moment, only a moment, it occurred to her that no one had called her beautiful in a very long time. She'd needed words like that once. Then she leaned back on the rail, planted her hands and aimed a killing look. She didn't need them now.

"I didn't choose to sleep with him. It might be difficult for you to accept, as you share the same face, but I didn't find Jerry irresistible."

"No?" As relaxed as she was tensed, Jonas reached into the cooler, offering her a beer. When she shook her head, he popped the top on one for himself. "What did you find him?"

"He was a drifter, and he happened to drift into my

life. I gave him a job because he had a quick mind and a strong back. The truth was, I never expected him to last over a month. Men like him don't."

Though he hadn't moved a muscle, Jonas had come to attention. "Men like him?"

"Men who look for the quickest way to easy street. He worked because he liked to eat, but he was always looking for the big strike—one he wouldn't have to sweat for."

"So you did know him," Jonas murmured. "What was he looking for here?"

"I tell you I don't know! For all I know he was looking for a good time and a little sun." Frustration poured out of her as she tossed a hand in the air. "I let him have a room because he seemed harmless and I could use the money. I wasn't intimate with him on any level. The closest he came to talking about what he was up to was bragging about diving for big bucks."

"Diving? Where?"

Fighting for control, she dragged a hand through her hair. "I wish you'd leave me alone."

"You're a realistic woman, aren't you, Elizabeth?"

Her chin was set when she looked back at him. "Yes."

"Then you know I won't. Where was he going to dive?"

"I don't know. I barely listened to him when he got started on how rich he was going to be."

"What did he say?" This time Jonas's voice was quiet, persuading. "Just try to think back and remember what he told you."

"He said something about making a fortune diving, and I joked about sunken treasure. And he said…" She strained to remember the conversation. It had been late in the evening, and she'd been busy, preoccupied. "I was working at home," Liz remembered. "I always seem to handle the books better at night. He'd been out, partying I thought, because he was a little unsteady when he came in. He pulled me out of the chair. I remember I started to swear at him but he looked so damn happy, I let it go. Really, I hardly listened because I was picking up all the papers he'd scattered, but he was saying something about the big time and buying champagne to celebrate. I told him he'd better stick to beer on his salary. That's when he talked about deals coming through and diving for big bucks. Then I made some comment about sunken treasure…"

"And what did he say?"

"Sometimes you make more putting stuff in than taking it out." With a line between her brows, she remembered how he'd laughed when she'd told him to go sleep it off. "He made a pass neither one of us took seriously, and then…I think he made a phone call. I went back to work."

"When was this?"

"A week, maybe one week after I took him on."

"That must have been when he called me." Jonas looked out to sea. And he hadn't paid much attention, either, he reminded himself. Jerry had talked about coming home in style. But then he had always been talking about coming home in style. And the call, as usual, had been collect.

"Did you ever see him with anyone? Talking, arguing?"

"I never saw him argue with anyone. He flirted with the women on the beach, made small talk with the clients and got along just fine with everyone he worked with. I assumed he spent most of his free time in San Miguel. I think he cruised a few bars with Luis and some of the others."

"What bars?"

"You'll have to ask them, though I'm sure the police already have." She took a deep breath. It was bringing it all back again, too close. "Mr. Sharpe, why don't you let the police handle this? You're running after shadows."

"He was my brother." And more, what he couldn't explain, his twin. Part of himself had been murdered. If he were ever to feel whole again, he had to know why. "Haven't you wondered why Jerry was murdered?"

"Of course." She looked down at her hands. They were empty and she felt helpless. "I thought he must've gotten into a fight, or maybe he bragged to the wrong person. He had a bad habit of tossing what money he had around."

"It wasn't robbery or a mugging, Elizabeth. It was professional. It was business."

Her heart began a slow, painful thud. "I don't understand."

"Jerry was murdered by a pro, and I'm going to find out why."

Because her throat was suddenly dry, she swallowed. "If you're right, then that's all the more reason to leave it to the police."

He drew out his cigarettes again, but stared ahead to where the sky met the water. "Police don't want revenge. I do." In his voice, she heard the calm patience and felt a shiver.

Staring, she shook her head. "Even if you found the person who did it, what could you do?"

He took a long pull from his beer. "As a lawyer, I suppose I'd be obliged to see they had their day in court. As a brother..." He trailed off and drank again. "We'll have to see."

"I don't think you're a very nice man, Mr. Sharpe."

"I'm not." He turned his head until his eyes locked on hers. "And I'm not harmless. Remember, if I make a pass, we'll both take it seriously."

She started to speak, then saw his line go taut. "You've got a fish, Mr. Sharpe," she said dryly. "You'd better strap in or he'll pull you overboard."

Turning on her heel, she went back to the bridge, leaving Jonas to fend for himself.

Chapter 3

It was sundown when Liz parked her bike under the lean-to beside her house. She was still laughing. However much trouble Jonas had caused her, however much he had annoyed her in three brief meetings, she had his two hundred dollars. And he had a thirty-pound marlin—whether he wanted it or not. *We deliver,* she thought as she jingled her keys.

Oh, it had been worth it, just to see his face when he'd found himself on the other end of the wire from a big, bad-tempered fish. Liz believed he'd have let it go if she hadn't taken the time for one last smirk. Stubborn, she thought again. Yes, any other time she'd have admired it, and him.

Though she'd been wrong about his not being able to handle a rod, he'd looked so utterly perplexed with the fish lying at his feet on the deck that she'd nearly felt sorry for him. But his luck, or the lack of it, had helped her make an easy exit once they'd docked. With all the people crowding around to get a look at his catch and congratulate him, Jonas hadn't been able to detain her.

Now she was ready for an early evening, she thought. And a rainy one if the clouds moving in from the east delivered. Liz let herself into the house, propping the door open to bring in the breeze that already tasted of rain. After the fans were whirling, she turned on the radio automatically. Hurricane season might be a few months off, but the quick tropical storms were unpredictable. She'd been through enough of them not to take them lightly.

In the bedroom she prepared to strip for the shower that would wash the day's sweat and salt from her skin. Because it was twilight, she was already reaching for the light switch when a stray thought stopped her. Hadn't she left the blinds up that morning? Liz stared at them, tugged snugly over the windowsill. Odd, she was sure she'd left them up, and why wasn't the cord wrapped around its little hook? She was fanatical about that kind of detail, she supposed because ropes on a boat were always secured.

She hesitated, even after light spilled into the room. Then she shrugged. She must have been more distracted that morning than she'd realized. Jonas Sharpe, she decided, was taking up too much of her time, and too many of her thoughts. A man like him was bound to do so, even under different circumstances. But she'd long since passed the point in her life where a man could dominate it. He only worried her because he was interfering in her time, and her time was a precious commodity. Now that he'd had his way, and his talk, there should be no more visits. She remembered, uncomfortably, the way he'd smiled at her. It would be best, she decided, if he went back to where he'd come from and she got on with her own routine.

To satisfy herself, Liz walked over to the first shade and secured the cord. From the other room, the radio announced an evening shower before music kicked in. Humming along with it, she decided to toss together a chicken salad before she logged the day's accounts.

As she straightened, the breath was knocked out of her by an arm closing tightly around her neck. The dying sun caught a flash of silver. Before she could react, she felt the quick prick of a knife blade at her throat.

"Where is it?"

The voice that hissed in her ear was Spanish. In reflex, she brought her hands to the arm around her neck. As her nails dug in, she felt hard flesh and a thin metal band. She gasped for air, but stopped struggling when the knife poked threateningly at her throat.

"What do you want?" In terror her mind skimmed forward. She had less than fifty dollars cash and no jewelry of value except a single strand of pearls left by her grandmother. "My purse is in on the table. You can take it."

The vicious yank on her hair had her gasping in pain. "Where did he put it?"

"Who? I don't know what you want."

"Sharpe. Deal's off, lady. If you want to live, you tell me where he put the money."

"I don't know." The knife point pricked the vulnerable skin at her throat. She felt something warm trickle down her skin. Hysteria bubbled up behind it. "I never saw any money. You can look—there's nothing here."

"I've already looked." He tightened his hold until her vision grayed from lack of air. "Sharpe died fast. You won't be so lucky. Tell me where it is and nothing happens."

He was going to kill her. The thought ran in her head. She was going to die for something she knew nothing about. Money…he wanted money and she only had fifty dollars. Faith. As she felt herself on the verge of unconsciousness, she thought of her daughter. Who would take care of her? Liz bit down on her lip until the pain cleared her mind. She couldn't die.

"Please…" She let herself go limp in his arms. "I can't tell you anything. I can't breathe."

His hold loosened just slightly. Liz slumped against him and when he shifted, she brought her elbow back with all her strength. She didn't bother to turn around but ran blindly. A rug slid under her feet, but she stumbled ahead, too terrified to look back. She was already calling for help when she hit the front door.

Her closest neighbor was a hundred yards away. She vaulted the little fence that separated the yards and sprinted toward the house. She stumbled up the steps, sobbing. Even as the door opened, she heard the sound of a car squealing tires on the rough gravel road behind her.

"He tried to kill me," she managed, then fainted.

"There is no further information I can give you, Mr. Sharpe." Moralas sat in his neat office facing the waterfront. The file on his desk wasn't as thick as he would have liked. Nothing in his investigation had turned up

a reason for Jerry Sharpe's murder. The man who sat
across from him stared straight ahead. Moralas had a
photo of the victim in the file, and a mirror image a
few feet away. "I wonder, Mr. Sharpe, if your brother's
death was a result of something that happened before
his coming to Cozumel."

"Jerry wasn't running when he came here."

Moralas tidied his papers. "Still, we have asked for
the cooperation of the New Orleans authorities. That
was your brother's last known address."

"He never had an address," Jonas murmured. Or a
conventional job, a steady woman. Jerry had been a
comet, always refusing to burn itself out. "I've told you
what Miss Palmer said. Jerry was cooking up a deal,
and he was cooking it up in Cozumel."

"Yes, having to do with diving." Always patient,
Moralas drew out a thin cigar. "Though we've already
spoken with Miss Palmer, I appreciate your bringing
me the information."

"But you don't know what the hell to do with it."

Moralas flicked on his lighter, smiling at Jonas over
the flame. "You're blunt. I'll be blunt, as well. If there
was a trail to follow to your brother's murder, it's cold.
Every day it grows colder. There were no fingerprints,
no murder weapon, no witnesses." He picked up the
file, gesturing with it. "That doesn't mean I intend to
toss this in a drawer and forget about it. If there is a
murderer on my island, I intend to find him. At the moment, I believe the murderer is miles away, perhaps in
your own country. Procedure now is to backtrack on
your brother's activities until we find something. To
be frank, Mr. Sharpe, you're not doing yourself or me
any good by being here."

"I'm not leaving."

"That is, of course, your privilege—unless you interfere with police procedure." At the sound of the buzzer on his desk, Moralas tipped his ash and picked up the phone.

"Moralas." There was a pause. Jonas saw the captain's thick, dark brows draw together. "Yes, put her on. Miss Palmer, this is Captain Moralas."

Jonas stopped in the act of lighting a cigarette and waited. Liz Palmer was the key, he thought again. He had only to find what lock she fit.

"When? Are you injured? No, please stay where you are, I'll come to you." Moralas was rising as he hung up the phone. "Miss Palmer has been attacked."

Jonas was at the door first. "I'm coming with you."

His muscles ached with tension as the police car raced out of town toward the shore. He asked no questions. In his mind, Jonas could see Liz as she'd been on the bridge hours before—tanned, slim, a bit defiant. He remembered the self-satisfied smirk she'd given him when he'd found himself in a tug-of-war with a thirty-pound fish. And how neatly she'd skipped out on him the moment they'd docked.

She'd been attacked. Why? Was it because she knew more than she'd been willing to tell him? He wondered if she were a liar, an opportunist or a coward. Then he wondered how badly she'd been hurt.

As they pulled down the narrow drive, Jonas glanced toward Liz's house. The door was open, the shades drawn. She lived there alone, he thought, vulnerable and unprotected. Then he turned his attention to the little stucco building next door. A woman in a cotton dress and apron came onto the porch. She carried a baseball bat.

"You are the police." She nodded, satisfied, when Moralas showed his identification. "I am Señora Alderez. She's inside. I thank the Virgin we were home when she came to us."

"Thank you."

Jonas stepped inside with Moralas and saw her. She was sitting on a patched sofa, huddled forward with a glass of wine in both hands. Jonas saw the liquid shiver back and forth as her hands trembled. She looked up slowly when they came in, her gaze passing over Moralas to lock on Jonas. She stared, with no expression in those deep, dark eyes. Just as slowly, she looked back at her glass.

"Miss Palmer." With his voice very gentle, Moralas sat down beside her. "Can you tell me what happened?"

She took the smallest of drinks, pressed her lips together briefly, then began as though she were reciting. "I came home at sunset. I didn't close the front door or lock it. I went straight into the bedroom. The shades were down, and I thought I'd left them up that morning. The cord wasn't secured, so I went over and fixed it. That's when he grabbed me—from behind. He had his arm around my neck and a knife. He cut me a little." In reflex, she reached up to touch the inch-long scratch her neighbor had already cleaned and fussed over. "I didn't fight because he had the knife at my throat and I thought he would kill me. He was going to kill me." She brought her head up to look directly into Moralas's eyes. "I could hear it in his voice."

"What did he say to you, Miss Palmer?"

"He said, 'Where is it?' I didn't know what he

wanted. I told him he could take my purse. He was choking me and he said, 'Where did he put it?' He said Sharpe." This time she looked at Jonas. When she lifted her head, he saw that bruises were already forming on her throat. "He said the deal was off and he wanted the money. If I didn't tell him where it was he'd kill me, and I wouldn't die quickly, the way Jerry had. He didn't believe me when I said I didn't know anything." She spoke directly to Jonas. As she stared at him he felt the guilt rise.

Patient, Moralas touched her arm to bring her attention back to him. "He let you go?"

"No, he was going to kill me." She said it dully, without fear, without passion. "I knew he would whether I told him anything or not, and my daughter—she needs me. I slumped as if I'd fainted, then I hit him. I think I hit him in the throat with my elbow. And I ran."

"Can you identify the man?"

"I never saw him. I never looked."

"His voice."

"He spoke Spanish. I think he was short because his voice was right in my ear. I don't know anything else. I don't know anything about money or Jerry or anything else." She looked back into her glass, abruptly terrified she would cry. "I want to go home."

"As soon as my men make certain it's safe. You'll have police protection, Miss Palmer. Rest here. I'll come back for you and take you home."

She didn't know if it had been minutes or hours since she'd fled through the front door. When Moralas took her back, it was dark with the moon just rising. An officer would remain outside in her driveway and all her doors and windows had been checked. Without a word, she went through the house into the kitchen.

"She was lucky." Moralas gave the living room another quick check. "Whoever attacked her was careless enough to be caught off guard."

"Did the neighbors see anything?" Jonas righted a table that had been overturned in flight. There was a conch shell on the floor that had cracked.

"A few people noticed a blue compact outside the house late this afternoon. Señora Alderez saw it drive off when she opened the door to Miss Palmer, but she couldn't identify the make or the plates. We will, of course, keep Miss Palmer under surveillance while we try to track it down."

"It doesn't appear my brother's killer's left the island."

Moralas met Jonas's gaze blandly. "Apparently whatever deal your brother was working on cost him his life. I don't intend for it to cost Miss Palmer hers. I'll drive you back to town."

"No. I'm staying." Jonas examined the pale pink shell with the crack spreading down its length. He thought of the mark on Liz's throat. "My brother involved her." Carefully, he set the damaged shell down. "I can't leave her alone."

"As you wish." Moralas turned to go when Jonas stopped him.

"Captain, you don't still think the murderer's hundreds of miles away."

Moralas touched the gun that hung at his side. "No, Mr. Sharpe, I don't. *Buenas noches.*"

Jonas locked her door himself, then rechecked the

windows before he went back to the kitchen. Liz was pouring her second cup of coffee. "That'll keep you up."

Liz drank half a cup, staring at him. She felt nothing at the moment, no anger, no fear. "I thought you'd gone."

"No." Without invitation, he found a mug and poured coffee for himself.

"Why are you here?"

He took a step closer, to run a fingertip gently down the mark on her throat. "Stupid question," he murmured.

She backed up, fighting to maintain the calm she'd clung to. If she lost control, it wouldn't be in front of him, in front of anyone. "I want to be alone."

He saw her hands tremble before she locked them tighter on the cup. "You can't always have what you want. I'll bunk in your daughter's room."

"No!" After slamming the cup down, she folded her arms across her chest. "I don't want you here."

With studied calm, he set his mug next to hers. When he took her shoulders, his hands were firm, not gentle. When he spoke, his voice was brisk, not soothing. "I'm not leaving you alone. Not now, not until they find Jerry's killer. You're involved whether you like it or not. And so, damn it, am I."

Her breath came quickly, too quickly, though she fought to steady it. "I wasn't involved until you came back and started hounding me."

He'd already wrestled with his conscience over that. Neither one of them could know if it were true. At the moment, he told himself it didn't matter. "However you're involved, you are. Whoever killed Jerry thinks you know something. You'll have an easier time convincing me you don't than you will them. It's time you started thinking about cooperating with me."

"How do I know you didn't send him here to frighten me?"

His eyes stayed on hers, cool and unwavering. "You don't. I could tell you that I don't hire men to kill women, but you wouldn't have to believe it. I could tell you I'm sorry." For the first time, his tone gentled. He lifted a hand to brush the hair back from her face and his thumb slid lightly over her cheekbone. Like the conch shell, she seemed delicate, lovely and damaged. "And that I wish I could walk away, leave you alone, let both of us go back to the way things were a few weeks ago. But I can't. We can't. So we might as well help each other."

"I don't want your help."

"I know. Sit down. I'll fix you something to eat."

She tried to back away. "You can't stay here."

"I am staying here. Tomorrow, I'm moving my things from the hotel."

"I said—"

"I'll rent the room," he interrupted, turning away to rummage through the cupboards. "Your throat's probably raw. This chicken soup should be the best thing."

She snatched the can from his hand. "I can fix my own dinner, and you're not renting a room."

"I appreciate your generosity." He took the can back from her. "But I'd rather keep it on a business level. Twenty dollars a week seems fair. You'd better take it, Liz," he added before she could speak. "Because I'm staying, one way or the other. Sit down," he said again and looked for a pot.

She wanted to be angry. It would help keep everything else bottled up. She wanted to shout at him, to throw him bodily out of her house. Instead she sat because her knees were too weak to hold her any longer.

What had happened to her control? For ten years she'd been running her own life, making every decision by herself, for herself. For ten years, she hadn't asked advice, she hadn't asked for help. Now something had taken control and decisions out of her hands, something she knew nothing about. Her life was part of a game, and she didn't know any of the rules.

She looked down and saw the tear drop on the back of her hand. Quickly, she reached up and brushed others from her cheeks. But she couldn't stop them. One more decision had been taken from her.

"Can you eat some toast?" Jonas asked her as he dumped the contents of the soup in a pan. When she didn't answer, he turned to see her sitting stiff and pale at the table, tears running unheeded down her face. He swore and turned away again. There was nothing he could do for her, he told himself. Nothing he could offer. Then, saying nothing, he came to the table, pulled a chair up beside her and waited.

"I thought he'd kill me." Her voice broke as she pressed a hand to her face. "I felt the knife against my throat and thought I was going to die. I'm so scared. Oh God, I'm so scared."

He drew her against him and let her sob out the fear. He wasn't used to comforting women. Those he knew well were too chic to shed more than a delicate drop or two. But he held her close during a storm of weeping that shook her body and left her gasping.

Her skin was icy, as if to prove the fact that fear made the blood run cold. She couldn't summon the pride to draw herself away, to seek a private spot as she'd always done in a crisis. He didn't speak to tell her everything would be fine; he didn't murmur quiet words of comfort. He was simply there. When she was drained, he still held her. The rain began slowly, patting the glass of the windows and pinging on the roof. He still held her.

When she shifted away, he rose and went back to the stove. Without a word, he turned on the burner. Minutes later he set a bowl in front of her then went back to ladle some for himself. Too tired to be ashamed, Liz began to eat. There was no sound in the kitchen but the slow monotonous plop of rain on wood, tin and glass.

She hadn't realized she could be hungry, but the bowl was empty almost before she realized it. With a little sigh, she pushed it away. He was tipped back in his chair, smoking in silence.

"Thank you."

"Okay." Her eyes were swollen, accentuating the vulnerability that always haunted them. It tugged at him, making him uneasy. Her skin, with its ripe, warm honey glow was pale, making her seem delicate and defenseless. She was a woman, he realized, that a man had to keep an emotional distance from. Get too close and you'd be sucked right in. It wouldn't do to care about her too much when he needed to use her to help both of them. From this point on, he'd have to hold the controls.

"I suppose I was more upset than I realized."

"You're entitled."

She nodded, grateful he was making it easy for her to skim over what she considered an embarrassing display of weakness. "There's no reason for you to stay here."

"I'll stay anyway."

She curled her hand into a fist, then uncurled it slowly. It wasn't possible for her to admit she wanted him to, or that for the first time in years she was frightened of being alone. Since she had to cave in, it was better to think of the arrangement on a practical level.

"All right, the room's twenty a week, first week in advance."

He grinned as he reached for his wallet. "All business?"

"I can't afford anything else." After putting the twenty on the counter, she stacked the bowls. "You'll have to see to your own food. The twenty doesn't include meals."

He watched her take the bowls to the sink and wash them. "I'll manage."

"I'll give you a key in the morning." She took a towel and meticulously dried the bowls. "Do you think he'll be back?" She tried to make her voice casual, and failed.

"I don't know." He crossed to her to lay a hand on her shoulder. "You won't be alone if he does."

When she looked at him, her eyes were steady again. Something inside him unknotted. "Are you protecting me, Jonas, or just looking for your revenge?"

"I do one, maybe I'll get the other." He twined the ends of her hair around his finger, watching the dark gold spread over his skin. "You said yourself I'm not a nice man."

"What are you?" she whispered.

"Just a man." When his gaze lifted to hers, she didn't

believe him. He wasn't just a man, but a man with patience, with power and with violence. "I've wondered the same about you. You've got secrets, Elizabeth."

She was breathless. In defense, she lifted her hand to his. "They've got nothing to do with you."

"Maybe they don't. Maybe you do."

It happened very slowly, so slowly she could have stopped it. Yet she seemed unable to move. His arms slipped around her, drawing her close with an arrogant sort of laziness that should have been his undoing. Instead, Liz watched, fascinated, as his mouth lowered to hers.

She'd just thought of him as a violent man, but his lips were soft, easy, persuading. It had been so long since she'd allowed herself to be persuaded. With barely any pressure, with only the slightest hint of power, he sapped the will she'd always relied on. Her mind raced with questions, then clouded over to a fine, smoky mist. She wasn't aware of how sweetly, how hesitantly her mouth answered his.

Whatever impulse had driven him to kiss her was lost in the reality of mouth against mouth. He'd expected her to resist, or to answer with fire and passion. To find her so soft, yielding, unsteady, had his own desire building in a way he'd never experienced. It was as though she'd never been kissed before, never been held close to explore what man and woman have for each other. Yet she had a daughter, he reminded himself. She'd had a child, she was young, beautiful. Other men had held her like this. Yet he felt like the first and had no choice but to treat her with care.

The more she gave, the more he wanted. He'd known needs before. The longer he held her, the longer he wanted to. He understood passions. But a part of himself he couldn't understand held back, demanded restraint. She wanted him—he could feel it. But even as his blood began to swim, his hands, as if under their own power, eased her away.

Needs, so long unstirred, churned in her. As she stared back at him, Liz felt them spring to life, with all their demands and risks. It wouldn't happen to her again. But even as she renewed the vow she felt the soft, fluttering longings waltz through her. It couldn't happen again. But the eyes that were wide and on his reflected confusion and hurt and hope. It was a combination that left Jonas shaken.

"You should get some sleep," he told her, and took care not to touch her again.

So that was all, Liz thought as the flicker of hope died. It was foolish to believe, even for a moment, anything could change. She brought her chin up and straightened her shoulders. Perhaps she'd lost control of many things, but she could still control her heart. "I'll give you a receipt for the rent and the key in the morning. I get up at six." She took the twenty-dollar bill she'd left on the counter and walked out.

Chapter 4

The jury was staring at him. Twelve still faces with blank eyes were lined behind the rail. Jonas stood before them in a small, harshly lit courtroom that echoed with his own voice. He carried stacks of law books, thick, dusty and heavy enough to make his arms ache. But he knew he couldn't put them down. Sweat rolled down his temples, down his back as he gave an impassioned closing plea for his client's acquittal. It was life and death, and his voice vibrated with both. The jury remained unmoved, disinterested. Though he struggled to hold them, the books began to slip from his grasp. He heard the verdict rebound, bouncing off the courtroom walls.

Guilty. Guilty. Guilty.

Defeated, empty-handed, he turned to the defendant. The man stood, lifting his head so that they stared, eye to eye, twin images. Himself? Jerry. Desperate, Jonas walked to the bench. In black robes, Liz sat above him, aloof with distance. But her eyes were sad as she slowly shook her head. "I can't help you."

Slowly, she began to fade. He reached up to grab her hand, but his fingers passed through hers. All he could see were her dark, sad eyes. Then she was gone, his brother was gone, and he was left facing a jury—twelve cold faces who smiled smugly back at him.

Jonas lay still, breathing quickly. He found himself staring back at the cluster of gaily dressed dolls on the shelf beside the bed. A flamenco dancer raised her castanets. A princess held a glass slipper. A spiffily dressed Barbie relaxed in a pink convertible, one hand raised in a wave.

Letting out a long breath, Jonas ran a hand over his face and sat up. It was like trying to sleep in the middle of a party, he decided. No wonder he'd had odd dreams. On the opposing wall was a collection of stuffed animals ranging from the dependable bear to something that looked like a blue dust rag with eyes.

Coffee, Jonas thought, closing his own. He needed coffee. Trying to ignore the dozens of smiling faces surrounding him, he dressed. He wasn't sure how or where to begin. The coin on his chain dangled before he pulled a shirt over his chest. Outside, birds were sending up a clatter. At home there would have been the sound of traffic as Philadelphia awoke for the day. He could see a bush close to the window where purple flowers seemed to crowd each other for room. There were no sturdy elms, no tidy evergreen hedges or chain-link fences. No law books would help him with what he had to do. There was nothing familiar, no precedents to follow. Each step he took would be taken blindly, but he had to take them. He smelled the coffee the moment he left the room.

Liz was in the kitchen dressed in a T-shirt and what appeared to be the bottoms of a skimpy bikini. Jonas wasn't a man who normally awoke with all batteries charged, but he didn't miss a pair of long, honey-toned legs. Liz finished buttering a piece of toast.

"Coffee's on the stove," she said without turning around. "There're some eggs in the refrigerator. I don't stock cereal when Faith's away."

"Eggs are fine," he mumbled, but headed for the coffee.

"Use what you want, as long as you replace it." She turned up the radio to listen to the weather forecast. "I leave in a half hour, so if you want a ride to your hotel, you'll have to be ready."

Jonas let the first hot taste of coffee seep into his system. "My car's in San Miguel."

Liz sat down at the table to go over that day's schedule. "I can drop you by the El Presidente or one of the other hotels on the beach. You'll have to take a cab from there."

Jonas took another sip of coffee and focused on her fully. She was still pale, he realized, so that the marks on her neck stood out in dark relief. The smudges under her eyes made him decide she'd slept no better than he had. He tossed off his first cup of coffee and poured another.

"Ever consider taking a day off?"

She looked at him for the first time. "No," she said simply and lowered her gaze to her list again.

So they were back to business, all business, and

don't cross the line. "Don't you believe in giving yourself a break, Liz?"

"I've got work to do. You'd better fix those eggs if you want to have time to eat them. The frying pan's in the cupboard next to the stove."

He studied her for another minute, then with a restless movement of his shoulders prepared to cook his breakfast. Liz waited until she was sure his back was to her before she looked up again.

She'd made a fool of herself the night before. She could almost accept the fact that she'd broken down in front of him because he'd taken it so matter-of-factly. But when she added the moments she'd stood in his arms, submissive, willing, hoping, she couldn't forgive herself. Or him.

He'd made her feel something she hadn't felt in a decade. Arousal. He'd made her want what she'd been convinced she didn't want from a man. Affection. She hadn't backed away or brushed him aside as she'd done with any other man who'd approached her. She hadn't even tried. He'd made her feel soft again, then he'd shrugged her away.

So it would be business, she told herself. Straight, impersonal business as long as he determined to stay. She'd put the rent money aside until she could manage the down payment on the aqua bikes. Jonas sat at the table with a plate of eggs that sent steam rising toward the ceiling.

"Your key." Liz slid it over to him. "And your receipt for the first week's rent."

Without looking at it, Jonas tucked the paper in his pocket. "Do you usually take in boarders?"

"No, but I need some new equipment." She rose to

pour another cup of coffee and wash her plate. The radio announced the time before she switched it off. She was ten minutes ahead of schedule, but as long as she continued to get up early enough, they wouldn't have to eat together. "Do you usually rent a room in a stranger's house rather than a hotel suite?"

He tasted the eggs and found himself vaguely dissatisfied with his own cooking. "No, but we're not strangers anymore."

Liz watched him over the rim of her cup. He looked a little rough around the edges this morning, she decided. It added a bit too much sexuality to smooth good looks. She debated offering him a razor, then rejected the notion. Too personal. "Yes, we are."

He continued to eat his eggs so that she thought he'd taken her at her word. "I studied law at Notre Dame, apprenticed with Neiram and Barker in Boston, then opened my own practice five years ago in Philadelphia." He added some salt, hoping it would jazz up his cooking. "I specialize in criminal law. I'm not married, and live alone. In an apartment," he added. "On weekends I'm remodeling an old Victorian house I bought in Chadd's Ford."

She wanted to ask him about the house—was it big, did it have those wonderful high ceilings and rich wooden floors? Were the windows tall and mullioned? Was there a garden where roses climbed on trellises? Instead she turned to rinse out her cup. "That doesn't change the fact that we're strangers."

"Whether we know each other or not, we have the same problem."

The cup rattled in the sink as it slipped from her hand. Silently, Liz picked it up again, rinsed it off and set it in the drainer. She'd chipped it, but that was a small matter at the moment. "You've got ten minutes," she said, but he took her arm before she could skirt around him.

"We do have the same problem, Elizabeth." His voice was quiet, steady. She could have hated him for that alone.

"No, we don't. You're trying to avenge your brother's death. I'm just trying to make a living."

"Do you think everything would settle down quietly if I were back in Philadelphia?"

She tugged her arm uselessly. "Yes!" Because she knew she lied, her eyes heated.

"One of the first impressions I had of you was your intelligence. I don't know why you're hiding on your pretty little island, Liz, but you've got a brain, a good one. We both know that what happened to you last night would have happened with or without me."

"All right." She relaxed her arm. "What happened wasn't because of you, but because of Jerry. That hardly makes any difference to my position, does it?"

He stood up slowly, but didn't release her arm. "As long as someone thinks you knew what Jerry was into, you're the focus. As long as you're the focus, I'm standing right beside you, because directly or indirectly, you're going to lead me to Jerry's killer."

Liz waited a moment until she was sure she could speak calmly. "Is that all people are to you, Jonas? Tools? Means to an end?" She searched his face and found it set and remote. "Men like you never look beyond their own interests."

Angry without knowing why, he cupped her face in his hand. "You've never known a man like me."

"I think I have," she said softly. "You're not unique, Jonas. You were raised with money and expectations, you went to the best schools and associated with the best people. You had your goal set and if you had to step on or over a few people on the way to it, it wasn't personal. That's the worst of it," she said on a long breath. "It's never personal." Lifting her chin, she pushed his hand from her face. "What do you want me to do?"

Never in his life had anyone made him feel so vile. With a few words she'd tried and condemned him. He remembered the dream, and the blank, staring eyes of the jury. He swore at her and turned to pace to the window. He couldn't back away now, no matter how she made him feel because he was right—whether he was here or in Philadelphia, she was still the key.

There was a hammock outside, bright blue and yellow strings stretched between two palms. He wondered if she ever gave herself enough time to use it. He found himself wishing he could take her hand, walk across the yard and lie with her on the hammock with nothing more important to worry about than swatting at flies.

"I need to talk to Luis," he began. "I want to know the places he went with Jerry, the people he may have seen Jerry talk to."

"I'll talk to Luis." When Jonas started to object, Liz shook her head. "You saw his reaction yesterday. He wouldn't be able to talk to you because you make him too nervous. I'll get you a list."

"All right." Jonas fished for his cigarettes and found with some annoyance that he'd left them in the bedroom. "I'll need you to go with me, starting tonight, to the places Luis gives you."

A feeling of stepping into quicksand came strongly. "Why?"

He wasn't sure of the answer. "Because I have to start somewhere."

"Why do you need me?"

And even less sure of this one. "I don't know how long it'll take, and I'm not leaving you alone."

She lifted a brow. "I have police protection."

"Not good enough. In any case, you know the language, the customs. I don't. I need you." He tucked his thumbs in his pockets. "It's as simple as that."

Liz walked over to turn off the coffee and move the pot to a back burner. "Nothing's simple," she corrected. "But I'll get your list, and I'll go along with you under one condition."

"Which is?"

She folded her hands. Jonas was already certain by her stance alone that she wasn't set to bargain but to lay down the rules. "That no matter what happens, what you find out or don't find out, you're out of this house and out of my life when my daughter comes home. I'll give you four weeks, Jonas—that's all."

"It'll have to be enough."

She nodded and started out of the room. "Wash your dishes. I'll meet you out front."

The police car still sat in the driveway when Jonas walked out the front door. A group of children stood on the verge of the road and discussed it in undertones. He heard Liz call one of them by name before she took out a handful of coins. Jonas didn't have to speak Spanish to recognize a business transaction. Moments later, coins in hand, the boy raced back to his friends.

"What was that about?"

Liz smiled after them. Faith would play with those same children throughout the summer. "I told them they were detectives. If they see anyone but you or the police around the house, they're to run right home and call Captain Moralas. It's the best way to keep them out of trouble."

Jonas watched the boy in charge pass out the coins. "How much did you give them?"

"Twenty pesos apiece."

He thought of the current rate of exchange and shook his head. "No kid in Philadelphia would give you the time of day for that."

"This is Cozumel," she said simply and wheeled out her bike.

Jonas looked at it, then at her. The bike would have sent a young teenager into ecstasies. "You drive this thing?"

Something in his tone made her want to smile. Instead, she kept her voice cool. "This thing is an excellent mode of transportation."

"A BMW's an excellent mode of transportation."

She laughed. He hadn't heard her laugh so easily since he'd met her. When she looked back at him, her eyes were warm and friendly. Jonas felt the ground shift dangerously under his feet. "Try to take your BMW on some of the back roads to the coast or into the interior." She swung a leg over the seat. "Hop on, Jonas, unless you want to hike back to the hotel."

Though he had his doubts, Jonas sat behind her. "Where do I put my feet?"

She glanced down and didn't bother to hide the grin. "Well, if I were you, I'd keep them off the ground." With this she started the engine then swung the bike around in the driveway. After adjusting for the added weight, Liz kept the speed steady. Jonas kept his hands lightly at her hips as the bike swayed around ruts and potholes.

"Are there roads worse than this?"

Liz sped over a bump. "What's wrong with this?"

"Just asking."

"If you want sophistication, try Cancun. It's only a few minutes by air."

"Ever get there?"

"Now and again. Last year Faith and I took the *Expatriate* over and spent a couple of days seeing the ruins. We have some shrines here. They're not well restored, but you shouldn't miss them. Still, I wanted her to see the pyramids and walled cities around Cancun."

"I don't know much about archaeology."

"You don't have to. All you need's an imagination."

She tooted the horn. Jonas saw an old, bent man straighten from the door of a shop and wave. "Señor Pessado," she said. "He gives Faith candy they both think I don't know about."

Jonas started to ask her about her daughter, then decided to wait for a better time. As long as she was being expansive, it was best to keep things less personal. "Do you know a lot of people on the island?"

"It's like a small town, I suppose. You don't necessarily have to know someone to recognize their face. I don't know a lot of people in San Miguel or on the east coast. I know a few people from the interior because we worked at the hotel."

"I didn't realize your shop was affiliated with the hotel."

"It's not." She paused at a stop sign. "I used to work

in the hotel. As a maid." Liz gunned the engine and zipped across the intersection.

He looked at her hands, lean and delicate on the handlebars. He studied her slender shoulders, thought of the slight hips he was even now holding. It was difficult to imagine her lugging buckets and pails. "I'd have thought you more suited to the front desk or the concierge."

"I was lucky to find work at all, especially during the off season." She slowed the bike a bit as she started down the long drive to El Presidente. She'd indulge herself for a moment by enjoying the tall elegant palms that lined the road and the smell of blooming flowers. She was taking one of the dive boats out today, with five beginners who'd need instruction and constant supervision, but she wondered about the people inside the hotel who came to such a place to relax and to play.

"Is it still gorgeous inside?" she asked before she could stop herself.

Jonas glanced ahead to the large stately building. "Lots of glass," he told her. "Marble. The balcony of my room looks out over the water." She steered the bike to the curb. "Why don't you come in? See for yourself."

She was tempted. Liz had an affection for pretty things, elegant things. It was a weakness she couldn't allow herself. "I have to get to work."

Jonas stepped onto the curb, but put his hand over hers before she could drive away. "I'll meet you at the house. We'll go into town together."

She only nodded before turning the bike back toward the road. Jonas watched her until the sound of the motor died away. Just who was Elizabeth Palmer?

he wondered. And why was it becoming more and more important that he find out?

By evening she was tired. Liz was used to working long hours, lugging equipment, diving, surfacing. But after a fairly easy day, she was tired. It should have made her feel secure to have had the young policeman identify himself to her and join her customers on the dive boat. It should have eased her mind that Captain Moralas was keeping his word about protection. It made her feel caged.

All during the drive home, she'd been aware of the police cruiser keeping a discreet distance. She'd wanted to run into her house, lock the door and fall into a dreamless, private sleep. But Jonas was waiting. She found him on the phone in her living room, a legal pad on his lap and a scowl on his face. Obviously a complication at his office had put him in a nasty mood. Ignoring him, Liz went to shower and change.

Because her wardrobe ran for the most part to beachwear, she didn't waste time studying her closet. Without enthusiasm, she pulled out a full cotton skirt in peacock blue and matched it with an oversized red shirt. More to prolong her time alone than for any other reason, she fiddled with her little cache of makeup. She was stalling, brushing out her braided hair, when Jonas knocked on her door. He didn't give her time to answer before he pushed it open.

"Did you get the list?"

Liz picked up a piece of notepaper. She could, of course, snap at him for coming in, but the end result wouldn't change. "I told you I would."

He took the paper from her to study it. He'd shaved,

she noticed, and wore a casually chic jacket over bone-
colored slacks. But the smoothness and gloss didn't
mesh with the toughness around his mouth and in his
eyes. "Do you know these places?"

"I've been to a couple of them. I don't really have a
lot of time for bar- or club-hopping."

He glanced up and his curt answer slipped away.
The shades behind her were up as she preferred them,
but the light coming through the windows was pink
with early evening. Though she'd buttoned the shirt
high over her throat, her hair was brushed back, away
from her face. She'd dawdled over the makeup, but
her hand was always conservative. Her lashes were
darkened, the lids lightly touched with shadow. She'd
brushed some color over her cheeks but not her lips.

"You should be careful what you do to your eyes,"
Jonas murmured, absently running his thumb along the
top curve of her cheek. "They're a problem."

She felt the quick, involuntary tug but stood still.
"A problem?"

"My problem." Uneasy, he tucked the paper in his
pocket and glanced around the room. "Are you ready?"

"I need my shoes."

He didn't leave her as she'd expected, instead wan-
dering around her room. It was, as was the rest of the
house, furnished simply but with jarring color. The
spicy scent he'd noticed before came from a wide green
bowl filled with potpourri. On the wall were two colored sketches, one of a sunset very much like the quietly brilliant one outside the window, and another of
a storm-tossed beach. One was all serenity, the other
all violence. He wondered how much of each were in-

side Elizabeth Palmer. Prominent next to the bed was a framed photograph of a young girl.

She was all smiles in a flowered blouse tucked at the shoulders. Her hair came to a curve at her jawline, black and shiny. A tooth was missing, adding charm to an oval, tanned face. If it hadn't been for the eyes, Jonas would never have connected the child with Liz. They were richly, deeply brown, slightly tilted. Still, they laughed out of the photo, open and trusting, holding none of the secrets of her mother's.

"This is your daughter."

"Yes." Liz slipped on the second shoe before taking the photo out of Jonas's hand and setting it down again.

"How old is she?"

"Ten. Can we get started? I don't want to be out late."

"Ten?" A bit stunned, Jonas stopped her with a look. He'd assumed Faith was half that age, a product of a relationship Liz had fallen into while on the island. "You can't have a ten-year-old child."

Liz glanced down at the picture of her daughter. "I do have a ten-year-old child."

"You'd have been a child yourself."

"No. No, I wasn't." She started to leave again, and again he stopped her.

"Was she born before you came here?"

Liz gave him a long, neutral look. "She was born six months after I moved to Cozumel. If you want my help, Jonas, we go now. Answering questions about Faith isn't part of our arrangement."

But he didn't let go of her hand. As it could become so unexpectedly, his voice was gentle. "He was a bastard, wasn't he?"

She met his eyes without wavering. Her lips curved, but not with humor. "Yes. Oh yes, he was."

Without knowing why he was compelled to, Jonas bent and just brushed her lips with his. "Your daughter's lovely, Elizabeth. She has your eyes."

She felt herself softening again, too much, too quickly. There was understanding in his voice without pity. Nothing could weaken her more. In defense she took a step back. "Thank you. Now we have to go. I have to be up early tomorrow."

The first club they hit was noisy and crowded with a high percentage of American clientele. In a corner booth, a man in a tight white T-shirt spun records on a turntable and announced each selection with a display of colored lights. They ordered a quick meal in addition to drinks while Jonas hoped someone would have a reaction to his face.

"Luis said they came in here a lot because Jerry liked hearing American music." Liz nibbled on hot nachos as she looked around. It wasn't the sort of place she normally chose to spend an evening. Tables were elbow to elbow, and the music was pitched to a scream. Still, the crowd seemed good-natured enough, shouting along with the music or just shouting to each other. At the table beside them a group of people experimented with a bottle of tequila and a bowl of lemon wedges. Since they were a group of young gringos, she assumed they'd be very sick in the morning.

It was definitely Jerry's milieu, Jonas decided. Loud, just this side of wild and crammed to the breaking point. "Did Luis say if he spoke with anyone in particular?"

"Women." Liz smiled a bit as she sampled a tortilla. "Luis was very impressed with Jerry's ability to… interest the ladies."

"Any particular lady?"

"Luis said there was one, but Jerry just called her baby."

"An old trick," Jonas said absently.

"Trick?"

"If you call them all baby, you don't mix up names and complicate the situation."

"I see." She sipped her wine and found it had a delicate taste.

"Could Luis describe her?"

"Only that she was a knockout—a Mexican knockout, if that helps. She had lots of hair and lots of hip. Luis's words," Liz added when Jonas gave her a mild look. "He also said there were a couple of men Jerry talked to a few times, but he always went over to them, so Luis didn't know what they spoke about. One was American, one was Mexican. Since Luis was more interested in the ladies, he didn't pay any attention. But he did say Jerry would cruise the bars until he met up with them, then he'd usually call it a night."

"Did he meet them here?"

"Luis said it never seemed to be in the same place twice."

"Okay, finish up. We'll cruise around ourselves."

By the fourth stop, Liz was fed up. She noticed that Jonas no more than toyed with a drink at each bar, but she was tired of the smell of liquor. Some places were quiet, and on the edge of seamy. Others were raucous and lit with flashing lights. Faces began to blur together. There were young people, not so young people.

There were Americans out for exotic nightlife, natives celebrating a night on the town. Some courted on dance floors or over tabletops. She saw those who seemed to have nothing but time and money, and others who sat alone nursing a bottle and a black mood.

"This is the last one," Liz told him as Jonas found a table at a club with a crowded dance floor and recorded music.

Jonas glanced at his watch. It was barely eleven. Action rarely heated up before midnight. "All right," he said easily, and decided to distract her. "Let's dance."

Before she could refuse, he was pulling her into the crowd. "There's no room," she began, but his arms came around her.

"We'll make some." He had her close, his hand trailing up her back. "See?"

"I haven't danced in years," she muttered, and he laughed.

"There's no room anyway." Locked together, jostled by the crowd, they did no more than sway.

"What's the purpose in all this?" she demanded.

"I don't know until I find it. Meantime, don't you ever relax?" He rubbed his palm up her back again, finding the muscles taut.

"No."

"Let's try it this way." His gaze skimmed the crowd as he spoke. "What do you do when you're not working?"

"I think about working."

"Liz."

"All right, I read—books on marine life mostly."

"Busman's holiday?"

"It's what interests me."

Her body shifted intimately against his. Jonas forgot to keep his attention on the crowd and looked down at her. "*All* that interests you?"

He was too close. Liz tried to ease away and found his arms very solid. In spite of her determination to remain unmoved, her heart began to thud lightly in her head. "I don't have time for anything else."

She wore no perfume, he noted, but carried the scent of powder and spice. He wondered if her body would look as delicate as it felt against his. "It sounds as though you limit yourself."

"I have a business to run," she murmured. Would it be the same if he kissed her again? Sweet, overpowering. His lips were so close to hers, closer still when he ran his hand through her hair and drew her head back. She could almost taste him.

"Is making money so important?"

"It has to be," she managed, but could barely remember why. "I need to buy some aqua bikes."

Her eyes were soft, drowsy. They made him feel invulnerable. "Aqua bikes?"

"If I don't keep up with the competition..." He pressed a kiss to the corner of her mouth.

"The competition?" he prompted.

"I...the customers will go someplace else. So I..." The kiss teased the other corner.

"So?"

"I have to buy the bikes before the summer season."

"Of course. But that's weeks away. I could make love with you dozens of times before then. Dozens," he repeated as she stared at him. Then he closed his mouth over hers.

He felt her jolt—surprise, resistance, passion—he

couldn't be sure. He only knew that holding her had led
to wanting her and wanting to needing. By nature, he
was a man who preferred his passion in private, quiet
spots of his own choosing. Now he forgot the crowded
club, loud music and flashing lights. They no longer
swayed, but were hemmed into a corner of the dance
floor, surrounded, pressed close. Oblivious.

She felt her head go light, heard the music fade. The
heat from his body seeped into hers and flavored the
kiss. Hot, molten, searing. Though they stood perfectly
still, Liz had visions of racing. The breath backed up in
her lungs until she released it with a shuddering sigh.
Her body, coiled like a spring, went lax on a wave of
confused pleasure. She strained closer, reaching up
to touch his face. Abruptly the music changed from
moody to rowdy. Jonas shifted her away from flailing arms.

"Poor timing," he murmured.

She needed a minute. "Yes." But she meant it in a
more general way. It wasn't a matter of time and place,
but a matter of impossibility. She started to move away
when Jonas's grip tightened on her. "What is it?" she
began, but only had to look at his face.

Cautiously, she turned to see what he stared at. A
woman in a skimpy red dress stared back at him. Liz
recognized the shock in her eyes before the woman
turned and fled, leaving her dance partner gaping.

"Come on." Without waiting for her, Jonas sprinted
through the crowd. Dodging, weaving and shoving
when she had to, Liz dashed after him.

The woman had barely gotten out to the street when
Jonas caught up to her. "What are you running away

from?" he demanded. His fingers dug into her arms as he held her back against a wall.

"Por favor, no comprendo," she murmured and shook like a leaf.

"Oh yes, I think you do." With his fingers bruising her arms, Jonas towered over her until she nearly squeaked in fear. "What do you know about my brother?"

"Jonas." Appalled, Liz stepped between them. "If this is the way you intend to behave, you'll do without my help." She turned away from him and touched the woman's shoulder. *"Lo siento mucho,"* she began, apologizing for Jonas. "He's lost his brother. His brother, Jerry Sharpe. Did you know him?"

She looked at Liz and whispered. "He has Jerry's face. But he's dead—I saw in the papers."

"This is Jerry's brother, Jonas. We'd like to talk to you."

As Liz had, the woman had already sensed the difference between Jonas and the man she'd known. She'd never have cowered away from Jerry for the simple reason that she'd known herself to be stronger and more clever. The man looming over her now was a different matter.

"I don't know anything."

"Por favor. Just a few minutes."

"Tell her I'll make it worth her while," Jonas added before she could refuse again. Without waiting for Liz to translate, he reached for his wallet and took out a bill. He saw fear change to speculation.

"A few minutes," she agreed, but pointed to an outdoor café. "There."

Jonas ordered two coffees and a glass of wine. "Ask her her name," he told Liz.

"I speak English." The woman took out a long, slim cigarette and tapped it on the tabletop. "I'm Erika. Jerry and I were friends." More relaxed, she smiled at Jonas. "You know, good friends."

"Yes, I know."

"He was very good-looking," she added, then caught her bottom lip between her teeth. "Lots of fun."

"How long did you know him?"

"A couple of weeks. I was sorry when I heard he was dead."

"Murdered," Jonas stated.

Erika took a deep drink of wine. "Do you think it was because of the money?"

Every muscle in his body tensed. Quickly, he shot Liz a warning look before she could speak. "I don't know—it looks that way. How much did he tell you about it?"

"Oh, just enough to intrigue me. You know." She smiled again and held out her cigarette for a light. "Jerry was very charming. And generous." She remembered the little gold bracelet he'd bought for her and the earrings with the pretty blue stones. "I thought he was very rich, but he said he would soon be much richer. I like charming men, but I especially like rich men. Jerry said when he had the money, we could take a trip." She blew out smoke again before giving a philosophical little shrug. "Then he was dead."

Jonas studied her as he drank coffee. She was, as Luis had said, a knockout. And she wasn't stupid. He was also certain her mind was focusing on one point, and one point alone. "Do you know when he was supposed to have the money?"

"Sure, I had to take off work if we were going away. He called me—it was Sunday. He was so excited. 'Erika,' he said, 'I hit the jackpot.' I was a little mad because he hadn't shown up Saturday night. He told me he'd done some quick business in Acapulco and how would I like to spend a few weeks in Monte Carlo?" She gave Jonas a lash-fluttering smile. "I decided to forgive him. I was packed," she added, blowing smoke past Jonas's shoulder. "We were supposed to leave Tuesday afternoon. I saw in the papers Monday night that he was dead. The papers said nothing about the money."

"Do you know who he had business with?"

"No. Sometimes he would talk to another American, a skinny man with pale hair. Other times he would see a Mexican. I didn't like him—he had *mal ojo*."

"Evil eye," Liz interpreted. "Can you describe him?"

"Not pretty," she said offhandedly. "His face was pitted. His hair was long in the back, over his collar and he was very thin and short." She glanced at Jonas again with a sultry smile that heated the air. "I like tall men."

"Do you know his name?"

"No. But he dressed very nicely. Nice suits, good shoes. And he wore a silver band on his wrist, a thin one that crossed at the ends. It was very pretty. Do you think he knows about the money? Jerry said it was lots of money."

Jonas merely reached for his wallet. "I'd like to find out his name," he told her and set a fifty on the table. His hand closed over hers as she reached for it. "His name, and the name of the American. Don't hold out on me, Erika."

With a toss of her head, she palmed the fifty. "I'll find out the names. When I tell you, it's another fifty."

"When you tell me." He scrawled Liz's number on the back of a business card. "Call this number when you have something."

"Okay." She slipped the fifty into her purse as she stood up. "You know, you don't look as much like Jerry as I thought." With the click of high heels, she crossed the pavement and went back into the club.

"It's a beginning," Jonas murmured as he pushed his coffee aside. When he looked over, he saw Liz studying him. "Problem?"

"I don't like the way you work."

He dropped another bill on the table before he rose. "I don't have time to waste on amenities."

"What would you have done if I hadn't calmed her down? Dragged her off to the nearest alley and beaten it out of her?"

He drew out a cigarette, struggling with temper. "Let's go home, Liz."

"I wonder if you're any different from the men you're looking for." She pushed back from the table. "Just as a matter of interest, the man who broke into my house and attacked me wore a thin band at his wrist. I felt it when he held the knife to my throat."

She watched as his gaze lifted from the flame at the end of the cigarette and came to hers. "I think you two might recognize each other when the time comes."

Chapter 5

"Always check your gauges," Liz instructed, carefully indicating each one on her own equipment as she spoke. "Each one of these gauges is vital to your safety when you dive. That's true if it's your first dive or your fiftieth. It's very easy to become so fascinated not only by the fish and coral, but the sensation of diving itself, that you can forget you're dependent on your air tank. Always be certain you start your ascent while you have five or ten minutes of air left."

She'd covered everything, she decided, in the hour lesson. If she lectured any more, her students would be too impatient to listen. It was time to give them a taste of what they were paying for.

"We'll dive as a group. Some of you may want to explore on your own, but remember, always swim in pairs. As a final precaution, check the gear of the diver next to you."

Liz strapped on her own weight belt as her group of novices followed instructions. So many of them, she knew, looked on scuba diving as an adventure. That was fine, as long as they remembered safety. Whenever she instructed, she stressed the what ifs just as thoroughly as the how tos. Anyone who went down under her supervision would know what steps to take under any circumstances. Diving accidents were most often the result of carelessness. Liz was never careless with herself or with her students. Most of them were talking excitedly as they strapped on tanks.

"This group." Luis hefted his tank. "Very green."

"Yeah." Liz helped him with the straps. As she did with all her employees, Liz supplied Luis's gear. It was checked just as thoroughly as any paying customer's. "Keep an eye on the honeymoon couple, Luis. They're more interested in each other than their regulators."

"No problem." He assisted Liz with her tank, then stepped back while she cinched the straps. "You look tired, kid."

"No, I'm fine."

When she turned, he glanced at the marks on her neck. The story had already made the rounds. "You sure? You don't look so fine."

She lifted a brow as she hooked on her diving knife. "Sweet of you."

"Well, I mean it. You got me worried about you."

"No need to worry." As Liz pulled on her mask, she glanced over at the roly-poly fatherly type who was struggling with his flippers. He was her bodyguard for the day. "The police have everything under control," she said, and hoped it was true. She wasn't nearly as sure about Jonas.

He hadn't shocked her the night before. She'd sensed that dangerously waiting violence in him from the first. But seeing his face as he'd grabbed Erika, hearing his voice, had left her with a cold, flat feeling in her stomach. She didn't know him well enough to be certain if he would choose to control the violence or let it free. More, how could she know he was capable of leashing it? Revenge, she thought, was never pretty. And that's what he wanted. Remembering the look in his eyes, Liz was very much afraid he'd get it.

The boat listed, bringing her back to the moment. She couldn't think about Jonas now, she told herself. She had a business to run and customers to satisfy.

"Miss Palmer." A young American with a thin chest and a winning smile maneuvered over to her. "Would you mind giving me a check?"

"Sure." In her brisk, efficient way, Liz began to check gauges and hoses.

"I'm a little nervous," he confessed. "I've never done this sort of thing before."

"It doesn't hurt to be a little nervous. You'll be more careful. Here, pull your mask down. Make sure it's comfortable but snug."

He obeyed, and his eyes looked wide and pale through the glass. "If you don't mind, I think I'll stick close to you down there."

She smiled at him. "That's what I'm here for. The depth here is thirty feet," she told the group in general. "Remember to make your adjustments for pressure and gravity as you descend. Please keep the group in sight at all times." With innate fluidity, she sat on the deck and rolled into the water. With Luis on deck, and Liz treading a few feet away, they waited until each student made his dive. With a final adjustment to her mask, Liz went under.

She'd always loved it. The sensation of weightlessness, the fantasy of being unimpeded, invulnerable. From near the surface, the sea floor was a spread of white. She loitered there a moment, enjoying the cathedral-like view. Then, with an easy kick, she moved down with her students.

The newlyweds were holding hands and having the time of their lives. Liz reminded herself to keep them in sight. The policeman assigned to her was plodding along like a sleepy sea turtle. He'd keep her in sight. Most of the others remained in a tight group, fascinated but cautious. The thin American gave her a wide-eyed look that was a combination of pleasure and nerves and stuck close by her side. To help him relax, Liz touched his shoulder and pointed up. In an easy motion, she turned on her back so that she faced the surface. Sunlight streaked thinly through the water. The hull of the dive boat was plainly visible. He nodded and followed her down.

Fish streamed by, some in waves, some on their own. Though the sand was white, the water clear, there was a montage of color. Brain coral rose up in sturdy mounds, the color of saffron. Sea fans, as delicate as lace, waved pink and purple in the current. She signaled to her companion and watched a school of coral sweepers, shivering with metallic tints, turn as a unit and skim through staghorn coral.

It was a world she understood as well as, perhaps better, than the one on the surface. Here, in the silence, Liz often found the peace of mind that eluded her from day to day. The scientific names of the fish and formations they passed were no strangers to her. Once she'd studied them diligently, with dreams of solving mysteries and bringing the beauty of the world of the sea to others. That had been another life. Now she coached tourists and gave them, for hourly rates, something memorable to take home after a vacation. It was enough.

Amused, she watched an angelfish busy itself by swallowing the bubbles rising toward the surface. To entertain her students, she poked at a small damselfish. The pugnacious male clung to his territory and nipped at her. To the right, she saw sand kick up and cloud the water. Signaling for caution, Liz pointed out the plate-like ray that skimmed away, annoyed by the intrusion.

The new husband showed off a bit, turning slow somersaults for his wife. As divers gained confidence, they spread out a little farther. Only her bodyguard and the nervous American stayed within an arm span at all times. Throughout the thirty-minute dive, Liz circled the group, watching individual divers. By the time the lesson was over, she was satisfied that her customers had gotten their money's worth. This was verified when they surfaced.

"Great!" A British businessman on his first trip to Mexico clambered back onto the deck. His face was reddened by the sun but he didn't seem to mind. "When can we go down again?"

With a laugh, Liz helped other passengers on board. "You have to balance your down time with your surface time. But we'll go down again."

"What was that feathery-looking stuff?" someone else asked. "It grows like a bush."

"It's a gorgonian, from the Gorgons of mythology."

She slipped off her tanks and flexed her muscles. "If you remember, the Gorgons had snakes for hair. The whip gorgonian has a resilient skeletal structure and undulates like a snake with the current."

More questions were tossed out, more answers supplied. Liz noticed the American who'd stayed with her, sitting by himself, smiling a little. Liz moved around gear then dropped down beside him.

"You did very well."

"Yeah?" He looked a little dazed as he shrugged his shoulders. "I liked it, but I gotta admit, I felt better knowing you were right there. You sure know what you're doing."

"I've been at it a long time."

He sat back, unzipping his wet suit to his waist. "I don't mean to be nosy, but I wondered about you. You're American, aren't you?"

It had been asked before. Liz combed her fingers through her wet hair. "That's right."

"From?"

"Houston."

"No kidding." His eyes lit up. "Hell, I went to school in Texas. Texas A and M."

"Really?" The little tug she felt rarely came and went. "So did I, briefly."

"Small world," he said, pleased with himself. "I like Texas. Got a few friends in Houston. I don't suppose you know the Dresscots?"

"No."

"Well, Houston isn't exactly small-town U.S.A." He stretched out long, skinny legs that were shades paler than his arms but starting to tan. "So you went to Texas A and M."

"That's right."

"What'd you study?"

She smiled and looked out to sea. "Marine biology."

"Guess that fits."

"And you?"

"Accounting." He flashed his grin again. "Pretty dry stuff. That's why I always take a long breather after tax time."

"Well, you chose a great place to take it. Ready to go down again?"

He took a long breath as if to steady himself. "Yeah. Hey, listen, how about a drink after we get back in?"

He was attractive in a mild sort of way, pleasant enough. She gave him an apologetic smile as she rose. "It sounds nice, but I'm tied up."

"I'll be around for a couple of weeks. Some other time?"

"Maybe. Let's check your gear."

By the time the dive boat chugged into shore, the afternoon was waning. Her customers, most of them pleased with themselves, wandered off to change for dinner or spread out on the beach. Only a few loitered near the boat, including her bodyguard and the accountant from America. It occurred to Liz that she might have been a bit brisk with him.

"I hope you enjoyed yourself, Mr. . . ."

"Trydent. But it's Scott, and I did. I might just try it again."

Liz smiled at him as she helped Luis and another of her employees unload the boat. "That's what we're here for."

"You, ah, ever give private lessons?"

Liz caught the look. Perhaps she hadn't been brisk enough. "On occasion."

"Then maybe we could—"

"Hey, there, missy."

Liz shaded her eyes. "Mr. Ambuckle."

He stood on the little walkway, his legs bulging out of the short wet suit. What hair he had was sleeked wetly back. Beside him, his wife stood wearily in a bathing suit designed to slim down wide hips. "Just got back in!" he shouted. "Had a full day of it."

He seemed enormously pleased with himself. His wife looked at Liz and rolled her eyes. "Maybe I should take you out as crew, Mr. Ambuckle."

He laughed, slapping his side. "Guess I'd rather dive than anything." He glanced at his wife and patted her shoulder. "Almost anything. Gotta trade in these tanks, honey, and get me some fresh ones."

"Going out again?"

"Tonight. Can't talk the missus into it."

"I'm crawling into bed with a good book," she told Liz. "The only water I want to see is in the tub."

With a laugh, Liz jumped down to the walkway. "At the moment, I feel the same way. Oh, Mr. and Mrs. Ambuckle, this is Scott Trydent. He just took his first dive."

"Well now." Expansive, Ambuckle slapped him on the back. "How'd you like it?"

"Well, I—"

"Nothing like it, is there? You want try it at night, boy. Whole different ball game at night."

"I'm sure, but—"

"Gotta trade in these tanks." After slapping Scott's

back again, Ambuckle hefted his tanks and waddled off toward the shop.

"Obsessed," Mrs. Ambuckle said, casting her eyes to the sky. "Don't let him get started on you, Mr. Trydent. You'll never get any peace."

"No, I won't. Nice meeting you, Mrs. Ambuckle." Obviously bemused, Scott watched her wander back toward the hotel. "Quite a pair."

"That they are." Liz lifted her own tanks. She stored them separately from her rental equipment. "Goodbye, Mr. Trydent."

"Scott," he said again. "About that drink—"

"Thanks anyway," Liz said pleasantly and left him standing on the walkway. "Everything in?" she asked Luis as she stepped into the shop.

"Checking it off now. One of the regulators is acting up."

"Set it aside for Jose to look at." As a matter of habit, she moved into the back to fill her tanks before storage. "All the boats are in, Luis. We shouldn't have too much more business now. You and the rest can go on as soon as everything's checked in. I'll close up."

"I don't mind staying."

"You closed up last night," she reminded him. "What do you want?" She tossed a grin over her shoulder. "Overtime? Go on home, Luis. You can't tell me you don't have a date."

He ran a fingertip over his mustache. "As a matter of fact…"

"A hot date?" Liz lifted a brow as air hissed into her tank.

"Is there any other kind?"

Chuckling, Liz straightened. She noticed Ambuckle

trudging across the sand with his fresh tanks. Her other employees talked among themselves as the last of the gear was stored. "Well, go make yourself beautiful then. The only thing I have a date with is the account books."

"You work too much," Luis mumbled.

Surprised, Liz turned back to him. "Since when?"

"Since always. It gets worse every time you send Faith back to school. Better off if she was here."

That her voice cooled only slightly was a mark of her affection for Luis. "No, she's happy in Houston with my parents. If I thought she wasn't, she wouldn't be there."

"She's happy, sure. What about you?"

Her brows drew together as she picked her keys from a drawer. "Do I look unhappy?"

"No." Tentatively, he touched her shoulder. He'd known Liz for years, and understood there were boundaries she wouldn't let anyone cross. "But you don't look happy either. How come you don't give one of these rich American tourists a spin? That one on the boat— his eyes popped out every time he looked at you."

The exaggeration made her laugh, so she patted his cheek. "So you think a rich American tourist is the road to happiness?"

"Maybe a handsome Mexican."

"I'll think about it—after the summer season. Go home," she ordered.

"I'm going." Luis pulled a T-shirt over his chest. "You look out for that Jonas Sharpe," he added. "He's got a different kind of look in his eyes."

Liz waved him off. *"Hasta luego."*

When the shop was empty, Liz stood, jingling her

keys and looking out onto the beach. People traveled in couples, she noted, from the comfortably married duo stretched out on lounge chairs, to the young man and woman curled together on a beach towel. Was it an easy feeling, she wondered, to be half of a set? Or did you automatically lose part of yourself when you joined with another?

She'd always thought of her parents as separate people, yet when she thought of one, the other came quickly to mind. Would it be a comfort to know you could reach out your hand and someone else's would curl around it?

She held out her own and remembered how hard, how strong, Jonas's had been. No, he wouldn't make a relationship a comfortable affair. Being joined with him would be demanding, even frightening. A woman would have to be strong enough to keep herself intact, and soft enough to allow herself to merge. A relationship with a man like Jonas would be a risk that would never ease.

For a moment, she found herself dreaming of it, dreaming of what it had been like to be held close and kissed as though nothing and no one else existed. To be kissed like that always, to be held like that whenever the need moved you—it might be worth taking chances for.

Stupid, she thought quickly, shaking herself out of it. Jonas wasn't looking for a partner, and she wasn't looking for a dream. Circumstances had tossed them together temporarily. Both of them had to deal with their own realities. But she felt a sense of regret and a stirring of wishes.

Because the feeling remained, just beyond her grasp,

Liz concentrated hard on the little details that needed
attending to before she could close up. The paperwork
and the contents of the cash box were transferred to a
canvas portfolio. She'd have to swing out of her way to
make a night deposit, but she no longer felt safe taking
the cash or the checks home. She spent an extra few
minutes meticulously filling out a deposit slip.

It wasn't until she'd picked up her keys again that she
remembered her tanks. Tucking the portfolio under the
counter, she turned to deal with her own gear.

It was perhaps her only luxury. She'd spent more on
her personal equipment than she had on all the contents of her closet and dresser. To Liz, the wet suit was
more exciting than any French silks. All her gear was
kept separate from the shop's inventory. Unlocking the
door to the closet, Liz hung up her wet suit, stored her
mask, weight belt, regulator. Her knife was sheathed
and set on a shelf. After setting her tanks side by side,
she shut the door and prepared to lock it again. After
she'd taken two steps away she looked down at the keys
again. Without knowing precisely why, she moved each
one over the ring and identified it.

The shop door, the shop window, her bike, the lock
for the chain, the cash box, the front and back doors of
her house, her storage room. Eight keys for eight locks.
But there was one more on her ring, a small silver key
that meant nothing to her at all.

Puzzled, she counted off the keys again, and again
found one extra. Why should there be a key on her ring
that didn't belong to her? Closing her fingers over it,
she tried to think if anyone had given her the key to
hold. No, it didn't make sense. Brows drawn together,
she studied the key again. Too small for a car or door

key, she decided. It looked like the key to a locker, or a box or... Ridiculous, she decided on a long breath. It wasn't her key but it was on her ring. Why?

Because someone put it there, she realized, and opened her hand again. Her keys were often tossed in the drawer at the shop for easy access for Luis or one of the other men. They needed to open the cash box. And Jerry had often worked in the shop alone.

With a feeling of dread, Liz slipped the keys into her pocket. Jonas's words echoed in her head. *"You're involved, whether you want to be or not."*

Liz closed the shop early.

Jonas stepped into the dim bar to the scent of garlic and the wail of a squeaky jukebox. In Spanish, someone sang of endless love. He stood for a moment, letting his eyes adjust, then skimmed his gaze over the narrow booths. As agreed, Erika sat all the way in the back, in the corner.

"You're late." She waved an unlit cigarette idly as he joined her.

"I passed it the first time. This place isn't exactly on the tourist route."

She closed her lips over the filter as Jonas lit her cigarette. "I wanted privacy."

Jonas glanced around. There were two men at the bar, each deep in separate bottles. Another couple squeezed themselves together on one side of a booth. The rest of the bar was deserted. "You've got it."

"But I don't have a drink."

Jonas slid out from the booth and bought two drinks at the bar. He set tequila and lime in front of Erika and settled for club soda. "You said you had something for me."

Erica twined a string of colored beads around her finger. "You said you would pay fifty for a name."

In silence, Jonas took out his wallet. He set fifty on the table, but laid his hand over it. "You have the name."

Erika smiled and sipped at her drink. "Maybe. Maybe you want it bad enough to pay another fifty."

Jonas studied her coolly. This was the type his brother had always been attracted to. The kind of woman whose hard edge was just a bit obvious. He could give her another fifty, Jonas mused, but he didn't care to be taken for a sucker. Without a word, he picked up the bill and tucked it into his pocket. He was halfway out of the booth when Erika grabbed his arm.

"Okay, don't get mad. Fifty." She sent him an easy smile as he settled back again. Erika had been around too long to let an opportunity slip away. "A girl has to make a living, *si?* The name is Pablo Manchez—he's the one with the face."

"Where can I find him?"

"I don't know. You got the name."

With a nod, Jonas took the bill out and passed it to her. Erika folded it neatly into her purse. "I'll tell you something else, because Jerry was a sweet guy." Her gaze skimmed the bar again as she leaned closer to Jonas. "This Manchez, he's bad. People got nervous when I asked about him. I heard he was mixed up in a couple of murders in Acapulco last year. He's paid, you know, to…" She made a gun out of her hand and pushed down her thumb. "When I hear that, I stop asking questions."

"What about the other one, the American?"

"Nothing. Nobody knows him. But if he hangs out with Manchez, he's not a Boy Scout." Erika tipped back her drink. "Jerry got himself in some bad business."

"Yeah."

"I'm sorry." She touched the bracelet on her wrist. "He gave me this. We had some good times."

The air in the bar was stifling him. Jonas rose and hesitated only a moment before he took out another bill and set it next to her drink. "Thanks."

Erika folded the bill as carefully as the first. *"De nada."*

She'd wanted him to be home. When Liz found the house empty, she made a fist over the keys in her hand and swore in frustration. She couldn't sit still; her nerves had been building all during the drive home. Outside, Moralas's evening shift was taking over.

For how long? she wondered. How long would the police sit patiently outside her house and follow her through her daily routine? In her bedroom, Liz closed the canvas bag of papers and cash in her desk. She regretted not having a lock for it, as well. Sooner or later, she thought, Moralas would back off on the protection. Then where would she be? Liz looked down at the key again. She'd be alone, she told herself bluntly. She had to do something.

On impulse, she started into her daughter's room. Perhaps Jerry had left a case, a box of some kind that the police had overlooked. Systematically she searched Faith's closet. When she found the little teddy bear with the worn ear, she brought it down from the shelf. She'd bought it for Faith before she'd been born. It was a vivid shade of purple, or had been so many years before. Now it was faded a bit, a little loose at the seams. The ear had been worn down to a nub because Faith had always carried him by it. They'd never named it, Liz recalled. Faith had merely called it *mine* and been satisfied.

On a wave of loneliness that rocked her, Liz buried her face against the faded purple pile. "Oh, I miss you, baby," she murmured. "I don't know if I can stand it."

"Liz?"

On a gasp of surprise, Liz stumbled back against the closet door. When she saw Jonas, she put the bear behind her back. "I didn't hear you come in," she said, feeling foolish.

"You were busy." He came toward her to gently pry the bear from her fingers. "He looks well loved."

"He's old." She cleared her throat and took the toy back again. But she found it impossible to stick it back on the top shelf. "I keep meaning to sew up the seams before the stuffing falls out." She set the bear down on Faith's dresser. "You've been out."

"Yes." He'd debated telling her of his meeting with Erika, and had decided to keep what he'd learned to himself, at least for now. "You're home early."

"I found something." Liz reached in her pocket and drew out her keys. "This isn't mine."

Jonas frowned at the key she indicated. "I don't know what you mean."

"I mean this isn't my key, and I don't know how it got on my ring."

"You just found it today?"

"I found it today, but it could have been put on anytime. I don't think I would've noticed." With the vain hope of distancing herself, Liz unhooked it from the others and handed it to Jonas. "I keep these in a drawer at the shop when I'm there. At home, I usually toss them on the kitchen counter. I can't think of any reason for someone to put it with mine unless they wanted to hide it."

Jonas examined the key. "'The Purloined Letter,'" he murmured.

"What?"

"It was one of Jerry's favorite stories when we were kids. I remember when he tested out the theory by putting a book he'd bought for my father for Christmas on the shelf in the library."

"So do you think it was his?"

"I think it would be just his style."

Liz picked up the bear again, finding it comforted her. "It doesn't do much good to have a key when you don't have the lock."

"It shouldn't be hard to find it." He held the key up by the stem. "Do you know what it is?"

"A key." Liz sat on Faith's bed. No, she hadn't distanced herself. The quicksand was bubbling again.

"To a safe-deposit box." Jonas turned it over to read the numbers etched into the metal.

"Do you think Captain Moralas can trace it?"

"Eventually," Jonas murmured. The key was warm in his hand. It was the next step, he thought. It had to be. "But I'm not telling him about it."

"Why?"

"Because he'd want it, and I don't intend to give it to him until I open the lock myself."

She recognized the look easily enough now. It was still revenge. Leaving the bear on her daughter's bed,

Liz rose. "What are you going to do, go from bank to bank and ask if you can try the key out? You won't have to call the police, they will."

"I've got some connections—and I've got the serial number." Jonas pocketed the key. "With luck, I'll have the name of the bank by tomorrow afternoon. You may have to take a couple of days off."

"I can't take a couple of days off, and if I could, why should I need to?"

"We're going to Acapulco."

She started to make some caustic comment, then stopped. "Because Jerry told Erika he'd had business there?"

"If Jerry was mixed up in something, and he had something important or valuable, he'd tuck it away. A safe-deposit box in Acapulco makes sense."

"Fine. If that's what you believe, have a nice trip." She started to brush past him. Jonas only had to shift his body to bar the door.

"We go together."

The word "together" brought back her thoughts on couples and comfort. And it made her remember her conclusion about Jonas. "Look, Jonas, I can't drop everything and follow you on some wild-goose chase. Acapulco is very cosmopolitan. You won't need an interpreter."

"The key was on your ring. The knife was at your throat. I want you where I can see you."

"Concerned?" Her face hardened, muscle by muscle. "You're not concerned with me, Jonas. And you're certainly not concerned *about* me. The only thing you care about is your revenge. I don't want any part of it, or you."

He took her by the shoulders until she was backed against the door. "We both know that's not true. We've started something." His gaze skimmed down, lingered on her lips. "And it's not going to stop until we're both finished with it."

"I don't know what you're talking about."

"Yes, you do." He pressed closer so that their bodies met and strained, one against the other. He pressed closer to prove something, perhaps only to himself. "Yes, you do," he repeated. "I came here to do something, and I intend to do it. I don't give a damn if you call it revenge."

Her heart was beating lightly at her throat. She wouldn't call it fear. But his eyes were cold and close. "What else?"

"Justice."

She felt an uncomfortable twinge, remembering her own feelings on justice. "You're not using your law books, Jonas."

"Law doesn't always equal justice. I'm going to find out what happened to my brother and why." He skimmed his hand over her face and tangled his fingers in her hair. He didn't find silk and satin, but a woman of strength. "But there's more now. I look at you and I want you." He reached out, taking her face in his hand so that she had no choice but to look directly at him. "I hold you and I forget what I have to do. Damn it, you're in my way."

At the end of the words, his mouth was crushed hard on hers. He hadn't meant to. He hadn't had a choice. Before he'd been gentle with her because the look in her eyes requested it. Now he was rough, desperate, because the power of his own needs demanded it.

He frightened her. She'd never known fear could be a source of exhilaration. As her heart pounded in her throat, she let him pull her closer, still closer to the edge. He dared her to jump off, to let herself tumble down into the unknown. To risk.

His mouth drew desperately from hers, seeking passion, seeking submission, seeking strength. He wanted it all. He wanted it mindlessly from her. His hands were reaching for her as if they'd always done so. When he found her, she stiffened, resisted, then melted so quickly that it was nearly impossible to tell one mood from the next. She smelled of the sea and tasted of innocence, a combination of mystery and sweetness that drove him mad.

Forgetting everything but her, he drew her toward the bed and fulfillment.

"No." Liz pushed against him, fighting to bring herself back. They were in her daughter's room. "Jonas, this is wrong."

He took her by the shoulders. "Damn it, it may be the only thing that's right."

She shook her head, and though unsteady, backed away. His eyes weren't cold now. A woman might dream of having a man look at her with such fire and need. A woman might toss all caution aside if only to have a man want her with such turbulent desire. She couldn't.

"Not for me. I don't want this, Jonas." She reached up to push back her hair. "I don't want to feel like this."

He took her hand before she could back away. His head was swimming. There had been no other time, no other place, no other woman that had come together to make him ache. "Why?"

"I don't make the same mistake twice."

"This is now, Liz."

"And it's my life." She took a long, cleansing breath and found she could face him squarely. "I'll go with you to Acapulco because the sooner you have what you want, the sooner you'll go." She gripped her hands together tightly, the only outward sign that she was fighting herself. "You know Moralas will have us followed."

He had his own battles to fight. "I'll deal with that."

Liz nodded because she was sure he would. "Do what you have to do. I'll make arrangements for Luis to take over the shop for a day or two."

When she left him alone, Jonas closed his hands over the key again. It would open a lock, he thought. But there was another lock that mystified and frustrated him. Idly, he picked up the bear Liz had left on the bed. He looked from it to the key in his hand. Somehow he'd have to find a way to bring them together.

Chapter 6

Acapulco wasn't the Mexico Liz understood and loved. It wasn't the Mexico she'd fled to a decade before, nor where she'd made her home. It was sophisticated and ultra modern with spiraling high-rise hotels crowded together and gleaming in tropical sunlight. It was swimming pools and trendy shops. Perhaps it was the oldest resort in Mexico, and boasted countless restaurants and nightclubs, but Liz preferred the quietly rural atmosphere of her own island.

Still she had to admit there was something awesome about the city, cupped in the mountains and kissed by a magnificent bay. She'd lived all her life in flat land, from Houston to Cozumel. The mountains made everything else seem smaller, and somehow protected. Over the water, colorful parachutes floated, allowing the adventurous a bird's-eye view and a stunning ride.

She wondered fleetingly if skimming through the sky would be as liberating as skimming through the water.

The streets were crowded and noisy, exciting in their own way. It occurred to her that she'd seen more people in the hour since they'd landed at the airport than she might in a week on Cozumel. Liz stepped out of the cab and wondered if she'd have time to check out any of the dive shops.

Jonas had chosen the hotel methodically. It was luxuriously expensive—just Jerry's style. The villas overlooked the Pacific and were built directly into the mountainside. Jonas took a suite, pocketed the key and left the luggage to the bellman.

"We'll go to the bank now." It had taken him two days to match the key with a name. He wasn't going to waste any more time.

Liz followed him out onto the street. True, she hadn't come to enjoy herself, but a look at their rooms and a bite of lunch didn't seem so much to ask. Jonas was already climbing into a cab. "I don't suppose you'd considered making that a request."

He gave her a brief look as she slammed the cab door. "No." After giving the driver their direction, Jonas settled back. He could understand Jerry drifting to Acapulco, with its jet-set flavor, frantic nightlife and touches of luxury. When Jerry landed in a place for more than a day, it was a city that had the atmosphere of New York, London, Chicago. Jerry had never been interested in the rustic, serene atmosphere of a spot like Cozumel. So since he'd gone there, stayed there, he'd had a purpose. In Acapulco, Jonas would find out what it was.

As to the woman beside him, he didn't have a clue.

Was she caught up in the circumstances formed before they'd ever met, or was he dragging her in deeper
than he had a right to? She sat beside him, silent and
a little sulky. Probably thinking about her shop, Jonas
decided, and wished he could send her safely back to
it. He wished he could turn around, go back to the villa
and make love with her until they were both sated.

She shouldn't have appealed to him at all. She wasn't
witty, flawlessly polished or classically beautiful. But
she did appeal to him, so much so that he was spending
his nights awake and restless, and his days on the edge
of frustration. He wanted her, wanted to fully explore
the tastes of passion she'd given him. He wanted to
arouse her until she couldn't think of accounts or customers or schedules. Perhaps it was a matter of wield-
ing power—he could no longer be sure. But mostly,
inexplicably, he wanted to erase the memory of how
she'd looked when he'd walked into her daughter's
room and found her clutching a stuffed bear.

When the cab rolled up in front of the bank, Liz
stepped out on the curb without a word. There were
shops across the streets, boutiques where she could
see bright, wonderful dresses on cleverly posed man-
nequins. Even with the distance, she caught the gleam
and glimmer of jewelry. A limousine rolled by, with
smoked glass windows and quiet engine. Liz looked
beyond the tall, glossy buildings to the mountains, and
space.

"I suppose this is the sort of place that appeals to you."

He'd watched her survey. She didn't have to speak
for him to understand that she'd compared Acapulco
with her corner of Mexico and found Acapulco lack-

ing. "Under certain circumstances." Taking her arm, Jonas led her inside.

The bank was, as banks should be, quiet and sedate. Clerks wore neat suits and polite smiles. What conversation there was, was carried on in murmurs. Jerry, he thought, had always preferred the ultraconservative in storing his money, just as he'd preferred the wild in spending it. Without hesitation, Jonas strolled over to the most attractive teller. "Good afternoon."

She glanced up. It only took a second for her polite smile to brighten. "Mr. Sharpe, *buenos días.* It's nice to see you again."

Beside him, Liz stiffened. He's been here before, she thought. Why hadn't he told her? She sent a long, probing look his way. Just what game was he playing?

"It's nice to see you." He leaned against the counter, urbane and, she noted, flirtatious. The little tug of jealousy was as unexpected as it was unwanted. "I wondered if you'd remember me."

The teller blushed before she glanced cautiously toward her supervisor. "Of course. How can I help you today?"

Jonas took the key out of his pocket. "I'd like to get into my box." He simply turned and stopped Liz with a look when she started to speak.

"I'll arrange that for you right away." The teller took a form, dated it and passed it to Jonas. "If you'll just sign here."

Jonas took her pen and casually dashed off a signature. Liz read: *Jeremiah C. Sharpe.* Though she looked up quickly, Jonas was smiling at the teller. Because her supervisor was hovering nearby, the teller stuck to procedure and checked the signature against the card in the files. They matched perfectly.

"This way, Mr. Sharpe."

"Isn't that illegal?" Liz murmured as the teller led them from the main lobby.

"Yes." Jonas gestured for her to precede him through the doorway.

"And does it make me an accessory?"

He smiled at her, waiting while the teller drew the long metal box from its slot. "Yes. If there's any trouble, I'll recommend a good lawyer."

"Great. All I need's another lawyer."

"You can use this booth, Mr. Sharpe. Just ring when you're finished."

"Thanks." Jonas nudged Liz inside, shut, then locked, the door.

"How did you know?"

"Know what?" Jonas set the box on a table.

"To go to that clerk? When she first spoke to you, I thought you'd been here before."

"There were three men and two women. The other woman was into her fifties. As far as Jerry would've been concerned, there would have been only one clerk there."

That line of thinking was clear enough, but his actions weren't. "You signed his name perfectly."

Key in hand, Jonas looked at her. "He was part of me. If we were in the same room, I could have told you what he was thinking. Writing his name is as easy as writing my own."

"And was it the same for him?"

It could still hurt, quickly and unexpectedly. "Yes, it was the same for him."

But Liz remembered Jerry's good-natured description of his brother as a stuffed shirt. The man Liz was beginning to know didn't fit. "I wonder if you understood each other as well as both of you thought." She looked down at the box again. None of her business, she thought, and wished it were as true as she'd once believed. "I guess you'd better open it."

He slipped the key into the lock, then turned it soundlessly. When he drew back the lid, Liz could only stare. She'd never seen so much money in her life. It sat in neat stacks, tidily banded, crisply American. Unable to resist, Liz reached out to touch.

"God, it looks like thousands." She swallowed. "Hundreds of thousands."

His face expressionless, Jonas flipped through the stacks. The booth became as quiet as a tomb. "Roughly three hundred thousand, in twenties and fifties."

"Do you think he stole it?" she murmured, too overwhelmed to notice Jonas's hands tighten on the money. "This must be the money the man who broke into my house wanted."

"I'm sure it is." Jonas set down a stack of bills and picked up a small bag. "But he didn't steal it." He forced his emotions to freeze. "I'm afraid he earned it."

"How?" she demanded. "No one earns this kind of money in a matter of days, and I'd swear Jerry was nearly broke when I hired him. I know Luis lent him ten thousand pesos before his first paycheck."

"I'm sure he was." He didn't bother to add that he'd wired his brother two hundred before Jerry had left New Orleans. Carefully, Jonas reached under the stack of money and pulled out a small plastic bag, dipped in a finger and tasted. But he'd already known.

"What is that?"

His face expressionless, Jonas sealed the bag. He couldn't allow himself any more grief. "Cocaine."

Horrified, Liz stared at the bag. "I don't understand. He lived in my house. I'd have known if he were using drugs."

Jonas wondered if she realized just how innocent she was of the darker side of humanity. Until that moment, he hadn't fully realized just how intimate he was with it. "Maybe, maybe not. In any case, Jerry wasn't into this sort of thing. At least not for himself."

Liz sat down slowly. "You mean he sold it?"

"Dealt drugs?" Jonas nearly smiled. "No, that wouldn't have been exciting enough." In the corner of the box was a small black address book. Jonas took it out to leaf through it. "But smuggling," he murmured. "Jerry could have justified smuggling. Action, intrigue and fast money."

Her mind was whirling as she tried to focus back on the man she'd known so briefly. Liz had thought she'd understood him, categorized him, but he was more of a stranger now than when he'd been alive. It didn't seem to matter anymore who or what Jerry Sharpe had been. But the man in front of her mattered. "And you?" she asked. "Can you justify it?"

He glanced down at her, over the book in his hands. His eyes were cold, so cold that she could read nothing in them at all. Without answering, Jonas went back to the book.

"He'd listed initials, dates, times and some numbers. It looks as though he made five thousand a drop. Ten drops."

Liz glanced over at the money again. It no longer seemed crisp and neat but ugly and ill used. "That only makes fifty thousand. You said there was three hundred."

"That's right." Plus a bag of uncut cocaine with a hefty street value. Jonas took out his own book and copied down the pages from his brother's.

"What are we going to do with this?"

"Nothing."

"Nothing?" Liz rose again, certain she'd stepped into a dream. "Do you mean just leave it here? Just leave it here in this box and walk away?"

With the last of the numbers copied, Jonas replaced his brother's book. "Exactly."

"Why did we come if we're not going to do anything with it?"

He slipped his own book into his jacket. "To find it."

"Jonas." Before he could close the lid she had her hand on his wrist. "You have to take it to the police. To Captain Moralas."

In a deliberate gesture, he removed her hand, then picked up the bag of coke. She understood rejection and braced herself against it. But it wasn't rejection she saw in his face; it was fury. "You want to take this on the plane, Liz? Any idea on what the penalty is in Mexico for carrying controlled substances?"

"No."

"And you don't want to." He closed the lid, locked it. "For now, just forget you saw anything. I'll handle this in my own way."

"No."

His emotions were raw and tangled, his patience thin. "Don't push me, Liz."

"Push you?" Infuriated, she grabbed his shirtfront and planted her feet. "You've pushed me for days. Pushed me right into the middle of something that's so opposed to the way I've lived I can't even take it all in. Now that I'm over my head in drug smuggling and something like a quarter of a million dollars, you tell me to forget it. What do you expect me to do, go quietly back and rent tanks? Maybe you've finished using me now, Jonas, but I'm not ready to be brushed aside. There's a murderer out there who thinks I know where the money is." She stopped as her skin iced over. "And now I do."

"That's just it," Jonas said quietly. For the second time, he removed her hands, but this time he held on to her wrists. Frightened, he thought. He was sure her pulse beat with fear as well as anger. "Now you do. The best thing for you to do now is stay out of it, let them focus on me."

"Just how am I supposed to do that?"

The anger was bubbling closer, the anger he'd wanted to lock in the box with what had caused it. "Go to Houston, visit your daughter."

"How can I?" she demanded in a whisper that vibrated in the little room. "They might follow me." She looked down at the long, shiny box. "They would follow me. I won't risk my daughter's safety."

She was right, and because he knew it, Jonas wanted to rage. He was boxed in, trapped between love and loyalty and right and wrong. Justice and the law. "We'll talk to Moralas when we get back." He picked up the box again, hating it.

"Where are we going now?"

Jonas unlocked the door. "To get a drink."

Rather than going with Jonas to the lounge, Liz took some time for herself. Because she felt he owed her, she went into the hotel's boutique, found a simple one-piece bathing suit and charged it to the room. She hadn't packed anything but a change of clothes and toiletries. If she was stuck in Acapulco for the rest of the evening, she was going to enjoy the private pool each villa boasted.

The first time she walked into the suite, she was dumbfounded. Her parents had been reasonably successful, and she'd been raised in a quietly middle-class atmosphere. Nothing had prepared her for the sumptuousness of the two-bedroom suite overlooking the Pacific. Her feet sank cozily into the carpet. Softly colored paintings were spaced along ivory-papered walls. The sofa, done in grays and greens and blues, was big enough for two to sprawl on for a lazy afternoon nap.

She found a phone in the bathroom next to a tub so wide and deep that she was almost tempted to take her dip there. The sink was a seashell done in the palest of pinks.

So this is how the rich play, she mused as she wandered to the bedroom where her overnight bag was set at the end of a bed big enough for three. The drapes of her balcony were open so that she could see the tempestuous surf of the Pacific hurl up and spray. She pulled the glass doors open, wanting the noise.

This was the sort of world Marcus had told her of so many years before. He'd made it seem like a fairy tale with gossamer edges. Liz had never seen his home, had never been permitted to, but he'd described it to her. The white pillars, the white balconies, the staircase that curved up and up. There were servants to bring you tea in the afternoons, a stable where grooms waited to saddle glossy horses. Champagne was drunk from French crystal. It had been a fairy tale, and she hadn't wanted it for herself. She had only wanted him.

A young girl's foolishness, Liz thought now. In her naive way, she'd made a prince out of a man who was weak and selfish and spoiled. But over the years she had thought of the house he'd talked of and pictured her daughter on those wide, curving stairs. That had been her sense of justice.

The image wasn't as clear now, not now that she'd seen wealth in a long metal box and understood where it had come from. Not when she'd seen Jonas's eyes when he'd spoken of his kind of justice. That hadn't been a fairy tale with gossamer edges, but grimly real. She had some thinking to do. But before she could plan for the rest of her life, and for her daughter's, she had to get through the moment.

Jonas. She was bound to him through no choice of her own. And perhaps he was bound to her in the same way. Was that the reason she was drawn to him? Because they were trapped in the same puzzle? If she could only explain it away, maybe she could stop the needs that kept swimming through her. If she could only explain it away, maybe she would be in control again.

But how could she explain the feelings she'd experienced on the silent cab ride back to the hotel? She had had to fight the desire to put her arms around him, to offer comfort when nothing in his manner had indicated he needed or wanted it. There were no easy answers—no answers at all to the fact that she was slowly, inevitably falling in love with him.

It was time to admit that, she decided, because you could never face anything until it was admitted. You could never solve anything until it was faced. She'd lived by that rule years before during the biggest crisis of her life. It still held true.

So she loved him, or very nearly loved him. She was no longer naive enough to believe that love was the beginning of any answer. He would hurt her. There were no ifs about that. He'd steal from her the one thing she'd managed to hold fast to for ten years. And once he'd taken her heart, what would it mean to him? She shook her head. No more than such things ever mean to those who take them.

Jonas Sharpe was a man on a mission, and she was no more to him than a map. He was ruthless in his own patient way. When he had finished what he'd come to do, he would turn away from her, go back to his life in Philadelphia and never think of her again.

Some women, Liz thought, were doomed to pick the men who could hurt them the most. Making her mind a blank, Liz stripped and changed to her bathing suit. But Jonas, thoughts of Jonas, kept slipping through the barriers.

Maybe if she talked to Faith—if she could touch her greatest link with normality, things would snap back into focus. On impulse, Liz picked up the phone beside her bed and began the process of placing the call. Faith would just be home from school, Liz calculated, growing more excited as she heard the clinks and buzzes on the receiver. When the phone began to ring, she sat on the bed. She was already smiling.

"Hello?"

"Mom?" Liz felt the twin surges of pleasure and guilt as she heard her mother's voice. "It's Liz."

"Liz!" Rose Palmer felt identical surges. "We didn't expect to hear from you. Your last letter just came this morning. Nothing's wrong, is it?"

"No, no, nothing's wrong." *Everything's wrong.* "I just wanted to talk to Faith."

"Oh, Liz, I'm so sorry. Faith's not here. She has her piano lesson today."

The letdown came, but she braced herself against it. "I forgot." Tears threatened, but she forced them back. "She likes the lessons, doesn't she?"

"She loves them. You should hear her play. Remember when you were taking them?"

"I had ten thumbs." She managed to smile. "I wanted to thank you for sending the pictures. She looks so grown up. Momma, is she…looking forward to coming back?"

Rose heard the need, felt the ache. She wished, not for the first time, that her daughter was close enough to hold. "She's marking off the days on her calendar. She bought you a present."

Liz had to swallow. "She did?"

"It's supposed to be a surprise, so don't tell her I told you."

"I won't." She dashed tears away, grateful she could keep her voice even. It hurt, but was also a comfort to be able to speak to someone who knew and understood Faith as she did. "I miss her. The last few weeks always seem the hardest."

Her voice wasn't as steady as she thought—and a mother hears what others don't. "Liz, why don't you come home? Spend the rest of the month here while she's in school?"

"No, I can't. How's Dad?"

Rose fretted impatiently at the change of subject, then subsided. She'd never known anyone as thoroughly stubborn as her daughter. Unless it was her granddaughter. "He's fine. Looking forward to coming down and doing some diving."

"We'll take one of the boats out—just the four of us. Tell Faith I...tell her I called," she finished lamely.

"Of course I will. Why don't I have her call you back when she gets home? The car pool drops her off at five."

"No. No, I'm not home. I'm in Acapulco—on business." Liz let out a long breath to steady herself. "Just tell her I miss her and I'll be waiting at the airport. You know I appreciate everything you're doing. I just—"

"Liz." Rose interrupted gently. "We love Faith. And we love you."

"I know." Liz pressed her fingers to her eyes. She did know, but was never quite sure what to do about it. "I love you, too. It's just that sometimes things get so mixed up."

"Are you all right?"

She dropped her hand again, and her eyes were dry. "I will be when you get there. Tell Faith I'm marking off the days, too."

"I will."

"Bye, Momma."

She hung up and sat until the churning emptiness had run its course. If she'd had more confidence in her parents' support, more trust in their love, would she have fled the States and started a new life on her own? Liz dragged a hand through her hair. She'd never be sure of that, nor could she dwell on it. She'd burned her own bridges. The only thing that was important was Faith, and her happiness.

An hour later, Jonas found her at the pool. She swam laps in long, smooth strokes, her body limber. She seemed tireless, and oddly suited to the private luxury. Her suit was a flashy red, but the cut so simple that it relied strictly on the form it covered for style.

He counted twenty laps before she stopped, and wondered how many she'd completed before he'd come down. It seemed to him as if she swam to drain herself of some tension or sorrow, and that with each lap she'd come closer to succeeding. Waiting, he watched her tip her head back in the water so that her hair slicked back. The marks on her neck had faded. As she stood, water skimmed her thigh.

"I've never seen you relaxed," Jonas commented. But even as he said the words, he could see her muscles tense again. She turned away from her contemplation of the mountains and looked at him.

He was tired, she realized, and wondered if she should have seen it before. There was a weariness around his eyes that hadn't been there that morning. He hadn't changed his clothes, and had his hands tucked into the pockets of bone-colored slacks. She wondered if he'd been up to the suite at all.

"I didn't bring a suit with me." Liz pushed against the side of the pool and hitched herself out. Water rained from her. "I charged this one to the room."

The thighs were cut nearly to the waist. Jonas caught himself wondering just how the skin would feel there. "It's nice."

Liz picked up her towel. "It was expensive."

He only lifted a brow. "I could deduct it from the rent."

Her lips curved a little as she rubbed her hair dry. "No, you can't. But since you're a lawyer, I imagine you can find a way to deduct it from something else. I saved the receipt."

He hadn't thought he could laugh. "I appreciate it. You know, I get the impression you don't think much of lawyers."

Something came and went in her eyes. "I try not to think of them at all."

Taking the towel from her, he gently dried her face. "Faith's father's a lawyer?"

Without moving, she seemed to shift away from him. "Leave it alone, Jonas."

"You don't."

"Actually I do, most of the time. Maybe it's been on my mind the past few weeks, but that's my concern."

He draped the towel around her shoulders and, holding the ends, drew her closer. "I'd like you to tell me about it."

It was his voice, she thought, so calm, so persuasive, that nearly had her opening both mind and heart. She could almost believe as she looked at him that he really wanted to know, to understand. The part of her that was already in love with him needed to believe he might care. "Why?"

"I don't know. Maybe it's that look that comes into your eyes. It makes a man want to stroke it away."

Her chin came up a fraction. "There's no need to feel sorry for me."

"I don't think sympathy's the right word." Abruptly weary, he dropped his forehead to hers. He was tired of fighting demons, of trying to find answers. "Damn."

Uncertain, she stood very still. "Are you all right?"

"No. No, I'm not." He moved away from her to walk to the end of the path where a plot of tiny orange flowers poked up through white gravel. "A lot of things you said today were true. A lot of things you've said all along are true. I can't do anything about them."

"I don't know what you want me to say now."

"Nothing." Hideously tired, he ran both hands over his face. "I'm trying to live with the fact that my brother's dead, and that he was murdered because he decided to make some easy money drug-trafficking. He had a good brain, but he always chose to use it in the wrong way. Every time I look in the mirror, I wonder why."

Liz was beside him before she could cut off her feelings. He hurt. It was the first time she'd seen below the surface to the pain. She knew what it was like to live with pain. "He was different, Jonas. I don't think he was bad, just weak. Mourning him is one thing—blaming yourself for what he did, or for what happened to him, is another."

He hadn't known he needed comfort, but her hand resting on him had something inside him slowly uncurling. "I was the only one who could reach him, keep him on some kind of level. There came a point where I just got tired of running both our lives."

"Do you really believe you could have prevented him from doing what he did?"

"Maybe. That's something else I have to live with."

"Just a minute." She took his shirtfront in much the same way she had that afternoon. There was no sympathy now, but annoyance on her face. He hadn't known he needed that, as well. "You were brothers, twins, but you were separate people. Jerry wasn't a child to be guided and supervised. He was a grown man who made his decisions."

"That's the trouble. Jerry never grew up."

"And you did," she tossed back. "Are you going to punish yourself for it?"

He'd been doing just that, Jonas realized. He'd gone home, buried his brother, comforted his parents and blamed himself for not preventing something he knew in his heart had been inevitable. "I have to find out who killed him, Liz. I can't set the rest aside until I do."

"We'll find them." On impulse, she pressed her cheek to his. Sometimes the slightest human contact could wash away acres of pain. "Then it'll be over."

He wasn't sure he wanted it to be, not all of it. He ran a hand down her arm, needing the touch of her skin. He found it chilled. "The sun's gone down." He wrapped the towel around her in a gesture that would have been mere politeness with another woman. With Liz, it was for protection. "You'd better get out of that wet suit. We'll have dinner."

"Here?"

"Sure. The restaurant's supposed to be one of the best."

Liz thought of the elegance of their suite and the contents of her overnight bag. "I didn't bring anything to wear."

He laughed and swung an arm around her. It was the

first purely frivolous thing he'd heard her say. "Charge something else."

"But—"

"Don't worry, I've got the best crooked accountant in Philadelphia."

Chapter 7

Because she'd been certain she would never sleep away from home, in a hotel bed, Liz was surprised to wake to full sunlight. Not only had she slept, she realized, she'd slept like a rock for eight hours and was rested and ready to go. True, it was just a little past six, and she had no business to run, but her body was tuned to wake at that hour. A trip to Acapulco didn't change that.

It had changed other things, she reminded herself as she stretched out in the too-big bed. Because of it, she'd become inescapably tangled in murder and smuggling. Putting the words together made her shake her head. In a movie, she might have enjoyed watching the melodrama. In a book, she'd have turned the page to read more. But in her own life, she preferred the more mundane. Liz was too practical to delude herself into believing she could distance herself from any part of the puzzle any longer. For better or worse, she was personally involved in this melodrama. That included Jonas Sharpe. The only question now was which course of action to take.

She couldn't run. That had never been a choice. Liz had already concluded she couldn't hide behind Moralas and his men forever. Sooner or later the man with the knife would come back, or another man more determined or more desperate. She wouldn't escape a second time. The moment she'd looked into the safe-deposit box, she'd become a full-fledged player in the game. Which brought her back full circle to Jonas. She had no choice but to put her trust in him now. If he were to give up on his brother's murder and return to Philadelphia she would be that much more alone. However much she might wish it otherwise, Liz needed him just as much as he needed her.

Other things had changed, she thought. Her feelings for him were even more undefined and confusing than they had started out to be. Seeing him as she had the evening before, hurt and vulnerable, had touched off more than impersonal sympathy or physical attraction. It had made her feel a kinship, and the kinship urged her to help him, not only for her own welfare, but for his. He suffered, for his brother's loss, but also for what his brother had done. She'd loved once, and had suffered, not only because of loss but because of disillusionment.

A lifetime ago? Liz wondered. Did we ever really escape from one lifetime to another? It seemed years could pass, circumstances could change, but we carried our baggage with us through each phase. If anything, with each phase we had to carry a bit more. There was little use in thinking, she told herself as she climbed from the bed. From this point on, she had little choice but to act.

Jonas heard her the moment she got up. He'd been awake since five, restless and prowling. For over an hour he'd been racking his brain and searching his conscience for a way to ease Liz out of a situation his brother, and he himself had locked her into. He'd already thought of several ways to draw attention away from her to himself, but that wouldn't guarantee Liz's safety. She wouldn't go to Houston, and he understood her feelings about endangering her daughter in any way.

As the days passed, he felt he was coming to understand her better and better. She was a loner, but only because she saw it as the safest route. She was a businesswoman, but only because she looked to her daughter's welfare first. Inside, he thought, she was a woman with dreams on hold and love held in bondage. She had steered both toward her child and denied herself. And, Jonas added, she'd convinced herself she was content.

That was something else he understood, because until a few weeks before he had also convinced himself he was content. It was only now, after he'd had the opportunity to look at his life from a distance, that he realized he had merely been drifting. Perhaps, when the outward trimmings were stripped away, he hadn't been so different from his brother. For both of them, success had been the main target, they had simply aimed for it differently. Though Jonas had a steady job, a home of his own, there had never been an important woman. He'd put his career first. Jonas wasn't certain he'd be able to do so again. It had taken the loss of his brother to make him realize he needed something more, something solid. Exploring the law was only a job. Winning cases was only a transitory satisfaction. Perhaps he'd known it for some time. After all, he'd bought the old house in Chadd's Ford to give himself something permanent. When had he started thinking about sharing it?

Still, thinking about his own life didn't solve the problem of Liz Palmer and what he was going to do with her. She couldn't go to Houston, he thought again, but there were other places she could go until he could assure her that her life could settle back the way she wanted it. His parents were his first thought, and the quiet country home they'd retired to in Lancaster. If he could find a way to slip her out of Mexico, she would be safe there. It would even be possible to have her daughter join her. Then his conscience would ease. Jonas had no doubt that his parents would accept them both, then dote on them.

Once he'd done what he'd come to do, he could go to Lancaster himself. He'd like to see Liz there, in surroundings he was used to. He wanted time to talk with her about simple things. He wanted to hear her laugh again, as she had only once in all the days he'd known her. Once they were there, away from the ugliness, he might understand his feelings better. Perhaps by then he'd be able to analyze what had happened inside him when she'd pressed her cheek against his and had offered unconditional support.

He'd wanted to hold on to her, to just hold on and the hell with the world. There was something about her that made him think of lazy evenings on cool porches and long Sunday afternoon walks. He couldn't say why. In

Philadelphia he rarely took time for such things. Even socializing had become business. And he'd seen for himself that she never gave herself an idle hour. Why should he, a man dedicated to his work, think of lazing days away with a woman obsessed by hers?

She remained a mystery to him, and perhaps that was an answer in itself. If he thought of her too often, too deeply, it was only because while his understanding was growing, he still knew so little. If it sometimes seemed that discovering Liz Palmer was just as important as discovering his brother's killer, it was only because they were tied together. How could he take his mind off one without taking his mind off the other? Yet when he thought of her now, he thought of her stretched out on his mother's porch swing, safe, content and waiting for him.

Annoyed with himself, Jonas checked his watch. It was after nine on the East Coast. He'd call his office, he thought. A few legal problems might clear his mind. He'd no more than picked up the receiver when Liz came out from her bedroom.

"I didn't know you were up," she said, and fiddled nervously with her belt. Odd, she felt entirely different about sharing the plush little villa with him than she did her home. After all, she reasoned, at home he was paying rent.

"I thought you'd sleep longer." He replaced the receiver again. The office could wait.

"I never sleep much past six." Feeling awkward, she wandered to the wide picture window. "Terrific view."

"Yes, it is."

"I haven't stayed in a hotel in…in years," she finished. "When I came to Cozumel, I worked in the same hotel where I'd stayed with my parents. It was an odd feeling. So's this."

"No urge to change the linen or stack the towels?"

When she chuckled, some of the awkwardness slipped away. "No, not even a twinge."

"Liz, when we're finished with all this, when it's behind us, will you talk to me about that part of your life?"

She turned to him, away from the window, but they both felt the distance. "When we're finished with this, there won't be any reason to."

He rose and came to her. In a gesture that took her completely by surprise, he took both of her hands. He lifted one, then the other, to his lips and watched her eyes cloud. "I can't be sure of that," he murmured. "Can you?"

She couldn't be sure of anything when his voice was quiet, his hands gentle. For a moment, she simply absorbed the feeling of being a woman cared for by a man. Then she stepped back, as she knew she had to. "Jonas, you told me once we had the same problem. I didn't want to believe it then, but it was true. It is true. Once that problem is solved, there really isn't anything else between us. Your life and mine are separated by a lot more than miles."

He thought of his house and his sudden need to share it. "They don't have to be."

"There was a time I might have believed that."

"You're living in the past." He took her shoulders, but this time his hands weren't as gentle. "You're fighting ghosts."

"I may have my ghosts, but I don't live in the past. I can't afford to." She put her hands to his wrists, but let them lie there only a moment before she let go. "I can't afford to pretend to myself about you."

He wanted to demand, he wanted to pull her with him to the sofa and prove to her that she was wrong. He resisted. It wasn't the first time he'd used courtroom skill, courtroom tactics, to win on a personal level. "We'll leave it your way for now," he said easily. "But the case isn't closed. Are you hungry?"

Unsure whether she should be uneasy or relieved, Liz nodded. "A little."

"Let's have breakfast. We've got plenty of time before the plane leaves."

She didn't trust him. Though Jonas kept the conversation light and passionless throughout breakfast, Liz kept herself braced for a countermove. He was a clever man, she knew. He was a man, she was certain, who made sure he got his own way no matter how long it took. Liz considered herself a woman strong enough to keep promises made, even when they were to herself. No man, not even Jonas, was going to make her change the course she'd set ten years before. There was only room enough for two loves in her life. Faith and her work.

"I can't get used to eating something at this hour of the morning that's going to singe my stomach lining."

Liz swallowed the mixture of peppers, onions and eggs. "Mine's flame resistant. You should try my chili."

"Does that mean you're offering to cook for me?"

When Liz glanced up she wished he hadn't been smiling at her in just that way. "I suppose I could make enough for two as easily as enough for one. But you don't seem to have any trouble in the kitchen."

"Oh, I can cook. It's just that once I've finished, it never seems worth the bother." He leaned forward to run a finger down her hand from wrist to knuckle. "Tell you what—I'll buy the supplies and even clean up the mess if you handle the chili."

Though she smiled, Liz drew her hand away. "The question is, can you handle the chili? It might burn right through a soft lawyer's stomach."

Appreciating the challenge, he took her hand again. "Why don't we find out? Tonight."

"All right." She flexed her fingers, but he merely linked his with them. "I can't eat if you have my hand."

He glanced down. "You have another one."

He made her laugh when she'd been set to insist. "I'm entitled to two."

"I'll give it back. Later."

"Hey, Jerry!"

The easy smile on Jonas's face froze. Only his eyes changed, locking on to Liz's, warning and demanding. His hand remained on hers, but the grip tightened. The message was very clear—she was to do nothing, say nothing until he'd tallied the odds. He turned, flashing a new smile. Liz's stomach trembled. It was Jerry's smile, she realized. Not Jonas's.

"Why didn't you tell me you were back in town?" A tall, tanned man with sandy blond hair and a trim beard dropped a hand on Jonas's shoulder. Liz caught the glint of a diamond on his finger. He was young, she thought, determined to store everything she could, barely into his thirties, and dressed with slick, trendy casualness.

"Quick trip," Jonas said as, like Liz, he took in every

detail. "Little business…" He cast a meaningful glance toward Liz. "Little pleasure."

The man turned and stared appreciatively at Liz. "Is there any other way?"

Thinking fast, Liz offered her hand. "Hello. Since Jerry's too rude to introduce us, we'll have to do it ourselves. I'm Liz Palmer."

"David Merriworth." He took her hand between both of his. They were smooth and uncallused. "Jerry might have trouble with manners, but he's got great taste."

She smiled, hoping she did it properly. "Thank you."

"Pull up a chair, Merriworth." Jonas took out a cigarette. "As long as you keep your hands off my lady." He said it in the good-natured, only-kidding tone Jerry had inevitably used, but his eyes were Jonas's, warning her to tread carefully.

"Wouldn't mind a quick cup of coffee." David pulled over a chair after he checked his watch. "Got a breakfast meeting in a few minutes. So how are things on Cozumel?" He inclined his head ever so slightly. "Getting in plenty of diving?"

Jonas allowed his lips to curve and kept his eyes steady. "Enough."

"Glad to hear it. I was going to check in with you myself, but I've been in the States for a couple weeks. Just got back last night." He used two sugars after the waiter set a fresh cup of coffee beside him. "Business is good, buddy. Real good."

"What business are you in, Mr. Merriworth?"

He gave Liz a big grin before he winked at Jonas. "Sales, sweetheart. Imports, you might say."

"Really." Because her throat was dry she drank more coffee. "It must be fascinating."

"It has its moments." He turned in his chair so that he could study her face. "So where did Jerry find you?"

"On Cozumel." She sent Jonas a steady look. "We're partners."

David lowered his cup. "That so?"

They were in too deep, Jonas thought, for him to contradict her. "That's so," he agreed.

David picked up his cup again with a shrug. "If it's okay with the boss, it doesn't bother me."

"I do things my way," Jonas drawled. "Or I don't do them."

Amused, and perhaps admiring, David broke into a smile. "That never changes. Look, I've been out of touch for a few weeks. The drops still going smooth?"

With those words, Jonas's last hopes died. What he'd found in the safe-deposit box had been real, and it had been Jerry's. He buttered a roll as though he had all the time in the world. Beneath the table, Liz touched his leg once, hoping he'd take it as comfort. He never looked at her. "Why shouldn't they?"

"It's the classiest operation I've ever come across," David commented, taking a cautious glance around to other tables. "Wouldn't like to see anything screw it up."

"You worry too much."

"You're the one who should worry," David pointed out. "I don't have to deal with Manchez. You weren't around last year when he took care of those two Colombians. I was. You deal with supplies, I stick with sales. I sleep better."

"I just dive," Jonas said, and tapped out his ciga-rette. "And I sleep fine."

"He's something, isn't he?" David sent Liz another grin. "I knew Jerry here was just the man the boss was looking for. You keep diving, kid." He tipped his cup at Jonas. "It makes me look good."

"Sounds like you two have known each other for a while," Liz said with a smile. Under the table, she twisted the napkin in her lap.

"Go way back, don't we, Jer?"

"Yeah. We go back."

"First time we hooked up was six, no, seven years ago. We were working a pigeon drop in L.A. We'd have had that twenty thousand out of that old lady if her daughter hadn't caught on." He took out a slim cigarette case. "Your brother got you out of that one, didn't he? The East Coast lawyer."

"Yeah." Jonas remembered posting the bond and pulling the strings.

"Now I've been working out of here for almost five. A real businessman." He slapped Jonas's arm. "Hell of a lot better than the pigeon drop, huh, Jerry?"

"Pays better."

David let out a roar of laughter. "Why don't I show you two around Acapulco tonight?"

"Gotta get back." Jonas signaled for the check. "Business."

"Yeah, I know what you mean." He nodded toward the restaurant's entrance. "Here's my customer now. Next time you drop down, give a call."

"Sure."

"And give my best to old Clancy." With another laugh, David gave them each a quick salute. They watched him stride across the room and shake hands with a dark-suited man.

"Don't say anything here," Jonas murmured as he signed the breakfast check. "Let's go."

Liz's crumpled napkin slid to the floor as she rose to walk out with him. He didn't speak again until they had the door of the villa closed behind them.

"You had no business telling him we were partners."

Because she'd been ready for the attack, she shrugged it off. "He said more once I did."

"He'd have said just as much if you'd made an excuse and left the table."

She folded her arms. "We have the same problem, remember?"

He didn't care to have his own words tossed back at him. "The least you could have done was to give him another name."

"Why? They know who I am. Sooner or later he's going to talk to whoever's in charge and get the whole story."

She was right. He didn't care for that either. "Are you packed?"

"Yes."

"Then let's check out. We'll go to the airport."

"And then?"

"And then we go straight to Moralas."

"You've been very busy." Moralas held on to his temper as he rocked back in his chair. "Two of my men wasted their valuable time looking for you in Acapulco. You might have told me, Mr. Sharpe, that you planned to take Miss Palmer on a trip."

"I thought a police tail in Acapulco might be inconvenient."

"And now that you have finished your own investigation, you bring me this." He held up the key and examined it. "This which Miss Palmer discovered several days ago. As a lawyer, you must understand the phrase 'withholding evidence.'"

"Of course." Jonas nodded coolly. "But neither Miss Palmer nor myself could know the key was evidence. We speculated, naturally, that it might have belonged to my brother. Withholding a speculation is hardly a crime."

"Perhaps not, but it is poor judgment. Poor judgment often translates into an offense."

Jonas leaned back in his chair. If Moralas wanted to argue law, they'd argue law. "If the key belonged to my brother, as executor of his estate, it became mine. In any case, once it was proved to me that the key did indeed belong to Jerry, and that the contents of the safe-deposit box were evidence, I brought both the key and a description of the contents to you."

"Indeed. And do you also speculate as to how your brother came to possess those particular items?"

"Yes."

Moralas waited a beat, then turned to Liz. "And you, Miss Palmer—you also have your speculations?"

She had her hands gripped tightly in her lap, but her voice was matter-of-fact and reasonable. "I know that whoever attacked me wanted money, obviously a great deal of money. We found a great deal."

"And a bag of what Mr. Sharpe…speculates is cocaine." Moralas folded his hands on the desk with the key under them. "Miss Palmer, did you at any time see Mr. Jeremiah Sharpe in possession of cocaine?"

"No."

"Did he at any time speak to you of cocaine or drug-trafficking?"

"No, of course not. I would have told you."

"As you told me about the key?" When Jonas started to protest, Moralas waved him off. "I will need a list of your customers for the past six weeks, Miss Palmer. Names and, wherever possible, addresses."

"My customers? Why?"

"It's more than possible that Mr. Sharpe used your shop for his contacts."

"My shop." Outraged, she stood up. "My boats? Do you think he could have passed drugs under my nose without me being aware?"

Moralas took out a cigar and studied it. "I very much hope you were unaware, Miss Palmer. You will bring me the list of clients by the end of the week." He glanced at Jonas. "Of course, you are within your rights to demand a warrant. It will simply slow down the process. And I, of course, am within my rights to hold Miss Palmer as a material witness."

Jonas watched the pale blue smoke circle toward the ceiling. It was tempting to call Moralas's bluff simply as an exercise in testing two ends of the law. And in doing so, he and the captain could play tug-of-war with Liz for hours. "There are times, Captain, when it's wiser not to employ certain rights. I think I'm safe in saying that the three of us in this room want basically the same thing." He rose and flicked his lighter at the end of Moralas's cigar. "You'll have your list, Captain. And more."

Moralas lifted his gaze and waited.

"Pablo Manchez," Jonas said, and was gratified to see Moralas's eyes narrow.

"What of Manchez?"

"He's on Cozumel. Or was," Jonas stated. "My brother met with him several times in local bars and clubs. You may also be interested in David Merriworth, an American working out of Acapulco. Apparently he's the one who put my brother onto his contacts in Cozumel. If you contact the authorities in the States, you'll find that Merriworth has an impressive rap sheet."

In his precise handwriting, Moralas noted down the names, though he wasn't likely to forget them. "I appreciate the information. However, in the future, Mr. Sharpe, I would appreciate it more if you stayed out of my way. *Buenas tardes,* Miss Palmer."

Moments later, Liz strode out to the street. "I don't like being threatened. That's what he was doing, wasn't it?" she demanded. "He was threatening to put me in jail."

Very calm, even a bit amused, Jonas lit a cigarette. "He was pointing out his options, and ours."

"He didn't threaten to put you in jail," Liz muttered.

"He doesn't worry as much about me as he does about you."

"Worry?" She stopped with her hand gripping the handle of Jonas's rented car.

"He's a good cop. You're one of his people."

She looked back toward the police station with a scowl. "He has a funny way of showing it." A scruffy little boy scooted up to the car and gallantly opened the door for her. Even as he prepared to hold out a hand, Liz was digging for a coin.

"Gracias."

He checked the coin, grinned at the amount and nodded approval. *"Buenas tardes, señorita."* Just as gallantly he closed the door for her while the coin disappeared into a pocket.

"It's a good thing you don't come into town often," Jonas commented.

"Why?"

"You'd be broke in a week."

Liz found a clip in her purse and pulled back her hair. "Because I gave a little boy twenty-five pesos?"

"How much did you give the other kid before we went into Moralas?"

"I bought something from him."

"Yeah." Jonas swung away from the curb. "You look like a woman who can't go a day without a box of Chiclets."

"You're changing the subject."

"That's right. Now tell me where I can find the best place for buying ingredients for chili."

"You want me to cook for you tonight?"

"It'll keep your mind off the rest. We've done everything we can do for the moment," he added. "Tonight we're going to relax."

She would have liked to believe he was right. Between nerves and anger, she was wound tight. "Cooking's supposed to relax me?"

"Eating is going to relax you. It's just an unavoidable circumstance that you have to cook it first."

It sounded so absurd that she subsided. "Turn left at the next corner. I tell you what to buy, you buy it, then you stay out of my way."

"Agreed."

"And you clean up."

"Absolutely."

"Pull over here," she directed. "And remember, you asked for it."

Liz never skimped when she cooked, even taking into account that authentic Mexican spices had more zing than the sort sold in the average American supermarket. She'd developed a taste for Mexican food and Yucatán specialties when she'd been a child, exploring the peninsula with her parents. She wasn't an elaborate cook, and when alone would often make do with a sandwich, but when her heart was in it, she could make a meal that would more than satisfy.

Perhaps, in a way, she wanted to impress him. Liz found she was able to admit it while she prepared a Mayan salad for chilling. It was probably very natural and harmless to want to impress someone with your cooking. After peeling and slicing an avocado, she found, oddly enough, she was relaxing.

So much of what she'd done in the past few days had been difficult or strange. It was a relief to make a decision no more vital than the proper way to slice her fruits and vegetables. In the end, she fussed with the arrangement a bit more, pleased with the contrasting colors of greens and oranges and cherry tomatoes. It was, she recalled, the only salad she could get Faith to eat because it was the only one Faith considered pretty enough. Liz didn't realize she was smiling as she began to sauté onions and peppers. She added a healthy dose of garlic and let it all simmer.

"It already smells good," Jonas commented as he strode through the doorway.

She only glanced over her shoulder. "You're supposed to stay out of my way."

"You cook, I take care of the table."

Liz only shrugged and turned back to the stove. She measured, stirred and spiced until the kitchen was filled with a riot of scent. The sauce, chunky with meat and vegetables, simmered and thickened on low heat. Pleased with herself, she wiped her hands on a cloth and turned around. Jonas was sitting comfortably at the table watching her.

"You look good," he told her. "Very good."

It seemed so natural, their being together in the kitchen with a pot simmering and a breeze easing its way through the screen. It made her remember how hard it was not to want such simple things in your life. Liz set the cloth down and found she didn't know what to do with her hands. "Some men think a woman looks best in front of a stove."

"I don't know. It's a toss-up with the way you looked at the wheel of a boat. How long does that have to cook?"

"About a half hour."

"Good." He rose and went to the counter where he'd left two bottles. "We have time for some wine."

A little warning signal jangled in her brain. Liz decided she needed a lid for the chili. "I don't have the right glasses."

"I already thought of that." From a bag beside the bottle, he pulled out two thin-stemmed wineglasses.

"You've been busy," she murmured.

"You didn't like me hovering over you in the market. I had to do something." He drew out the cork, then let the wine breathe.

"These candles aren't mine."

He turned to see Liz fiddling with the fringe of one of the woven mats he'd set on the table. In the center were two deep blue tapers that picked up the color in the border of her dishes.

"They're ours," Jonas told her.

She twisted the fringe around one finger, let it go, then twisted it again. The last time she'd burned candles had been during a power failure. These didn't look sturdy, but slender and frivolous. "There wasn't any need to go to all this trouble. I don't—"

"Do candles and wine make you uneasy?"

Dropping the fringe, she let her hands fall to her sides. "No, of course not."

"Good." He poured rich red wine into both glasses. Walking to her, he offered one. "Because I find them relaxing. We did agree to relax."

She sipped, and though she wanted to back away, held her ground. "I'm afraid you may be looking for more than I can give."

"No." He touched his glass to hers. "I'm looking for exactly what you can give."

Recognizing when she was out of her depth, Liz turned toward the refrigerator. "We can start on the salad."

He lit the candles and dimmed the lights. She told herself it didn't matter. Atmosphere was nothing more than a pleasant addition to a meal.

"Very pretty," Jonas told her when she'd mixed the dressing and arranged avocado slices. "What's it called?"

"It's a Mayan salad." Liz took the first nibble and was satisfied. "I learned the recipe when I worked at the hotel. Actually, that's where most of my cooking comes from."

"Wonderful," Jonas decided after the first bite. "It makes me wish I'd talked you into cooking before."

"A one time only." She relaxed enough to smile. "Meals aren't—"

"Included in the rent," Jonas finished. "We might negotiate."

This time she laughed at him and chose a section of grapefruit. "I don't think so. How do you manage in Philadelphia?"

"I have a housekeeper who'll toss together a casserole on Wednesdays." He took another bite, enjoying the contrast of crisp greens and spicy dressing. "And I eat out a lot."

"And parties? I suppose you go to a lot of parties."

"Some business, some pleasure." He'd almost forgotten what it was like to sit in a kitchen and enjoy a simple meal. "To be honest, it wears a bit. The cruising."

"Cruising?"

"When Jerry and I were teenagers, we might hop in the car on a Friday night and cruise. The idea was to see what teenage girls had hopped in their cars to cruise. The party circuit's just adult cruising."

She frowned a bit because it didn't seem as glamorous as she'd imagined. "It seems rather aimless."

"Doesn't seem. Is."

"You don't appear to be a man who does anything without a purpose."

"I've had my share of aimless nights," he murmured. "You come to a point where you realize you don't want too many more." That was just it, he realized. It wasn't the work, the hours spent closeted with law books or in a courtroom. It was the nights without meaning that left him wanting more. He lifted the wine to top off her glass, but his eyes stayed on hers. "I came to that realization very recently."

Her blood began to stir. Deliberately, Liz pushed her wine aside and rose to go to the stove. "We all make decisions at certain points in our lives, realign our priorities."

"I have the feeling you did that a long time ago."

"I did. I've never regretted it."

That much was true, he thought. She wasn't a woman for regrets. "You wouldn't change it, would you?"

Liz continued to spoon chili into bowls. "Change what?"

"If you could go back eleven years and take a different path, you wouldn't do it."

She stopped. From across the room he could see the flicker of candlelight in her eyes as she turned to him. More, he could see the strength that softness and shadows couldn't disguise. "That would mean I'd have to give up Faith. No, I wouldn't do it."

When she set the bowls on the table, Jonas took her hand. "I admire you."

Flustered, she stared down at him. "What for?"

"For being exactly what you are."

Chapter 8

No smooth phrases, no romantic words could have affected her more deeply. She wasn't used to flattery, but flattery, Liz was sure, could be brushed easily aside by a woman who understood herself. Sincere and simple approval was a different matter. Perhaps it was the candlelight, the wine, the intimacy of the small kitchen in the empty house, but she felt close to him, comfortable with him. Without being aware of it happening, Liz dropped her guard.

"I couldn't be anything else."

"Yes, you could. I'm glad you're not."

"What are you?" she wondered as she sat beside him.

"A thirty-five-year-old lawyer who's just realizing he's wasted some time." He lifted his glass and touched it to hers. "To making the best of whatever there is."

Though she wasn't certain she understood him, Liz drank, then waited for him to eat.

"You could fuel an engine with this stuff." Jonas dipped his spoon into the chili again and tasted. Hot spice danced on his tongue. "It's great."

"Not too hot for your Yankee stomach?"

"My Yankee stomach can handle it. You know, I'm surprised you haven't opened a restaurant, since you can cook like this."

She wouldn't have been human if the compliment hadn't pleased her. "I like the water more than I like the kitchen."

"I can't argue with that. So you picked this up in the kitchen when you worked at the hotel?"

"That's right. We'd take a meal there. The cook would show me how much of this and how much of that. He was very kind," Liz remembered. "A lot of people were kind."

He wanted to know everything—the small details, the feelings, the memories. Because he did, he knew he had to probe with care. "How long did you work there?"

"Two years. I lost count of how many beds I made."

"Then you started your own business?"

"Then I started the dive shop." She took a thin cracker and broke it in two. "It was a gamble, but it was the right one."

"How did you handle it?" He waited until she looked over at him. "With your daughter?"

She withdrew. He could hear it in her voice. "I don't know what you mean."

"I wonder about you." He kept the tone light, knowing she'd never respond to pressure. "Not many women could have managed all you've managed. You were alone, pregnant, making a living."

"Does that seem so unusual?" It made her smile to think of it. "There are only so many choices, aren't there?"

"A great many people would have made a different one."

With a nod, she accepted. "A different one wouldn't have been right for me." She sipped her wine as she let her mind drift back. "I was frightened. Quite a bit at first, but less and less as time when on. People were very good to me. It might have been different if I hadn't been lucky. I went into labor when I was cleaning room 328." Her eyes warmed as if she'd just seen something lovely. "I remember holding this stack of towels in my hand and thinking, 'Oh God, this is it, and I've only done half my rooms.'" She laughed and went back to her meal. Jonas's bowl sat cooling.

"You worked the day your baby was born?"

"Of course. I was healthy."

"I know men who take the day off if they need a tooth filled."

She laughed again and passed him the crackers. "Maybe women take things more in stride."

Only some women, he thought. Only a few exceptional women. "And afterward?"

"Afterward I was lucky again. A woman I worked with knew Señora Alderez. When Faith was born, her youngest had just turned five. She took care of Faith during the day, so I was able to go right back to work."

The cracker crumbled in his hand. "It must have been difficult for you."

"The only hard part was leaving my baby every

morning, but the señora was wonderful to Faith and to me. That's how I found this house. Anyway, one thing led to another. I started the dive shop."

He wondered if she realized that the more simply she described it, the more poignant it sounded. "You said the dive shop was a gamble."

"Everything's a gamble. If I'd stayed at the hotel, I never would have been able to give Faith what I wanted to give her. And I suppose I'd have felt cheated myself. Would you like some more?"

"No." He rose to take the bowls himself while he thought out how to approach her. If he said the wrong thing, she'd pull away again. The more she told him, the more he found he needed to know. "Where did you learn to dive?"

"Right here in Cozumel, when I was just a little older than Faith." As a matter of habit she began to store the leftovers while Jonas ran water in the sink. "My parents brought me. I took to it right away. It was like, I don't know, learning to fly I suppose."

"Is that why you came back?"

"I came back because I'd always felt peaceful here. I needed to feel peaceful."

"But you must have still been in school in the States."

"I was in college." Crouching, Liz shifted things in the refrigerator to make room. "My first year. I was going to be a marine biologist, a teacher who'd enlighten class after class on the mysteries of the sea. A scientist who'd find all the answers. It was such a big dream. It overwhelmed everything else to the point where I studied constantly and rarely went out. Then I—" She caught herself. Straightening slowly, she closed the refrigerator. "You'll want the lights on to do those dishes."

"Then what?" Jonas demanded, taking her shoulder as she hit the switch.

She stared at him. Light poured over them without the shifting shadows of candles. "Then I met Faith's father, and that was the end of dreams."

The need to know eclipsed judgment. He forgot to be careful. "Did you love him?"

"Yes. If I hadn't, there'd have been no Faith."

It wasn't the answer he'd wanted. "Then why are you raising her alone?"

"That's obvious, isn't it?" Anger surged as she shoved his hand aside. "He didn't want me."

"Whether he did or didn't, he was responsible to you and the child."

"Don't talk to me about responsibility. Faith's my responsibility."

"The law sees things otherwise."

"Keep your law," she snapped. "He could quote it chapter and verse, and it didn't mean a thing. We weren't wanted."

"So you let pride cut you off from your rights?" Impatient with her, he stuck his hands in his pockets and strode back to the sink. "Why didn't you fight for what you were entitled to?"

"You want the details, Jonas?" Memory brought its own particular pain, its own particular shame. Liz concentrated on the anger. Going back to the table, she picked up her glass of wine and drank deeply.

"I wasn't quite eighteen. I was going to college to study exactly what I wanted to study so I could do exactly what I wanted to do. I considered myself a great deal more mature than some of my classmates who flitted around from class to class more concerned about where the action would be that night. I spent most of my evenings in the library. That's where I met him. He was in his last year and knew if he didn't pass the bar there'd be hell to pay at home. His family had been in law or politics since the Revolution. You'd understand about family honor, wouldn't you?"

The arrow hit the mark, but he only nodded.

"Then you should understand the rest. We saw each other every night in the library, so it was natural that we began to talk, then have a cup of coffee. He was smart, attractive, wonderfully mannered and funny." Almost violently, she blew out the candles. The scent carried over and hung in the room. "I fell hard. He brought me flowers and took me for long quiet drives on Saturday nights. When he told me he loved me, I believed him. I thought I had the world in the palm of my hand."

She set the wine down again, impatient to be finished. Jonas said nothing. "He told me we'd be married as soon as he established himself. We'd sit in his car and look at the stars and he'd tell me about his home in Dallas and the wonderful rooms. The parties and the servants and the chandeliers. It was like a story, a lovely happily-ever-after story. Then one day his mother came." Liz laughed, but gripped the back of her chair until her knuckles were white. She could still feel the humiliation.

"Actually, she sent her driver up to the dorm to fetch me. Marcus hadn't said a thing about her visiting, but I was thrilled that I was going to meet her. At the curb was this fabulous white Rolls, the kind you only see in movies. When the driver opened the door for me, I was floating. Then I got in and she gave me the facts of life. Her son had a certain position to maintain, a certain image to project. She was sure I was a very nice girl, but hardly suitable for a Jensann of Dallas."

Jonas's eyes narrowed at the name, but he said nothing. Restless, Liz went to the stove and began to scrub the surface. "She told me she'd already spoken with her son and he understood the relationship had to end. Then she offered me a check as compensation. I was humiliated, and worse, I was pregnant. I hadn't told anyone yet, because I'd just found out that morning. I didn't take her money. I got out of the Rolls and went straight to Marcus. I was sure he loved me enough to toss it all aside for me, and for our baby. I was wrong."

Her eyes were so dry that they hurt. Liz pressed her fingers to them a moment. "When I went to see him, he was very logical. It had been nice; now it was over. His parents held the purse strings and it was important to keep them happy. But he wanted me to know we could still see each other now and again, as long as it was on the side. When I told him about the baby, he was furious. How could I have done such a thing? *I*."

Liz tossed the dishrag into the sink so that hot, soapy water heaved up. "It was as though I'd conceived the baby completely on my own. He wouldn't have it, he wouldn't have some silly girl who'd gotten herself pregnant messing up his life. He told me I had to get rid of it. It—as though Faith were a thing to be erased and forgotten. I was hysterical. He lost his temper. There were threats. He said he'd spread word that I was sleeping around and his friends would back him up. I'd never be able to prove the baby was his. He said my parents would be embarrassed, perhaps sued if I tried to press it. He tossed around a lot of legal phrases that I couldn't understand, but I understood he was finished with me. His family had a lot of pull at the college, and he said he'd see that I was dismissed. Because I was foolish enough to believe everything he said, I was terrified. He gave me a check and told me to go out of state— better, out of the country—to take care of things. That way no one would have to know.

"For a week I did nothing. I went through my classes in a daze, thinking I'd wake up and find out it had all been a bad dream. Then I faced it. I wrote my parents, telling them what I could. I sold the car they'd given me when I graduated from high school, took the check from Marcus and came to Cozumel to have my baby."

He'd wanted to know, even demanded, but now his insides were raw. "You could have gone to your parents."

"Yes, but at the time Marcus had convinced me they'd be ashamed. He told me they'd hate me and consider the baby a burden."

"Why didn't you go to his family? You were entitled to be taken care of."

"Go to them?" He'd never heard venom in her voice before. "Be taken care of by them? I'd have gone to hell first."

He waited a moment, until he was sure he could speak calmly. "They don't even know, do they?"

"No. And they never will. Faith is mine."

"And what does Faith know?"

"Only what she has to know. I'd never lie to her."

"And do you know that Marcus Jensann has his sights set on the senate, and maybe higher?"

Her color drained quickly and completely. "You know him?"

"By reputation."

Panic came and went, then returned in double force. "He doesn't know Faith exists. None of them do. They can't."

Watching her steadily, he took a step closer. "What are you afraid of?"

"Power. Faith is mine, she's going to stay mine. None of them will ever touch her."

"Is that why you stay here? Are you hiding from them?"

"I'll do whatever's necessary to protect my child."

"He's still got you running scared." Furious for her, Jonas took her arms. "He's got a frightened teenager strapped inside of you who's never had the chance to stretch and feel alive. Don't you know a man like that wouldn't even remember who you are? You're still running away from a man who wouldn't recognize you on the street."

She slapped him hard enough to make his head snap back. Breathing fast, she backed away from him, appalled by a show of violence she hadn't been aware of possessing. "Don't tell me what I'm running from," she whispered. "Don't tell me what I feel." She turned and fled. Before she'd reached the front door he had her again, whirling her around, gripping her hard. He no longer knew why his anger was so fierce, only that he was past the point of controlling it.

"How much have you given up because of him?" Jonas demanded. "How much have you cut out of your life?"

"It's my life!" she shouted at him.

"And you won't share it with anyone but your daughter. What the hell are you going to do when she's grown? What the hell are you going to do in twenty years when you have nothing but your memories?"

"Don't." Tears filled her eyes too quickly to be blinked away.

He grabbed her close again, twisting until she had to look at him. "We all need someone. Even you. It's about time someone proved it to you."

"No."

She tried to turn her head but he was quick. With his mouth crushed on hers she struggled, but her arms were trapped between their bodies and his were iron-like around her. Emotions already mixed with fear and anger became more confused with passion. Liz fought not to give in to any of them as his mouth demanded both submission and response.

"You're not fighting me," he told her. His eyes were close, searing into hers. "You're fighting yourself. You've been fighting yourself since the first time we met."

"I want you to let me go." She wanted her voice to be strong, but it trembled.

"Yes. You want me to let you go just as much as you want me not to. You've been making your own decisions for a long time, Liz. This time I'm making one for you."

Her furious protest was lost against his mouth as he pressed her down to the sofa. Trapped under him, her body began to heat, her blood began to stir. Yes, she was fighting herself. She had to fight herself before she could fight him. But she was losing.

She heard her own moan as his lips trailed down

her throat, and it was a moan of pleasure. She felt the hard line of his body against hers as she arched under him, but it wasn't a movement of protest. *Want me,* she seemed to say. *Want me for what I am.*

Her pulse began to thud in parts of her body that had been quiet for so many years. Life burst through her like a torrid wind through thin glass until every line of defense was shattered. With a desperate groan, she took his face in her hands and dragged his mouth back to hers.

She could taste the passion, the life, the promises. She wanted them all. Recklessness, so long chained within, tore free and ruled. A sound bubbled in her throat she wasn't even aware was a laugh as she wrapped herself around him. She wanted. He wanted. The hell with the rest.

He wasn't sure what had driven him—anger, need, pain. All he knew now was that he had to have her, body, soul and mind. She was wild beneath him, but no longer in resistance. Every movement was a demand that he take more, give more, and nothing seemed fast enough. She was a storm set to rage, a fire desperate to consume. Whatever he'd released inside of her had whipped out and taken him prisoner.

He pulled the shirt over her head and tossed it aside. His heartbeat thundered. She was so small, so delicate. But he had a beast inside him that had been caged too long. He took her breast in his mouth and sent them both spinning. She tasted so fresh: a cool, clear glass of water. She smelled of woman at her most unpampered and most seductive. He felt her body arch against his, taut as a bowstring, hot as a comet. The innocence that remained so integral a part of her trembled just beneath wanton passion. No man alive could have resisted it; any man alive might have wished for it. His mouth was buried at her throat when he felt the shirt rip away from his back.

She hardly knew what she was doing. Touching him sent demands to her brain that she couldn't deny. She wanted to feel him against her, flesh to flesh, to experience an intimacy she'd so long refused to allow herself. There'd been no one else. As Liz felt her skin fused to his she understood why. There was only one Jonas. She pulled his mouth back to hers to taste him again.

He drew off her slacks so that she was naked, but she didn't feel vulnerable. She felt invulnerable. Hardly able to breathe, she struggled with his. Then she gave him no choice. Desperate for that final release, she wrapped her legs around him and drew him into her until she was filled. At the shock of that first ragged peak, her eyes flew open. Inches away, he watched her face. Her mouth trembled open, but before she could catch her breath, he was driving her higher, faster. She couldn't tell how long they balanced on the edge, trapped between pleasure and fulfillment. Then his arms came around her, hers around his. Together, they broke free.

She didn't speak. Her system leveled slowly, and she was helpless to hurry it. He didn't move. He'd shifted his weight, but his arms had come around her and stayed there. She needed him to speak, to say something that would put what had happened in perspective. She'd only had one other lover and had learned not to expect.

Jonas rested his forehead against her shoulder a moment. He was wrestling with his own demons. "I'm sorry, Liz."

He could have said nothing worse. She closed her eyes and forced her emotions to drain. She nearly succeeded. Steadier, she reached for the tangle of clothes on the floor. "I don't need an apology." With her clothes in a ball in her arm, she walked quickly to the bedroom.

On a long breath, Jonas sat up. He couldn't seem to find the right buttons on Liz Palmer. Every move he made seemed to be a move in reverse. It still stunned him that he'd been so rough with her, left her so little choice in the final outcome. He'd be better off hiring her a private bodyguard and moving himself back to the hotel. It was true he didn't want to see her hurt and felt a certain responsibility for her welfare, but he didn't seem to be able to act on it properly. When she'd stood in the kitchen telling him what she'd been through, something had begun to boil in him. That it had taken the form of passion in the end wasn't something easily explained or justified. His apology had been inadequate, but he had little else.

Drawing on his pants, Jonas started for his room. It shouldn't have surprised him to find himself veering toward Liz's. She was just pulling on a robe. "It's late, Jonas."

"Did I hurt you?"

She sent him a look that made guilt turn over in his stomach. "Yes. Now I want to take a shower before I go to bed."

"Liz, there's no excuse for being so rough, and there's no making it up to you, but—"

"Your apology hurt me," she interrupted. "Now if you've said all you have to say, I'd like to be alone."

He stared at her a moment, then dragged a hand through his hair. How could he have convinced himself he understood her when she was now and always had been an enigma? "Damn it, Liz, I wasn't apologizing for making love to you, but for the lack of finesse. I practically tossed you on the ground and ripped your clothes off."

She folded her hands and tried to keep calm. "I ripped yours."

His lips twitched, then curved. "Yeah, you did."

Humor didn't come into her eyes. "And do you want an apology?"

He came to her then and rested his hands on her shoulders. Her robe was cotton and thin and whirling with bright color. "No. I guess what I'd like is for you to say you wanted me as much as I wanted you."

Her courage weakened, so she looked beyond him. "I'd have thought that was obvious."

"Liz." His hand was gentle as he turned her face back to his.

"All right. I wanted you. Now—"

"Now," he interrupted. "Will you listen?"

"There's no need to say anything."

"Yes, there is." He walked with her to the bed and drew her down to sit. Moonlight played over their hands as he took hers. "I came to Cozumel for one reason. My feelings on that haven't changed but other things have. When I first met you I thought you knew something, were hiding something. I linked everything about you to Jerry. It didn't take long for me to see there was something else. I wanted to know about you, for myself."

"Why?"

"I don't know. It's impossible not to care about you."
At her look of surprise, he smiled. "You project this
image of pure self-sufficiency and still manage to look
like a waif. Tonight, I purposely maneuvered you into
talking about Faith and what had brought you here.
When you told me I couldn't handle it."

She drew her hand from his. "That's understandable.
Most people have trouble handling unwed mothers."

Anger bubbled as he grabbed her hand again. "Stop
putting words in my mouth. You stood in the kitchen
talking and I could see you, young, eager and trusting, being betrayed and hurt. I could see what it had
done to you, how it had closed you off from things you
wanted to do."

"I told you I don't have any regrets."

"I know." He lifted her hand and kissed it. "I guess
for a moment I needed to have them for you."

"Jonas, do you think anyone's life turns out the way
they plan it as children?"

He laughed a little as he slipped an arm around her
and drew her against him. Liz sat still a moment, unsure how to react to the casual show of affection. Then
she leaned her head against his shoulder and closed her
eyes. "Jerry and I were going to be partners."

"In what?"

"In anything."

She touched the coin on the end of his chain. "He
had one of these."

"Our grandparents gave them to us when we were
kids. They're identical five-dollar gold pieces. Funny,
I always wore mine heads up. Jerry wore his heads
down." He closed his fingers over the coin. "He stole
his first car when we were sixteen."

Her fingers crept up to his. "I'm sorry."

"The thing was he didn't need to—we had access to any car in the garage. He told me he just wanted to see if he could get away with it."

"He didn't make life easy for you."

"No, he didn't make life easy. Especially for himself. But he never did anything out of meanness. There were times I hated him, but I never stopped loving him."

Liz drew closer. "Love hurts more than hate."

He kissed the top of her head. "Liz, I don't suppose you've ever talked to a lawyer about Faith."

"Why should I?"

"Marcus has a responsibility, a financial responsibility at the least, to you and Faith."

"I took money from Marcus once. Not again."

"Child support payments could be set up very quietly. You could stop working seven days a week."

Liz took a deep breath and pulled away until she could see his face. "Faith is my child, has been my child only since the moment Marcus handed me a check. I could have had the abortion and gone back to my life as I'd planned it. I chose not to. I chose to have the baby, to raise the baby, to support the baby. She's never given me anything but pleasure from the moment she was born, and I have no intention of sharing her."

"One day she's going to ask you for his name."

Liz moistened her lips, but nodded. "Then one day I'll tell her. She'll have her own choice to make."

He wouldn't press her now, but there was no reason he couldn't have his law clerk begin to investigate child support laws and paternity cases. "Are you going to let me meet her? I know the deal is for me to be out of the house and out of your life when she gets back. I will, but I'd like the chance to meet her."

"If you're still in Mexico."

"One more question."

The smile came more easily. "One more."

"There haven't been any other men, have there?"

The smile faded. "No."

He felt twin surges of gratitude and guilt. "Then let me show you how it should be."

"There's no need—"

Gently, he brushed the hair back from her face. "Yes, there is. For both of us." He kissed her eyes closed. "I've wanted you from the first." His mouth on hers was as sweet as spring rain and just as gentle. Slowly, he slipped the robe from her shoulders, following the trail with warm lips. "Your skin's like gold," he murmured, then traced a finger over her breasts where the tone changed. "And so pale. I want to see all of you."

"Jonas—"

"All of you," he repeated, looking into her eyes until the heat kindled again. "I want to make love with all of you."

She didn't resist. Never in her life had anyone ever touched her with such reverence, looked at her with such need. When he urged her back, Liz lay on the bed, naked and waiting.

"Lovely," Jonas murmured. Her body was milk and honey in the moonlight. And her eyes were dark—dark and open and uncertain. "I want you to trust me." He began a slow journey of exploration at her ankles. "I want to know when I look at you that you're not afraid of me."

"I'm not afraid of you."

"You have been. Maybe I've even wanted you to be. No more."

His tongue slid over her skin and teased the back of her knees. The jolt of power had her rising up and gasping. "Jonas."

"Relax." He ran a hand lightly up her hip. "I want to feel your bones melt. Lie back, Liz. Let me show you how much you can have."

She obeyed, only because she hadn't the strength to resist. He murmured to her, stroking, nibbling, until she was too steeped in what he gave to give in return. But he wanted her that way, wanted to take her as though she hadn't been touched before. Not by him, not by anyone. Slowly, thoroughly and with great, great patience he seduced and pleasured. He thought as his mouth skimmed up her thigh that he could hear her skin hum.

She'd never known anything could be like this—so deep, so dark. There was a freedom here, she discovered, that she'd once only associated with diving down through silent fathoms. Her body could float, her limbs could be weightless, but she could feel every touch, every movement. Dreamlike, sensations drifted over her, so soft, so misty, each blended into the next. How long could it go on? Perhaps, after all, there were forevers.

She was lean, with muscles firm in her legs. Like a dancer's he thought, disciplined and trained. The scent from the bowl on her dresser spiced the air, but it was her fragrance, cool as a waterfall, that swam in his head. His mind emptied of everything but the need to delight her. Love, when unselfish, has incredible power.

His tongue plunged into the heat and his hands gripped hers as she arched, stunned at being flung

from a floating world to a churning one. He drew from
her, both patient and relentless, until she shuddered to
climax and over. When her hands went limp in his, he
brought them back to his body and pleasured himself.

She hadn't known passion could stretch so far or a
body endure such a barrage of sensations. His hands,
rough at the palm, showed her secrets she'd never had
the chance to imagine. His lips, warmed from her own
skin, opened mysteries and whispered the answers. He
gentled her, he enticed her, he stroked with tenderness
and he devoured. Gasping for air, she had no choice
but to allow him whatever he wanted, and to strain for
him to show her more.

When he was inside of her she thought it was all, and
more, than she could ever want. If this was love, she'd
never tasted it. If this was passion, she'd only skimmed
its surface. Now it was time to risk the depths. Willing, eager, she held on to him.

It was trust he felt from her, and trust that moved
him unbearably. He thought he'd needed before, desired
before, but never so completely. Though he knew what
it was to be part of another person, he'd never expected
to feel the merger again. Strong, complex, unavoidable,
the emotion swamped him. He belonged to her as fully
as he'd wanted her to belong to him.

He took her slowly, so that the thrill that coursed
through her seemed endless. His skin was moist when
she pressed her lips to his throat. The pulse there was
as quick as her own. A giddy sense of triumph moved
through her, only to be whipped away with passion
before it could spread.

Then he drew her up to him, and her body, liquid
and limber with emotion, rose like a wave to press

against his. Wrapped close, mouths fused, they moved together. Her hair fell like rain down her back. She could feel his heartbeat fast against her breast.

Still joined, they lowered again. The rhythm quickened. Desperation rose. She heard him breathe her name before the gates burst open and she was lost in the flood.

Chapter 9

She woke slowly, with a long, lazy stretch. Keeping her eyes closed, Liz waited for the alarm to ring. It wasn't often she felt so relaxed, even when waking, so she pampered herself and absorbed the luxury of doing nothing. In an hour, she mused, she'd be at the dive shop shifting through the day's schedule. The glass bottom, she thought, frowning a little. Was she supposed to take it out? Odd that she couldn't remember. Then with a start, it occurred to her that she didn't remember because she didn't know. She hadn't handled the schedule in two days. And last night...

She opened her eyes and looked into Jonas's.

"I could watch your mind wake up." He bent over and kissed her. "Fascinating."

Liz closed her fingers over the sheet and tugged it a little higher. What was she supposed to say? She'd never spent the night with a man, never awoken with one. She cleared her throat and wondered if every man awoke as sexily disheveled as Jonas Sharpe. "How did you sleep?" she managed, and felt ridiculous.

"Fine." He smiled as he brushed her hair from her cheek with a fingertip. "And you?"

"Fine." Her fingers moved restlessly on the sheet until he closed his hands over them. His eyes were warm and heavy and made her heart pound.

"It's a little late to be nervous around me, Elizabeth."

"I'm not nervous." But color rose to her cheeks when he pressed his lips to her naked shoulder.

"Still, it's rather flattering. If you're nervous…" He turned his head so the tip of his tongue could toy with her ear. "Then you're not unmoved. I wouldn't like to think you felt casually about being with me—yet."

Was it possible to want so much this morning what she'd sated herself with the night before? She didn't think it should be, and yet her body told her differently. She would, as she always did, listen to her intellect first. "It must be almost time to get up." One hand firmly on the sheets, she rose on her elbows to look at the clock. "That's not right." She blinked and focused again. "It can't be eight-fifteen."

"Why not?" He slipped a hand beneath the sheet and stroked her thigh.

"Because." His touch had her pulses speeding. "I always set it for six-fifteen."

Finding her a challenge, Jonas brushed light kisses over her shoulder, down her arm. "You didn't set it last night."

"I always—" She cut herself off. It was hard enough to try to think when he was touching her, but when she remembered the night before, it was nearly impossible to understand why she had to think. Her mind hadn't been on alarms and schedules and customers when her body had curled into Jonas's to sleep. Her mind, as it was now, had been filled with him.

"Always what?"

She wished he wouldn't distract her with fingertips sliding gently over her skin. She wished he could touch her everywhere at once. "I always wake up at six, whether I set it or not."

"You didn't this time." He laughed as he eased her back down. "I suppose I should be flattered again."

"Maybe I flatter you too much," she murmured and started to shift away. He simply rolled her back to him. "I have to get up."

"No, you don't."

"Jonas, I'm already late. I have to get to work."

Sunlight dappled over her face. He wanted to see it over the rest of her. "The only thing you have to do is make love with me." He kissed her fingers, then slowly drew them from the sheet. "I'll never get through the day without you."

"The boats—"

"Are already out, I'm sure." He cupped her breast, rubbing his thumb back and forth over the nipple. "Luis seems competent."

"He is. I haven't been in for two days."

"One more won't hurt."

Her body vibrated with need that slowly wound itself into her mind. Her arms came up to him, around him. "No, I guess it won't."

* * *

She hadn't stayed in bed until ten o'clock since she'd been a child. Liz felt as irresponsible as one as she started the coffee. True, Luis could handle the shop and the boats as well as she, but it wasn't his job. It was hers. Here she was, brewing coffee at ten o'clock, with her body still warm from loving. Nothing had been the same since Jonas Sharpe had arrived on her doorstep.

"It's useless to give yourself a hard time for taking a morning off," Jonas said from behind her.

Liz popped bread into the toaster. "I suppose not, since I don't even know today's schedule."

"Liz." Jonas took her by the arms and firmly turned her around. He studied her, gauging her mood before he spoke. "You know, back in Philadelphia I'm considered a workaholic. I've had friends express concern over the workload I take on and the hours I put in. Compared to you, I'm retired."

Her brows drew together as they did when she was concentrating. Or annoyed. "We each do what we have to do."

"True enough. It appears what I have to do is harass you until you relax."

She had to smile. He said it so reasonably and his eyes were laughing. "I'm sure you have a reputation for being an expert on harassment."

"I majored in it at college."

"Good for you. But I'm an expert at budgeting my own time. And there's my toast." He let her pluck it out, waited until she'd buttered it, then took a piece for himself.

"You mentioned diving lessons."

She was still frowning at him when she heard the

coffee begin to simmer. She reached for one cup, then relented and took two. "What about them?"

"I'll take one. Today."

"Today?" She handed him his coffee, drinking her own standing by the stove. "I'll have to see what's scheduled. The way things have been going, both dive boats should already be out."

"Not a group lesson, a private one. You can take me out on the *Expatriate*."

"Luis usually takes care of the private lessons."

He smiled at her. "I prefer dealing with the management."

Liz dusted crumbs from her fingers. "All right then. It'll cost you."

He lifted his cup in salute. "I never doubted it."

Liz was laughing when Jonas pulled into a narrow parking space at the hotel. "If he'd picked your pocket, why did you defend him?"

"Everyone's entitled to representation," Jonas reminded her. "Besides, I figured if I took him on as a client, he'd leave my wallet alone."

"And did he?"

"Yeah." Jonas took her hand as they crossed the sidewalk to the sand. "He stole my watch instead."

She giggled, a foolish, girlish sound he'd never heard from her. "And did you get him off?"

"Two years probation. There, it looks like business is good."

Liz shielded her eyes from the sun and looked toward the shop. Luis was busily fitting two couples with snorkel gear. A glance to the left showed her only the

Expatriate remained in dock. "Cozumel's becoming very popular," she murmured.

"Isn't that the idea?"

"For business?" She moved her shoulders. "I'd be a fool to complain."

"But?"

"But sometimes I think it would be nice if I could block out the changes. I don't want to see the water choked with suntan oil. *Hola,* Luis."

"Liz!" His gaze passed over Jonas briefly before he grinned at her. "We thought maybe you deserted us. How did you like Acapulco?"

"It was…different," she decided, and was already scooting behind the counter to find the daily schedule. "Any problems?"

"Jose took care of a couple repairs. I brought Miguel back to fill in, but I keep an eye on him. Got this— what do you call it—brochure on the aqua bikes." He pulled out a colorful pamphlet, but Liz only nodded.

"The Brinkman party's out diving. Did we take them to Palancar?"

"Two days in a row. Miguel likes them. They tip good."

"Hmm. You're handling the shop alone."

"No problem. Hey, there was a guy." He screwed up his face as he tried to remember the name. "Skinny guy, American. You know the one you took out on the beginners' trip?"

She flipped through the receipts and was satisfied. "Trydent?"

"*Sí,* that was it. He came by a coupla times."

"Rent anything?"

"No." Luis wiggled his eyebrows at her. "He was looking for you."

Liz shrugged it off. If he hadn't rented anything, he didn't interest her. "If everything's under control here, I'm going to take Mr. Sharpe out for a diving lesson."

Luis looked quickly at Jonas, then away. The man made him uneasy, but Liz looked happier than she had in weeks. "Want me to get the gear?"

"No, I'll take care of it." She looked up and smiled at Jonas. "Write Mr. Sharpe up a rental form and give him a receipt for the gear, the lesson and the boat trip. Since it's..." She trailed off as she checked her watch. "Nearly eleven, give him the half-day rate."

"You're all heart," Jonas murmured as she went to the shelves to choose his equipment.

"You got the best teacher," Luis told him, but couldn't manage more than another quick look at Jonas.

"I'm sure you're right." Idly, Jonas swiveled the newspaper Luis had tossed on the counter around to face him. He missed being able to sit down with the morning paper over coffee. The Spanish headlines told him nothing. "Anything going on I should know about?" Jonas asked, indicating the paper.

Luis relaxed a bit as he wrote. Jonas's voice wasn't so much like Jerry's when you weren't looking at him. "Haven't had a chance to look at it yet. Busy morning."

Going with habit, Jonas turned the paper over. There, in a faded black-and-white picture, was Erika. Jonas's fingers tightened. He glanced back and saw that Liz was busy, her back to him. Without a word, he slid the paper over the receipt Luis was writing.

"Hey, that's the—"

"I know," Jonas said in an undertone. "What does it say?"

Luis bent over the paper to read. He straightened again very slowly, and his face was ashen. "Dead," he whispered. "She's dead."

"How?"

Luis's fingers opened and closed on the pen he held. "Stabbed."

Jonas thought of the knife held at Liz's throat. "When?"

"Last night." Luis had to swallow twice. "They found her last night."

"Jonas," Liz called from the back, "how much do you weigh?"

Keeping his eyes on Luis, Jonas turned the paper over again. "One seventy. She doesn't need to hear this now," he added under his breath. He pulled bills from his wallet and laid them on the counter. "Finish writing the receipt."

After a struggle, Luis mastered his own fear and straightened. "I don't want anything to happen to Liz."

Jonas met the look with a challenge that held for several humming seconds before he relaxed. The smaller man was terrified, but he was thinking of Liz. "Neither do I. I'm going to see nothing does."

"You brought trouble."

"I know." His gaze shifted beyond Luis to Liz. "But if I leave, the trouble doesn't."

For the first time, Luis forced himself to study Jonas's face. After a moment, he blew out a long breath. "I liked your brother, but I think it was him who brought trouble."

"It doesn't matter anymore who brought it. I'm going to look out for her."

"Then you look good," Luis warned softly. "You look real good."

"First lesson," Liz said as she unlocked her storage closet. "Each diver carries and is responsible for his own gear." She jerked her head back to where Jonas's was stacked. With a last look at Luis, he walked through the doorway to gather it up.

"Preparing for a dive is twice as much work as diving itself," she began as she hefted her tanks. "It's a good thing it's worth it. We'll be back before sundown, Luis. *Hasta luego.*"

"Liz." She stopped, turning back to where Luis hovered in the doorway. His gaze passed over Jonas, then returned to her. *"Hasta luego,"* he managed, and closed his fingers over the medal he wore around his neck.

The moment she was on board, Liz restacked her gear. As a matter of routine, she checked all the *Expatriate*'s gauges. "Can you cast off?" she asked Jonas.

He ran a hand down her hair, surprising her. She looked so competent, so in charge. He wondered if by staying close he was protecting or endangering. It was becoming vital to believe the first. "I can handle it."

She felt her stomach flutter as he continued to stare at her. "Then you'd better stop looking at me and do it."

"I like looking at you." He drew her close, just to hold her. "I could spend years looking at you."

Her arms came up, hesitated, then dropped back to her sides. It would be so easy to believe. To trust again, give again, be hurt again. She wanted to tell him of the love growing inside her, spreading and strengthening with each moment. But if she told him she'd no longer have even the illusion of control. Without control, she was defenseless.

"I clocked you on at eleven," she said, but couldn't resist breathing deeply of his scent and committing it to memory.

Because she made him smile again, he drew her back. "I'm paying the bill, I'll worry about the time."

"Diving lesson," she reminded him. "And you can't dive until you cast off."

"Aye, aye, sir." But he gave her a hard, breath-stealing kiss before he jumped back on the dock.

Liz drew air into her lungs and let it out slowly before she turned on the engines. All she could hope was that she looked more in control than she felt. He was winning a battle, she mused, that he didn't even know he was fighting. She waited for Jonas to join her again before she eased the throttle forward.

"There are plenty of places to dive where we don't need the boat, but I thought you'd enjoy something away from the beaches. Palancar is one of the most stunning reefs in the Caribbean. It's probably the best place to start because the north end is shallow and the wall slopes rather than having a sheer vertical drop-off. There are a lot of caves and passageways, so it makes for an interesting dive."

"I'm sure, but I had something else in mind."

"Something else?"

Jonas took a small book out of his pocket and flipped through it. "What do these numbers look like to you?"

Liz recognized the book. It was the same one he'd used in Acapulco to copy down the numbers from his brother's book in the safe-deposit box. He still had his priorities, she reminded herself, then drew back on the throttle to let the boat idle.

The numbers were in precise, neat lines. Any child who'd paid attention in geography class would recognize them. "Longitude and latitude."

He nodded. "Do you have a chart?"

He'd planned this since he'd first seen the numbers, she realized. Their being lovers changed nothing else. "Of course, but I don't need it for this. I know these waters. That's just off the coast of Isla Mujeres." Liz adjusted her course and picked up speed. Perhaps, she thought, the course had already been set for both of them long before this. They had no choice but to see it through. "It's a long trip. You might as well relax."

He put his hands on her shoulders to knead. "We won't find anything, but I have to go."

"I understand."

"Would you rather I go alone?"

She shook her head violently, but said nothing.

"Liz, this had to be his drop point. By tomorrow, Moralas will have the numbers and send his own divers down. I have to see for myself."

"You're chasing shadows, Jonas. Jerry's gone. Nothing you can do is going to change that."

"I'll find out why. I'll find out who. That'll be enough."

"Will it?" With her hand gripping the wheel hard, she looked over her shoulder. His eyes were close, but they held that cool, set look again. "I don't think so—not for you." Liz turned her face back to the sea. She would take him where he wanted to go.

Isla Mujeres, Island of Women, was a small gem in the water. Surrounded by reefs and studded with untouched lagoons, it was one of the perfect retreats of the Caribbean. Party boats from the continental coast or one of the other islands cruised there daily to offer their customers snorkeling or diving at its best. It had once been known by pirates and blessed by a goddess. Liz anchored the boat off the southwest coast. Once again, she became the teacher.

"It's important to know and understand both the name and the use of every piece of equipment. It's not just a matter of stuffing in a mouthpiece and strapping on a tank. No smoking," she added as Jonas took out a cigarette. "It's ridiculous to clog up your lungs in the first place, and absurd to do it before a dive."

Jonas set the pack on the bench beside him. "How long are we going down?"

"We'll keep it under an hour. The depth here ranges to eighty feet. That means the nitrogen in your air supply will be over three times denser than what your system's accustomed to. In some people at some depths, this can cause temporary imbalances. If you begin to feel light-headed, signal to me right away. We'll descend in stages to give your body time to get used to the changes in pressure. We ascend the same way in order to give the nitrogen time to expel. If you come up too quickly, you risk decompression sickness. It can be fatal." As she spoke, she spread out the gear with the intention of explaining each piece. "Nothing is to be taken for granted in the water. It is not your milieu. You're dependent on your equipment and your own good sense. It's beautiful and it's exciting, but it's not an amusement park."

"Is this the same lecture you give on the dive boat?"

"Basically."

"You're very good."

"Thank you." She picked up a gauge. "Now—"

"Can we get started?" he asked and reached for his wet suit.

"We are getting started. You can't dive without a working knowledge of your equipment."

"That's a depth gauge." He nodded toward her hand as he stripped down to black briefs. "A very sophisticated one. I wouldn't think most dive shops would find it necessary to stock that quality."

"This is mine," she murmured. "But I keep a handful for rentals."

"I don't think I mentioned that you have the best-tended equipment I've ever seen. It isn't in the same league with your personal gear, but it's quality. Give me a hand, will you?"

Liz rose to help him into the tough, stretchy suit. "You've gone down before."

"I've been diving since I was fifteen." Jonas pulled up the zipper before bending over to check the tanks himself.

"Since you were fifteen." Liz yanked off her shirt and tossed it aside. Fuming, she pulled off her shorts until she wore nothing but a string bikini and a scowl. "Then why did you let me go on that way?"

"I liked hearing you." Jonas glanced up and felt his blood surge. "Almost as much as I like looking at you."

She wasn't in the mood to be flattered, less in the mood to be charmed. Without asking for assistance, she tugged herself into her wet suit. "You're still paying for the lesson."

Jonas grinned as he examined his flippers. "I never doubted it."

She strapped on the rest of her gear in silence. It was difficult even for her to say if she were really angry. All she knew was the day, and dive, weren't as simple as they had started out to be. Lifting the top of a bench, she reached into a compartment and took out two short metal sticks shaped like bats.

"What's this for?" Jonas asked as she handed him one.

"Insurance." She adjusted her mask. "We're going down to the caves where the sharks sleep."

"Sharks don't sleep."

"The oxygen content in the water in the cave keeps them quiescent. But don't think you can trust them."

Without another word, she swung over the side and down the ladder.

The water was as clear as glass, so she could see for more than a hundred feet. As she heard Jonas plunge in beside her, Liz turned to assure herself he did indeed know what he was doing. Catching her skeptical look, Jonas merely circled his thumb and forefinger, then pointed down.

He was tense. Liz could feel it from him, though she understood it had nothing to do with his skill underwater. His brother had dived here once—she was as certain of it as Jonas. And the reason for his dives had been the reason for his death. She no longer had to think whether she was angry. In a gesture as personal as a kiss, she reached out a hand and took his.

Grateful, Jonas curled his fingers around hers. He didn't know what he was looking for, or even why he continued to look when already he'd found more than he'd wanted to. His brother had played games with the rules and had lost. Some would say there was justice

in that. But they'd shared birth. He had to go on looking, and go on hoping.

Liz saw the first of the devilfish and tugged on
Jonas's hand. Such things never failed to touch her
spirit. The giant manta rays cruised together, feeding on plankton and unconcerned with the human in-
truders. Liz kicked forward, delighted to swim among
them. Their huge mouths could crush and devour crustaceans. Their wingspan of twenty feet and more was
awesome. Without fear, Liz reached out to touch. Pleasure came easily, as it always did to her in the sea. Her
eyes were laughing as she reached out again for Jonas.

They descended farther, and some of his tension
began to dissolve. There was something different about
her here, a lightness, an ease that dissolved the sadness
that always seemed to linger in her eyes. She looked
free, and more, as happy as he'd ever seen her. If it were
possible to fall in love in a matter of moments, Jonas
fell in love in those, forty feet below the surface with
a mermaid who'd forgotten how to dream.

Everything she saw, everything she could touch
fascinated her. He could see it in the way she moved,
the way she looked at everything as though it were
her first dive. If he could have found a way, he would
have stayed with her there, surrounded by love and
protected by fathoms.

They swam deeper, but leisurely. If something evil
had been begun, or been ended there, it had left no
trace. The sea was calm and silent and full of life too
lovely to exist in the air.

When the shadow passed over, Liz looked up. In all
her dives, she'd never seen anything so spectacular.
Thousands upon thousands of silvery grunts moved

together in a wave so dense that they might have been one creature. Eyes wide with the wonder of it, Liz lifted her arms and took her body up. The wave swayed as a unit, avoiding intrusion. Delighted, she signaled for Jonas to join her. The need to share the magic was natural. This was the pull of the sea that had driven her to study, urged to explore and invited her once to dream. With her fingers linked with Jonas's, she propelled them closer. The school of fish split in half so that it became two unified forms swirling on either side of them. The sea teemed with them, thick clouds of silver so tightly grouped that they seemed fused together.

For a moment she was as close to her own fantasies as she had ever been, floating free, surrounded by magic, with her lover's hand in hers. Impulsively, she wrapped her arms around Jonas and held on. The clouds of fish swarmed around them, linked into one, then swirled away.

He could feel her pulse thud when he reached for her wrist. He could see the fascinated delight in her eyes. Hampered by his human frailty in the water, he could only touch his hand to her cheek. When she lifted her own to press it closer, it was enough. Side by side they swam toward the seafloor.

The limestone caves were eerie and compelling. Once Jonas saw the head of a moray eel slide out and curve, either in curiosity or warning. An old turtle with barnacles crusting his back rose from his resting place beneath a rock and swam between them. Then at the entrance to a cave, Liz pointed and shared another mystery.

The shark moved across the sand, as a dog might on a hearth rug. His small, black eyes stared back at them as his gills slowly drew in water. While they huddled just inside the entrance, their bubbles rising up through the porous limestone and toward the surface, the shark shifted restlessly. Jonas reached for Liz's hand to draw her back, but she moved a bit closer, anxious to see.

In a quick move, the shark shot toward the entrance. Jonas was grabbing for Liz and his knife, when she merely poked at the head with her wooden bat. Without pausing, the shark swam toward the open sea and vanished.

He wanted to strangle her. He wanted to tell her how fascinating she was to watch. Since he could do neither, Jonas merely closed a hand over her throat and gave her a mock shake. Her laughter had bubbles dancing.

They swam on together, parting from time to time to explore separate interests. He decided she'd forgotten his purpose in coming, but thought it was just as well. If she could take this hour for personal freedom, he was glad of it. For him, there were demands.

The water and the life in it were undeniably beautiful, but Jonas noticed other things. They hadn't seen another diver and their down time was nearly up. The caves where the sharks slept were also a perfect place to conceal a cache of drugs. Only the very brave or the very foolish would swim in their territory at night. He thought of his brother and knew Jerry would have considered it the best kind of adventure. A man with a reason could swim into one of the caves while the sharks were out feeding, and leave or take whatever he liked.

Liz hadn't forgotten why Jonas had come. Because she thought she could understand a part of what he was feeling, she gave him room. Here, eighty feet below the surface, he was searching for something, anything, to help him accept his brother's death. And his brother's life.

It would come to an end soon, Liz reflected. The police had the name of the go-between in Acapulco. And the other name that Jonas had given them, she remembered suddenly. Where had he gotten that one? She looked toward him and realized there were things he wasn't telling her. That, too, would end soon, she promised herself. Then she found herself abruptly out of air.

She didn't panic. Liz was too well trained to panic. Immediately, she checked her gauge and saw that she had ten full minutes left. Reaching back, she ran a hand down her hose and found it unencumbered. But she couldn't draw air.

Whatever the gauge said, her life was on the line. If she swam toward the surface, her lungs would be crushed by the pressure. Forcing herself to stay calm, she swam in a diagonal toward Jonas. When she caught his ankle, she tugged sharply. The smile he turned with faded the moment he saw her eyes. Recognizing her signal, he immediately removed his regulator and passed it to her. Liz drew in air. Nodding, she handed it back to him. Their bodies brushing, her hand firm on his shoulder, they began their slow ascent.

Buddy-breathing, they rose closer to the surface, restraining themselves from rushing. What took only a matter of minutes seemed to drag on endlessly. The moment Liz's head broke water, she pushed back her mask and gulped in fresh air.

"What happened?" Jonas demanded, but when he felt her begin to shake, he only swore and pulled her with him to the ladder. "Take it easy." His hand was firm at her back as she climbed up.

"I'm all right." But she collapsed on a bench, without the energy to draw off her tanks. Her body shuddered once with relief as Jonas took the weight from her. With her head between her knees, she waited for the mists to clear. "I've never had anything like that happen," she managed. "Not at eighty feet."

He was rubbing her hands to warm them. "What did happen?"

"I ran out of air."

Enraged, he took her by the shoulders and dragged her back to a sitting position. "Ran out of air? That's unforgivably careless. How can you give lessons when you haven't the sense to watch your own gauges?"

"I watched my gauge." She drew air in and let it out slowly. "I should have had another ten minutes."

"You rent diving equipment, for God's sake! How can you be negligent with your own? You might've died."

The insult to her competence went a long way toward smothering the fear. "I'm never careless," she snapped at him. "Not with rental equipment or my own." She dragged the mask from her head and tossed it on the bench. "Look at my gauge. I should have had ten minutes left."

He looked, but it didn't relieve his anger. "Your equipment should be checked. If you go down with a faulty gauge you're inviting an accident."

"My equipment has been checked. I check it myself after every dive, and it was fine before I stored it. I filled those tanks myself." The alternative came to her even as she finished speaking. Her face, already pale, went white. "God, Jonas, I filled them myself. I checked every piece of equipment the last time I went down."

He closed a hand over hers hard enough to make her wince. "You keep it in the shop, in that closet."

"I lock it up."

"How many keys?"

"Mine—and an extra set in the drawer. They're rarely used because I always leave mine there when I go out on the boats."

"But the extra set would have been used when we were away?"

The shaking was starting again. This time it wasn't as simple to control it. "Yes."

"And someone used the key to the closet to get in and tamper with your equipment."

She moistened her lips. "Yes."

The rage ripped inside him until he was nearly blind with it. Hadn't he just promised to watch out for her, to keep her safe? With intensely controlled movements, he pulled off his flippers and discarded his mask. "You're going back. You're going to pack, then I'm putting you on a plane. You can stay with my family until this is over."

"No."

"You're going to do exactly what I say."

"No," she said again and managed to draw the strength to stand. "I'm not going anywhere. This is the second time someone's threatened my life."

"And they're not going to have a chance to do it again."

"I'm not leaving my home."

"Don't be a fool." He rose. Knowing he couldn't touch her, he unzipped his wet suit and began to strip it off. "Your business isn't going to fall apart. You can come back when it's safe."

"I'm not leaving." She took a step toward him. "You came here looking for revenge. When you have it, you can leave and be satisfied. Now I'm looking for answers. I can't leave because they're here."

Struggling to keep his hands gentle, he took her face between them. "I'll find them for you."

"You know better than that, don't you, Jonas? Answers don't mean anything unless you find them yourself. I want my daughter to be able to come home. Until I find those answers, until it's safe, she can't." She lifted her hands to his face so that they stood as a unit. "We both have reasons to look now."

He sat, took his pack of cigarettes and spoke flatly. "Erika's dead."

The anger that had given her the strength to stand wavered. "What?"

"Murdered." His voice was cold again, hard again. "A few days ago I met her, paid her for a name."

Liz braced herself against the rail. "The name you gave to the captain."

Jonas lit his cigarette, telling himself he was justified to put fear back into her eyes. "That's right. She asked some questions, got some answers. She told me this Pablo Manchez was bad, a professional killer. Jerry was killed by a pro. So, it appears, was Erika."

"She was shot?"

"Stabbed," Jonas corrected and watched Liz's hand reach involuntarily for her own neck. "That's right." He drew violently on the cigarette then hurled it overboard before he rose. "You're going back to the States until this is all over."

She turned her back on him a moment, needing to be certain she could be strong. "I'm not leaving, Jonas. We have the same problem."

"Liz—"

"No." When she turned back her chin was up and her eyes were clear. "You see, I've run from problems before, and it doesn't work."

"This isn't a matter of running, it's a matter of being sensible."

"You're staying."

"I don't have a choice."

"Then neither do I."

"Liz, I don't want you hurt."

She tilted her head as she studied him. She could believe that, she realized, and take comfort in it. "Will you go?"

"I can't. You know I can't."

"Neither can I." She wrapped her arms around him, pressed her cheek to his shoulder in a first spontaneous show of need or affection. "Let's go home," she murmured. "Let's just go home."

Chapter 10

Every morning when Liz awoke she was certain Captain Moralas would call to tell her it was all over. Every night when she closed her eyes, she was certain it was only a matter of one more day. Time went on.

Every morning when Liz awoke she was certain Jonas would tell her he had to leave. Every night when she slept in his arms, she was certain it was the last time. He stayed.

For over ten years her life had had a certain purpose. Success. She'd started the struggle toward it in order to survive and to provide for her child. Somewhere along the way she'd learned the satisfaction of being on her own and making it work. In over ten years, Liz had gone steadily forward without detours. A detour could mean failure and the loss of independence. It had been barely a month since Jonas had walked into her house and her life. Since that time the straight road she had followed had forked. Ignoring the changes hadn't helped, fighting them hadn't worked. Now it no longer seemed she had the choice of which path to follow.

Because she had to hold on to something, she worked every day, keeping stubbornly to her old routine. It was the only aspect of her life that she could be certain she could control. Though it brought some semblance of order to her life, it didn't keep Liz's mind at rest. She found herself studying her customers with suspicion. Business thrived as the summer season drew closer. It didn't seem as important as it had even weeks before, but she kept the shop open seven days a week.

Jonas had taken the fabric of her life, plucked at a few threads and changed everything. Liz had come to the point that she could admit nothing would ever be quite the same again, but she had yet to come to the point that she knew what to do about it. When he left, as she knew he would, she would have to learn all over again how to suppress longings and black out dreams.

They would find Jerry Sharpe's killer. They would find the man with the knife. If she hadn't believed that, Liz would never have gone on day after day. But after the danger was over, after all questions were answered, her life would never be as it had been. Jonas had woven himself into it. When he went away, he'd leave a hole behind that would take all her will to mend.

Her life had been torn before. Liz could comfort herself that she had put it together again. The shape had been different, the texture had changed, but she had put it together. She could do so again. She would have to.

There were times when she lay in bed in the dark, in the early hours of the morning, restless, afraid she would have to begin those repairs before she was strong enough.

Jonas could feel her shift beside him. He'd come to understand she rarely slept peacefully. Or she no longer slept peacefully. He wished she would lean on him, but knew she never would. Her independence was too vital, and opposingly, her insecurity was too deep to allow her to admit a need for another. Even the sharing of a burden was difficult for her. He wanted to soothe. Through his adult life, Jonas had carefully chosen companions who had no problems, required no advice, no comfort, no support. A woman who required such things required an emotional attachment he had never been willing to make. He wasn't a selfish man, simply a cautious one. Throughout his youth, and through most of his adult life, he'd picked up the pieces his brother had scattered. Consciously or unconsciously, Jonas had promised himself he'd never be put in the position of having to do so for anyone else.

Now he was drawing closer and closer to a woman who elicited pure emotion, then tried to deflect it. He was falling in love with a woman who needed him but refused to admit it. She was strong and had both the intelligence and the will to take care of herself. And she had eyes so soft, so haunted, that a man would risk anything to protect her from any more pain.

She had completely changed his life. She had altered the simple, tidy pattern he'd been weaving for himself. He *needed* to soothe, to protect, to share. There was nothing he could do to change that. Whenever he touched her, he came closer to admitting there was nothing he would do.

The bed was warm and the room smelled of the

flowers that grew wild outside the open window. Their scent mixed with the bowl of potpourri on Liz's dresser. Now and then the breeze ruffled through palm fronds so that the sound whispered but didn't disturb. Beside him was a woman whose body was slim and restless. Her hair spread over her pillow and onto his, carrying no more fragrance than wind over water. The moonlight trickled in, dipping into corners, filtering over the bed so he could trace her silhouette. As she tossed in sleep, he drew her closer. Her muscles were tense, as though she were prepared to reject the gift of comfort even before it was offered. Slowly, as her breath whispered at his throat, he began to massage her shoulders. Strong shoulders, soft skin. He found the combination irresistible. She murmured, shifting toward him, but he didn't know if it was acceptance or request. It didn't matter.

She felt so good there; she felt right there. All questions, all doubts could wait for the sunrise. Before dawn they would share the need that was in both of them. In the moonlight, in the quiet hours, each would have what the other could offer. He touched his mouth lightly, ever so lightly, to hers.

She sighed, but it was only a whisper of a sound— a sigh in sleep as her body relaxed against his. If she dreamed now, she dreamed of easy things, calm water, soft grass. He trailed a hand down her back, exploring the shape of her. Long, lean, slender and strong. He felt his own body warm and pulse. Passion, still sleepy, began to stir.

She seemed to wake in stages. First her skin, then her blood, then muscle by muscle. Her body was alert and throbbing before her mind raced to join it. She found herself wrapped around Jonas, already aroused, already hungry. When his mouth came to hers again, she answered him.

There was no hesitation in her this time, no moment of doubt before desire overwhelmed reason. She wanted to give herself to him as fully as it was possible to give. It wouldn't be wise to speak her feelings out loud. It couldn't be safe to tell him with words that her heart was stripped of defenses and open for him. But she could show him, and by doing so give them both the pleasure of love without restrictions.

Her arms tightened around him as her mouth roamed madly over his. She drew his bottom lip inside the heat, inside the moistness of her mouth and nibbled, sucked until his breath came fast and erratic. She felt the abrupt tension as his body pressed against hers and realized he, too, could be seduced. He, too, could be aroused beyond reason. And she realized with a heady sort of wonder that she could be the seducer, she could arouse.

She shifted her body under his, tentatively, but with a slow rhythm that had him murmuring her name and grasping for control. Instinctively she sought out vulnerabilities, finding them one by one, learning from them, taking from them. Her tongue flicked over his throat, seeking then enjoying the subtle, distinct taste of man. His pulse was wild there, as wild as hers. She shifted again until she lay across him and his body was hers for the taking.

Her hands were inexperienced so that her stroking was soft and hesitant. It drove him mad. No one had ever been so sweetly determined to bring him pleasure. She pressed kisses over his chest, slowly, experimentally, then rubbed her cheek over his skin so that the touch both soothed and excited.

His body was on fire, yet it seemed to float free so that he could feel the passage of air breathe cool over his flesh. She touched, and the heat spread like brushfire. She tasted and the moisture from her lips was like the whisper of a night breeze, cooling, calming.

"Tell me what you want." She looked up and her eyes were luminous in the moonlight, dark and beautiful. "Tell me what to do."

It was almost more than he could bear, the purity of the request, the willingness to give. He reached up so that his hands were lost in her hair. He could have kept her there forever, arched above him with her skin glowing gold in the thin light, her hair falling pale over her shoulders, her eyes shimmering with need. He drew her down until their lips met again. Hunger exploded between them. She didn't need to be told, she didn't need to be taught. Her body took over so that her own desire drove them both.

Jonas let reason go, let control be damned. Gripping her hips, he drew her up, then brought her to him, brought himself into her with a force that had her gasping in astonished pleasure. As she shuddered again, then again, he reached for her hands. Their fingers linked as she arched back and let her need set the pace. Frantic. Desperate. Uncontrollable. Pleasure, pain, delight, terror all whipped through her, driving her on, thrusting her higher.

He couldn't think, but he could feel. Until that moment, he wouldn't have believed it possible to feel so much so intensely. Sensations racked him, building and building and threatening to explode until the only sound he could hear was the roar of his own heart inside his head. With his eyes half open he could see her above him, naked and glorious in the moonlight. And when she plunged him beyond sensation, beyond sight and reason, he could still see her. He always would.

It didn't seem possible. It didn't, Liz thought, seem reasonable that she could be managing the shop, dealing with customers, stacking equipment when her system was still soaking up every delicious sensation she'd experienced just before dawn. Yet she was there, filling out forms, giving advice, quoting prices and making change. Still it was all mechanical. She'd been wise to delegate the diving tours and remain on shore.

She greeted her customers, some old and some new, and tried not to think too deeply about the list she'd been forced to give Moralas. How many of them would come to the Black Coral for equipment or lessons if they knew that by doing only that they were under police investigation? Jerry Sharpe's murder, and her involvement in it, could endanger her business far more than a slow season or a rogue hurricane.

Over and above her compassion, her sympathy and her hopes that Jonas could put his mind and heart at rest was a desperate need to protect her own, to guard what she'd built from nothing for her daughter. No matter how she tried to bury it, she couldn't completely block out the resentment she felt for being pulled into a situation that had been none of her making.

Yet there was a tug-of-war waging inside of her. Resentment for the disruption of her life battled against the longing to have Jonas remain in it. Without the disruption, he never would have come to her. No matter how much she tried, she could never regret the weeks they'd had together. She promised herself that she never would. It was time to admit that she had a great scope of love that had been trapped inside her. Rejected once, it had refused to risk again. But Jonas had released it, or perhaps she'd released it herself. Whatever happened, however it ended, she'd been able to love again.

"You're a hard lady to pin down."

Startled out of her own thoughts, Liz looked up. It took her a moment to remember the face, and a moment still to link a name with it. "Mr. Trydent." She rose from her desk to go to the counter. "I didn't realize you were still on the island."

"I only take one vacation a year, so I like to make the most of it." He set a tall paper cup that bounced with ice on the counter. "I figured this was the only way to get you to have a drink with me."

Liz glanced at the cup and wondered if she'd been businesslike or rude. At the moment she would have liked nothing better than to be alone with her own thoughts, but a customer was a customer. "That's nice of you. I've been pretty tied up."

"No kidding." He gave her a quick smile that showed straight teeth and easy charm. "You're either out of town or out on a boat. So I thought about the mountain and Mohammed." He glanced around. "Things are pretty quiet now."

"Lunchtime," Liz told him. "Everyone who's going out is already out. Everyone else is grabbing some food or a siesta before they decide how to spend the afternoon."

"Island living."

She smiled back. "Exactly. Tried any more diving?"

He made a face. "I let myself get talked into a night dive with Mr. Ambuckle before he headed back to Texas. I'm planning on sticking to the pool for the rest of my vacation."

"Diving's not for everyone."

"You can say that again." He drank from the second cup he'd brought, then leaned on the counter. "How about dinner? Dinner's for everyone."

She lifted a brow, a little surprised, a little flattered that he seemed bent on a pursuit. "I rarely eat out."

"I like home cooking."

"Mr. Trydent—"

"Scott," he corrected.

"Scott, I appreciate the offer, but I'm…" How did she put it? Liz wondered. "I'm seeing someone."

He laid a hand on hers. "Serious?"

Not sure whether she was embarrassed or amused, Liz drew her hand away. "I'm a serious sort of person."

"Well." Scott lifted his cup, watching her over the rim as he drank. "I guess we'd better stick to business then. How about explaining the snorkeling equipment to me?"

With a shrug, Liz glanced over her shoulder. "If you can swim, you can snorkel."

"Let's just say I'm cautious. Mind if I come in and take a look?"

She'd been ungracious enough for one day, Liz decided. She sent him a smile. "Sure, look all you want." When he'd skirted around the counter and through the door, she walked with him to the back shelves. "The snorkel's just a hollow tube with a mouthpiece," she began as she took one down to offer it. "You put this lip between your teeth and breathe normally through your mouth. With the tube attached to a face mask, you can paddle around on the surface indefinitely."

"Okay. How about all the times I see these little tubes disappear under the water?"

"When you want to go down, you hold your breath and let out a bit of air to help you descend. The trick is to blow out and clear the tube of water when you surface. Once you get the knack, you can go down and up dozens of times without ever taking your face out of the water."

Scott turned the snorkel over in his hand. "There's a lot to see down there."

"A whole world."

He was no longer looking at the snorkel, but at her. "I guess you know a lot about the water and the reefs in this area. Know much about Isla Mujeres?"

"Excellent snorkeling and diving." Absently, Liz took down a mask to show him how to attach the snorkel. "We offer full- and half-day trips. If you're adventurous enough, there are caves to explore."

"And some are fairly remote," he said idly.

"For snorkeling you'd want to stay closer to the reefs, but an experienced diver could spend days around the caves."

"And nights." Scott passed the snorkel through his fingers as he watched her. "I imagine a diver could go down there at night and be completely undisturbed."

She wasn't certain why she felt a trickle of alarm. Automatically, she glanced over his shoulder to where her police guard half dozed in the sun. Silly, she told herself with a little shrug. She'd never been one to jump at shadows. "It's a dangerous area for night diving."

"Some people prefer danger, especially when it's profitable."

Her mouth was dry, so she swallowed as she replaced the mask on the shelf. "Perhaps. I don't."

This time his smile wasn't so charming or his eyes so friendly. "Don't you?"

"I don't know what you mean."

"I think you do." His hand closed over her arm. "I think you know exactly what I mean. What Jerry Sharpe skimmed off the top and dumped in that safe-deposit box in Acapulco was petty cash, Liz." He leaned closer as his voice lowered. "There's a lot more to be made. Didn't he tell you?"

She had a sudden, fierce memory of a knife probing against her throat. "He didn't tell me anything. I don't know anything." Before she could evade, he had her backed into a corner. "If I scream," she managed in a steady voice, "there'll be a crowd of people here before you can take a breath."

"No need to scream." He held up both hands as if to show her he meant no harm. "This is a business discussion. All I want to know is how much Jerry told you before he made the mistake of offending the wrong people."

When she discovered she was trembling, Liz forced herself to stop. He wouldn't intimidate her. What weapon could he hide in a pair of bathing trunks and an open shirt? She straightened her shoulders and looked him directly in the eye. "Jerry didn't tell me anything. I said the same thing to your friend when he had the knife at my throat. It didn't satisfy him, so he put a damaged gauge on my tanks."

"My partner doesn't understand much about finesse," Scott said easily. "I don't carry knives, and I don't know enough about your diving equipment to mess with the gauges. What I know about is you, and I know plenty. You work too hard, Liz, getting up at dawn and hustling until sundown. I'm just trying to give you some options. Business, Liz. We're just going to talk business."

It was his calm, reasonable attitude that had her temper whipping out. He could be calm, he could be reasonable, and people were dead. "I'm not Jerry and I'm not Erika, so keep that in mind. I don't know anything about the filthy business you're into, but the police do, and they'll know more. If you think you can frighten me by threatening me with a knife or damaging my equipment, you're right. But that doesn't stop me from wishing every one of you to hell. Now get out of my shop and leave me alone."

He studied her face for a long ten seconds, then backed an inch or two away. "You've got me wrong, Liz. I said this was a business discussion. With Jerry gone, an experienced diver would come in handy, especially one who knows the waters around here. I'm authorized to offer you five thousand dollars. Five thousand American dollars for doing what you do best. Diving. You go down, drop off one package and pick up another. No names, no faces. Bring the package back to me unopened and I hand you five thousand in cash. Once or twice a week, and you can build up a nice little nest egg. I'd say a woman raising a kid alone could use some extra money."

Fear had passed into fury; she clenched her hands together. "I told you to get out," she repeated. "I don't want your money."

He smiled and touched a finger to her cheek. "Give it some thought. I'll be around if you change your mind."

Liz waited for her breathing to level as she watched him walk away. With deliberate movements, she locked the shop, then walked directly to her police guard. "I'm going home," she told him as he sprang to attention. "Tell Captain Moralas to meet me there in half an hour." Without waiting for a reply, she strode across the sand.

Fifteen minutes later, Liz slammed into her house. The ride home hadn't calmed her. At every turn she'd been violated. At every turn, her privacy and peace had been disrupted. This last incident was the last she'd accept. She might have been able to handle another threat, another demand. But he'd offered her a job. Offered to pay her to smuggle cocaine, to take over the position of a man who'd been murdered. Jonas's brother.

A nightmare, Liz thought as she paced from window to window. She wished she could believe it was a nightmare. The cycle was drawing to a close, and she felt herself being trapped in the center. What Jerry Sharpe had started, she and Jonas would be forced to finish, no matter how painful. No matter how deadly. Finish it she would, Liz promised herself. The cycle would be broken, no matter what she had to do. She would be finished with it so her daughter could come home safely. Whatever she had to do, she would see to that.

At the sound of a car approaching, Liz went to the front window. Jonas, she thought, and felt her heart sink. Did she tell him now that she'd met face-to-face with the man who might have killed his brother? If he had the name, if he knew the man, would he race off in a rage for the revenge he'd come so far to find? And if he found his revenge, could the cycle ever be broken? Instead, she was afraid it would revolve and revolve around them, smothering everything else. She saw Jonas, a man of the law, a man of patience and compassion, shackled forever within the results of his own violence. How could she save him from that and still save herself?

Her hand was cold as she reached for the door and opened it to meet him. He knew there was something wrong before he touched her. "What are you doing home? I went by the shop and it was closed."

"Jonas." She did the only thing she knew how. She drew him against her and held on. "Moralas is on his way here."

"What happened?" A little skip of panic ran through him before he could stop it. He held her away, searching her face. "Did something happen to you? Were you hurt?"

"No, I'm not hurt. Come in and sit down."

"Liz, I want to know what happened."

She heard the sound of a second engine and looked down the street to see the unmarked car. "Moralas is here," she murmured. "Come inside, Jonas. I'd rather go through this only once."

There was really no decision to be made, Liz told herself as she moved away from the door to wait. She would give Moralas and Jonas the name of the man who had approached her. She would tell them exactly what he'd said. By doing so she would take herself one step further away from the investigation. They would have a name, a face, a location. They would have motive. It was what the police wanted, it was what she wanted. She glanced at Jonas as Moralas came up the front walk. It was what Jonas wanted. What he needed. And by giving it to him, she would take herself one step further way from him.

"Miss Palmer." Moralas took off his hat as he entered, glanced briefly at Jonas and waited.

"Captain." She stood by a chair but didn't sit. "I have some information for you. There's an American, a man named Scott Trydent. Less than an hour ago he offered me five thousand dollars to smuggle cocaine off the reef of Isla Mujeres."

Moralas's expression remained impassive. He tucked his hat under his arm. "And have you had previous dealings with this man?"

"He joined one of my diving classes. He was friendly. Today he came by the shop to talk to me. Apparently he believed that I…" She trailed off to look at Jonas. He stood very still and very quiet just inside the door. "He thought that Jerry had told me about the operation. He'd found out about the safe-deposit box. I don't know how. It was as though he knew every move I've made for weeks." As her nerves began to fray, she dragged a hand through her hair. "He told me that I could take over Jerry's position, make the exchange in the caves near Isla Mujeres and be rich. He knows…" She had to swallow to keep her voice from trembling. "He knows about my daughter."

"You would identify him?"

"Yes. I don't know if he killed Jerry Sharpe." Her gaze shifted to Jonas again and pleaded. "I don't know, but I could identify him."

Moralas watched the exchange before crossing the room. "Please sit down, Miss Palmer."

"You'll arrest him?" She wanted Jonas to say something, anything, but he continued to stand in silence. "He's part of the cocaine ring. He knows about Jerry Sharpe's murder. You have to arrest him."

"Miss Palmer." Moralas urged her down on the sofa, then sat beside her. "We have names. We have faces. The smuggling ring currently operating in the Yucatan Peninsula is under investigation by both the Mexican and the American governments. The names you and Mr. Sharpe have given me are not unfamiliar. But there is one we don't have. The person who organizes, the person who undoubtedly ordered the murder of Jerry Sharpe. This is the name we need. Without it, the arrest of couriers, of salesmen, is nothing. We need this name, Miss Palmer. And we need proof."

"I don't understand. You mean you're just going to let Trydent go? He'll just find someone else to make the drops."

"It won't be necessary for him to look elsewhere if you agree."

"No." Before Liz could take in Moralas's words, Jonas was breaking in. He said it quietly, so quietly that chills began to race up and down her spine. He took out a cigarette. His hands were rock steady. Taking his time, he flicked his lighter and drew until the tip glowed red. He blew out a stream of smoke and locked his gaze on Moralas. "You can go to hell."

"Miss Palmer has the privilege to tell me so herself."

"You're not using her. If you want someone on the inside, someone closer to the names and proof, I'll make the drop."

Moralas studied him, saw the steady nerves and untiring patience along with simmering temper. If he'd had a choice, he'd have preferred it. "It isn't you who has been asked."

"Liz isn't going down."

"Just a minute." Liz pressed both hands to her temples. "Are you saying you want me to see Trydent again, to tell him I'll take the job? That's crazy. What purpose could there be?"

"You would be a decoy." Moralas glanced down at her hands. Delicate, yes, but strong. There was nothing about Elizabeth Palmer he didn't know. "The investigation is closing in. We don't want the ring to change locations at this point. If the operation appears to go smoothly, there should be no move at this time. You've been the stumbling block, Miss Palmer, for the ring, and the investigation."

"How?" Furious, she started to stand. Moralas merely put a hand on her arm.

"Jerry Sharpe lived with you, worked for you. He had a weakness for women. Neither the police nor the smugglers have been sure exactly what part you played. Jerry Sharpe's brother is now living in your home. The key to the safe-deposit box was found by you."

"Guilty by association, Captain?" Her voice took on that ice-sharp edge Jonas had heard only once or twice before. "Have I had police protection, or have I been under surveillance?"

Moralas's tone never altered. "One serves the same purpose as the other."

"If I'm under suspicion, haven't you considered that I might simply take the money and run?"

"That's precisely what we want you to do."

"Very clever." Jonas wasn't certain how much longer he could hold on to his temper. It would have given him great satisfaction to have picked Moralas up bodily and thrown him out of the house. Out of Liz's life. "Liz double-crosses them, annoying the head of the operation. It's then necessary to eliminate her the way my brother was eliminated."

"Except that Miss Palmer will be under police protection at all times. If this one drop goes as we plan, the investigation will end, and the smugglers, along with your brother's killer, will be caught and punished. This is what you want?"

"Not if it means risking Liz. Plant your own pigeon, Moralas."

"There isn't time. With your cooperation, Miss Palmer, we can end this. Without it, it could take months."

Months? she thought. Another day would be a lifetime. "I'll do it."

Jonas was beside her in a heartbeat, pulling her off the couch. "Liz—"

"My daughter comes home in two weeks." She put her hands on his arms. "She won't come back to anything like this."

"Take her someplace else." Jonas gripped her shoulders until his fingers dug into flesh. "We'll go someplace else."

"Where?" she demanded. "Every day I tell myself I'm pulling away from this thing and every day it's a lie. I've been in it since Jerry walked in the door. We can't change that. Until it's over, really over, nothing's going to be right."

He knew she was right, had known it from the first moment. But too much had changed. There was a desperation in him now that he'd never expected to feel.

It was all for her. "Come back to the States with me. It will be over."

"Will it? Will you forget your brother was murdered? Will you forget the man who killed him?" His fingers tightened, his eyes darkened, but he said nothing. Her breath came out in a sigh of acceptance. "No, it won't be over until we finish it. I've run before, Jonas. I promised myself I'd never run again."

"You could be killed."

"I've done nothing and they've nearly killed me twice." She dropped her head on his chest. "Please help me."

He couldn't force her to bend his way. Two of the things he most admired in her were her capacity to give and her will to stand firm. He could plead with her, he could argue, but he could never lie. If she ran, if they ran, they'd never be free of it. His arm came around her. Her hair smelled of summer and sea air. And before the summer ended, he promised himself, she'd be free. They'd both be free.

"I go with her." He met Moralas's eyes over her head.

"That may not be possible."

"I'll make it possible."

Chapter 11

She'd never been more frightened in her life. Every day she worked in the shop, waiting for Scott Trydent to approach. Every evening she locked up, went home and waited for the phone to ring. Jonas said little. She no longer knew what he did with the hours they were apart, but she was aware that he was planning his own move, in his own time. It only frightened her more.

Two days passed until her nerves were stretched thinner and tighter than she would have believed possible. On the beach, people slept or read novels, lovers walked by arm in arm. Children chattered and ran. Snorkelers splashed around the reef. She wondered why nothing seemed normal, or if it ever would again. At sundown she emptied her cash box, stacked gear and began to lock up.

"How about that drink?"

Though she'd thought she'd braced herself for the moment when it would begin, Liz jolted. Her head began to throb in a slow, steady rhythm she knew would last for hours. In the pit of her stomach she felt the twist come and go from panicked excitement. From this point on, she reminded herself, she had no room to panic. She turned and looked at Scott. "I was wondering if you'd come back."

"Told you I'd be around. I always figure people need a couple of days to mull things over."

She had a part to play, Liz reminded herself. She had to do it well. Carefully, she finished locking up, then turned back to him. She didn't smile. It was to be a business discussion, cut-and-dried. "We can get a drink over there." She pointed to the open-air thatched-roof restaurant overhanging the reef. "It's public."

"Suits me." Though he offered his hand, she ignored it and began to walk.

"You used to be friendlier."

"You used to be a customer." She sent him a sideways look. "Not a business partner."

"So…" She saw him glance right, then left. "You've mulled."

"You need a diver, I need money." Liz walked up the two wooden stairs and chose a chair that had her back to the water. Seconds after she sat, a man settled himself into a corner table. One of Moralas's, she thought, and ordered herself to be calm. She'd been briefed and rebriefed. She knew what to say, how to say it, and that the waiter who would serve them carried a badge and a gun. "Jerry didn't tell me a great deal," she began, and ordered an American soft drink. "Just that he made the drop and collected the money."

"He was a good diver."

Liz swallowed the little bubble of fear. "I'm better."

Scott grinned at her. "So I'm told."

A movement beside her had her glancing over, then freezing. A dark man with a pitted face took the chair beside her. Liz knew he wore a thin silver band on his wrist before she looked for it.

"Pablo Manchez, Liz Palmer. Though I think you two have met."

"Señorita." Manchez's thin mouth curved as he took her hand.

"Tell your friend to keep his hands to himself." Calmly, Jonas pulled a chair up to the table. "Why don't you introduce me, Liz?" When she could do no more than stare at him, he settled back. "I'm Jonas Sharpe. Liz and I are partners." He leveled his gaze to Manchez. This was the man, he thought, whom he'd come thousands of miles to see. This was the man he'd kill. Jonas felt the hatred and the fury rise. But he knew how to strap the emotions and wait. "I believe you knew my brother."

Manchez's hand dropped from Liz's and went to his side. "Your brother was greedy and stupid."

Liz held her breath as Jonas reached in his pocket. Slowly, he pulled out his cigarettes. "I'm greedy," he said easily as he lit one. "But I'm not stupid. I've been looking for you." He leaned across the table. With a slow smile, he offered Manchez the cigarettes.

Manchez took one and broke off the filter. His hands were beautiful, with long spidery fingers and narrow palms. Liz fought back a shudder as she looked at them. "So you found me."

Jonas was still smiling as he ordered a beer. "You need a diver."

Scott sent Manchez a warning look. "We have a diver."

"What you have is a team. Liz and I work together." Jonas blew out a stream of smoke. "Isn't that right, Liz?"

He wanted them. He wasn't going to back off until he had them. And she had no choice. "That's right."

"We don't need no team." Manchez started to rise.

"You need us." Jonas took his beer as it was served. "We already know a good bit about your operation. Jerry wasn't good at keeping secrets." Jonas took a swig from the bottle. "Liz and I are more discreet. Five thousand a drop?"

Scott waited a beat, then held a hand up, signaling Manchez. "Five. If you want to work as a team, it's your business how you split it."

"Fifty-fifty." Liz spread her fingers around Jonas's beer. "One of us goes down, one stays in the dive boat."

"Tomorrow night. Eleven o'clock. You come to the shop. Go inside. You'll find a waterproof case. It'll be locked."

"So will the shop," Liz put in. "How does the case get inside?"

Manchez blew smoke between his teeth. "I got no problem getting in."

"Just take the case," Scott interrupted. "The coordinates will be attached to the handle. Take the boat out, take the case down, leave it. Then come back up and wait exactly an hour. That's when you dive again.

All you have to do is take the case that's waiting for you back to the shop and leave it."

"Sounds smooth," Jonas decided. "When do we get paid?"

"After you do the job."

"Half up front." Liz took a long swallow of beer and hoped her heart would settle. "Leave twenty-five hundred with the case or I don't dive."

Scott smiled. "Not as trusting as Jerry."

She gave him a cold, bitter look. "And I intend to stay alive."

"Just follow the rules."

"Who makes them?" Jonas took the beer back from Liz. Her hand slipped down to his leg and stayed steady.

"You don't want to worry about that," Manchez advised. The cigarette was clamped between his teeth as he smiled. "He knows who you are."

"Just follow the coordinates and keep an eye on your watch." Scott dropped bills on the table as he rose. "The rest is gravy."

"Stay smart, Jerry's brother." Manchez gave them both a slow smile. *"Adios, señorita."*

Jonas calmly finished his beer as the two men walked away.

"You weren't supposed to interfere during the meeting," Liz began in a furious undertone. "Moralas said—"

"The hell with Moralas." He crushed out his cigarette, watching as the smoke plumed up. "Is that the man who put the bruises on your neck?"

Her hand moved up before she could stop it. Halfway to her throat, Liz curled her fingers into a ball and set her hand on the table. "I told you I didn't see him."

Jonas turned his head. His eyes, as they had before, reminded her of frozen smoke. "Was it the man?"

He didn't need to be told. Liz leaned closer and spoke softly. "I want it over, Jonas. And I don't need revenge. You were supposed to let me meet with Scott and set things up by myself."

In an idle move, he tilted the candle on the table toward him and lit it. "I changed my mind."

"Damn you, you could've messed everything up. I don't want to be involved but I am. The only way to get uninvolved is to finish it. How do we know they won't just back off now that you've come into it?"

"Because you're right in the middle, and you always have been." Before she could speak, he took her arm. His face was close, his voice cool and steady. "I was going to use you. From the minute I walked into your house, I was going to use you to get to Jerry's killer. If I had to walk all over you, if I had to knock you out of the way or drag you along with me, I was going to use you. Just the way Moralas is going to use you. Just the way the others are going to use you." The heat of the candle flickered between them as he drew her closer. "The way Jerry used you."

She swallowed the tremor and fought against the pain. "And now?"

He didn't speak. They were so close that he could see himself reflected in her eyes. In them, surrounding his own reflection, he saw the doubts and the defiance. His hand came to the back of her neck, held there until he could feel the rhythm of her pulse. With a simmering violence, he pulled her against him and covered her mouth with his. A flare that was passion, a glimmer that was hope—he didn't know which to reach for. So he let her go.

"No one's going to hurt you again," he murmured. "Especially not me."

It was the longest day of her life. Liz worked and waited as the hours crawled by. Moralas's men mixed with the vacationers on the beach. So obviously, it seemed to Liz, that she wondered everyone else didn't notice them as though they wore badges around their necks. Her boats went out, returned and went out again. Tanks and equipment were checked and rented. She filled out invoices and accepted credit cards as if there were some importance to daily routine. She wished for the day to end. She hoped the night would never come.

A thousand times she thought of telling Moralas she couldn't go through with it. A thousand times she called herself a coward. But as the sun went down and the beach began to clear, she realized courage wasn't something that could be willed into place. She would run, if she had the choice. But as long as she was in danger, Faith was in danger. When the sun went down, she locked the shop as if it were the end of any ordinary day. Before she'd pocketed her keys, Jonas was beside her.

"There's still time to change your mind."

"And do what? Hide?" She looked out at the beach, at the sea, at the island that was her home. And her prison. Why had she never seen it as a prison until Jonas had come to it? "You've already told me how good I am at hiding."

"Liz—"

She shook her head to stop him. "I can't talk about it. I just have to do it."

They drove home in silence. In her mind, Liz went over her instructions, every point, every word Moralas had pushed at her. She was to follow the routine, make the exchange, then turn the case with the money over to the police who'd be waiting near the dock. She'd wait for the next move. And while she waited, she'd never be more than ten feet away from a cop. It sounded foolproof. It made her stomach churn.

There was a man walking a dog along the street in front of her house. One of Moralas's men. The man whittling on her neighbor's porch had a gun under his denim vest. Liz tried to look at neither of them.

"You're going to have a drink, some food and a nap," Jonas ordered as he steered her inside.

"Just the nap."

"The nap first then." After securing the lock, Jonas followed her into the bedroom. He lowered the shades. "Do you want anything?"

It was still so hard to ask. "Would you lie down with me?"

He came to her. She was already curled on her side, so he drew her back against him and wrapped her close. "Will you sleep?"

"I think so." In sleep she could find escape, if only temporarily. But she didn't close her eyes. "Jonas?"

"Hmm?"

"After tonight—after we've finished, will you hold me like this again?"

He pressed his lips to her hair. He didn't think he could love her any more. He was nearly certain if he told her she'd pull away. "As long as you want. Just sleep."

Liz let her eyes close and her mind empty.

The case was small, the size of an executive brief-case. It seemed too inconspicuous to be the catalyst for so much danger. Beside it, on the counter of Liz's shop, was an envelope. Inside was a slip of paper with longitude and latitude printed. With the slip of paper were twenty-five one-hundred-dollar bills.

"They kept their part of the bargain," Jonas commented.

Liz merely shoved the envelope into a drawer. "I'll get my equipment."

Jonas watched her. She'd rather do this on her own, he reflected. She'd rather not think she had someone to lean on, to turn to. He took her tanks before she could heft them. She was going to learn, he reminded himself, that she had a great deal more than that. "The coordinates?"

"The same that were in Jerry's book." She found herself amazingly calm as she waited to lock the door behind him. They were being watched. She was aware that Moralas had staked men in the hotel. She was just as certain Manchez was somewhere close. She and Jonas didn't speak again until they were on the dive boat and had cast off. "This could end it." She glanced at him as she set her course.

"This could end it."

She was silent for a moment. All during the evening hours she'd thought about what she would say to him, how she would say it. "Jonas, what will you do?"

The flame of his lighter hissed, flared, then was quiet. "What I have to do."

The fear tasted like copper in her mouth, but it had nothing to do with herself and everything to do with Jonas. "If we make the exchange tonight, turn the second case over to Moralas. They'll have to come out in the open. Manchez, and the man who gives the orders."

"What are you getting at, Liz?"

"Manchez killed your brother."

Jonas looked beyond her. The sea was black. The sky was black. Only the hum of the motor broke the silence. "He was the trigger."

"Are you going to kill him?"

Slowly, he turned back to her. The question had been quiet, but her eyes weren't. They sent messages, posed argument, issued pleas. "It doesn't involve you."

That hurt deeply, sharply. With a nod, she followed the shimmer of light on the water. "Maybe not. But if you let hate rule what you do, how you think, you'll never be free of it. Manchez will be dead, Jerry will still be dead and you..." She turned to look at him again. "You'll never really be alive again."

"I didn't come all this way, spend all this time, to let Manchez walk away. He kills for money and because he enjoys it. He enjoys it," Jonas repeated viciously. "You can see it in his eyes."

And she had. But she didn't give a damn about Manchez. "Do you remember telling me once that everyone was entitled to representation?"

He remembered. He remembered everything he'd once believed in. He remembered how Jerry had looked in the cold white light of the morgue. "It didn't have anything to do with this."

"I suppose you change the rules when it's personal."

"He was my brother."

"And he's dead." With a sigh she lifted her face so that the wind could cool her skin. "I'm sorry, Jonas. Jerry's dead and if you go through with what you've planned, you're going to kill something in yourself." And, though she couldn't tell him, something in her. "Don't you trust the law?"

He tossed his cigarette into the water, then leaned on the rail. "I've been playing with it for years. It's the last thing I'd trust."

She wanted to go to him but didn't know how. Still, no matter what he did, she was beside him. "Then you'll have to trust yourself. And so will I."

Slowly, he crossed to her. Taking her face in his hands, he tried to understand what she was telling him, what she was still holding back. "Will you?"

"Yes."

He leaned to press a kiss to her forehead. Inside there was a need, a fierce desire to tell her to head the boat out to sea and keep going. But that would never work, not for either of them. They stood on the boat together, and stood at the crossroads. "Then start now." He kissed her again before he turned and lifted one of the compartment seats. Liz frowned as she saw the wet suit.

"What are you doing?"

"I arranged to have Luis leave this here for me."

"Why? We can't both go down."

Jonas stripped down to his trunks. "That's right. I'm diving, you're staying with the boat."

Liz stood very straight. It wouldn't do any good to

lose her temper. "The arrangements were made on all sides, Jonas. I'm diving."

"I'm changing the arrangements." He tugged the wet suit up to his waist before he looked at her. "I'm not taking any more chances with you."

"You're not taking chances with me. I am. Jonas, you don't know these waters. I do. You've never gone down here at night. I have."

"I'm about to."

"The last thing we need right now is for you to start behaving like an overprotective man."

He nearly laughed as he snapped the suit over his shoulders. "That's too bad, then, because that's just what we've got."

"I told Manchez and Trydent I was going down."

"I guess your reputation's shot when you lie to murderers and drug smugglers."

"Jonas, I'm not in the mood for jokes."

He strapped on his diver's knife, adjusted his weight belt, then reached for his mask. "Maybe not. And maybe you're not in the mood to hear this. I care about you. Too damn much." He reached out, gripping her chin. "My brother dragged you into this because he never wasted two thoughts about anyone else in his life. I pulled you in deeper because all I was thinking about was payback. Now I'm thinking about you, about us. You're not going down. If I have to tie you to the wheel, you're not going down."

"I don't want you to go." She balled her fists against his chest. "If I was down, all I'd think about was what I was doing. If I stay up here, I won't be able to stop thinking about what could happen to you."

"Time me." He lifted the tanks and held them out to her. "Help me get them on."

Hadn't she told herself weeks before that he wasn't a man who'd lose an argument? Her hands trembled a bit as she slipped the straps over his shoulders. "I don't know how to handle being protected."

He hooked the tanks as he turned back to her. "Practice."

She closed her eyes. It was too late for talk, too late for arguments. "Bear northeast as you dive. The cave's at eighty feet." She hesitated only a moment, then picked up a spear gun. "Watch out for sharks."

When he was over the side, she lowered the case to him. In seconds, he was gone and the sea was black and still. In her mind, Liz followed him fathom by fathom. The water would be dark so that he would be dependent on his gauges and the thin beam of light. Night creatures would be feeding. Squid, the moray, barracuda. Sharks. Liz closed her mind to it.

She should have forced him to let her go. How? Pacing the deck, she pushed the hair back from her face. He'd gone to protect her. He'd gone because he cared about her. Shivering, she sat down to rub her arms warm again. Was this what it was like to be cared for by a man? Did it mean you had to sit and wait? She was up again and pacing. She'd lived too much of her life doing to suddenly become passive. And yet... To hear him say he cared. Liz sat again and waited.

She'd checked her watch four times before she heard him at the ladder. On a shudder of relief, she dashed over to the side to help him. "I'm going down the next time," she began.

Jonas pulled off his light, then his tanks. "Forget

it." Before she could protest, he dragged her against him. "We've got an hour," he murmured against her ear. "You want to spend it arguing?"

He was wet and cold. Liz wrapped herself around him. "I don't like being bossed around."

"Next time you can boss me around." He dropped onto a bench and pulled her with him. "I'd forgotten what it was like down there at night. Fabulous." And it was nearly over, he told himself. The first step had been taken, the second one had to follow. "I saw a giant squid. Scared the hell out of him with the light. I swear he was thirty feet long."

"They get bigger." She rested her head on his shoulder and tried to relax. They had an hour. "I was diving with my father once. We saw one that was nearly sixty."

"Made you nervous?"

"No. I was fascinated. I remember I swam close enough to touch the tentacles. My father gave me a twenty-minute lecture when we surfaced."

"I imagine you'd do the same thing with Faith."

"I'd be proud of her," Liz began, then laughed. "Then I'd give her a twenty-minute lecture."

For the first time that night he noticed the stars. The sky was alive with them. It made him think of his mother's porch swing and long summer nights. "Tell me about her."

"You don't want to get me started."

"Yes, I do." He slipped an arm around her shoulder. "Tell me about her."

With a half smile, Liz closed her eyes. It was good to think of Faith, to talk of Faith. A picture began to emerge for Jonas of a young girl who liked school because there was plenty to do and lots of people. He heard the love and the pride, and the wistfulness. He saw the dark, sunny-faced girl in the photo and learned she spoke two languages, liked basketball and hated vegetables.

"She's always been sweet," Liz reflected. "But she's no angel. She's very stubborn, and when she's crossed, her temper isn't pretty. Faith wants to do things herself. When she was two she'd get very annoyed if I wanted to help her down the stairs."

"Independence seems to run in the family."

Liz moved her shoulders. "We've needed it."

"Ever thought about sharing?"

Her nerves began to hum. Though she shifted only a bit, it was away from him. "When you share, you have to give something up. I've never been able to afford to give up anything."

It was an answer he'd expected. It was an answer he intended to change. "It's time to go back down."

Liz helped him back on with his tanks. "Take the spear gun. Jonas..." He was already at the rail before she ran to him. "Hurry back," she murmured. "I want to go home. I want to make love with you."

"Hell of a time to bring that up." He sent her a grin, curled and fell back into the water.

Within five minutes Liz was pacing again. Why hadn't she thought to bring any coffee? She'd concentrate on that. In little more than an hour they could be huddled in her kitchen with a pot brewing. It wouldn't matter that there would be police surrounding the house. She and Jonas would be inside. Together. Perhaps she was wrong about sharing. Perhaps... When she heard the splash at the side of the boat, she was at the rail like a shot.

"Jonas, did something happen? Why—" She found herself looking down the barrel of a .22.

"Señorita." Manchez tossed his mask and snorkel onto a bench as he climbed over the side. *"Buenas noches."*

"What are you doing here?" She struggled to sound indignant as the blood rushed from her face. No, she wasn't brave, she realized. She wasn't brave at all. "We had a deal."

"You're an amateur," he told her. "Like Sharpe was an amateur. You think we'd just forget about the money?"

"I don't know anything about the money Jerry took." She gripped the rail. "I've told you that all along."

"The boss decided you were a loose end, pretty lady. You do us a favor and make this delivery. We do you a favor. We kill you quickly."

She didn't look at the gun again. She didn't dare. "If you keep killing your divers, you're going to be out of business."

"We're finished in Cozumel. When your friend brings up the case, I take it and go to Merida. I live in style. You don't live at all."

She wanted to sit because her knees were shaking. She stood because she thought she might never be able to again. "If you're finished in Cozumel, why did you set up this drop?"

"Clancy likes things tidy."

"Clancy?" The name David Merriworth had mentioned, Liz remembered, and strained to hear any sound from the water.

"There's a few thousand in cocaine down there, that's all. A few thousand dollars in the case coming up. The boss figures it's worth the investment to make it look like you were doing the dealing with Sharpe. Then you two have an argument and shoot each other. Case closed."

"You killed Erika, too, didn't you?"

"She asked too many questions." He lowered the gun. "You ask too many questions."

Light flooded the boat and the water so quickly that Liz's first instinct was to freeze. Before the next re-action had fully registered, she was tumbling into the water and diving blind.

How could she warn Jonas? Liz groped frantically in the water as lights played on the surface above her. She had no tanks, no mask, no protection. Any moment he'd be surfacing, unaware of any danger. He had no protection but her.

Without equipment, she'd be helpless in a matter of moments. She fought to stay down, keeping as close to the ladder as she dared. Her lungs were ready to burst when she felt the movement in the water. Liz turned toward the beam of light.

When he saw her, his heart nearly stopped. She looked like a ghost clinging to the hull of the boat. Her hair was pale and floating out in the current, her face was nearly as white as his light. Before his mind could begin to question, he was pushing his mouth-piece between her lips and giving her air. There could be no communication but emotion. He felt the fear. Jonas steadied the spear gun in his arm and surfaced.

"Mr. Sharpe." Moralas caught him in the beam of a spotlight. Liz rose up beside him. "We have every-thing under control." On the deck of her boat, Liz saw Manchez handcuffed and flanked by two divers. "Perhaps you will give my men and their prisoner a ride back to Cozumel."

She felt Jonas tense. The spear gun was set and aimed. Even through the mask, she could see his eyes burning, burning as only ice can. "Jonas, please." But he was already starting up the ladder. She hauled herself over the rail and tumbled onto the deck, cold and dripping. "Jonas, you can't. Jonas, it's over."

He barely heard her. All his emotion, all his concentration was on the man who stood only feet away. Their eyes were locked. It gave him no satisfaction to watch the blood drain from Manchez's face, or the knowledge leap frantically into his eyes. It was what he'd come for, what he'd promised himself. The medallion on the edge of his chain dangled and reminded him of his brother. His brother was dead. No satisfaction. Jonas lowered the gun.

Manchez tossed back his head. "I'll get out," he said quietly. The smile started to spread. "I'll get out."

The spear shot out and plowed into the deck between Manchez's feet. Liz saw the smile freeze on his face an instant before one formed on Jonas's. "I'll be waiting."

Could it really be over? It was all Liz could think when she awoke, warm and dry, in her own bed. She was safe, Jonas was safe and the smuggling ring on Cozumel was broken. Of course, Jonas had been furious. Manchez had been watched, they had been watched, but the police had made their presence known only after Liz had been held at gunpoint.

But he'd gotten what he'd come for, she thought. His brother's killer was behind bars. He'd face a trial and justice. She hoped it was enough for Jonas.

The morning was enough for her. The normality of it. Happy, she rolled over and pressed her body against Jonas's. He only drew her closer.

"Let's stay right here until noon."

She laughed and nuzzled against his throat. "I have—"

"A business to run," he finished.

"Exactly. And for the first time in weeks I can run it without having this urge to look over my shoulder. I'm happy." She looked at him, then tossed her arms around his neck and squeezed. "I'm so happy."

"Happy enough to marry me?"

She went still as a stone, then slowly, very slowly drew away. "What?"

"Marry me. Come home with me. Start a life with me."

She wanted to say yes. It shocked her that her heart burned to say yes. Pulling away from him was the hardest thing she'd ever done. "I can't."

He stopped her before she could scramble out of bed. It hurt, he realized, more than he could possibly have anticipated. "Why?"

"Jonas, we're two different people with two totally separate lives."

"We stopped having separate lives weeks ago." He took her hands. "They're not ever going to be separate again."

"But they will." She drew her hands away. "After you're back in Philadelphia for a few weeks, you'll barely remember what I look like."

He had her wrists handcuffed in his hands. The fury that surfaced so seldom in him seemed always on simmer when he was around her. "Why do you do that?" he demanded. "Why can't you ever take what you're given?" He swung her around until she was beneath him on the bed. "I love you."

"Don't." She closed her eyes as the wish nearly eclipsed the reason. "Don't say that to me."

Shut out. She was shutting him out. Jonas felt the panic come first, then the anger. Then the determination. "I will say it. If I say it enough, sooner or later you'll start to believe it. Do you think all these nights have been a game? Haven't you felt it? Don't you feel anything?"

"I thought I felt something once before."

"You were a child." When she started to shake her head, he gripped her tighter. "Yes, you were. In some ways you still are, but I know what goes through you when you're with me. I know. I'm not a ghost, I'm not a memory. I'm real and I want you."

"I'm afraid of you," she whispered. "I'm afraid because you make me want what I can't have. I won't marry you, Jonas, because I'm through taking chances with my life and I won't take chances with my child's life. Please let me go."

He released her, but when she stood, his arms went around her. "It isn't over for us."

She dropped her head against his chest, pressed her cheek close. "Let me have the few days we have left. Please let me have them."

He lifted her chin. Everything he needed to know was in her eyes. A man who knew and who planned to win could afford to wait. "You haven't dealt with anyone as stubborn as you are before this. And you haven't nearly finished dealing with me." Then his hand gentled as he stroked her hair. "Get dressed. I'll take you to work."

Because he acted as though nothing had been said, Liz relaxed. It was impossible, and she knew it. They'd known each other only weeks, and under circumstances that were bound to intensify any feelings. He cared. She believed that he cared, but love—the kind of love needed to build a marriage—was too much to risk.

She loved. She loved so much that she pushed him away when she wanted to pull him closer. He needed to go back to his life, back to his world. After time had passed, if he thought of her he'd think with gratitude that she had closed a door he'd opened on impulse. She would think of him. Always.

By the time Liz was walking toward the shop, she'd settled her mind. "What are you going to do today?"

"Me?" Jonas, too, had settled his mind. "I'm going to sit in the sun and do nothing."

"Nothing?" Incredulous, Liz stared at him. "All day?"

"It's known as relaxing, or taking a day off. If you do it several days running, it's called a vacation. I was supposed to have one in Paris."

Paris, she thought. It would suit him. She wondered briefly how the air smelled in Paris. "If you get bored, I'm sure one of the boats could use the extra crew."

"I've had enough diving for a few days, thanks." Jonas plopped down on a chaise in front of the shop. It was the best place to keep an eye on her.

"Miguel." Liz automatically looked around for Luis. "You're here early."

"I came with Luis. He's checking out the dive boat— got an early tour."

"Yes, I know." But she wouldn't trust Miguel to run

the shop alone for long. "Why don't you help him? I'll take care of the counter."

"*Bueno.* Oh, there were a couple of guys looking at the fishing boat. Maybe they want to rent."

"I'll take a look. You go ahead." Walking back, she crouched beside Jonas. "Keep an eye on the shop for me, will you? I've got a couple of customers over by the *Expatriate*."

Jonas adjusted his sunglasses. "What do you pay per hour?"

Liz narrowed her eyes. "I might cook dinner tonight."

With a smile, he got up to go behind the counter. "Take all the time you need."

He made her laugh. Liz strolled down the walkway and to the pier, drinking up the morning. She could use a good fishing cruise. The aqua bikes had been ordered, but they still had to be paid for. Besides, she'd like the ride herself. It made her think of Jonas and his unwanted catch a few weeks before. Liz laughed again as she approached the men beside her boat.

"*Buenos días,*" she began. "Mr. Ambuckle." Beaming a smile, Liz held out a hand. "I didn't know you were back. Is this one of your quick weekend trips?"

"That's right." His almost bald head gleamed in the sun as he patted her hand. "When the mood strikes me I just gotta move."

"Thinking about some big-game fishing this time around?"

"Funny you should mention it. I was just saying to my associate here that I only go for the big game."

"Only the big game." Scott Trydent turned around and pushed back his straw hat. "That's right, Clancy."

"Now don't turn around, honey." Ambuckle's fingers clamped over hers before she could move. "You're going to get on the boat, nice and quiet. We have some talking to do, then we might just take a little ride."

"How long have you been using my dive shop to smuggle?" Liz saw the gun under Scott's jacket. She couldn't signal to Jonas, didn't dare.

"For the past couple of years I've found your shop's location unbeatable. You know, they ship that stuff up from Colombia and dump in Miami. The way the heat's been on the past few years, you take a big chance using the regular routes. It takes longer this way, but I lose less merchandise."

"And you're the organizer," she murmured. "You're the man the police want."

"I'm a businessman," he said with a smile. "Let's get on board, little lady."

"The police are watching," Liz told him as she climbed on deck.

"The police have Manchez. If he hadn't tried to pull a double cross, the last shipment would have gone down smooth."

"A double cross?"

"That's right," Scott put in as he flanked her. "Pablo decided he could make more freelancing than by being a company man."

"And by reporting on his fellow employee, Mr. Trydent moves up in rank. I work my organization on the incentive program."

Scott grinned at Ambuckle. "Can't beat the system."

"You had Jerry Sharpe killed." Struggling to believe what was happening, Liz stared at the round little man who'd chatted with her and rented her tanks. "You had him shot."

"He stole a great deal of money from me." Ambuckle's face puckered as he thought of it. "A great deal. I had Manchez dispose of him. The truth is, I'd considered you as a liaison for some time. It seemed simpler, however, just to use your shop. My wife's very fond of you."

"Your wife." Liz thought of the neat, matronly woman in skirted bathing suits. "She knows you smuggle drugs, and she knows you kill people?"

"She thinks we have a great stockbroker." Ambuckle grinned. "I've been moving snow for ten years, and my wife wouldn't know coke from powdered sugar. I like to keep business and family separate. The little woman's going to be sick when she finds out you had an accident. Now we're going to take a little ride. And we're going to talk about the three hundred thousand our friend Jerry slipped out from under my nose. Cast off, Scott."

"No!" Thinking only of survival, Liz made a lunge toward the dock. Ambuckle had her on the deck with one shove. He shook his head, dusted his hands and turned to her. "I'd wanted to keep this from getting messy. You know, I switched gauges on your tanks, figuring you'd back off. Always had a soft spot for you, little lady. But business is business." With a wheezy sigh, he turned to Scott. "Since you've taken over Pablo's position, I assume you know how to deal with this."

"I certainly do." He took out a revolver. His eyes locked on Liz's. When she caught her breath, he turned the barrel toward Ambuckle. "You're under arrest." With his other hand, he pulled out a badge. "You have the right to remain silent..." It was the last thing Liz heard before she buried her face in her hands and wept.

Chapter 12

"I want to know what the hell's been going on." They were in Moralas's office, but Jonas wouldn't sit. He stood behind Liz's chair, his fingers curled tight over the back rung. If anyone had approached her, he would have struck first and asked questions later. He'd already flattened the unfortunate detective who'd tried to hold him back when he'd seen Liz on the deck of the *Expatriate* with Scott.

With his hands folded on his desk, Moralas gave Jonas a long, quiet look. "Perhaps the explanation should come from your countryman."

"Special Agent Donald Scott." The man Liz had known as Scott Trydent sat on the corner of Moralas's desk. "Sorry for the deception, Liz." Though his voice was calm and matter-of-fact, it couldn't mask the excitement that bubbled from him. As he sipped his cof-

fee, he glanced up at Jonas. Explanations wouldn't go
over easily with this one, he thought. But he'd always
believed the ends justified the means. "I've been after
that son of a bitch for three years." He drank again,
savoring triumph. "It took us two before we could in-
filtrate the ring, and even then I couldn't make contact
with the head man. To get to him I had to go through
more channels than you do with the Company. He's
been careful. For the past eight months I've been working with Manchez as Scott Trydent. He was the closest
I could get to Ambuckle until two days ago."

"You used her." Jonas's hand went to Liz's shoulder.
"You put her right in the middle."

"Yeah. The problem was, for a long time we weren't
sure just how involved she was. We knew about your
shop, Liz. We knew you were an experienced diver. In
fact, there isn't anything about you my organization
didn't know. For some time, you were our number-
one suspect."

"Suspect?" She had her hands folded neatly in her
lap, but the anger was boiling. "You suspected me."

"You left the U.S. over ten years ago. You've never
been back. You have both the contacts and the means
to have run the ring. You keep your daughter off the island for most of the year and in one of the best schools
in Houston."

"That's my business."

"Details like that become our business. When you
took Jerry Sharpe in and gave him a job, we leaned
even further toward you. He thought differently, but
then we weren't using him for his opinions."

She felt Jonas's fingers tighten and reached up to
them as she spoke. "Using him?"

"I contacted Jerry Sharpe in New Orleans. He was someone else we knew everything about. He was a con, an operator, but he had style." He took another swig of coffee as he studied Jonas. "We made him a deal. If he could get on the inside, feed us information, we'd forget about a few…indiscretions. I liked your brother," Scott said to Jonas. "Really liked him. If he'd been able to settle a bit, he'd have made a hell of a cop. 'Conning the bad guys,' he called it."

"Are you saying Jerry was working for you?" Jonas felt his emotions race toward the surface. The portrait he'd barely been able to force himself to accept was changing.

"That's right." Scott took out a cigarette and watched the match flare as he struck it. "I liked him—I mean that. He had a way of looking at things that made you forget they were so lousy."

That was Jerry, Jonas thought. To give himself a moment, he walked to the window. He could see the water lapping calmly against the hulls of boats. He could see the sun dancing down on it and children walking along the sea wall. The scene had been almost the same the day he'd arrived on Cozumel. Some things remained the same; others altered constantly. "What happened?"

"He had a hard time following orders. He wanted to push them too fast too far. He told me once he had something to prove, to himself and to the other part of him. The better part of him."

Jonas turned slowly. The pain came again, an ache. Liz saw it in his eyes and went to stand with him. "Go on."

"He got the idea into his head to rip off the money from a shipment. I didn't know about it until he called me from Acapulco. He figured he'd put the head man in a position where he'd have to deal personally. I told him to stay put, that we were scrubbing him. He'd have been taken back to the States and put somewhere safe until the job was over." He tossed the match he'd been holding into an ashtray on Moralas's desk. "He didn't listen. He came back to Cozumel and tried to deal with Manchez himself. It was over before I knew. Even if I'd have known, I can't be sure I could've stopped it. We don't like to lose civilians, Mr. Sharpe. I don't like to lose friends."

The anger drained from him degree by degree. It would have been so like Jerry, Jonas thought. An adventure, the excitement, the impulsiveness. "Go on."

"Orders came down to put the pressure on Liz." Scott gave a half laugh that had nothing to do with humor. "Orders from both sides. It wasn't until after your trip to Acapulco that we were sure you weren't involved in the smuggling. You stopped being a suspect and became the decoy."

"I came to the police." She looked at Moralas. "I came to you. You didn't tell me."

"I wasn't aware of Agent Scott's identity until yesterday. I knew only that we had a man on the inside and that it was necessary to use you."

"You were protected," Scott put in. "There wasn't a day you weren't guarded by Moralas's men and by mine. Your being here complicated things," he said to Jonas. "You were pushing too close to the bone. I guess you and Jerry had more in common than looks."

Jonas felt the weight on the chain around his neck. "Maybe we did."

"Well, we'd come to the point where we had to settle for Manchez and a few others or go for broke. We went for broke."

"The drop we made. It was a setup."

"Manchez had orders to do whatever he had to to get back the money Jerry had taken. They didn't know about the safe-deposit box." He blew out a stream of smoke. "I had to play it pretty fast and loose to keep that under wraps. But then we didn't know about it either, until you led us to it. As far as Ambuckle was concerned, you had the money, and he was going to get it back. He wanted it to look as though you'd been running the smuggling operation together. When you were found dead, the heat would be off of him. He planned to lie low awhile, then pick up business elsewhere. I had that from Manchez. You were set up," he agreed. "So was he. I got to Merriworth, made enough noise about how Manchez was about to double-cross to set him off. When Manchez was snorkeling to your boat, I was on the phone with the man I knew as Clancy. I got a promotion, and Clancy came back to deal with you himself."

Liz tried to see it as he did, as a chess game, as any game with pawns. She couldn't. "You knew who he was yesterday morning and you still had me get on that boat."

"There were a dozen sharpshooters in position. I had a gun, Ambuckle didn't. We wanted him to order Liz's murder, and we wanted him to tell her as much as possible. When this goes to court, we want it tidy. We want him put away for a long time. You're a lawyer, Sharpe. You know how these things can go. We can make a clean collar, have a stack of evidence and lose. I've watched too many of these bastards walk."

He blew out smoke between set teeth. "This one's not walking anywhere but into federal prison."

"There is still the question of whether these men will be tried in your country or mine." Moralas spoke softly, and didn't move when Scott whirled on him.

"Look, Moralas—"

"This will be discussed later. You have my thanks and my apologies," he said to Jonas and Liz. "I regret we saw no other way."

"So do I," Liz murmured, then turned to Scott. "Was it worth it?"

"Ambuckle brought thousands of pounds of cocaine into the States. He's responsible for more than fifteen murders in the U.S. and Mexico. Yeah, it was worth it."

She nodded. "I hope you understand that I never want to see you again." After closing her hand around Jonas's she managed a smile. "You were a lousy student."

"Sorry we never had that drink." He looked back at Jonas. "Sorry about a lot of things."

"I appreciate what you told me about my brother. It makes a difference."

"I'm recommending him for a citation. They'll send it to your parents."

"It'll mean a great deal to them." He offered his hand and meant it. "You were doing your job—I understand that. We all do what we have to do."

"That doesn't mean I don't regret it."

Jonas nodded. Something inside him was free, completely free. "As to putting Liz through hell for the past few weeks…" Very calmly, Jonas curled his hand into a fist and planted it solidly on Scott's jaw. The thin man snapped a chair in half as he crashed into it on his way to the floor.

"Jonas!" Stunned, Liz could do no more than stare. Then, incredibly, she felt the urge to giggle. With one hand over her mouth, she leaned into Jonas and let the laughter come. Moralas remained contentedly at his desk, sipping coffee.

Scott rubbed his jaw gingerly. "We all do what we have to do," he murmured.

Jonas only turned his back. "Goodbye, Captain."

Moralas stayed where he was. "Goodbye, Mr. Sharpe." He rose and, in a rare show of feeling, took Liz's hand and kissed it. *"Vaya con dios."*

He waited until the door had shut behind them before he looked down at Scott again. "Your government will, of course, pay for the chair."

He was gone. She'd sent him away. After nearly two weeks, Liz awoke every morning with the same thoughts. Jonas was gone. It was for the best. After nearly two weeks she awoke every morning struggling to convince herself. If she'd followed her heart, she would have said yes the moment he'd asked her to marry him. She would have left everything she'd built behind and gone with him. And ruined his life, perhaps her own.

He was already back in his own world, poring through law books, facing juries, going to elegant dinner parties. By now, she was sure his time in Cozumel was becoming vague. After all, he hadn't written. He hadn't called. He'd left the day after Ambuckle had been taken into custody without another word about love. He'd conquered his ghosts when he'd faced Manchez and had walked away whole.

He was gone, and she was once more standing on her own. As she was meant to, Liz thought. She'd have no regrets. That she'd promised herself. What she'd given to Jonas had been given without conditions or expectations. What he'd given to her she'd never lose.

The sun was high and bright, she thought. The air was as mellow as quiet music. Her lover was gone, but she, too, was whole. A month of memories could be stretched to last a lifetime. And Faith was coming home.

Liz pulled her bike into a parking space and listened to the thunder of a plane taking off. Even now Faith and her parents were crossing the Gulf. Liz left her bike and walked toward the terminal. It was ridiculous to feel nervous, she told herself, but she couldn't prevent it. It was ridiculous to arrive at the airport nearly an hour early, but she'd have gone mad at home. She skirted around a bed of marigolds and geraniums. She'd buy flowers, she decided. Her mother loved flowers.

Inside the terminal, the air was cool and full of noise. Tourists came and went but rarely passed the shops without a last-minute purchase. Liz started in the first store and worked her way down, buying consistently and strictly on impulse. By the time she arrived at the gate, she carried two shopping bags and an armful of dyed carnations.

Any minute, she thought. She'd be here any minute. Liz shifted both bags to one hand and nervously brushed at her hair. Passengers waited for their flights by napping in the black plastic chairs or reading guidebooks. She watched a woman check her lipstick in a compact mirror and wondered if she had time to run into the ladies room to examine her own face. Gnawing on her lip, she decided she couldn't leave, even for a moment. Neither could she sit, so she paced back and forth in front of the wide windows and watched the planes come and go. It was late. Planes were always late when you were waiting for them. The sky was clear and blue. She knew it was equally clear in Houston because she'd been checking the weather for days. But the plane was late. Impatient, she walked back to security to ask about the status. She should have known better.

Liz got a shrug and the Mexican equivalent of *It'll be here when it comes.* In another ten minutes, she was ready to scream. Then she saw it. She didn't have to hear the flight announcement to know. With her heart thudding dully, she waited by the door.

Faith wore blue striped pants and a white blouse. Her hair's grown, Liz thought as she watched her daughter come down the steps. She's grown—though she knew it would never do to tell Faith so. She'd just wrinkle her nose and roll her eyes. Her palms were wet. *Don't cry, don't cry,* Liz ordered herself. But the tears were already welling. Then Faith looked up and saw her. With a grin and a wave she was racing forward. Liz dropped her bags and reached out for her daughter.

"Mom, I got to sit by the window, but I couldn't see our house." As she babbled, Faith held her mother's neck in a stranglehold. "I brought you a present."

With her face buried against Faith's throat, Liz drew in the scents—powder, soap and chocolate from the streak on the front of the white blouse. "Let me look at you." Drawing her back, Liz soaked up the sight of her.

She's beautiful, Liz realized with a jolt. Not just cute or sweet or pretty any longer. Her daughter was beautiful.

I can't let her go again. It hit her like a wall. *I'll never be able to let her go again.* "You've lost a tooth," Liz managed as she brushed back her daughter's hair.

"Two." Faith grinned to show the twin spaces. "Grandma said I could put them under my pillow, but I brought them with me so I can put them under my real pillow. Will I get pesos?"

"Yes." Liz kissed one cheek, then the other. "Welcome home."

With her hand firmly in Faith's, Liz rose to greet her parents. For a moment she just looked at them, trying to see them as a stranger would. Her father was tall and still slim, though his hairline was creeping back. He was grinning at her the way he had whenever she'd done something particularly pleasing to him. Her mother stood beside him, lovely in her tidy way. She looked now, as she'd always looked to Liz, like a woman who'd never had to handle a crisis more stressful than a burned roast. Yet she'd been as solid and as sturdy as a rock. There were tears in her eyes. Liz wondered abruptly if the beginning of the summer left her mother as empty as the end of the summer left her.

"Momma." Liz reached out and was surrounded. "Oh, I've missed you. I've missed you all so much." *I want to go home.* The thought surged up inside her and nearly poured out. She needed to go home.

"Mom." Faith tugged on the pocket of her jeans. "Mom."

Giddy, Liz turned and scooped her up. "Yes." She covered her face with kisses until Faith giggled. "Yes, yes, yes!"

Faith snuggled in. "You have to say hello to Jonas."

"What?"

"He came with us. You have to say hi."

"I don't—" Then she saw him, leaning against the window, watching—waiting patiently. The blood rushed out of her head to her heart until she was certain something would burst. Holding onto Faith, Liz stood where she was. Jonas walked to her, took her face in both hands and kissed her hard.

"Nice to see you," he murmured, then bent down to pick up the bags Liz had dropped. "I imagine these are for you," he said as he handed Liz's mother the flowers.

"Yes." Liz tried to gather the thoughts stumbling through her mind. "I forgot."

"They're lovely." She sent her daughter a smile. "Jonas is going to drive us to the hotel. I invited him to dinner tonight. I hope you don't mind. You always make enough."

"No, I... Of course."

"We'll see you then." She gave Liz another brief kiss. "I know you want to get Faith home and have some time together. We'll see you tonight."

"But I—"

"Our bags are here. We're going to deal with customs."

Before Liz could say another word, she was alone with her daughter.

"Can we stop by and see Señor Pessado?"

"Yes," Liz said absently.

"Can I have some candy?"

Liz glanced down to the chocolate stain on Faith's blouse. "You've already had some."

Faith just smiled. She knew she could depend on Señor Pessado. "Let's go home now."

Liz waited until Faith was unpacked, until the crystal bird Faith had bought her was hanging in the window and her daughter had consumed two tacos and a pint of milk.

"Faith…" She wanted her voice to be casual. "When did you meet Mr. Sharpe?"

"Jonas? He came to Grandma's house." Faith turned the doll Liz had brought her this way and that for inspection.

"To Grandma's? When?"

"I don't know." She decided to call the doll Cassandra because it was pretty and had long hair. "Can I have my ice cream now?"

"Oh—yes." Liz walked over to get it out of the freezer. "Faith, do you know why he went to Grandma's?"

"He wanted to talk to her, I guess. To Grandpa, too. He stayed for dinner. I knew Grandma liked him because she made cherry pies. I liked him, too. He can play the piano really good." Faith eyed the ice cream and was satisfied when her mother added another scoop. "He took me to the zoo."

"What?" The bowl nearly slipped out of Liz's hand as she set it down. "Jonas took you to the zoo?"

"Last Saturday. We fed popcorn to the monkeys, but mostly we ate it." She giggled as she shoveled in ice cream. "He tells funny stories. I scraped my knee." Remembering suddenly, Faith pulled up her slacks to show off her wound.

"Oh, baby." It was small and already scabbed over,

but Liz brushed a kiss over it anyway. "How'd you do this?"

"At the zoo. I was running. I can run really fast in my new sneakers, but I fell down. I didn't cry."

Liz rolled the slacks down. "I'm sure you didn't."

"Jonas didn't get mad or anything. He cleaned it all up with his handkerchief. It was pretty messy. I bled a lot." She smiled at that, pleased with herself. "He said I have pretty eyes just like you."

A little thrill of panic raced through her, but she couldn't stop herself. "Did he? What else did he say?"

"Oh, we talked about Mexico and about Houston. He wondered which I liked best."

Liz rested her hands on her daughter's knees. *This is what matters,* she realized. This was all that really mattered. "What did you tell him?"

"I like it best where you are." She scraped the bottom of the bowl. "He said he liked it best there, too. Is he going to be your boyfriend?"

"My—" Liz managed, just barely, to suppress the laugh. "No."

"Charlene's mother has a boyfriend, but he isn't as tall as Jonas and I don't think he ever took Charlene to the zoo. Jonas said sometime maybe we could go see the Liberty Bell. Do you think we can?"

Liz picked up the ice cream dish and began to wash it. "We'll see," she muttered.

"Listen, someone's coming." Faith was up like a shot and dashing for the front door. "It's Jonas!" With a whoop, she was out of the door and running full steam.

"Faith!" Liz hurried from the kitchen and reached the porch in time to see Faith hurl herself at Jonas. With a laugh, he caught her, tossed her in the air then set her down again in a move so natural that it seemed he'd been doing so all his life. Liz knotted the dishcloth in her hands.

"You came early." Pleased, Faith hung on to his hand. "We were talking about you."

"Were you?" He tousled Faith's hair but looked up at Liz. "That's funny, because I was thinking about you."

"We're going to make paella because that's what Grandpa likes best. You can help."

"Faith—"

"Love to," Jonas interrupted. "After I talk to your mother." At the foot of the stairs he crouched down to Faith's level. "I'd really like to talk to your mom alone."

Faith's mouth screwed up. "Why?"

"I have to convince her to marry me."

He ignored Liz's gasp and watched for Faith's reaction. Her eyes narrowed and her mouth pursed. "She said you weren't her boyfriend. I asked."

He grinned and leaned closer. "I just have to talk her into it."

"Grandma says nobody can ever talk my mom into anything. She has a hard head."

"So do I, and I make a living talking people into things. But maybe you could put in a few good words for me later."

As Faith considered, her eyes brightened. "Okay. Mom, can I see if Roberto's home? You said he had new puppies."

Liz stretched out the cloth then balled it again. "Go ahead, but just for a little while."

Jonas straightened as he watched Faith race toward the house across the street. "You've done an excellent job with your daughter, Elizabeth."

"She's done a great deal of it herself."

He turned and saw the nerves on her face. It didn't displease him. But he remembered the way she'd looked when she had opened her arms to Faith at the airport. He wanted, he would, see her look that way again. "Do you want to talk inside?" he began as he walked up the steps. "Or right here?"

"Jonas, I don't know why you've come back, but—"

"Of course you know why I've come back. You're not stupid."

"We don't have anything to talk about."

"Fine." He closed the distance quickly. She didn't resist, though she told herself she would. When he dragged her against him, she went without hesitation. Her mouth locked hungrily to his, and for a moment, just for a moment, the world was right again. "If you don't want to talk, we'll go inside and make love until you see things a little more clearly."

"I see things clearly." Liz put her hands on his arms and started to draw away.

"I love you."

He felt the shudder, saw the flash of joy in her eyes before she looked away. "Jonas, this isn't possible."

"Wrong. It's entirely possible—in fact, it's already done. The point is, Liz, you need me."

Her eyes narrowed to slits. "What I need I take care of."

"That's why I love you," he said simply and took the wind out of her sails.

"Jonas—"

"Are you going to tell me you haven't missed me?" She opened her mouth, then shut it again. "Okay, so you take the Fifth on that one." He stepped back from her. "Are you going to deny that you've spent some sleepless nights in the past couple of weeks, that you've thought about what happened between us? Are you going to stand here and look at me now and tell me you're not in love with me?"

She'd never been able to lie well. Liz turned and meticulously spread the dishcloth over the porch rail. "Jonas, I can't run my life on my feelings."

"From now on you can. Did you like the present Faith brought you?"

"What?" Confused, she turned back. "Yes, of course I did."

"Good. I brought you one, too." He took a box out of his pocket. Liz saw the flash of diamond and nearly had her hand behind her back before he caught it in his. Firmly, he slipped the ring on. "It's official."

She wouldn't even look at it. She couldn't stop herself. The diamond was shaped in a teardrop and as white and glossy as a wish. "You're being ridiculous," she told him, but couldn't make herself take it off.

"You're going to marry me." He took her shoulders and leaned her back against a post. "That's not negotiable. After that, we have several options. I can give up my practice and live in Cozumel. You can support me."

She let out a quick breath that might have been a laugh. "Now you're really being ridiculous."

"You don't like that one. Good, I didn't care for it either. You can come back to Philadelphia with me. I'll support you."

Her chin went up. "I don't need to be supported."

"Excellent. We agree on the first two options." He ran his hands through her hair and discovered he wasn't feeling as patient as he'd thought he would. "Now, you can come back to the States. We'll take a map and you can close your eyes and pick a spot. That's where we'll live."

"We can't run our lives this way." She pushed him aside to walk down the length of the porch and back. But part of her was beginning to believe they could. "Don't you see how impossible it is?" she demanded as much of herself as of him. "You have your career. I have my business. I'd never be a proper wife for someone like you."

"You're the only wife for someone like me." He grabbed her shoulders again. No, he wasn't feeling patient at all. "Damn it, Liz, you're the only one. If the business is important to you, keep it. Have Luis run it. We can come back a half a dozen times a year if you want. Start another business. We'll go to Florida, to California, anywhere you want where they need a good dive shop. Or…" He waited until he was sure he had her full attention. "You could go back to school."

He saw it in her eyes—the surprise, the dream, then the denial. "That's over."

"The hell it is. Look at you—it's what you want. Keep the shop, build another, build ten others, but give yourself something for yourself."

"It's been more than ten years."

He lifted a brow. "You said once you wouldn't change anything."

"And I meant it, but to go back now, after all this time."

"Afraid?"

Her eyes narrowed; her spine stiffened. "Yes."

He laughed, delighted with her. "Woman, in the past

few weeks, you've been through hell and out again. And you're afraid of a few college courses?"

With a sigh, she turned away. "I might not be able to make it."

"So what?" He whirled her back again. "So you fall flat on your face. I'll be right there falling down with you. It's time for risking, Liz. For both of us."

"Oh, I want to believe you." She lifted a hand to rest it on his face. "I want to. I do love you, Jonas. So much."

She was locked against him again, lost in him. "I need you, Liz. I'm not going back without you."

She clung to him a moment, almost ready to believe. "But it's not just me. You have to understand I can't do whatever I'd like."

"Faith?" He drew her back again. "I've spent the past weeks getting to know her. My main objective when I started was to ingratiate myself. I figured the only way to get to you was through her."

So she'd already surmised. "Afternoons at the zoo?"

"That's right. Thing was, I didn't know she was as easy to fall for as her mother. I want her."

The hand Liz had lifted to her hair froze. "I don't understand."

"I want her to be mine—legally, emotionally. I want you to agree to let me adopt her."

"Adopt…" Whatever she might have expected from him, it hadn't been this. "But she's—"

"Yours?" he interrupted. "No, she's going to be ours. You're going to have to share her. And if you're set on her going to school in Houston, we'll live in Houston. Within the year I expect she should have a brother or sister because she needs family as much as we do."

He was offering her everything, everything she'd ever wanted and had refused to believe in. She had only to hold out her hand. The idea terrified her. "She's another man's child. How will you be able to forget that?"

"She's your child," he reminded her. "You told me yourself she was your child only. Now she's going to be mine." Taking her hands, he kissed them. "So are you."

"Jonas, do you know what you're doing? You're asking for a wife who'll have to start from scratch and a half-grown daughter. You're complicating your life."

"Yeah, and maybe I'm saving it."

And hers. Her blood was pumping again, her skin was tingling. For the first time in years she could look at her life and see no shadows. She closed her eyes and breathed deeply before she turned. "Be sure," she whispered. "Be absolutely sure. If I let myself go, if I say yes and you change your mind, I'll hate you for the rest of my life."

He took her by the shirtfront. "In one week, we're going to my parents' farm in Lancaster, calling the local minister, justice of the peace or witch doctor and we're getting married. Adoption papers are being drawn up. When we settle in as a family, we're all having the same name. You and Faith and I."

With a sigh, Liz leaned back again against the post and studied his face. It was beautiful, she decided. Strong, passionate, patient. Her life was going to be bound up with that face. It was as real as flesh and blood and as precious as dreams. Her lover was back, her child was with her and nothing was impossible.

"When I first met you, I thought you were the kind of man who always got what he wanted."

"And you were right." He took her hands again and held them. "Now what are we going to tell Faith?" he demanded.

Her lips curved slowly. "I guess we'd better tell her you talked me into it."

* * * * *